Copyright © 2024 by Holly Roberds

Edited by: Theresa Paolo

Cover by: Opulent Swag & Designs

Proofreading: The Havoc Archives

All rights reserved.

No part of this book may be reproduced in any form or by any electronic or mechanical means, including information storage and retrieval systems, without written permission from the author, except for the use of brief quotations in a book review.

IGNITING CINDER

HOLLY ROBERDS

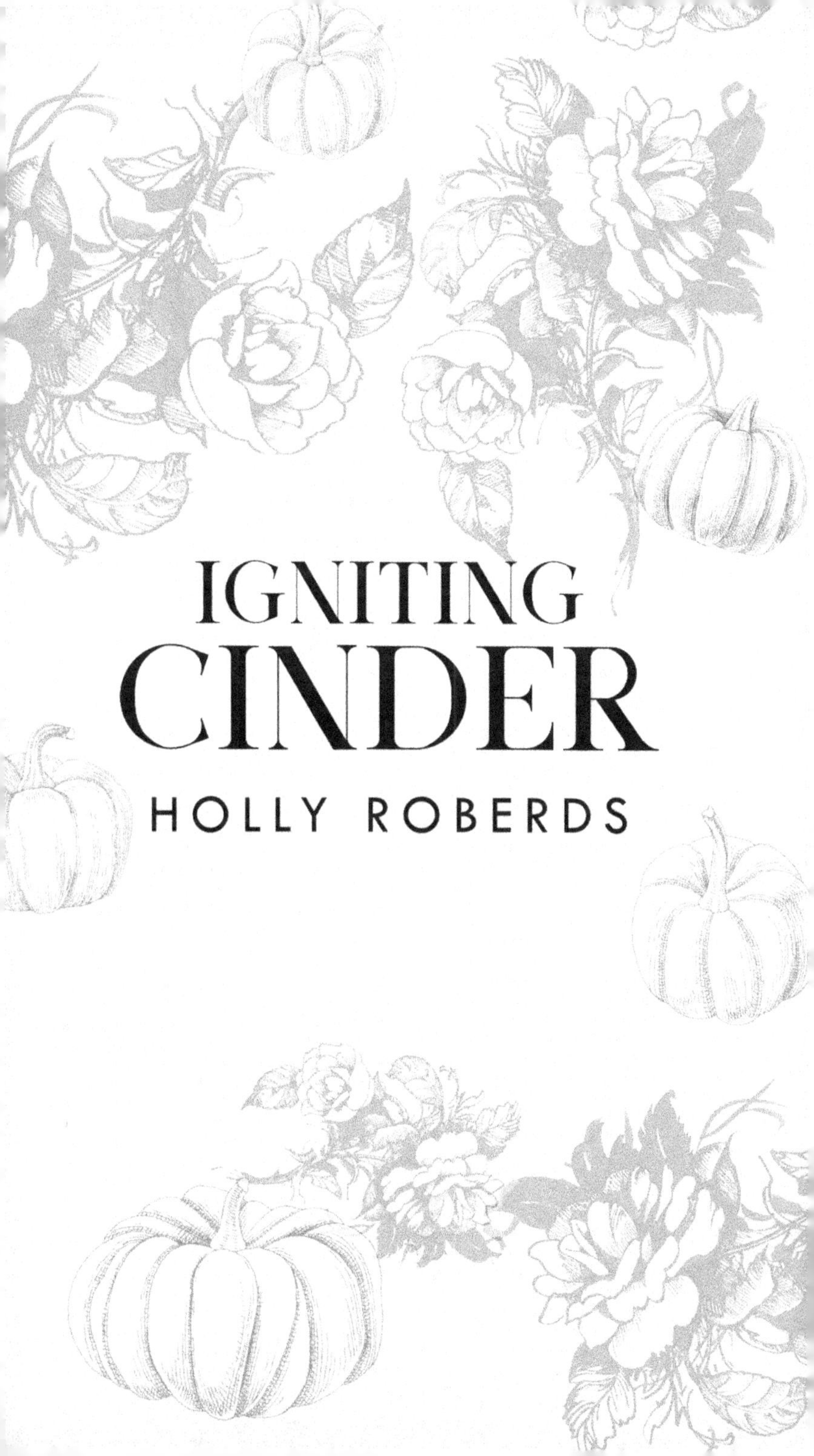

BOOKS BY HOLLY ROBERDS

<u>**VEGAS IMMORTALS**</u>

Death and the Last Vampire

Book 1 - Bitten by Death

Book 2 - Kissed by Death

Book 3 - Seduced by Death

The Beast & the Badass

Book 1 - Breaking the Beast

Book 2 - Claiming the Beast

<u>**DEMON KNIGHTS**</u>

Book 1 - One Savage Knight

Book 2 - One Bad Knight

<u>**LOST GIRLS SERIES**</u>

Book 1 - Tasting Red

Book 2 - Chasing Goldie

Book 3 - Igniting Cinder

Book 4 - Blackmailing Belle

<u>**THE FIVE ORDERS**</u>

Book 0.5 – The Knight Watcher

Book 1 - Prophecy Girl

Book 2 - Soulless Son

Book 3 - Tear in the World

Book 4 – Into Darkness

Book 4.5 - Touch of Hell

Book 5 - End Game

* For recommended reading order, visit www.hollyroberds.com

To those who believe in their Prince Charming (or Cinder), no matter how out of fashion romance is in our present day.

Romance is real. Never settle.

CHAPTER 1

BIBBIDI-BOBBIDI-BITCH IS IN DANGER

CINDER

The Fairy Godmother assured me these glass slippers would not shatter and slice my feet off into bloody nubbins.

When I initially asked, her nose and forehead wrinkled, taken aback in open disgust. But if I was going to step into the fairy realm of Midnight, I needed to make sure I could run without becoming an instant amputee.

Though the option of using the jagged edge of a broken glass shoe to stab anyone who dared come at me held a certain appeal. My look has always been on the stabbier side anyway—chains, spikes, dog collars, and fish nets. Nothing says *fuck off, don't touch or talk to me* like goth fashion.

Tonight I traded in my six-inch platform combat boots for dainty footwear to get me where I need to go. The Fairy Godmother also forced me to forgo my usual black lipstick, cover up any visible tattoos with makeup, and take out my many facial piercings—the goal being to blend in.

I've penetrated the society ball and now I just need to get what I came for and get.

As I weave through the throng of fairy aristocrats, a passing elbow jabs into my ribs. I flinch, my breath catching in my throat. The unwelcome contact sends a jolt of panic through me and I quickly sidestep, putting distance between myself and the offending party. My skin crawls, a prickling sensation that lingers long after the touch is gone.

I grab a glass of champagne from a silver tray, not meeting the human server's gaze. Their sightless eyes freak me out. The humans in the fairy realm are little more than automatons, running on autopilot to serve their master, the King.

Maybe I should have snuck in disguised as a human servant, but my pride wouldn't let me pretend to be one of their familiars.

The lace face-covering distorts the upper half of my features. I doubt I'll be recognized, but capitalizing on the outlandish fashion here only works to my benefit. In the kingdom of Midnight, most days it is acceptable to dress as if one is attending a gothic masquerade.

My skin, a ghostly shade of pale that's damn near translucent, helps me blend seamlessly into the monochromatic crowd. On my side of the world, Boston doesn't feature many sunny days and I tend to be a night owl, thanks to my upbringing here in the kingdom. Since the Midnight fairies live in a land of perpetual night, no one around me is sporting a tan either.

Once, years ago, I walked among the Midnight fairies as an equal.

Okay, at the very least as a tolerated presence.

But then my father died, and all protection and

pretense of tolerance disappeared before I could say Bibbidi-Bobbidi-Butthurt. I'd been degraded by these fairy fuck faces enough for one lifetime, yet here I am again.

Flickering candelabras and chandeliers cast a warm glow over the ballroom. The attire varies in shades of black, deep blues, and purples—the royal colors of Midnight. The castle is near freezing since the Midnight fairies are not bothered by temperature. Like the Common World, it has slipped into the chill of autumn.

Crossing realms into Midnight is like stepping back into the early nineteenth century. The faint echo of clip-clopping filters in from the courtyard, reminding me horses are still the primary mode of transportation.

After seceding onto their own astral plane from the Common World several hundred years ago, the fairy lands forbade technologies like electricity and tightly controlled their borders to keep out humans, mages, and the more common fae creatures like ogres and shifters.

Fairies are pure-blood bastards with a superiority complex.

Sipping the sharp citrus bubbles that likely came from a priceless vintage, I take a moment to be grateful there are libations available other than the usual.

A couple adorned in matching eggplant colors next to me put their lips to dark, blue glass coupe glasses. Despite their attempts to mask a color the kingdom views as vulgar, I know exactly what thick viscous liquid they drink.

Blood.

The woman laughs at something the man says, throwing her head back with just the right amount of tilt to show off the jewels dripping around her pale throat. Her upper lip curls, showcasing a pair of long, sharp canines that gleam under the candlelight.

I swallow hard.

The Common World has another name for the Midnight fairies.

Vampires.

Fear snakes up my spine and winds around and down to land with an icy drip in my stomach.

You won't let fear get the best of you, Cinder. You are here for a reason, and this may be your only chance.

Is it idiotic to try and blend in amongst the fanged when I am so painfully human and my veins overrunneth with what they subsist on?

Yes.

Am I going to pick up my skirts and click away in my little glass heels?

Fuck no.

As I make my way through the crowd, I can't help but overhear the giggles from a group of young ladies.

"Prince Charming looks absolutely delicious tonight," one of them gushes. "It's no wonder he's bedded over half the court already."

Her companion titters behind her fan. "Well, can you blame them? With that smoldering gaze and wicked smile, I'd let him ravish me whenever he wished."

I roll my eyes, trying to block out their inane chatter. The last thing I need is to get caught up in the drama of the playboy prince and his gaggle of admirers. I have my own mission to focus on.

A third lady chimes in, her tone conspiratorial. "I heard he once seduced a duchess and her daughter on the same night, convincing them to engage in scandalous play with *each other*. The man has no shame."

The first one turns to the second girl. "I heard that rumor too and it was about you, Lady Felicia."

I freeze mid-step, my ears straining to catch every juicy detail. The temptation to eavesdrop overpowers my urgency to get what I came for.

The second fairy's face contorts, her features twisting into a pinched and stricken expression. She looks as though she sucked down some spoiled blood.

Oh witchtits, it's true! And that girl was just outed so hard.

Wait, with her own mom?

Yikes.

Okay, maybe I enjoy a little bit of gossip. I blame my bestie Goldie for making me watch so many trashy reality mage shows where a bunch of egotistical, power-hungry hotties have to live in the same house together.

Unable to help myself, I glide closer to the group. "Oh, that's just a typical Tuesday for us," I chime in nonchalantly. "We usually have our romps in the stable with a strap-on at his insistence and his exotic pet monkey as an audience."

I float away, leaving behind the collective gasp of shock and awe.

Okay, so I'm here to steal something but it doesn't mean I can't have a little fun. Especially at the expense of Prince Charming.

Walking to the far side of the ballroom, I approach the art expanding across the entirety of the wall in front of me. All amusement drops away as my heart jerks up into my throat.

Nostalgia is quickly followed by a warm prickling sensation attacking my stomach with a painful vengeance. Tears burn at the backs of my eyes. I'm not sentimental or a crier, but this damn near pushes me to the brink.

Strong, wide brush strokes travel along the canvas with

iridescent splendor. Its textured colors rise off the canvas, tempting the viewer to run their fingers across the surface and feel the layers of paint. The painting seems to glow with an otherworldly luminescence as if the very essence of the moonlight has been woven into the work.

The landscape of the Midnight Kingdom unfolds before me, captured with an almost ethereal beauty. The misty moors stretch out to the horizon, their edges softened by the gentle caress of starlight. The colors are rich and vivid, yet there's a dreamlike quality to them as if they might shift and dance at any moment.

I'm swept away in an ocean of magic just looking at it.

More than the art itself is the memory of my father once bent over this piece, brush in hand, paint flecked in his dark hair and unkempt goatee. I can almost smell the smoke of the cigarillo that always hung off his lips. I miss him so badly it nearly rocks me off my feet.

It also reminds me of what I came for.

"Do you think it's in poor taste of our King to use Byung-He's art as the backdrop for our social season?" a woman asks her partner in a low tone to my left.

It takes all my wherewithal not to stiffen at the mention of my father's name. Thankfully, the couple doesn't take any note of my presence as they do the forbidden—question their King.

The male answers. "He may have been human, but it is undeniable his art is transcendent. And seeing as he was the King's confidant and familiar, I can't say it's that surprising to commemorate the day of the man's death."

"Yes, well," she hedges with obvious distaste. "It has been ten years. At least this is his only lapse in judgment when it comes to humans. The idea of them intermingling with us as equals is repulsive." The tone of her words radiates with contempt, mirroring the disdainful expression on her face.

"This pittance of a rebellion will not take hold, my dear. The Mice shall be exterminated," the man assures his partner.

"Of course they shall be taken care of," a new voice joins in, cold as the grave and accented with the tones of Mandarin.

My entire body seizes with fear and I slowly, carefully, tilt away to hide my face, not wanting to catch the attention of King Charming who is flanked by one of his aides.

CHAPTER 2
MEET THE CHARMINGS

CINDER

f I was forced to pick a fight between the tall, broad, beefy aide to the King, and King Charming himself who is a shriveled man who appears to be in his seventies, I'd take on the side of beef without a second thought.

The King's features, though worn by time, still bear the hallmarks of his Asian ancestry, a remnant of the Midnight Realm's origins before it seceded from the Common World.

Despite appearing as a wrinkled, white-haired man, I know better than to underestimate the ruler of Midnight. His skull seems ready to cave in trying to hold up that impressively large silver crown adorned with blood-red rubies, but King Valdor Charming, ruler of the Midnight fairies, is anything but weak.

Judging by the wild fear in the eyes of the couple who made the unforgivable mistake of questioning the King, they know it too.

"My King, of course," the woman rushes, her tongue tripping over the words. "We harbor no doubts as to your power."

The King's silky voice drips with danger. "Only doubts as to my judgment, la?" he says, employing the Mandarin exclamation to punctuate his statement.

"My lady did not know what she was saying, Your Majesty," the man interjects. "She has been imbibing too much on your generous spirits."

"I do not believe spiked blood is the issue here, Lord Thornby." The King's tone is deceptively soft, but it carries an undercurrent of menace that makes my skin crawl. "I believe the issue may be that she needs to be reminded how my judgment has served this kingdom the past two hundred and sixty-three years." A sharp edge enters his last words.

Panic bubbles in my chest, suffocating me as I stand mere inches away from the most powerful and feared vampire in existence. I clench my fists tightly, trying to control the tremble in my hands. Every instinct screams at me to run, to flee, but I know that any sudden movement will only draw their attention. So I force myself to stand still even as fear courses through my veins.

What the fae fucks was I thinking coming back here? I've put myself in a stupid amount of danger.

Every muscle in my body tenses as I try to keep completely still, not even daring to breathe. I'm frozen, bracing for what I know comes next.

Despite not looking directly at him, I know how the King's pupils expand to swallow up the irises until they are bottomless black pits. The King's power builds, a crackling energy pressing against my skin. I instinctively close my eyes in an attempt to shield myself. But even though I'm not looking, I can feel the piercing chill as his words slide through the air like a deadly blade.

"Change out of that frivolous gown, Lady Thornby," his voice has dropped into a layered, hypnotizing timbre, "and don the lowly attire of my familiars. You shall serve your peers as if you were nothing more than a human for the next fortnight, taking on the vilest, most despised of tasks. Use the time of servitude to remember your place. You do *not* think, you do *not* question. You are a servant. Your sole purpose is to serve your King and kingdom."

Only when he is done speaking do I chance a look to the side. The woman stiffens, her eyes glazing over as she turns and walks away, a puppet on invisible strings.

The effect of thrall.

I want to run, to hide, to be anywhere but here. But I'm rooted to the spot, paralyzed by a primal fear that goes beyond reason.

"Do you wish to join your wife, Lord Thornby?" the King asks, his voice carrying a mocking edge.

There is a wrong answer and an even *more* wrong answer.

Any response is about to get Thornby thralled alongside his wife. Then they'll both endure the humiliation of debasement in front of the fairy court.

Even after the Thornbys are released from service, the rest of the vicious bloodsuckers won't soon let one of their own forget such degradation.

"I shall serve you however Your Majesty sees fit." The male bows deeply.

The King dismisses him, and Lord Thornby scurries away like a whipped dog.

The one correct answer. The only answer when answering the Crown.

I'm half surprised he didn't strip the Thornbys of their title before having them executed. That's far more the King's style. But he seems to be ruling with a softer hand.

A scary, all-powerful hand that can crush anyone with ease, but one that has definitely been moisturized.

Though some of the humans here are willing and grateful to serve the Midnight court, all familiars have been subject to the King's unique ability to put others under his thrall. It's what makes his reign so terrifying and impenetrable. He isn't afraid to use it on familiars or fairies.

Then again, back when I was a kid, no one dared breathe a word against the monarchy. Apparently, some things have changed.

Charming isn't just the royal surname, it's what makes the King undeniably more powerful than any other. He's the only one with the power of thrall.

It's what has me trembling almost violently even as I pretend to be invisible. Without the protection of my father I'm as vulnerable as a lamb for slaughter.

I really wish I had my combat boots right about now. They'd at least give me the illusion of being a badass.

A part of me wonders if it might be more than an illusion soon. Sometimes I swear I can feel something stirring deep within, waiting to be unleashed. Thanks to eating a magic cookie a powerful mage baked, it's possible I could sprout a magical ability when I least expect it.

But for now, I'm terribly human.

"Your Majesty may want to remember that the ambassadors from the Common World are in attendance tonight," the King's aide reminds him quietly, giving me the opportunity to take my first hesitant step away from the threat.

"Pah," the King huffs. "Those fools will not notice one of the court amongst the servants. The interfering beaters are too busy drinking our champagne and enjoying their inside look into our way of life." His words are dark, underlined with resentment.

I'm not the least bit surprised to hear the King use the derogatory name for beings who have beating hearts. My own big red organ does its best to thump its way up my throat and out of my mouth so it can splat on the marble floor and give me away.

Damn heart. I should have cut it out years ago.

"The rumors of your rule being unchecked and despotic, while untrue, are spreading." The aide continues diplomatically. "We do not want the attention, Your Majesty."

Whatever the King says next is lost to me as the two walk away.

I finally take in big swallowing gulps of air as I desperately attempt to feed my starving lungs.

I'm suddenly glad for the forced makeover I received earlier tonight.

When I would have phoned it in on the dress, the Fairy Godmother wouldn't hear of it.

The Fairy Godmother, aka Dame Kiki Eleganza, the best drag queen in the greater Boston area, was my best bet at getting entry into the Midnight realm. I just hadn't realized the deal would come with a makeover.

I glance down at the daringly low-cut neckline that frames my collarbones and is adorned with ornamental black flowers, hoping like hell my pulse isn't visible. At least the black dress placates my goth girl's heart. You can take the girl out of Midnight, but she'll still have a weird affinity for Tim Burton aesthetics the rest of her life.

Sweat beads along my hairline as I navigate the crowded ballroom. The tight fabric encasing my arms covers the tattoos but feels like a straitjacket. My voluminous skirt brushes against a chair, the sudden squeak making me flinch.

As effective as the Fairy Godmother was at getting me here, I'm the only one who can get me home.

The need to get the fae fucks out of this ballroom as soon as possible grips me with a desperate edge. Even as fear claws at my throat, I remind myself I didn't come this far just to run now.

So I force my feet forward, keeping my head down and my movements casual as I continue to search the fringes of the ballroom for what I came for.

A hush falls over the room, forcing me to stop. The King and Queen stand before the indigo velvet thrones that sparkle with something shiny like glitter to create the illusion of stars. The small, yet terrifying King is now poised on the dais at the far side of the room, his coal-black eyes sharply scanning the crowd.

Even shorter than her husband at under five feet, the Asian queen's jet-black hair is now streaked with silver. She's otherwise unchanged down to the same vacant expression she always wears.

"Greetings, my friends and fairies." The King's voice travels to the far corners of the ballroom. "I thank you all for attending tonight's ball. The beginning of the Midnight fairy social season is of particular import. Not only have we opened our borders to host several esteemed ambassadors from the Common World," he gestures to a small cluster of humans, mages, and even a fae elf with false graciousness, "but this is also the season in which my son shall pick his bride. The future princess and eventual Queen of Midnight."

My fingers stiffen on the cold flute. Ascending the stairs onto the dais in a long-legged gait is Prince Kaison Charming himself. He stands next to his father, dwarfing him with over a foot of extra height. For some reason my heart pounds so hard, my ribs rattle under the impact of each beat.

Thump. Thump. Thump.

I'm not sure why seeing him has such an effect on me.

Okay, maybe I have some idea.

Prince Charming lives up to his name. The smirk that stretches one side of his mouth is as sharp as it is devastating. Like cocking a gun, he uses it on the crowd, holding them in suspense.

Everyone leans in.

I take a step back.

A hand has recently swept his jet-black hair away from his face, but rebellious pieces fall forward into his dark eyes. There is a mischievous glint and a devil-may-care attitude in the way he scans the crowd. As if we are all here for his amusement and indeed, he is amused. His features are angular, precise and so very *pretty*.

More unforgivable is that he knows it.

The luxurious form-fitting coat of black stops at his knees and features a high collar. It's tailored to perfection, accentuating the wide set of his shoulders to his tapered waist. A subtle brocade pattern weaves through the material of his outfit, visible only at certain angles. Silver filigree buttons run down the center of his vest, ending at the belt buckle cinching his hips with the insignia of the Midnight Kingdom. A chalice of blood set against the stars.

"The playboy prince, find a bride?" someone to my right

scoffs under their breath. "We've a better chance of turning vegan than he does of turning over his partying ways."

"This is our chance," a woman murmurs to her daughter off to my left.

As the prince waits for the chatter to die down, my stomach begins folding in on itself like origami. I look down into my drink at the minuscule bubbles rising to kiss the surface. An irrational fear grips me that his roaming eyes will find me.

It's a ridiculous thought. I'm in a crowd of at least two hundred, with my face half obscured. Not to mention, he hasn't seen me since I was twelve. He's filled out since I last saw him, but I knew that already from the social media pics that show he missed his calling as a model.

While I managed to get away from Midnight, Prince Charming has haunted me through the years. With such a public persona and his university years spent in the Common World, I can't scroll fast enough to avoid his gorgeous, infuriating face on my own damn phone.

Every time I see him, there's the familiar burn of shame and humiliation heating my skin. That familiar bad taste seeps into my mouth whenever I think of him. He had no trouble making it known what a waste of space I was in our youth. He wouldn't recognize me even if I were stark naked and strutting around.

Yet that's how I feel right now. Naked.

I lift my head and my gaze connects with the prince's dark eyes which are trained directly on me.

A jolt of electricity shoots through me, igniting a fire in my belly that I've never felt before. I try to look away, to break the connection, but I can't make myself.

The entire room around me turns hazy, almost fading into the background while my heartbeat booms loudly in my ears. In this moment there is only him and me, a connection pulsing with an undeniable magnetism.

The prince's cocky grin doesn't disappear but slips slightly. A dark calculation crosses his face, belying the playboy carelessness he exuded a moment ago.

We are practically strangers yet his gaze bores into me as if he knows me better than anyone ever has. I feel an undeserved sense of familiarity, as if he's letting me see the real him. As if I'm the *only* one who gets to see the real him.

The only thing I should be is disgusted with his playboy prince routine—oh, and the fact he sucks blood from zombified people. Yeah, disgusted, not tingly, hot, or thrilling.

I finally force myself to look away. My heart rate doubles when I notice the gloved hand flexing at his side.

No. He couldn't know it's me. There's absolutely no fae fucking way. He must be lost in thought and only appears to be looking directly at me.

Suddenly, this whole plan is the stupidest idea I've ever had.

The fae fucks am I thinking, crashing a ball for blood-drinking fairies? If I get caught, I'll be thralled, imprisoned, or worse.

I didn't even tell my friends I was coming here. They wouldn't know where to look for my body, that is until the Fairy Godmother squeals on my dumbass.

The King clears his throat and Prince Charming's smile is back on full blast, the invisible tether in my direction now broken.

"Thank you all for coming," he echoes the King's sentiment in a rich, resonant English accent. "Allow me to present my mother, the Queen." He takes his mother's slim, pale hand into his leather-clad palm and pulls her forward. Prince Charming directs his mother between him and his father as he introduces her. "Queen Mei-Ling Charming."

We all bow or curtsy in her direction, but I don't take my eyes off the royal family.

I've rarely seen the Queen even when I was a child. There's an emptiness to her expression that used to make me wonder if she was under thrall as well. But seeing her now, I know exactly what her deal is. I've seen it in the mirror too many times to count.

Disassociation.

It's the only way I survived those four years. Disconnecting from myself so I wouldn't be fully aware of what was happening to me.

The Queen doesn't walk, she floats as Prince Charming leads her to her throne. I can't help but wonder if she even knows what's going on, or if she is completely in her own little world.

Just then, she connects gazes with her son and gives him a slight nod of the head and a kind smile, which he returns. I guess there's one person she's willing to break the surface of her mind for. But just like that, her expression glazes over and she's gone again. To somewhere that is not here.

The orchestra in the corner strikes up the music and couples take to the dance floor. I turn on my heel to hightail it out of the ballroom. My heart pounds in my throat, and heat rushes through my veins until my skin burns.

The way the prince found me in the crowd leaves me unsettled.

Nope, he didn't see me. He doesn't know me. I'm just being a paranoid squirrel because I want to get out of here.

I turn my attention back to my father's massive paintings that adorn the walls. All I need to do is follow the display until I find *the one*.

Once I do, I'll find a way to grab it and get the fae fucks out of here. Before I get dead.

I turn to make my escape and nearly slam into a solid wall of muscle. The scent of frosted pine needles and leather envelops me. The prince dips his head, more hair falling forward. "Hello Cinder," he practically purrs, "May I have this dance?"

CHAPTER 3

WALTZING WITH PRINCE SLUT

CHARMING

Cinder's mouth parts in surprise then closes. I give her the time she needs to recover.

Though fae lords know I haven't yet. Recovered.

I can't believe it's really her, and a strange rush of relief sweeps through me.

All eyes are on us, and if she refuses my invitation it will create a stir.

After several beats, the woman wearing the veil gives a nod and slips her hand into my outstretched glove. I grip her hand a little too tight as I lead her onto the dance floor, my head spinning like a top at finding her. Like discovering a gem amidst rocks.

She's really alive.

I set my hand on her hip and launch us both into an easy waltz. To her credit, Cinder doesn't miss a step, though her lips purse with displeasure.

"How did you know it was me?" she asks in a low tone.

How *did* I know it was her?

The veil she wears hides half her face, and she is dressed as any of the kingdom's aristocrats. Yet I knew. She stood out as clearly as a blaze of fire amidst a sea of ice cubes. Something in the way she holds herself, something in the way her eyes burn me from behind her face covering, or perhaps it's that perfect cupid's bow of a mouth that catches my attention, reminding me of a certain human girl I once knew.

The daughter of my father's close personal friend. His *only* human friend.

While we didn't interact very often, Cinder was always in my sphere, orbiting around the edges until her father died. I sometimes weirdly felt our situations were opposite sides of the same coin.

Then I never saw her again or knew what became of her. It niggled at me until one day I asked around and got various versions of a rumor that she'd been sucked dry and left for dead by rogue vampires in the woods.

That night I didn't sleep. For even longer, I'd be visited by intrusive thoughts imagining her discarded drained body just lying in the woods. Nobody seemed to care, but I did. If no one else would, I would be the one who remembered the girl who was always dotted or smeared with paint stains and often sat on the cliffs, humming to herself when she thought no one was around.

Instead of confessing any of that, I shoot the very alive and warm-blooded human girl a cocky grin. "I know everyone of course."

"You mean you've banged every woman here but me?" Her words come out flat and bored. They are meant to be a jab. An attack I'm more than used to.

"Are you calling me a slut?" I ask in mock offense as I sweep her across the dance floor.

Her lips tighten. As much as she lets me lead, Cinder's body is tense beneath my touch, her movements stiff and unyielding. She leans away slightly, maintaining a careful distance even as I guide her through our dance.

"I'm well aware of my reputation," I say to put her at ease. "I'm the one who earned it, after all. I learned early on," *maybe too early*, "that everyone wants to sleep with a prince. I'm nothing if not a philanthropist, giving the people what they want."

It's difficult to ignore the heat of her hand permeating through my leather gloves, or how much I like having her in my hold.

Even as she begins to lean into the dance, I sense a lingering hesitation in her movements, a guardedness that never quite disappears. It's like trying to hold onto a wild creature, poised to bolt at the slightest provocation.

"I would never slut shame anyone. I'm only repeating the headlines, Your Highness." She is somehow scathing and smug even in a monotone delivery.

Sparks of excitement pop off in my chest. A woman unafraid to call me on my bullshit. How interesting.

"Well then, it seems you've missed a couple of articles. Otherwise, you'd know I've seduced a number of men as well."

"Even more hearts to be broken over your pending nuptials, how tragic." Her words are as dry as an empty glass in a desert amid a draught.

She's savage.

I love it.

I bite the inside of my cheek to keep from grinning. Appearances matter at events like these, and I have a specific, cultivated look. If she keeps throwing so many zingers my way, I might ruin all of that with a full belly laugh.

We've already exchanged more words on this dance floor than we have in our entire lives, yet the banter swings back and forth as timely as our dance steps, with an easy familiarity I can't account for.

I heave a dramatic sigh for effect. "Yes, so many will be devastated." Then my lips curve up. "But who's to say anyone should be deprived of my fantastic dicking skills even if I'm married?"

She snorts, and it's suddenly my favorite sound.

Despite keeping the conversation light, a weight presses on my chest.

I will have to pick a bride this season. My father needs me to do my part to show the face of strength and commit to growing up. He demands I make a serious commitment to the monarchy and get to work making an heir.

If only he knew how serious I was about the monarchy.

Darkness curls like smoke inside my chest, but I school my features to not let that part of me show.

My dance partner's shoulders stiffen and rise several inches as she does a quick, almost imperceptible scan of the room. I don't have to look to know that everywhere eyes press hungrily into us, watching with greedy need and covetous desire. The first dance of the evening, on the first night of a season where I am to pick my bride, I might as well have thrown a spotlight and a gallon of red paint on us.

While I don't love the feeling, I'm used to it.

"Why me?" Cinder asks in a low, self-conscious voice.

It's not the question of a woman who does not value

her own worth enough to be picked in a crowd. It's the complaint of someone who wishes I hadn't singled her out.

"I wanted a dance with the mystery woman." Then I lower my voice conspiratorially. "It will drive the rest of them crazy, not knowing who you are."

"If they find out a human has snuck in..." There is a slight waver in her voice. Fear. "I'll be—"

"*No one* will touch you while I'm with you." A hard edge entered my voice before I could check it, but I meant it. No one will do her any harm; I will make sure of it. Though why she's snuck back into Midnight, a human girl among Midnight fairies who'd just as soon step into daylight than endure treating her as an equal, is beyond me.

"What *are* you doing here, anyway?" I finally ask. The question burns me.

Cinder's hand tightens, and I suddenly wish my palm was naked against hers. I want to feel her bare skin. I can already tell her fingers are slender, but I want to know if they are soft or calloused, smooth or chapped.

A weird thing to want. Usually, women or men who entice me don't inspire an interest in their hands, only what their hands can do *to* me.

I tell myself the reason I'm thinking about her digits is because her appearance has thrown me. I pride myself on rolling with the punches, on being flexible and able to think on my feet, but she is completely unexpected. But now I'm thinking of a human's fingers and of lifting her veil to see if I remember the shade of her eyes correctly.

"That's none of your business," Cinder says. Even through the lace fabric, I can tell she's addressing the spot over my shoulder.

My hand slides from her waist to her lower back, drawing her closer to me. I can't help but inhale her unique scent. It reminds me of vanilla orchids with a hint of something deeper, darker, like charred cedar. I'm becoming almost addicted to the heat emanating through her dress.

As I pull her closer, she stiffens, her breath catching in her throat. For a moment, I think she might push me away, but she holds her ground, even as I sense the effort it takes for her to endure my proximity.

Others usually swoon when I pull them near. Her head turns to the side, the only part she can pull away with.

She truly is unlike anyone else I've ever met, a puzzle I've never been able to figure out. Her aversion to touch intrigues me as much as it frustrates me, and I find myself wanting to unravel the mystery that lies beneath her prickly exterior.

I almost concede by giving her those inches back, but I don't want anyone to overhear us.

Being this close only fuels a fire within me that I can't explain. Every nerve in my body is on edge, buzzing with raw desire. Not just lust or attraction, but it's as if my entire being is coming to life, recognizing something in her my brain isn't smart enough to comprehend yet. Her lips are magnets, drawing my gaze and thoughts to them over and over again like they are stuck in a loop.

As a prince, I have been taught to recognize power and dominance. People think I'm important. They don't know the meaning of the word.

Cinder effortlessly exudes a force that money and status can't buy. She undeniably knows who she is, and now I'm desperate to know her too.

"Au contraire, it is my business," I continue to tease. "You have come to my bride-finding party. I can only assume you are here because you are one of the hopefuls wishing to tame the famous playboy prince." I say the last part in a conspiratorial whisper.

Her lips twitch, and I can't tell if she is fighting a smile or a disgusted grimace.

"Aside from the fact you are fae and I'm a human, I can't say I'm the marrying type, your *highness*." She loads my title with open irreverence. As if she meant to say, *your lowly scumliness.*

It's delicious.

But she makes a point I share. Marriage is not on my 'to do' list either.

"That makes two of us," I grumble. "But that still doesn't answer the question of why you are here."

She inhales deeply. "My father—" Cinder abruptly cuts herself off, not completing the explanation as if she doesn't trust herself to speak.

My brows knit. Her father died ten years ago.

Then my forehead smooths.

She must know what I've suspected all this time.

"So you've come back to find out who killed him," I say the obvious in a hushed tone.

Cinder's head snaps up toward me as her body stiffens under my hands. She misses a step and then another. I practically lift her off her feet and continue moving to keep pace with the other couples. Even with all her full skirts, she's so light.

"Milady," I say, even though she isn't a noblewoman to warrant the moniker. "If you don't move your feet, we may be in danger of being trampled by the rest of the dancers."

Her chest jerks up and down in unsteady movements, and I key in on a jumping beat that reaches my ears. Cinder's heartbeat. It's erratic, like a bird repeatedly trying to land but can't actually settle.

The scent of her blood hits me like a freight train. Suddenly my pants are too tight and my mouth waters with a thirst that is needy as it is urgent.

Witchtits. I need to get a hold of myself.

More importantly, *she* needs to calm down, or that heady copper and vanilla scent is going to arouse the interest of nearby dancers.

I lower my voice to a more intimate tone that I hope is soothing. "Cinder, I need you to breathe."

There is a slight shake of her head.

I put a little more force into my words. "Breathe in, yes, thattagirl, and now breathe out," I coach. She follows my instructions, though it takes three full breaths for them to turn somewhat even.

Shit, she didn't know about her father.

Not that I know for sure, but the likelihood her father was murdered is too probable that it's a damn near certainty.

But then why is she here?

I need to get Cinder alone, somewhere private, then I can get the truth behind her unexpected appearance.

The song comes to an end and instead of the melody flowing into the next, a silence falls over the room.

The dancing couples have parted and receded, and I find my father standing next to us.

My gloved hand tightens around hers as my spine stiffens.

The urge to haul Cinder over my shoulder and get as far away from him as possible grips me by the scruff of my neck.

Because despite the years apart, some part of me still feels responsible for Cinder. And I'll be damned if I let any harm come to her, not while she's within the reach of my admittedly limited power.

"Your Majesty," I force myself to say, turning us both to face my father. I take a step forward, putting myself in between my father and Cinder. I keep hold of her hand, gripping it tight behind me. I feel it tremble against my fingers.

The King regards us with an appraising look, but I recognize that expression. He is a shark scenting blood. "Ah, I did not recognize your first choice of dance partner for the evening. The two of you danced beautifully together and I simply could not stay in suspense as to the identity of your companion."

We both stand there, stock still.

Cinder was right. I shouldn't have put so much attention on her. Going to her had been thoughtless, my feet carrying me to her like a magnetic pull before I fully knew what I was doing. She's not welcome here, not by the Midnight court, and not by my father who views humans as a mere means to an end.

My hands clench and release as I throw all my effort into maintaining a neutral demeanor.

I meant what I said. I won't let anyone hurt her. Still, there is no going back now.

I reach forward and my fingers pinch the edges of black lace that cover the top half of her face. Slowly, oh so painfully slowly, I peel it back, revealing that pert little nose and violet eyes that always held an undercurrent of violence and defiance. The downward angle of her dark lashes gives her eyes a mysterious, half-lidded allure.

Her graceful, almost ethereal Korean beauty contrasts sharply with her forbidding, gothic allure, creating a striking duality. It's a contrast that draws me in, making me want to discover all her hidden facets. She's like a beautiful graveyard of secrets.

Fuck, when did I get so poetic?

Still, it feels like I'm looking at a ghost. And in her dress, she certainly resembles a spirit that might roam the halls, intent on haunting the palace.

A sharp intake of breath comes from my father beside me. "Why you are my old friend, Byung-He's, daughter."

The collective gasp around us lets me know I've fully and completely blown Cinder's cover.

Good job, Charming.

Cinder tenses as if awaiting the backlash. In fact the entire room holds its breath as if everyone is waiting for the axe to fall.

Which is mildly hilarious, considering almost no one here but Cinder needs to breathe.

My father takes Cinder's hand in his. Lifting it to his lips, he brushes a light kiss along the back of it. I want to rip his hold off her. Judging by her tight expression, she doesn't care much for the attention either.

I have no doubt the second the King is out of sight, he'll be rubbing his lips to get them clean. But he's trying to keep the peace, especially with the ambassadors here. If a spectacle blows up, he could draw the wrong kind of attention from the Common World. It would also be more difficult for the ball to proceed which would delay my finding a bride. Nothing is done without calculation.

My hatred slithers through me like an old familiar serpent chased by another swell of protectiveness toward the woman by me.

I am determined to protect Cinder, even after all these years. Despite my attempts to always keep everyone at a distance, I couldn't help but always feel drawn to her.

Like now. I couldn't resist being near her, and I've created this mess.

The King's eyes drop to her bare fingertips stained with what appears to be red paint. The top of his lip twitches, and I know he is suppressing a sneer. To him, red is vulgar. Feeding is private. Even though we sip the finest, richest blood at the parties, the color must always be obscured by tinted glass. The fairy court is careful not to let it stain their lips or teeth.

It doesn't do to arouse the thirst publicly. There's a difference between sipping a glass of blood thinned with liqueur and an actual feeding.

Even I know it's a piss poor attempt to hide our monstrous side in a farce to exhibit civility. My father and I both know what we are. The only difference between us is I don't relish it like he does.

For a moment, I think his controlled demeanor will snap and he'll express his displeasure in all his favored ways.

Public humiliation.

Pain.

Thrall.

My muscles coil with tension, ready to intervene on Cinder's behalf.

Frustration at my attempts to get out from under his tyranny for the last three years grates against my nerves and makes it hard to compose myself. Cinder may be vulnerable here in the viper's den, but the King doesn't know he has a fox in his own hen house.

It would be a mistake to show my hand, or fang as it were. To keep him from hurting Cinder, I'd be throwing away any chance of burning this court to the ground. And yet, I am on the edge of action.

Thankfully, my father releases her hand. I relax ever so slightly.

"My dear friend's daughter. As you can see, this year's social season will be set to the backdrop of his masterpieces, in commemoration of his talent." He holds an arm out to the paintings along the wall.

The show is for the ambassadors from the Common World. My father is putting on a fantastic performance of how open-minded and hospitable he is to beaters.

Cinder bows her head. "He would be honored by the gesture."

My father smiles, but his eyes are sharp. "May I ask how you came to be here tonight?"

Aka *how the fuck did you get in here, little human girl?*

The portals to our realm are heavily monitored by our guards, and the outskirts of our land are plagued by feral rogue vampires.

To her credit, Cinder keeps her face neutral as she simply says, "I am from this land."

"Ah yes, of course," he says as if he sees.

He doesn't know shit. Not even I know how she got here, which leaves me deeply impressed.

The King's eyes narrow slightly. "The borders are not as treacherous as they once were. There used to be so many. . . incidents back then. I heard a particularly disturbing rumor about your own journey out of our lands, my dear. That the rogues had gotten you. But I am pleased to find you made it out and back, alive."

"Sounds like an important lesson in listening to gossip because I'm here now." The words are even, and her expression gives nothing away.

Shock electrocutes me in an almost titillating way.

Holy witchtits, she must be fearless. Or stupid. Maybe both?

The King smiles, but there's no warmth in it. "Indeed, you are," he murmurs thoughtfully as if to himself. "Indeed," he repeats, this time loud enough to be heard by all. "We are honored to have the daughter of my esteemed friend and artist Byung-He and she is most welcome."

My fuck face of a father is using Cinder's presence as a way to pander to the crowd. Though he and most of those here don't believe humans to be much better than livestock, Cinder's father notwithstanding.

An old-fashioned mentality of an antiquated, savage society. One I loathe but cannot change nor escape, not with *him* under the crown. A snarl of hot hatred runs through me but I push it deep down with all the other dark feelings I have caged over the years.

The ambassadors are here because the Common World has begun to question his methods. Cinder is a perfectly wrapped political moment to show my father extends consideration. He is using her to prove to them he is not bigoted, that he is fair and gracious.

The only reason he can tolerate putting on this little show is because she is the daughter of his old friend. I doubt he could manage it with any of the familiars working here.

It takes work to unclench my jaw even as I continue to smile.

Maybe he's not wrong. Maybe Cinder has presented a perfect moment, a rare opportunity for political. . .

No, I couldn't.

I'm not like *him*.

She's different too.

Not only from everyone here but from who she was.

Otherwise, why the fae fucks would a human girl willingly walk into this ballroom knowing what she knows? My dark princess isn't afraid of the Midnight court and meets my father's gaze with her head held high.

My princess. . .

I must be what everyone says, spoiled, indulgent, rash, because suddenly I can't stop the gears running in my heat that pull Cinder into my own plans.

It's ill-advised and it's wicked, yet my body knows with solid certainty it's the only way I will get the support of the rebels.

The King's last announcement is a signal. The orchestra and the festivities resume with a little more titter of interest than before. I lead Cinder off the floor before he can question her any further.

"Before I take another turn on the dance floor with a new partner," I say loud enough for most to hear, as I lead her through the throng, "there is a piece of art of your father's I think you will much appreciate seeing again."

Now that she's been ousted as a human, barely restrained disdain shows on the faces we pass by. Cinder is in danger.

I pull her down a hallway, past a set of guards. As soon as we are out of sight of them, Cinder rips her hand from mine. I reach for it again. Because I don't think she'll follow me, or because I simply want to cling to her hand, is uncertain even to me.

"I don't like being touched," she snaps, dodging my grasp.

"Noted," I say, opening a door and ushering her inside.

Without light from a fire or candlelight, the drawing room is awash in blue hues of moonlight. It's empty and even colder than the ballroom. Cinder is poised by one of the dozens of settees, her fingers clutched in her skirts.

That perfect cupid's bow mouth purses. Cinder blinks twice, and I can tell she's debating whether she should make a break for it and try to run past me, out of the room.

"What is the art piece you wanted me to see?"

There is an edge to her question I don't quite understand. An almost fearful anticipation? Maybe she thinks I was lying, which I am. Or maybe it's something else?

"I must return to the ball, but you'll be safe here for now. I'll be back as soon as I can. If anyone comes, well scratch that, no one will come. Just wait for me. We need to talk."

I'm not done with her, but if I stay, they will come looking for me. I must perform my princely duties and dance with more eligible young ladies.

As I turn to go, Cinder makes a sound in her throat. I halt and look at her.

"I'm here for the Ember of Midnight."

I don't know what that is, but I damn well intend to find out.

"Thirty minutes," I say, before slipping out of the room. Then to make sure she is extra secure, I pull a master key from my pocket and turn the lock.

First, I'll entertain five—maybe three dances if I can manage it—and then I'll come right back and find out how a very human Cinder got here, and what the Ember of Midnight is.

As the music swells and the dance floor blurs around me with a faceless partner, I let my mind drift to the seeds of a plan I've been nurturing in secret. It could change everything. It's a gamble far greater than any I've made before, and I've lost millions at a poker table, along with the pair of pants off my ass.

But with Cinder's unexpected return, I can't help but think fate is trying to tell me something.

Do it. Push the envelope. Show the Mice you mean business.

And it all hinges on Cinder being part of my plan.

Excitement thrums through me like a live wire. Because I can finally get some traction or because it will result in spending more time with a woman who has me twitching with hunger in more places than just my fangs or pants?

Yes, is all my brain says back.

Something tells me persuading her won't be easy. Cinder is different from everyone else, and not just because she's human. The fact she was ballsy enough to sneak in here shows she's not to be underestimated. So I'll need to dangle something she desires more than anything else as bait, to rope her into my terrible, no-good scheme.

I have just the thing.

CHAPTER 4
THE PISS IN THE BOOTS

CINDER

I wait until I hear Prince Charming's footsteps fade away, then I lunge for the door.

Well, duck fucks. He locked it.

Retreating back into the shadows of the room, I can't help but mentally kick myself.

Great, Cinder, trapped in a room by the Most Eligible Prince of Midnight. Way to stay under the radar.

My limbs still feel like lead weights. The familiar dizziness washes over me forcing me to sit again. I grip the armrest to steady myself. Another day of battling this damn anemia. I don't love the combined effects of a large pumpkin spice latte, not enough food, and a whooping emotional shock that just about laid me out on the ballroom floor.

And considering why the Prince bothered to whisk me away to the safety of this room, hurts my brain.

Or maybe it's the bomb he dropped about my father being murdered.

My father died of a heart attack. The prince is crazy.

Something niggles at my gut like a worm feasting on a corpse, eating away at the part of me that's never felt right about his sudden passing. I've tried to convince myself that death is always sudden, always too soon. Now that the prince has said something out loud I haven't been able to even admit in my own mind, the chomping worm of doubt is joined by a hundred buddies that wriggle and bite away at the fragile peace I built in myself.

Nope. We aren't going there, Cinder. So I move to the more immediate issue.

Is the playboy prince going to come back and feed on me? Not willing to share a live meal with anyone else?

No, you know that's not it.

There were all kinds of cues, like the way he protectively put himself a little more in front of me when his father showed up. The way he didn't treat me like dirt, even joking with me. He didn't seem to want to hurt me.

It doesn't make any sense. He has to want something from me. No one helps someone else without wanting something in return.

But I don't know what he wants. The serious-faced boy I barely knew as a child grew up to be a bit of a partying ho-bag who shirks his responsibilities.

That may all be according to the gossip, but he openly admitted it to me just now. Plus there was that vampire girl who clearly had a tryst with him and her mom.

A shudder of disgust rolls through me again.

Yuck. I take a second to lean against the fancy couch, to get a grip on my spinning head. In the few interactions I've had with the prince, I felt like I was meeting different people each time.

There is the cock-sure pleasure seeker who can joke

about his sexual activities, but then there are moments when his expression darkens and I think something is lurking underneath that veneer.

But mostly, I remember the Kaison Charming of when I was eight years old. It was still several years before my father died, and I was often pushed to socialize with other kids in the castle while my father and the King met. Though hanging on the outskirts while the fairy children went about their lives was more accurate.

We'd all been shuffled outside. As the boys darted past me playing tag, their laughter ringing in my ears, the weight of my solitude pressed down on me like a leaden cloak. I hugged my arms around myself, trying to ward off the chill that seeped into my bones. The scent of Midnight-grass and moon flowers enveloped me, filling my nostrils with their heady perfume.

The bright full moon filled the sky and cast brilliant silvery light over everything, a muted sun that was always present, always hugging the horizon, making it seem more massive.

I was pretty good at silencing the pang of longing deep within my chest. A yearning for connection, for companionship, for some sense of belonging. But in that moment, surrounded by laughter, I was painfully aware of just how alone I truly was. For once, I couldn't keep to myself any longer.

Knowing the girls wouldn't let me hang out with them, I asked the boys if I could join.

A white kid with impossibly blond hair and silvery eyes shot me a cruel smile that reminded me of a snake. "What do you know, boys? The meat snack wants to play with us."

A shorter, pudgy boy with dark hair flanked me on the

other side. The press of sweaty odors from the musky boys closed in around me. I immediately regretted asking.

"If we catch you, do we get to feed from you?" the pudgy boy asked, his expression hungry and mouth wet. His pale cheeks were ruddy from running around.

My heart jumped up to lodge in my throat. I'd made a big, huge, massive mistake.

They closed in around me with unsettling gleams in their eyes. The metallic tang of fear spread on my tongue.

"I've heard in the olden days when we chased our prey, it would make the blood more delicious," the pudgy one offered.

"Y-you can't," I protested weakly. "My father is friends with the King."

The blond one licked his canines. "I bet the King likes his blood fresh and that's why he converses with a filthy human like your father. If we want to be kingly, we must follow his example, eh boys?"

My back hit something solid. I turned to find the tallest, biggest boy with ebony skin leering down at me.

"Yeah fellas, let's have a fun chase, shall we?" His voice cracked from hormones, but that didn't make it any less terrifying.

The beating of my heart thundered in my ears. My stomach turned sour. I should have run as far and fast as I could, but I was closer to vomiting on my shoes.

"You all are disgusting," another voice interrupted.

The small gang of boys all turned toward the lanky, dark-haired prince who leaned casually against a tree. A tingle of fear and unease ran down my spine as the prince's gaze shifted toward me, causing my skin to prickle with a mix of excitement and dread. He'd never given me much of a second glance, but now his dark eyes seared into my skin. Even as a pre-teen, intensity and power radiated from him.

"Why would you want to drink from *her*? That's repulsive."

The prince's words cut through me like a knife, straight through my belly button. The way he said it made it sound as if they suggested drinking from a slimy toad-infested pond. While most of the kids usually treated me with cold, polite indifference, the prince gave voice to what everyone was thinking.

The boys nearly tripped over themselves agreeing with him before they followed him off to practice sparring.

In that moment our eyes locked and I saw something intense and raw in his gaze that took my breath away. Was it revulsion or was it something more? Something unspoken? My breath caught in my throat as I struggled to interpret the complex emotions burning in his stare.

Kaison Charming's words ignited a fiery anger within me but also gave me a sense of relief. Because of his insult, the boys lost interest in torturing me and moved on.

But I never forgot how that moment made me feel. The fact that the child of my father's best friend openly scorned me hurt more than I wanted to admit.

It was then that I knew for sure that I would always be an outsider in Midnight, no matter how long I lived there. No matter what special concessions the King gave my father, I was too different. *Repulsive.*

The days following filled me with a crushing weight of loneliness that burrowed deep into my soul, gnawing and tearing at my insides until I was nothing but a hollow shell.

And now, over a decade later, Charming waltzed me around the ballroom in front of the entire Midnight court, chatting with me as if we were old friends who could joke about any one of his character flaws.

Old instincts kicked in as he led me onto the dance floor. I detached, the world blurring into a peripheral sideshow. I hovered somewhere above, my body going through the motions mechanically. I floated there, an observer of my own life, watching as if through a film projector.

Gradually, certain sensory details—the muscled shoulder under my hand, the firmness of his grip on my hip, the faint scent of his expensive cologne—seeped into my awareness, anchoring me once more to the here and now.

Even I can't deny that my artist's eye is drawn to the balanced proportions of his face that have successfully calibrated the sharpness of his father's and his mother's soft, round one. It perfectly straddles the masculine and feminine to create irresistibly androgynous features, making him universally appealing.

The golden flecks in his dark brown eyes pulled me back in further. Then there were the snakes of ink sneaking out from under his high collar. His Highness had neck tattoos.

Midnight Kingdom? More like I'd entered the Twilight Zone.

Then I began to have a stupid episode, my heart tripping over itself, a stupid bout of faintness, until Charming practically carried me on the dance floor. Prince Kaison Charming had saved me from an incredibly embarrassing moment and even made me feel almost. . . safe in my moment of weakness.

Pushing my consideration of Prince Charming's true character out the window, I remind myself I came here for a reason. The Ember of Midnight.

I have two options. Option one: wait for Prince Charming to come back and be subject to his nosiness.

With that last look, I got the impression he planned for more than just an interrogation. I can't imagine what, but I'm not sure I want to find out. The prince's plans for me could range from mild inconvenience to hideously fatal.

Not to mention, I run the risk of the fairies changing their mind and deciding to thrall or snack on me. The King said I was welcome, but I'm not stupid enough to believe what anyone says in this place. My father had the King's favor, not me. And after what the prince said...

An invisible fist reaches in and grabs my guts, giving them a sharp twist.

Murder.

No, I can't think about that. I have to focus on the present.

Option two: I cut my losses and get the hell out of here and try my luck another day.

The second option galls the witchtits out of me after I made such an effort to come all this way, but I've waited years to get the Ember. But it's the only way. What's a couple more days?

Next time, I'll be more careful and put a wide berth between the prince and myself.

I lift my skirts and stare down at my feet, still encased in the glass slippers.

The slippers shimmer in the dim light, a mesmerizing blend of silver filigree and deep, amethyst hues that dance along the glass like living shadows. Delicate yet sturdy, the intricate dark roses etched into the glass weave around my feet, holding them securely in place.

Each step I take in these heels is a balance between

fragility and strength, a reminder of the thin line I walk. I can almost feel the magic thrumming through the glass.

These babies are my ticket home.

The Fairy Godmother's instructions come back to me. *Just picture where you need to be.*

So simple, yet. . . not.

My brain suddenly transforms into a doomsday machine, thinking of all the places I don't want to end up.

Don't teleport into a volcano. Boston. Boston. Not a volcano.

More scary bizarre intrusive thoughts crowd their way in.

I could teleport to the bottom of an ocean, to the middle of an underground supernatural fight club where I'd be mauled. Or worse, to that horrifying Build a Bunny shop where they hang the empty skins for children to fill with the fluff equivalent of viscera. Stuff animal fun, my ass. And people think *I'm* morbid.

Calm down, Cinder, you are freaking yourself out.

Taking a breath, I try to rally my scattered thoughts, aiming for Boston. My dingy apartment never sounded so good. I think of the smell of acrylic paints that practically suffocate my small bedroom and the dirty cereal bowl I left in the sink this morning.

I concentrate on the slippers, envisioning my escape. Nothing happens. I glare at them. "Come on, you glorified paperweights, do your thing."

I take a hesitant step, and suddenly, the room blurs.

Oh, it's working!

Or I'm having a stroke.

The slippers light up like a disco floor, and I feel that unmistakable tug in my navel, the one that says, *You're about to go on an unplanned trip. Hope you packed clean underwear.*

But in my disorienting walk forward, my foot snags on. . . something. Knowing my luck, it's probably a priceless rug.

There's a weird sensation of being pulled in half, like a magician's assistant in a particularly gruesome trick.

And then, just as quickly, I snap back into one piece. I find myself standing in my apartment, staring at a very confused cat who seems to be questioning my mode of entry. Sitting back, its hind leg is stuck up in a near-seductive pose.

The stray black cat with malicious, glowing green eyes keeps finding its way into my apartment, no matter how many times I lock the windows. Its long fur sticks out at all angles, making me wonder if it doesn't stick its little kitty claw into a socket to shock itself just for the fun of it.

I'm convinced the feline belongs to Satan himself because the cat loves pulling out our garbage on the kitchen floor, hissing at me, scratching up the furniture, and peeing on my sheets.

Therefore, I dubbed thee Lucifer.

I look down. One slipper on, one slipper very much not on.

Fantastic. I've left a shoe behind like an intoxicated pop star.

I flop onto my thrift-store couch in a pouf of skirts, trying not to hyperventilate.

The night was a disaster.

"So much for flying under the radar," I mutter to the cat, who returns to avidly licking its privates. A comforting thought cuts through the fog of my disastrous evening. "At least I'm back in the land of pumpkin spice."

It's a small, almost laughable thing to find solace in, yet the idea of savoring the treat at my favorite time of year is a lifeline I can cling to. A modest pleasure, but it may be the thing I love most in the Common World. Right after my friends.

Or it might be a tie.

My girlfriends probably wouldn't be too offended by the hierarchy.

But I better not tell them.

Snow pads in barefoot from the second bedroom. The mass of pure white hair is bound up in an oversized, messy bun. My petite roommate wears a set of worn pale blue sweats that contrast and complement her ebony skin. The logo of Grandma's House, intricately embroidered on her shirt above her right breast, matches the brand of the chocolate snack cake she holds in her hand, already half-eaten.

"Hey Cinder," she greets me though her focus is on the phone in her hand, "can I borrow your leather mini skirt for work tomorrow night? I haven't had a chance to hit the laundromat this week."

When Snow finally looks up, crystal blue eyes widen. "Well shit, I'm not sure I'm ready to level up to your fashion game." A quick glance at the cat has the corner of her mouth turning down. "By the way, Lucifer pissed in your boots again."

What a fantastic finish to a spectacular failure of a day.

CHAPTER 5
SHACKLES CLOSING AROUND MY DICK

CHARMING

Stalking is not a word I like to use, but *following* is a somewhat acceptable term.

I *follow* Cinder's trail to the Common World.

That trail being the glass slipper Cinder left behind.

As I hold it up, I marvel over the tiny, delicate footwear. The guy I know who helps me with random jobs from time to time had commented on what a terrifying thing to put on one's feet.

Then he did a little research with some forbidden tech to get me details on where my missing lady might have magically disappeared to. Judging by the energetic thrum I feel whenever I touch her shoe, I suspect it might have played a part in helping her flee.

The Poison Apple is more than a bar, it is the heart hub of Boston. While I've never been before, I've heard of it. Not in Midnight, but in my semi-regular escapes to the Common World.

The humans-only establishment has a line wrapped

around the block, but I easily make my way past the velvet ropes. It's a talent and a gift that most any prince probably knows how to wield. Though I make sure not to smile too wide and give the security guards too good a look at my fangs.

I step out of the crisp autumn chill and into the warmth of an establishment with wooden beams, gleaming gold metal railings, and a bar that rises several stories high. The back-lit liquor bottles are transformed into glowing jewels. Overhead is a beautiful, complex network of windows that make for quite the glass ceiling.

Off to one side is a massive live tree that stretches over several red tufted couches. Golden bistro lights weave through the upper branches while Chinese lanterns hang over the patrons who drink and laugh. Perfumes and something sweet, like ripe apples, waft in the air as I make my way through the crowd.

Packs of young women decked in sparkling glitzy dresses that barely touch the tops of their thighs writhe on the crowded dance floor, while men with gelled hair drink their beers on the outskirts. It's like a scene from a nature documentary I know all too well. The key is to grab the eye of one of the females and then separate her from the pack, so none of her girlfriends interfere.

Though in my case, I can often reel in an entire pack at a time.

More than one set of eyes tracks me as I cross the bar, and I feel the gravitational pull of the unspoken invitations. But I'm not here for that tonight.

I'm here to see a girl about a shoe.

A shoe currently half-buried in my shallow back pocket that is beginning to be a literal pain in my ass.

Searching for a certain violet-eyed human, I push my

way up to the bar, surprised to find it completely untended. I set my hands on the bar and lean in, looking side to side, waiting for someone to show up.

"Don't worry," a woman sitting at the barstool next to me says even as her attention is fastened to the book she's reading. The subtle scent of rose perfume lingers around her.

"I'm sorry?"

The woman looks up at me through a pair of black-rimmed glasses. She's heavyset, giving her face a full and smooth look. The woman's skin is creamy porcelain. Chestnut brown hair is pulled back into a low bun, and she wears a tasteful black turtleneck that downplays yet complements her generous bosom. Something about her reminds me of a librarian, though her fire engine red lips suggest with some light persuasion she could easily be the naughty kind.

Big brown eyes blink up at me and I know she didn't expect what she found.

I traded out the ornate ensembles I wear in the Midnight Kingdom for a more casual suit jacket and slacks. The white button-down is only halfway fastened, allowing for the tattoos that expand across my chest and up my neck to be on display. Metal rings adorn each of my fingers, spike earrings dangle from my lobes, and the piercing that loops over my lower lip is back in.

Titanium jewelry of course. I don't much fancy a silver burn.

Her eyes catch on my bare chest, her red lips parting a moment as her eyes glaze over. Or maybe she's looking at the opal gemstone I wear on a chain. With my own teleportation key hanging from my neck, I don't have to go through the castle checkpoints to travel from the

Midnight plane to the Common World. The perks of being a prince.

Cinder's not the only one with tricks.

Then the woman's attention snaps back to the blue bound book in her hand. "I said don't worry. You'll get a drink in a minute. They are making their midnight entrance." The woman's voice is soft but confident, her words reaching my ears with a soothing tone. If she recognizes me, she doesn't let on.

Before I can ask her anything else, the lights dim and the crowd's murmur dips into an anticipatory hush. A spotlight ignites, centering on a small stage near the bar where a man stands, his presence as flamboyant and vibrant as a peacock. His suit, a riot of colors that somehow doesn't clash, glitters under the spotlight. His smile is wide and infectious.

"Ladies, gents, and creatures of the night, welcome to the sanctuary of The Poison Apple, where the lost are found and solace is brewed in a cocktail glass. Under Rapunzel's watchful eye, our bar has become a haven for souls seeking refuge and a bit of magic. Tonight, let me introduce the enchantresses of our bar, the guardians of gallantry, hand-picked by Rap herself. Once adrift, each has found a home here, weaving spells of comfort and courage with every pour. Celebrate with us the artistry and allure of our bewitching belles, as they guide us through the night's revelry."

A soft pink glow emanates from the stage, casting a warm and inviting atmosphere. With her head held high, a woman confidently struts forward onto the bar, exuding an air of self-assurance. She is a plus-sized woman with tanned skin that glows under the lights. Her blonde hair cascades down, providing a striking contrast to the daring pink leather jacket. Underneath, a shimmering black dress playfully flirts with every step she takes.

"Here's Goldie, a vision in pink and leather," the genie announces with all the drama of a talented MC. "She's our goddess of the golden pour! Don't be fooled by her sweet exterior—her mixes are as bold as she."

Goldie winks at the crowd, her presence captivating yet playful.

The spotlight spirals away only to land and bathe the other end of the bar in an ethereal blue light which enhances the next woman's eyes. They are two frozen lakes, piercing and alive. Pure white hair frames her ebony face and sets off the deep, beautiful cool undertones of her skin that shimmer under the spotlight.

"And here's Snow, our petite powerhouse with a gaze as piercing as ice and a feral spirit. She might look like a winter fairy, but her concoctions will warm you to your core!" Snow's ice-blue eyes scan the crowd with an intensity that promises adventure and a hint of danger.

Dressed in a cerulean velvet corset and leather mini skirt, she lifts a middle finger, nails painted bright candy apple red, and kisses it before lifting it out to the crowd.

They go wild. I can't help the chuckle that escapes me. I love a good show. Usually, it's me putting on the theatrics so this is an unexpected delight.

The spotlight turns violet and sweeps away to the other end of the bar yet again.

"And now, the enchantress of the evening, Cinder," the genie's voice, laced with a hint of awe, fills the space. "With her bewitching gaze and a touch that can spark a flame in the darkest of hearts, she's the gothic princess who reigns supreme over the night. Her creations behind the bar are as mesmerizing as her legend, each one a spell waiting to be cast."

Cinder steps into the light, sporting impossibly high platform boots covered in massive metal and rubber spikes.

My chest seizes.

I've always been drawn to Cinder, when we were young and when I saw her across the ballroom, but it's only now that I feel I'm looking at the fullest expression of her. Before me is a spooky goth babe, a creature from another world. With each step, she draws me up into her hypnotic spell. Invisible shackles close around my ankles, wrists, and not too surprisingly, my dick.

Her razor-straight bangs fall over her brows and the rest of her hair falls in silken waterfalls from two high pigtails. Those slim arms that were once concealed by long dressy sleeves are now exposed to show off exquisite ink designs of skulls, cherry blossoms, and imagery I'm way too keen to get a closer look at. Embedded on her shoulder is the Poison Apple logo of a half-skull, half-apple mashup with crossbones and the words 'Pick Your Poison' around it.

A heavily chained and spiked dog collar wraps around her delicate neck. Facial piercings glint as she moves, each one a star in the constellation of her face. My heart races, my body heats up despite the cool air in the bar, and I thicken in my slacks. Tonight, her perfect cupid's bow mouth is covered with a sheen of glossy purplish black lipstick that is absolutely forbidding.

Everything about her screams *look but do not touch*.

Rebel I am, I am seized by the extreme need to kiss it anyway and smear that glossy sheen over her face. Or to see that moody color smudged over other more intimate places.

But what the fuck is she wearing?

And why does it have such an intense effect on me?

The baggy violet cargo pants sit so low, the top half of a black string thong shows. A partial corset that cinches her already tiny waist encases her middle with a plethora of belts, buckles, and zippers. A strip of pale flesh is the only buffer between that and the tiny string bra she wears. If one were to remove the boots and pants. . .

Bad prince. I'm not here to get her out of her pants. I'm here to get her in on my plan.

My cock sticks its proverbial fingers in its invisible ears and starts yelling *lalala!* very loudly, unwilling to hear my command as it swells further against my zipper.

While I'm caught up in the complexity and forbidden effect of her outfit, her face remains completely placid. As if she couldn't care less whether anyone else was here or not.

But that indifference only adds to Cinder's allure, only enhances her mystique in a shroud of enigma that surrounds her.

Everywhere I go I command the attention of the room, whether I'm a prince or simply a man who exudes sexual confidence and power. But at this human girl's boots, I'm nothing. I'm no one. And she is everything. All that matters.

The power I've always innately held slides over until she sucks it up like a sponge, absorbing it all.

And for some reason, I find that impossibly and unforgivably hot.

"As enchanting as they are elusive, our Lost Girls," the genie declares, his arms sweeping toward the three girls with dramatic flair. "Each night they weave magic behind the bar, serving concoctions that dazzle and delight. But beware," he adds, his tone dropping into a conspiratorial whisper, "for their charms are potent, and their tales are as intoxicating as the drinks they pour."

The crowd cheers, riled by the introduction as the Lost Girls dance and sway, urging them on. Goldie raises her arms over her head as if commanding the beat that controls the room like a living pulse. Snow leans over and pours liquor directly into someone's mouth.

Cinder clomps several feet across the bar before dropping her ass like it's hot. The move is so fast and slick it acts as a defibrillator to my heart, jolting it so hard I think it might actually beat. She rises slowly from the crouch, her slim hips rolling. A guy reaches out and clamps a hand on her boot. Cinder's head snaps in his direction, violet eyes narrowing with danger. She tilts her head slightly as if considering the man at her feet. Then she pushes a single finger into the center of his forehead, pushing him back until he stumbles away, releasing her. She struts off without looking back.

Using the stairs on either side, the Lost Girls descend and take their positions behind the bar. In an instant, the atmosphere shifts from anticipation to exhilaration. Bottles fly, liquids swirl and glasses clink—a dance of spirits orchestrated by the trio.

As the genie steps down, blending into the background from whence he came, the bar erupts into a whirlwind of activity, the Lost Girls at its heart.

A whoosh of air flows over my face. Once, then twice.

I turn to find the hot librarian chick fanning me with her book. "Thought you could use a cool down after that."

Hot librarian is right.

CHAPTER 6

A PROPOSAL FROM PRINCE HOT PANTS

CINDER

Of course, the prince of persuasion is wearing leather pants. I hate the way they cling to him because it makes my mouth water.

It takes every bit of my control not to gape at Kaison as I take my place behind the bar. In the Common World, Prince Charming shows up as a different persona, and seeing this side of him rocks me to my core.

And my core gives an involuntary clench having suddenly become very hot, wet, and *wanty*.

Traitorous bitch.

Tonight, spikes dangle from Kaison's earlobes and a line of metal studs curve along the shell of his ear. Not silver of course—unlike mine. My knees weaken when I drink in the tattoos spreading like a web of temptation across his chest, exposed by the unbuttoned shirt. The intricate feathers of the wings were crafted by a master tattoo artist. They almost look like they are about to flutter and ruffle in the wind.

My temperature shoots up as my heart is strangled by an invisible hand, and desire rushes downward toward my belly.

I fucking hate it.

I especially despise the twinkle in his eye. It's as if he knows just how devastating his boyish charm mixes with his dangerous, taboo energy. He looks as though he's stepped straight from the pages of a dark mafia romance novel, complete with the billowing shirt.

Since when am I attracted to men who exude sex and schmooze whether in Hessian boots or leather and piercings?

Now apparently. Right freaking now.

I've had my fair share of sexual partners, but not a single one of them affected me to this degree. Not even when they were shoving their dicks between my legs did I feel this level of heat or internal volatility.

It has always been about scratching an itch, experimenting with touch and pleasure, nothing more.

It's... fine.

The thrill I get out of a vibrating needle jetting ink into my flesh or a fresh piercing has always been far more of a high for me.

The last guy I considered getting serious with was based on the fact we were both art majors at Boston University and were in all the same classes. I enjoyed our shared discourse on art, though he got too pretentious for even me at times.

I should have known he was an irredeemable douche when he slighted my favorite artist, Lala Drona. Her blunt yet sharp-edged depiction of women and how we experience our bodies, how we commodify the flesh, is genius, brutal, and beautiful all at once. She boldly showcases the complex and often oppressive relationship between women, their bodies, and even each other.

Growing up in a land where the population must depend on the bodies of humans for sustenance, her messages hit me on so many levels I felt hammers drilling into my chest when confronted with her depictions.

Anyone who doesn't recognize Lala Drona's masterful blend of raw truth and bold beauty is an automatic red flag.

Then it turned out the guy was secretly fixated on my best friend, Goldie.

Ugh.

I wasn't heartbroken even a little bit, just pissed off over the deceit.

Before I knew that, I gave up the cookie.

After that spectacularly mediocre sex, I remember thinking we should stick to discourse on art. My vibrator can do ten times the work he could in a quarter of the time. And I don't have to fake it at the end with the vibrator.

I prefer the efficiency of a good sex toy to work off any tension I might have, so I can get back to other daily activities I enjoy more. Like painting, bartending, or plotting ways to catch Lucifer so I can fling him into the Atlantic Ocean for that present he left on my pillow this morning.

Yet, I have a strong suspicion it wouldn't be that way with Prince Kaison Charming.

The sex, not the cat murder.

I would never actually hurt a cat, but I'm damned close to finding a black-market vendor of curses so I can make Lucifer believe he's always wet even when he isn't. Or see cucumbers that aren't there. I heard cats hate cucumbers. Something to annoy the ever-loving shit out of the feline devil, the way he does to me.

The prince's eyes lock on mine and the world fades into

blurry watercolors around me again, like it did that first time. He has the power to make me feel like the only person in the room, the only one who matters in the entire world.

Being that important to someone makes my heart pound double-time and my palms sweat. I'm not sure if it's because I find the prospect terrifying or thrilling.

At least he seems thrown too. His pupils are blown as he watches me with rapt attention. I pretend being the object of his focus doesn't send a thrill of excitement through me.

"Hey Isabelle." I ignore the prince she is currently fanning with a book to top off her favorite prosecco though the drink is barely down an inch. "How is the bookselling business?"

Belle swivels back to face me on her stool and half her mouth curves up. "Living the dream as always."

Belle owns the romance bookstore across the street. After she closes her shop, she walks over here for a nightcap and reads a few chapters before she heads home. It's part of her routine, something she takes very seriously.

The prince sets an arm on the counter, his white shirt buckling to reveal more of his inked pectoral. A hot shiver runs through me.

Seriously, who cranked up the thermostat in here?

"Can I get her next drink?" the prince asks me before he turns to Belle. "You sell books?"

How does the ring curving over his bottom lip make his mouth even more magnetic and inviting?

A fully expressed infectious smile spreads across Belle's face this time. "I own the romance bookstore across the street. It's called Chapter Three."

He lights up with recognition. "Oh, the one with the gorgeous sign of a rose in an open book?"

Worse than being naturally magnetic and handsome, the prince can take an interest in others.

"Why is it called Chapter Three?" Kaison asks Belle, leaning in. The low lighting highlights the contours of his perfect face and dark tousled hair.

Disgusting.

A woman wearing forbidding black eyeshadow with a styled rainbow-streaked, banana-blonde mohawk walks up to the bar. My boss and the bar owner, Rapunzel aka Rap, answers for Belle. "Because her favorite chapter of her favorite romance book is chapter three where the female protagonist realizes the man she's lusting after is actually a prince."

Belle blushes, her cheeks turning a deep crimson. "You know me so well, Rap."

Rap gives her shy friend a tight smile. It exudes more friendliness and encouragement than I've ever seen her share. "That's why we're friends. Both business owners and badasses."

"A prince you say." Charming perks up. "Why what a coincidence because—"

"He's always hoped to find his own prince charming," I cut in.

Kaison shoots me a knowing smirk. "You know me so well," he purrs, echoing the exchange between Belle and Rap.

Every inch of Kaison oozes blatant sexuality that promises twisted pleasures beyond imagination. Depravity and fun, likely to leave the participant dazed, shamed, and rocked by the aftermath of Kaison's havoc.

The hooded eyes tracking him from around the bar only prove that he commands the room. I don't doubt he could draw in a line of people ready to fall on his bed and suck and lick anything he asks of them with a mere look.

The thing is, the tingling in my Iron Maiden lets me know part of me is very willing to do the same. So I keep my face an implacable mask because I refuse to give him the satisfaction of thinking he has any effect on me.

Oh yeah, I've decided to call my neither region "Iron Maiden" because it's metal as fuck, and I'm sure it will remind me that I'm foreboding and untouchable.

The glare I shoot him could make daisies curl up and die.

While Kaison remains unfazed by my murderous cutting gaze, I focus on cleaning glasses behind the bar.

But then he pulls out something from his back pocket and dangles it in front of me on one finger.

"I thought you might like this back," he says coyly, his deep brown eyes sparkling.

Fae fucks. The shoe I tripped out of. My irritation turns into full-blown frustration as I reach for it, only for him to pull it out of reach.

I hadn't told the Fairy Godmother I lost one of her magical shoes and I'd been dreading it. But now it's here and a knot in my belly loosens. I reach again, but he dodges my grasp a second time.

The look in his eyes lets me know what the price will be.

We need to talk.

Ugggghhhhhh. I don't wanna.

"Hey Rap, do you think I could take my break right now?" I ask through gritted teeth, glaring at the playboy prince I am seriously considering stabbing once I get a hold of that shoe with the very pointy heel.

Rap glances over the activity of the bar to assess if

Goldie and Snow can handle it. I wouldn't ask if I didn't think they could.

Or maybe I would.

Because right now, I need to get Prince Charming's ass the hell out of here.

Rap nods, signaling I'm good to go and I don't waste any time dragging Prince High-and-Mighty to the back. The loud, lively atmosphere of the Poison Apple fades as we hit the corridor, our steps quick and my heart doing that annoying race thing it does whenever he's near.

I shove the door open to the breakroom, not bothering to hold it for him. The room lined in hot pink lockers—Goldie spray painted herself—suddenly feels claustrophobic. Giving him as wide a berth as I can, I decide I need even more space. Or at least, an exit at the ready.

I slink around the prince before propping the door to keep it ajar.

"Scared to be alone with me?" Kaison grins.

I shift nervously. His smile falters.

"I'm not going to bite you," he says with all seriousness.

I fiddle with the buckles on my corset. "I know."

I don't know.

At least I know if he comes at me, he won't enjoy the contact. The silver piercings adorning me wouldn't really be enough to stop him, but they'd certainly hurt. They'd leave nasty burn marks behind. Of course he'd only need to drink some blood, and he'd be healed in seconds.

His mouth parts like he's going to say something else, but I cut him off.

"What are you doing here?"

Whatever he'd been about to say is chased away by my question, and he rolls back his shoulders as if he's going to make an important announcement.

He has ten seconds before I squeal on his non-human ass and get him kicked out of the bar by security. Not that we are truly humans-only. Not with Goldie living with a bear shifter, and her having magic powers now qualifying as a level five mage.

Thanks to some magic cookies I ate, I could be popping powers any day now too.

Again, did someone crank up the heat? I'm sweating.

The need to step in closer to the room temperature being next to me is suddenly more appealing than it should be.

Kaison steeples his fingers. "I have a proposal for you."

"What kind of proposal?" I say, urging him to get on with it.

He's giving me big earnest goo-goo eyes and I melt under his boyish charm. But I don't let it show.

I refuse to let myself fall for his magnetism or good looks. Not when he's holding something over my head, not when he doesn't take a single thing seriously. He's not a person. He's a bloodsucker who enjoys being everyone's favorite clickbait. When he lived in the Common World there was always some new story breaking out about a party, an orgy, or that legendary time when he peddled on a miniature bike down a main street in the nude because someone dared him to.

I'm not falling into his trap of attractive allure because it could only lead to feeling like a used tissue and a couple of STDs, at best.

Okay, so Midnight fairies can't get STDs, but I bet he would if he could.

No one grows up with those kinds of looks and powers without becoming an utter narcissist and sociopath. It's not a judgment, it's just science. Or is it statistics? I was always shit at math.

"The literal kind." He beams. As proud as a cat who's brought home a dead rat for their owner. "A marriage proposal."

I wait for the punch line.

His silence stretches out with expectation.

Har fucking har.

CHAPTER 7

A MURDER IN MIDNIGHT?

CINDER

I raise an eyebrow, letting Prince Charming know I don't appreciate him wasting my time.

"I'm serious. I wish to propose to you. In front of everyone."

He says it all so cavalierly. There isn't a chance I'm taking this seriously.

My mind blanks and all I can do is blink. It must be a defense mechanism to keep my brain from shattering when my psyche encounters something impossible.

"Tell me, Cinder," he murmurs, his voice becoming low and rough. "Don't you feel it too? This fire that consumes us, that draws us together even though it's forbidden?" His gaze drops to my lips, a silent invitation, a challenge.

I swallow hard, my heart pounding a frantic rhythm against my ribs. "I don't feel anything." I lie. "Anything other than contempt for you and everything you represent." I'd rather die than let on that my body has been waking up in ways I never anticipated since laying eyes on him in Midnight.

The corner of the prince's mouth lifts in a knowing smirk and I curse myself for the heat that pools in my belly, the traitorous want that pulses through me like a second heartbeat.

Who slipped me the drugs? This is not normal.

He reaches for my hand, his fingers grazing my wrist.

I jerk back, snatching my hand away as if burned. The contact sends a shockwave through me, a visceral reminder of the vulnerability that comes with being touched. I wrap my arms around myself and level a glare at him.

"Back up there, *Prince Charming*," I say, dripping his name with all the disdain I can muster. "Are you high or just bored?"

Pretty, rich princes must do the best kind of designer drugs. Ones that make them say stupid, ridiculous things with all the confidence in the world.

Maybe the world will get lucky and break from being under his spell when his teeth go soft from the drugs and fall out.

Though knowing my luck, he'll remain beautifully attractive and simply make the toothless look a fad.

"You should call me Kaison, or better yet, Kai. I'm not bored, and I don't do drugs." His tone is suddenly serious as if it's imperative I know he means that.

Oh sure, I'll call the Prince of the Midnight Kingdom by his first name.

Next we can braid each other's hair and watch trashy reality mage TV shows while bingeing junk food.

Actually, I am overdue for a chill night in. . .

The prince takes a step closer to me, his proximity forcing me to drop my arms, or we'll touch.

I don't like being touched. Especially not by vampires.

"I need a bride. As you know, my father insists. So I figure why not give the old man what he wants."

While Prince Charming rambles on about his outrageous proposal, I stealthily slide over to the small kitchenette corner of the break room. I flick on a lighter and set the wick of a little orange candle aflame. In mere seconds, the spicy-sweet aroma of pumpkin apple spice wraps around me like a comforting hug.

So sonny boy wants to rebel and punish dear old daddy. I turn to face him again. "And why not give him the most unsuitable bride, eh?"

Kaison's lips quirk up on one side, but his eyes remain untouched by the half-smile. As if he is having a very serious thought about something I just said.

"You're perfect." The words come out in a low husk, and I don't like how they land in my belly and explode in a bevy of warm tingles.

Panic rises in my chest as I struggle to catch my breath and fight off the overwhelming urge to give in to him completely. Desperate for space, I shove him aside to get some air closer to the open door. He moves, but only because he wants to, not because I made him. He'd been steadily backing me up against the lockers, and I can't think like that, all caged in.

Turning back to face him, I say, "What's in it for me?"

With a smirk and a suggestive tone, he asks me, "What do you want?"

The Ember of Midnight.

I don't say it out loud. I've said it to him once before, I won't say it again. It's a secret need, something I've tried to go without for so long, but I can't stand it. It's like having a piece of my soul missing.

There is no use explaining it to Prince Kaison Charming. If he has a soul, it's been spoiled under riches, wild sex, and privilege.

I learned a long time ago to not make myself vulnerable in front of others. Especially not anyone from Midnight. Bloodsuckers can't be trusted.

Instead of repeating what I went to the Midnight realm for, I ask about the other thing that has been ripping at the inside of my brain since he said it. "What makes you think my father was murdered?"

Kaison's hands slip into his pockets. "Toward the end, your father had a contentious relationship with my father, that much was no secret. It's the stuff of palace intrigue and whispers in dark corridors." He leans back against the lockers, his gaze direct, unflinching. "But the night before he was found. . ." he trails off.

Dead.

I don't know why he thinks he needs to protect me from the word.

". . .there was a fervor to their argument that I'd never seen before."

"Byung-He was working on something for the King. The way your father was sequestered the days leading up to his. . . passing, and the tension it brewed, it never sat right with me." He meets my eyes, and there's a solemnity in them that wasn't there before.

His pause is telling, a quiet space that lets the weight of his words hang in the air. As if sure I understand his meaning. I do. I don't like it, but I do.

"Plus, the morning after he died, I saw one of the King's advisors burning documents in the courtyard. Early morning, before anyone else was around. Maybe it was nothing.

Or maybe it was everything." There's steel in his voice, a conviction that's hard to deny.

There's a moment when everything pauses—the sound, the breath in my lungs, the very beating of my heart—and I hover in that space, disconnected from the agony of reality. His words echo like distant thunder, a storm I'm desperate to avoid by folding into the gray shadows of my detached self.

He watches me closely now, gauging my reaction.

"They said he died of heart failure." The words that escape my lips feel like they belong to someone else.

My father was everything to me. My mother died in childbirth, so he was all I had. While I didn't exactly belong in the Midnight Kingdom, it had been okay because we had been together.

My dad made sure we took regular trips back to the Common World to get ice cream. He took me to the movies, taught me to ride a bike, and most importantly, we painted together. While he made masterpieces on massive spans of canvas, he was never too fussy to stop and fingerpaint with me.

When he died, my world fell apart.

And then it morphed into a hell I never saw coming.

My breath turns ragged and shallow. Anxiety squeezes around me like a python, making me light-headed. I glance at the prince to see if he's noticed, but he only scoffs and goes on. "Yeah, technically that's not wrong. His heart stopped, but I doubt his ticker gave out for no reason. The timing was too convenient with the shit I saw."

A part of me yearns to slip into the void between thoughts, where the harshness of his theories can't reach me.

I point first at him, "You think your father," then at myself, "killed my father."

Kaison pushes off the lockers, frustration etched into every line of his face as he runs a hand through his hair. "I don't know," he admits. "But if I were you, I sure as hell would want to find out."

My chest constricts and my breath catches in my throat, as if my lungs are collapsing under the weight of all the air rushing out. A sense of unease settles over me, creeping up my spine like a cold hand. "I don't know that he was murdered."

And yet, deep down, I couldn't shake the nagging feeling that something wasn't right about my father's death.

I had avoided thinking about it for so long, pushing the thoughts away in order to survive in my personal hell with my stepmother and stepsisters. The idea of my father being killed was too much to bear on top of everything else.

Even now, ten years later, I struggle to accept the possibility.

My entire nervous system trembles with the knowledge as if acknowledging it would shatter me completely. The emotions welling up inside—anger, rage, fear—seem almost tangible, ready to consume me whole. To know that my father was murdered, to face that brutal reality head-on, could very well crush me.

It's only been six years since I escaped to the Common World, and it took a long time to get my head out from under water. Not to mention to get my health back.

My heart flutters in my chest and my breathing becomes ragged, but I've become an expert at masking these reactions around others.

I begin to shut down, retreating again to a place where his theories and my fears turn hazy. Reality becomes slippery and distant as if I'm watching us from the other end of a long, dark tunnel.

"We can both get what we want here," he goes on. "You need safe, protected access to the castle, to the fairies of Midnight to find out what happened. And I don't want to spend the social season entertaining young ladies and their mothers who want to land me as their prize." Kaison's face blanches as if the thought makes him physically ill. "If I'm engaged, I'll be left alone. Plus, bonus points for following the letter of the law while staunchly giving the traditional spirit of it the middle finger. There is no law that says I can't choose a human as my bride. Getting engaged to you will drive my father up a wall." He waggles his eyebrows at me.

"You really think he'd let an engagement between us stand?" I ask.

"You would be the sole exception as the daughter to his only human friend. If he got all racist over you, let's just say it would look very bad for him politically. It would damage relations with the Common World, and we are getting *a lot* of attention right now."

The words of King Charming and his advisor return to me, about having to tolerate the ambassadors. That tensions were high as his rule was in question.

"And if I find my father's killer?" I say slowly.

A storm moves in over Charming's face, and it reminds me of that moment he found me in the crowd at the ball. Suddenly, he's unrecognizable. Whatever carefree façade he's been touting is not the whole of Prince Kaison Charming. Not even close.

"Well, I know what I'd do, but you choose to do what

you wish with that information. And when the time comes, we'll call off the engagement. Or better yet, I'll cause a scandal that forces us to part ways." Kaison explains, and a flicker of mischief dances in his dark eyes as if the thought amuses him.

"Like having a threesome with some chick and her mom?" I ask, cocking a hand on my hip.

He doesn't even have the decency to pretend to look ashamed. His eyes glaze a little as if remembering something pleasant, while he runs his tongue over his teeth.

Um. Gross.

"Something like that," he muses before his focus sharpens back on me. "My father will annul the engagement himself, leaving you blameless. You'll be free with a sigh of relief from the court, and I'll be the prodigal son who can't do anything right, once again."

Kaison shrugs, a cavalier lift of his shoulders that somehow conveys both the weight of his position and the lightness with which he's learned to carry it. "Of course, we'll time it right—after you've had a chance to investigate and get whatever information you need about your father. And after the social season has passed. That way I won't spend all season as chicken bits baiting the piranhas of Midnight society."

I stare at him, trying to piece together the man before me. There's a dance of shadows and light in his words, a delicate balance between the persona he projects and the gears turning behind the façade. And in that balance, I find a sliver of common ground.

He's offering a partnership of sorts, one with an endgame that serves us both. And though I don't trust him, there's an honesty in his plan that resonates with the part of me that wants answers.

"I understand your plan," I say slowly, going over all the angles and curves of it in my mind.

"So you'll do it?" His voice ticks up with hopefulness as he practically bounces on the balls of his feet.

"Absolutely fucking not."

CHAPTER 8
THE SHITTY STEPS

CINDER

Stepping back into the Midnight realm is like slipping into a recurring dream that is as opulent as it is dangerous. Last time I was caught up in the spectacle, but tonight I'm a ghost moving through the crowd, dodging anyone who might notice me.

Ornate carriages drawn by pairs of elegant horses arrive at the castle gates, depositing finely dressed guests for the evening's festivities. I transported directly into the castle in a corridor I knew would be deserted to avoid the grand entrance space.

I'm back to my original mission—to find the Ember of Midnight and reclaim the family I lost the only way I can now that they are dead and gone. With an added objective —*avoid the crazy Prince of Midnight and stay out of his insane plan at all costs.*

Despite the logic of how our common interests could line up, there is no denying that sex, blood, and fame have turned his brain into warped mush. How else would he come up with such an idiotic plan?

Besides, I don't like the way I feel when he's near. My skin heats, my breathing trips, and I...

...want.

I want stupid things, like for him to keep teasing me, to keep feeding me attention like I'm the only being in the universe. I want to discover the full expanse of his tattoos. I want to press my lips to the curve of his grin.

Whoa, Cinder. What is that hot tingling between your legs? That special feeling is reserved for when we sweep brush over canvas and guzzle pumpkin spice lattes.

Both of which I did avidly after my shift last night, well into midmorning until I was dizzy and a little high from the fumes trapped in my small bedroom. I glance down at my fingertips, still stained with acrylic paint despite my attempts to wash it off.

Despite my base attraction to the prince, I've not forgotten what he is. Not for a second.

Once a bloodsucker, always a bloodsucker.

My throat tightens, choking off my breath as it grows heavy and labored.

I don't want to be here.

Summoning every ounce of will, I shove aside the suffocating thought that I'm utterly surrounded, an island of isolation in a sea of glittering hostility. The last remaining piece of my family is hidden somewhere in these castle walls, and I'll bring them all down if that's what it takes to find it.

A part of me drifts away as I navigate the ballroom, watching from a chilling distance. Is the girl in the black ballgown really me? Fear seems to peel me out of my body, leaving only a specter in my place, detached and numb, hovering just out of reach.

Candlelight dances off crystal chandeliers, throwing shadows across the ancient stone walls that blend with the soft murmur of conversations and the rustle of silk and satin. It's like witnessing a scene from another world—one where I don't belong.

My gaze darts as I scan the crowd, searching for the source of my unease. For a fleeting second, I spot a familiar silhouette—a flash of dark hair framed by cruel, pink-painted lips. I blink, and she vanishes, absorbed by the swirling mass of gowns and jewels.

They aren't here.

They can't be.

After my father's death, my stepmother and her daughters fell out of favor with the King. King Charming's disdain for my stepmother's naked ambition had swiftly removed them from the circles of power, their invitations to court revoked. With no one left to impress, she turned her frustrations and cruelty upon me with renewed vigor.

An unexpected brush from a passerby's shoulder jolts me back to my harsh reality. The simple contact sears like a hot iron, slicing through the haze of detachment. My heart slams and batters my ribs, trapped within the confines of my corset as fear spikes through my veins.

My shudder is a visceral attempt to ward off the flood of memories clawing at the edges of my mind. *Teeth, blood, pain, submission. Cold iron cuffed around my ankle. Lying on the ground, looking into the fathomless depths of a fireplace long burnt out.*

The past must remain where it lies—there's too much at stake tonight.

Despite my resolve, I can't shake the crawling dread that tightens my stomach. Each step forward is like wading through treacle, fighting an invisible force that threatens to pull me into the nightmares I've struggled so long to escape.

Every part of me is on high alert. Not only am I avoiding shadows, I'm also avoiding Charming's crazy scheme of a fake engagement.

Like I'd be engaged to *him* in any universe.

Ha!

I skirt the edges of the ballroom, always moving, always watching. The women preen and pomp themselves up. They'll all be vying to dance and charm the prince into a proposal.

Yet I'm the human girl he proposed to over any of them.

A strange slip of heat and smug satisfaction snakes through me. It's an unfamiliar warmth, a grounding force that pulls me slightly back into myself, towards the here and now.

I could be here playing the part of the doting fiancée right now. I could be on Charming's arm, pissing everyone off with my general presence. Kaison would look at me the same way he did when we were dancing. As if he were intrigued and delighted, like I'm something truly unique and worthwhile of his attention.

The exact way I look at a pumpkin spice treat.

The memory of his words tethers me to the present moment despite my desire to flee. The way his voice turned rough when he promised no one would hurt me. . . my skin heats up as my belly flip flops.

With disgust. Definitely disgust.

The fact he grew up to be mildly amusing as well as drop-dead gorgeous means nothing. It means less than nothing.

That nothing is only made worse by the fact he's tatted and wears heavy lethal jewelry.

And I have zero interest in finding more about that dangerous glint that passes over his face when his cocky playboy attitude drops for a moment.

A shiver travels up my spine, leaving a tingling warmth in its wake.

I didn't come back here to get tangled in his mess. I came for my family's legacy. It rightfully belongs to me, not the Midnight fairies. The Ember is here somewhere, among all these gaudy displays of wealth and power. It *has* to be.

A hush falls over the room as the King makes another introduction like he did at the last ball. Everyone stills to listen, so I'm forced to slow my pace even as I back away from the dais where the royal family stands.

The Fairy Godmother dressed me again, and this time we used elaborate dark eye makeup under a lace eye mask to hide my features since the lace veil didn't do the trick. Thankfully the narcissists in this room don't give me a second glance despite my big reveal last time.

"—and I encourage as many of you young ladies to court my son. Take a turn about the dance floor to impress him with your most charming. . . assets." There's a leer in the King's words even as his eyes scan some of the younger attendees.

Gross.

The Midnight Kingdom really needed to get the *smash the patriarchy* memo.

Even as I think it, women pat their hair or adjust their breasts to push up further in their corsets.

Beneath my disgust for these outdated protocols, a dark coiling snake of doubt and anger begins to rise.

Is Kaison right? Was my father murdered? Is the killer here?

Is it the King?

If the King did it, why would he use my father's art as the backdrop to the social season?

It was more than my father's life that was stolen. I was thrust into a living hell after his death, and while I thought I'd moved on, a deep dark need for retribution still pounds in my blood.

With each violent throb of my heart, my hands turn slick with sweat and the promise of a headache kicks up at my temples. Trying to shut down the pain and emotions fueling my anger, I strain to twist the spigot closed. It only intensifies the feelings bubbling up inside me with relentless force.

A shift in a trio of women nearby draws my attention and the bottom drops out from under me. It's as if I'm free-falling directly into hell. The sounds around me distort into a dull, incomprehensible roar. What started as clammy palms turns into a full-body cold sweat. Primal fear grabs me by the scruff of my neck, capturing me in a chokehold.

My focus snaps to the cruel, beautifully twisted faces of my former family.

There stands my stepmother, Marisela, in a gown as dark as her soul, its fabric clinging to her like a second skin. Her beauty, undiminished by the centuries, belies the malevolence lurking beneath. Her eyes sweep the room, cold and calculating. The way she holds herself with a Queen's disdain converts me back into that shy, unsure little girl.

To her right, my eldest stepsister, Anastasia, mirrors her mother's chilling elegance. The cascade of midnight blue silk slithers around her as she moves, seeming almost alive. Ice-cold blonde hair is pulled into an elegant updo that offsets her pale eyes. Her face has always reminded me of a snake, which is fitting to her personality.

And then there's Drusilla, the youngest, who takes perverse pleasure in her own brand of sadism. Clad in a gown of inky black, she stands slightly apart, her head tilted in a mock show of innocence that doesn't fool me for a second. Her colorless eyes match her sister's, though her hair is a deep chestnut brown like her mother's.

Memories of cold, hunger, and pain dance before my eyes. They took everything from me and left me with scars that no amount of time or distance can heal.

I thought we were family.

I was wrong.

Forcing my burning lungs to commence breathing again, I remind myself that I'm not that little girl under their control anymore.

Fuckity frog wads. This is a terrible time to remember I forgot to take my iron supplements. Faintness sweeps through me and I struggle to feel the floor under my feet.

They wear expressions of shock and displeasure at seeing me. Except for Drusilla. She looks as though she's rediscovered a long, lost forgotten toy that used to be her favorite.

As I come back to my senses, a thought occurs to me.

Maybe Marisela killed my father.

The constant undercurrent inside me compacts into a dark ball of concentrated fury. Heat washes over me, and for a second I smell something burning.

Prince Kaison interrupts the King, drawing everyone's attention. "I hate to disappoint the many lovely ladies here tonight." He opens a hand to the crowd where women openly preen, including my stepsisters.

It takes everything in me to pull away from the hellish

memories to calm my turmoil at being near *them* enough to focus on Kaison's words.

"But I have an announcement," he says, taking another commanding step forward. "I have made an unexpected love match and have chosen my bride."

I briefly wonder what other perfectly unsuitable bride he's picked out to piss off daddy. She has to be a real piece of work.

Then Kaison's eyes find mine in the crowd, hitting me like an arrow connecting with the bullseye of a target.

Oh.

Oh no.

A gloved hand stretches out toward me.

I clench my fists into tight balls. *Don't you dare fucking do it.*

"Cinder Park, daughter of my father's dearest friend Byung-He Park, has agreed to join me in holy matrimony and begin a new era in the Midnight Kingdom."

Outraged and shocked mutters race through the room.

I'm keenly aware of my stepmother and stepsisters wheeling around to look at me again. Even enduring their eyes on my skin makes my stomach turn into a boiling cauldron of discomfort.

My vision blurs as my head becomes so light I fear it will float off my shoulders. In contrast, my body turns heavy and unbalanced.

Oh no. Not now.

I refuse to let my body betray me in front of all these bloodsuckers. Focusing on my breath and my feet on the ground, I work to stay even and in the present moment.

Despite the uproar, Kaison wastes no time stepping off the platform and striding straight toward me.

What the hell do I do?

Scream out I agreed to no such thing?

Call the prince a liar in front of everyone?

Pick up my skirts and run like hell?

Oh right, I could smash one of my shoes against a table until there's a jagged edge I could cut him with. That was my original plan if cornered, right? Shank my way out of this.

My brain is stuck on the possibilities, unable to reach a conclusion before he is right in front of me.

Prince Kaison Charming's publicity-friendly smile drops for just a moment as his eyes ask the question.

Will you do this with me?

His gloved hand is open before me, an invitation to join him in his idiotic plan.

A plan that will help me find who killed my father. That will explain why my entire life fell to shit.

I notice the King temper his reaction to the announcement, mindful of the ambassadors' watchful gaze. A wrath like no other is being reigned in, and I feel it stab at me from across the room.

I can't trust the undercurrent between us as the Prince proposes we join forces and share a secret, a lie, that will connect us. It would be us against everyone else in this ballroom, likely in this kingdom.

His fingers close around mine. His stage smile turns into a genuine grin that makes butterflies take flight in my belly.

Except all the butterflies are on fire.

CHAPTER 9
A SIMPLE NO WOULD SUFFICE

CHARMING

Taking Cinder's hand, I guide her back up to the dais where my mother and father are. The King's expression is unreadable, but his eyes flash with barely contained fury. His posture is regal and composed, but I can sense the rage simmering beneath the surface.

I fight the urge to let a smug smile slip onto my face, knowing that it would only stoke his anger further. He may be the King, but I have outmaneuvered him in more ways than one.

Our engagement alone would be scandalous enough—a human and a fairy betrothed? Unheard of.

But to add fuel to the fire, Cinder is also the daughter of my father's close personal friend. It means something.

This is an alliance that could potentially shift the delicate balance of power between humans and fairies.

If the King tries to deny our union, it will come off badly in front of the ambassadors from the Common World.

Common/fairy politics have reached a tense impasse. There have been too many rumors making their way to the Common World about the treatment of humans that have incited conversations about the Midnight Kingdom needing to be checked.

More scrutiny will fall on his autocratic rule, and the Common World might just do something about it.

Our kingdom's strength lies in its isolation. The more attention we draw to ourselves, the more our independence is threatened.

The Common World is a hundred times bigger than Midnight and only a fraction of that power could crack or overwhelm us if they decide the Charming rule has gone on for long enough.

My father knows this too, and the lines creasing the corners of his eyes betray his inner turmoil. Though he wants to lash out, he is trapped. At this moment, I hold all the power, and he knows it.

I'll pay for this later. Dearly.

Squeezing Cinder's hand in mine, I murmur, "Do try to look as if you are a besotted bride."

"I think I'm doing a rather excellent job," she whispers back, her fingers twitching agitatedly in mine. "Not actively stabbing you and all."

Bringing her hand to my mouth, I kiss the delicate bones of her knuckles. She jerks it away.

The room draws in a collective breath.

"Don't put your mouth on my skin," she hisses under her breath. While her eyes are normally a cold wall giving away nothing that goes on inside, there is a look of wild panic in them now. Her scent intensifies in the air around us, its sweetness mixing with the tanginess of her fear.

What? Did she seriously think I was going to sink my fangs into her right here before everyone?

Not to say the idea of devouring her hasn't crossed my mind, in more ways than one...

The room is seething with palpable tension, a volatile mix of fear and anger swirling around me. No one disrespects the royal family, especially not a human. Cinder's eyes dart about and I know she senses everything is on the verge.

My muscles tense and my senses are on high alert as I feel the weight of all eyes on us. I can almost taste the tinge of violence lingering in the air. It threatens to explode at any moment.

So, I do what I always do in moments of crisis. I throw my head back and laugh.

"You are right, it's best to save kisses for when we are in private," I first address Cinder, then the room, "Who would think I'd be taken with someone so chaste to be my bride?" Sure to make eye contact with those around us, I allow my easy-going nature to permeate the atmosphere until it is so infectious no one can resist.

And just like that, the tension dissipates—shattered like fragile glass under my unflappable command.

Cinder doesn't fight me when I take her hand again and continue to guide her to the platform where my parents wait.

As soon as we ascend the steps, I pull my mother into an embrace, and she returns the gesture with kisses on each of my cheeks. Her usual distant demeanor sharpens into focus. Her gaze lingers on Cinder longer than normal, scrutinizing as if she's peering into my bride's very soul or sifting through distant memories.

"My mother, the Queen," I introduce.

Cinder drops into a deep curtsy.

My mother's eyes, usually glazed and unfocused, bore into Cinder with an intensity I've never seen her exhibit. She steps forward, a move so out of character that it sends a ripple of unease through me.

The Queen sets a finger under Cinder's chin, drawing her back up to a standing position. Then, as if caught in a moment, she traces the curve of Cinder's face.

My mother is the one who taught me to respect all beings equally, so I can only imagine the importance of this engagement has penetrated the fog that is usually about her.

Then, just as quickly as the moment arrives, my mother's sharpness dissipates and she drifts back, resuming her usual disengaged repose.

A pang shoots through my heart. My mother deserves so much more.

Then I meet my father's stony expression. I'm well over a foot taller and use the height to my advantage.

Silent communication passes between us, and I can tell he is not impressed with my power play, but nor is he intimidated.

He is, however, pissed off and irritated.

Again, I will pay a price for this little show, but it's worth it.

This alliance is more than just a scandal—it's a strategic move in a game of political chess. With Cinder as my Queen, I'm one step closer to checkmate.

The smile my father cracks nearly breaks his face as he turns to the room. "Let us rejoice! My son, the prince, has chosen the child of my former friend and familiar, Byung-He Park."

To further cement the image of a love match, I turn to openly glow at my bride.

Cinder doesn't look exactly psyched to announce her engagement. As always, her expression remains neutral and unreadable, giving away no hint of her inner thoughts or emotions.

Needing to sell this, I pull her to my side. The way her slight frame fits perfectly to me takes me by surprise as I feel an inaudible click at the connection. Her body is near scalding even through our clothes, making me wonder—do all humans run this hot?

No, I've had humans before. They are significantly warmer, but Cinder is running at a near volcanic temperature. I can't say I don't enjoy the burn.

Despite our perfect fit, a murderous gleam broadcasts from her violet eyes.

My father goes on with his announcements. "We shall continue with the social season, in celebration of the prince's pending nuptials. At the end of which, we shall hold the biggest wedding celebration this land or any other has seen."

He's putting on a show for the ambassadors, masking his true feelings behind a façade of acceptance. I relish how uncomfortable I know he is. He's almost always able to act however he sees fit, but right now he has to play a part. A part that he abhors but is necessary for his survival.

I can relate.

My father's piercing gaze now falls upon Cinder, and my skin prickles with anticipation. "And I shall be glad to host Cinder Park in our abode until that day comes."

His words hang heavy in the air, effectively trapping Cinder in our realm, in our castle. While I possess a great, if not inexplicable, desire to keep her close, I know deep down that my father is not announcing her stay out of genuine hospitality.

No, it's just another way for him to assert his control over her like he does with me and everyone else. All under the guise of false kindness and hospitality.

Then with a flick of the King's wrist, the orchestra strikes up a song and fairies take to the dance floor.

Cinder stumbles next to me, her eyes glazed and unfocused. I pull her arm into mine, steadying her.

Something's wrong. She's even paler than usual, if that's possible. This close I can hear her heart beating in an excited arrhythmic pattern.

"I think the excitement might be a bit too much for my bride," I announce to my father, mother, and those close enough to hear. "We shall take a moment to get our bearings before returning."

My hand firmly connects to her lower back so I can steer her past the scrutiny of a court consumed by suspicion, disgust, and envy. As soon as I touch her, Cinder stiffens. With a sharp inhale her lips flatten, as if she's enduring some kind of torture from my physical contact.

As we leave the ballroom, I spot the ambassadors whispering among themselves, their expressions calculating. They know as well as I do that this engagement is a political move, one that could shift the balance of power between our worlds.

I close the doors behind us in a warmly lit library with a roaring fireplace that is nearly as tall as me.

"Are you okay?" I ask once we are alone.

She darts away from me with a wild look in her eyes. "I'm fine. I just need a minute."

Letting out a shaky breath, she grips the back of the

couch with white knuckles. Her chest heaves as she tries to calm herself down, inhaling deeply through her nose.

Something is definitely wrong, but I don't push. I simply give her a chance to recover. I use the time to study her more closely.

The skinny little girl I knew is still there, but there is a jaded darkness that she wears like a mantle. I imagine it came after her father died.

Seeming to recover somewhat, Cinder comes over to stand before me in front of the firelight.

The light of the dancing flames plays along Cinder's face, making her look ethereal and inviting. Those lips purse slightly, and I'm suddenly desperate to close the distance and kiss her senseless.

I want to make her mine. As if we really were—

A sharp smack across my face interrupts my thoughts.

I touch my stinging cheek.

"You presumptuous asshole." Her eyes are a cutting glare. "Is that your normal tactic? Put a girl on the spot so they can't refuse you?"

Can't say I didn't see this reaction coming.

Can't even say I don't deserve it.

I cross to a chair and flop down in it unceremoniously, giving her a shrug. "You said yes, didn't you?"

"Because you put me on the spot," she reiterates through clenched teeth. "I'm pretty sure if I turned down the very public proposal of the Prince of Midnight, I'd be immediately executed." She paces back and forth in front of the fire. The flames flicker and sway, almost as if they want to reach out toward her.

To be fair, her turning me down definitely would have made tonight an ugly affair. But I knew it would all turn out alright.

I lean over, nearly toppling over the chair, but unwilling to stand up to reach the decanter of clear liquor on a nearby table. The glasses are too far, so I unstop the bottle and take a swig directly from the glass neck, allowing the sweet anise flavor to burn down my throat. "If you didn't want to go in on my proposal, why did you come back?"

The glower she throws in my direction is so intense I instantly give it a name—the purple death.

"I told you. I came here for my own reasons."

The Ember of Midnight. I remember. I don't know what it is, but I know it's why she's here.

When she entered the ballroom, I felt her. I pretended not to, but all my senses were keenly tuned into where Cinder was at any given moment. Beyond that, a need, from deep down at the bottom of my gut, urged me to do it, to put her on the spot and lock her in.

I need her.

For my plan, of course. She's the only one that will do.

The fact I also want her is irrelevant.

Then there was the stricken way she froze when she caught sight of her stepmother and stepsisters. Anastasia and Drusilla had spent a considerable amount of time and energy throwing themselves in my path with hopes of becoming the next princess of Midnight, even before my marriage season was announced. Despite their flattery and perfect manners over the years, I've always sensed a cruelty that turned my insides to stone.

"Well, it's done now," I say. I take a longer pull from the bottle, feeling the warmth spread out through my cold limbs. Stretching, I stand again. "So you pose as my bride and get the opportunity to find out what really happened to your father."

"While you supremely piss yours off," she adds, heavy skepticism in her tone.

And a wee bit more than that, but the details of my plan don't need to concern her.

"I am sorry you are trapped here now," I add with true remorse.

To be honest, I'm still not sure how she's been traveling back and forth between the Common World and the Midnight realm. But I've no doubt her ability to move freely went up in a puff of smoke the second I suckered her into an engagement.

Cinder doesn't deserve to be under my father's thumb, but I also can't help but feel better about having her nearby so I can keep tabs.

Huh. I've really developed a noble side.

"Trapped? You think this is just about being trapped?" Her voice is a mix of disbelief and anger. "I have a life beyond this. . . this charade. One that doesn't include playing pretend with you."

I nod, understanding more than she could imagine. "I know, and I'm not blind to how unfair this is to you. But," I say, nearing her until there is but a step between us. "We could also reap the extra benefits of our arrangement."

She barely contains her sneer. "What extra benefits?"

She's so mean.

I'm obsessed.

I drop my voice to a low husk. "The carnal kind, of course." Deliberately dragging my eyes over her from head to toe, pausing on all the most delicious spots like her lips, her chest, hips, and surprisingly her wrists, I make my meaning known. "If we are going to sell this, I think it's a good idea for us to," I lean in closer, hoping to drag the word over the shell of her ear like a velvet temptation, "fuck."

A sudden blow lands between my legs, striking me in my most sensitive area. The intense pain shoots through my body, sending my head off in a tailspin. I struggle to catch my breath and regain my balance as tears sting the backs of my eyes.

"That won't be happening, Your Highness," she says as she steps back.

"A simple *no* would have sufficed," I wheeze, guiding myself into the nearest chair to help with the recovery.

"You're too handsy." She crosses her arms over her chest, reminding me of a petulant child. "And I don't fuck vampires. Your kind disgusts me."

Between her words and her attack on the family jewels, I'd be inclined to believe her except there had been that instant when I first leaned in, so brief I almost missed it. Her lips parted on a sharp inhale as her pupils dilated to dark pools. Her heartbeat picked up speed and her scent intensified, drugging me with vanilla orchid and cedar. It made my mouth water.

Some part of her wants me, and all I can think of is cracking that part of her open so I can work my way inside.

Not just because I'm used to the challenge of routine sexual conquests.

There's something so deliciously intriguing about Cinder that I can't ignore. There is a raw edge to this attraction that's sparked an interest, a curiosity I've only felt once before.

And that was toward a young, skinny human who always hung around the outskirts of my life.

I'd ask why she hates my kind so much now, but I've seen the way she's been treated over the years. A barely tolerated entity that my kind looks down upon with thinly veiled disgust. If I were her, I'd hate me too.

Well, not me particularly. I'm charming, after all.

Before I can say anything else, there is a knock on the door. One of my father's advisors.

It's time to face the music and take the next step in my plan.

Overthrow my father and take the crown.

CHAPTER 10
CAN'T DRINK AWAY THE MEMORIES

CHARMING

After enduring hours of polite congratulations on my fake engagement, we retire for the night. As my father decreed, Cinder would stay in the castle. She was set up in a room adjoining mine, though no one would be likely to hand me the key to open that door anytime soon.

Like I need a key. *Ha!*

Turning down a corridor, I nearly run into my father. He's shed his public persona, his face now mottled with untamed rage.

"I know what you are doing." He seethes the words, but his eyes are cold and merciless.

"Picking a bride, just as you asked, father—"

The impact of the blow to my face reverberates through my whole body, sending me stumbling backward. The force of his hit is a cannonball of fiery pain.

My vision blurs as I struggle to regain my balance, frantically reaching for the wall to steady myself. For a moment, I'm sure my eyeball has exploded into jelly.

"You think you can outsmart me?" His words are now as cold as his gaze. "You want to start a pissing contest to see who will win, but I don't play games, son."

Unlike Cinder, my father can pack a punch. I already know my skin will darken and bruise, my eyelid will likely swell. Yet another of the precious gifts I receive from dear old dad on the regular.

A bit of blood and it will heal right up. Like it never happened.

I wish I could as easily drink away the memories.

"You really should indulge in a game or two. It might lighten you up." I can't help but mouth off.

His fist connects again. My lips cut against my teeth, filling my mouth with the metallic taste of my blood.

I rub my crackling jaw as he bears down on me.

"You've created yet *another* mess," he spits the words out with distaste and disappointment, but he's spoken to me like this since I was a child. "Now you will follow my every order. You will not leave the kingdom, nor leave this castle until further notice. Do you understand me?"

Before I can respond, he grabs the chain around my neck, breaking it away with ease. The opal stone embedded within glints in the dim light as he snatches it, leaving me without my means of traveling between realms.

Fury simmers inside of me, but I'm not surprised by his actions. This is how it's always been. Still hunched over, nursing my wounds, I find myself at the mercy of this diminutive man who dominates almost every part of my world.

Everyone always comments that I have my father's eyes and his high cheekbones. They say it as a compliment. The constant reminder of our similarities once drove me to press a sharp pen knife against my skin as I faced my reflection. It took all my willpower to resist the urge to mutilate myself, to erase the resemblance.

Slowly, I'd shifted my focus from all the things that made me like him to all the features that weren't his. Where his chin is weak and narrow, mine is squared, and I have my mother's nose, ears, and smile.

After shifting the perspective, I was finally able to unclench my fist and release the knife from my shaking fingers.

"You both will do exactly as I say when I say it. If either she or you attempt to leave the premises, the guards are instructed to stop you both by any means necessary. If you don't abide, someone might get... hurt."

I am in no doubt as to what he's implying.

My father turns on his heel to leave.

Still holding myself up against the wall, I call after him. "So you'll permit it? The marriage?" I can't help my surprise or skepticism. It's too much to hope his only retaliation will be a house arrest.

He pauses, looking over his shoulder but not back at me. "This union would be an abomination. The day this kingdom is handed over to a lowly human will be the day I'm rotting in the ground."

My lips curve up in a grimace. That's the general idea.

"Don't worry," he sniffs, "I'll take care of your mess like I always do." A chill runs down my spine at those final words. I know him and can anticipate his intention all too well—stopping the wedding at any cost, even if it means targeting Cinder.

Doubts flood my mind and guilt gnaws at me for

bringing her into such danger. Unlike my father, I'm not willing to hurt others to further my agenda.

But deep down, I also know that I couldn't resist the opportunity she presented.

A human bride will help everything move along quicker and sway the odds in my favor.

I just need to make sure she survives long enough to fulfill her purpose. Which means I can't let her out of my sight.

CHAPTER 11
A WALKING SEXUAL INNUENDO

CINDER

I wake up feeling the full force of how my life turned upside down when Prince Too-Handsy paraded me about in front of the Midnight court.

I was received by barely tolerant fairies who would rather swallow their tongues than acknowledge me as the future Princess of Midnight.

If only they knew I share the sentiment.

After hours of enduring half-hearted congratulations and waiting for someone to rip my throat out, I was finally led to my new jail cell.

I mean my bed chambers.

Exhausted, I shimmied out of the massive ballgown and cracked into the bottle of iron supplements I brought. Leaving my clutch on the side table next to my phone, a useless brick without cell service, I slipped between the impossibly soft sheets in only my panties and fell into an uneasy sleep.

My room in the castle is something I always dreamed of having as a little girl. Of course, in my fantasy, I wasn't a pseudo prisoner.

The soft flickering light of the candles casts a warm glow over the elegant furnishings and rich tapestries lining the walls. The plush canopy bed is fit for a Queen, with its luxurious velvet drapes and soft down pillows. The huge windows offer a stunning view of the rolling hills bathed in silver moonlight. In the distance, I spot a group of riders on sleek, midnight-black steeds, their coats gleaming under the perpetual full moon. The stars twinkle above, winking at me with assurance.

A fist closes around my heart with an unwelcome feeling. Nostalgia.

While I spent the worst years of my life here, I also spent some of the best. Though never socially accepted, I found solace in the stars and moonlight. I had loved the dark embrace of the Midnight Kingdom.

I remember sneaking out when everyone was asleep to explore, like an adventurer on a secret mission. The moon was always my guide as I roamed through the gardens and stumbled upon hidden nooks and crannies that only seemed to reveal themselves in the darkness.

I often found myself sitting by the edge of the cliff that overlooked the sea, watching as the waves crashed against the rocks below. The wind would whisper secrets to me, and it was like I became part of something bigger than myself.

Then there were the endless hours creating, painting, and sculpting with my father. A cigarillo always hung from his lips, though he often forgot to keep it burning. Too busy squinting at his canvas, willing it to open up its potential to him. I learned to love the smokiness ingrained in his skin and clothes.

Without the rise and fall of the sun, there was nothing to interrupt our time of creation. We'd only pause to hastily make peanut butter and jelly sandwiches to stop our stomachs from complaining.

The food for humans in Midnight is limited—canned or usually on the cusp of expiration, but I remember those stale sandwiches tasting better than almost anything else I've known.

Not willing to pull the massive dress back over my body, I open the closet and find a plethora of clothes, including a silk robe. Pulling the cold material around my too-hot body—must be the stress—I remember the stretches of my childhood filled with fear and loneliness. In this kingdom where darkness reigns supreme, it's easy to feel lost and forgotten.

Once my father became engaged in one of his pieces, he barely came up for air. Without any friends or other humans, it was often just me and my thoughts.

When I learned he would marry, which meant a new mom and not one but two new sisters, I thought my solitude would come to an end.

Boy, was I fucking wrong.

Flinging the nostalgia off like a tattered blanket, I remind myself this place lacks the greatest things of all—my friends, autumn, and pumpkin spice.

I rummage through my small clutch, fishing out the bottle of iron pills I never leave home without. Swallowing them dry, I hope they'll give me enough energy to make it through the day without collapsing. The constant battle against fatigue is exhausting in itself.

I still mean to get my hands on the Ember of Midnight, but right now, I was cutting it close to getting back to the Common World. Yesterday was my night off, but I had work tonight. Royal engagement or not, I wasn't going to miss my shift.

A metal jangling precedes the creak of a door that was locked a minute ago. I instinctively tense, my nerves spiking with alertness as I ready myself for anything.

Prince Charming leans against the doorjamb in a tight black T-shirt and jeans. With a black eye and a split lip.

My brows knit. "Holy fae fucks, what happened to you?"

He brushes a thumb along the red line on his lower lip, his eyes turning unfocused. "A little run-in with a lover's significant other."

How terribly predictable. It thankfully reinforces my ideas about him that he can't take anything seriously or keep it in his pants. My Iron Maiden needs the reminder to keep cool. Even with a busted face, he trains that unerring gaze on me which threatens to suck me under his fuck boy spell. *Not today, Satan.*

"Don't worry, it'll heal soon enough. I just need a little breakfast," he adds.

I suppress a shiver. He means a little blood.

There is something absent-minded about his words that makes me doubt what he's telling me, but why would he lie?

"That's what you get for being a slut," I give him a pointed look.

Despite what I said, I can't ignore the fact that my dark clam of seduction tingles whenever he's near. I might even fuck him if it weren't for the one big thing that has me wary to keep my distance.

Those flesh piercing fangs.

My gaze drifts over his carved triceps, admiring the intricate tattoos that wind their way out from beneath his shirt and over the backs of his hands. Elegant lines of detailed snakes, dragons, and lotus flowers adorn his skin. It's a maze of patterns that I want to follow to their conclusion.

The ones creeping up from his collar are like a living work of art, swirling gracefully around a larger lotus flower at the base of his throat. Some people get tattooed to remember something significant in their lives, but for Prince Kaison, it seems like every inch of his body is a canvas for personal expression. He is a masterpiece in motion, and I can't help but admire that.

Then I see past him to another bedroom. His bedroom. "Wait, our rooms are adjoined?" A flood of dread shoots through me.

Charming begins to smile but after he winces in pain, he works harder to suppress the smirk. As his eyes flow over my body.

"Worried, my little spooky babe?"

"The hell did you call me?"

He pushes off from the door frame and saunters into my room. "Would you prefer goth girl? Gloom cookie? Shadow pup? Sparky?"

"Wh-what? Are you having a stroke?" Each nickname is worse than the last, so bad they make my teeth hurt.

"If we are to be engaged, we must present as a couple. Endearments are a must." He attempts a stern look, but he can't hide the sly smirk threatening to break through as well as split his lip again.

Crossing the space between us, his lithe muscle flexes under his shirt. Like a panther moving in on his prey.

"But if you don't like those, how about my dark angel, my spooky darling, my ghost boo?"

How are these getting so much worse? And how is he making them still sound somewhat sexy?

"Gloomy goddess, Shadow Queen?"

If this jungle kitty gets any closer, he'll find out I have no problems smacking him on the snout.

Still, my body instinctually wants to recoil at his approach. It knows exactly what he could do to me.

Yet there is another part that requests something else he could do to my body altogether.

No. No, we are *not* interested in the slutty playboy.

"Does that mean I get to call you slut muffin?" I bat my eyes at him.

He tilts his head as if considering it. "Perhaps best not to let that out in polite society, but in private? You can call me anything you want." This time a real smirk blooms and his skin tears, causing red to stream over his bottom lip. He licks it up without even a wince. I suppress an involuntary shiver.

Because of how sensual he makes that one little gesture? Or because I'm reminded that he subsists on blood to live?

Fear and arousal mix inside of me. Fearousal.

If it hasn't been a thing before, I'm making it a thing now.

"You know what I'd love to hear you call me?" His voice drops into a low confession.

I don't trust myself to speak.

The way he says it, the way his scent of leather and icy pine surrounds me, it threatens to drown me.

"Kai." It comes out in a rough husk.

Oh fuck. What is happening to my insides? Heat kicks up at the bottom of my gut, like a pile of burning coals.

I thank god this castle is so cold, as I break out into a sweat. Even so, I refuse to let him see he's gotten to me.

"I think I'll stick with Your Majesty," I mock, just to get his goat. Because he's got mine—by the throat.

His eyes bore into mine as if he sees through all my walls and into the depths of my being. It's a look he's given me since we were kids—an enigmatic gaze that always has me questioning what he sees in me.

My skin itches and shrinks under his focus.

"Why don't you like my kind?" he asks, switching the topic so fast I almost get whiplash.

"Apart from the fact bloodsucking fairies have a superiority complex and old-fashioned racist sensibilities?"

"Of course, aside from that." He easily concedes the point which only makes him more likeable—damn him.

I tap my teeth, my black nail clicking against my very human canine.

The humor halfway drains from his face. "I wouldn't bite you, Cinder."

"You'll have to excuse my inability to trust or believe you." The words are flat and cold. Though the memory of him telling the other kids how disgusting it would be to drink my blood returns to me in high definition.

I believed him then. Why won't I believe him now?

Because my trust was shattered after my father, and it's limped along like an animal with a broken leg ever since then. Only able to minimally function because of the life and the friends I made in the Common World after what happened.

He shakes his head. "We drink ethically sourced blood, donated by familiars."

I knew that. My father had a never-ending supply of dedicated groupies who followed him in the Common World, and he'd persuaded hundreds to cross the border and take the vow to be a familiar. It was the reason my father had such a close relationship with the king. His artistic fame and notoriety brought in a lot of new blood to the Midnight Kingdom—literally.

In the Common World, it was often suggested that my father had been a cult leader. Not that I was cognizant of that as a child. Only much later in life did I realize he was a more complicated figure.

But regardless of Charming's claim, he's still dead wrong.

"Some people like to play with their food," I say, though the words come out weak.

"Oh, I want to play with you, maybe eat you alive." That cheeky tone is back in his voice as his tongue curls over his teeth, a wicked glint in his eye.

I flush as I feel my panties dampen. Prince Charming is everything the tabloids say. A walking sexual innuendo.

Despite knowing that, his words still have such an effect on me.

Though part of me really, *really* wants him to do what he says, vulnerability, danger, and primal fear braids in with my desire.

"But okay," he shrugs and takes a step back. "I won't touch you."

A pang of disappointment shoots through me, almost causing my body to sway towards him.

Almost.

Then I narrow my eyes. There's something about the way he says it that tells me that's not all. He has something up his sleeve. The tension in the air thickens despite his retreat.

If I hadn't been sure of a hidden agenda before, the half-smile that kicks up confirms it.

With a few long-legged strides, he falls splayed in one of the bedroom's sitting chairs. He hooks a leg over the arm of the seat, as if he's posing for a provocative painting.

"But what if I *tell* you how I would touch you?" A positively devilish grin curls up until he's showing off his fangs.

CHAPTER 12

FLUTTERS IN THE IRON MAIDEN

CINDER

A dark chunk of hair falls over Kaison's gaze, his eyes hooded with lust.

I want to say something, but my throat constricts, cutting off anything from coming out.

"I would start," he murmurs, his voice low and husky, "by tracing the curve of your jaw with my fingertips. Slowly, so you can feel every movement, every caress as if it were a whisper against your skin."

He can't be serious.

Kaison's eyes darken with intensity. "I want that robe in a puddle at your feet. I want to discover all the secrets you hide under there. More ink, maybe a bit of metal?" He lifts an eyebrow in suggestion.

No. Tell him to stop. This is ridiculous. We aren't really involved, it's just for show.

"I'd drag my fingers over your bare arms. Trace the petals of the cherry blossom tattoos along the smooth skin and follow the skulls no matter where they lead." His words become languid, each syllable drugging me.

Phantom sensations caress my tattoo, swooping down my rib cage where it swirls under my breast.

The coals in my stomach burn brighter, hotter, heating the blood in my veins. My heartbeat slows, pounding in heavy, rhythmic thumps. In moments, I'm hypnotized. The room fades around us and there is only the space between us and the words traveling from him to me.

Kaison's eyes drop down my body with open desire, leaving a trail of heat in its wake. "I want to slip my fingers under that silk robe until I find your sweet little nipples. Find out if they are shades of rosy pink or a dusky brown. Though," a wicked grin curves his mouth, "based on the outline I'm highly keyed in on right now, I can see I'll have little bars to play with as well because, like me you have a penchant for piercings."

My breath catches in my throat. The tips of my breasts screw up into little buds, clenching around the piercings and intensifying the arousal shooting through me like an electric shock. Goosebumps wash over my entire body. Even though I'm still in panties and the robe, I feel completely naked and exposed.

My mouth parts then shuts.

Tell him to stop. Tell him you don't like this.

But oh, I do. I like it very much.

I like it too much.

The sensations his words are creating are as pleasurable as the act of arming my body in silver or tattoos.

I'm frozen to the spot, afraid if I move, he'll stop speaking.

Kaison rubs a hand along his thigh and the movement is absurdly erotic. I want to know the texture of his slacks. I want to feel the cords of his thigh muscles underneath, and then later try to sketch his form based on memory.

Without my protest, he continues. "I roll my thumbs over them until they tighten into peaks before I flick them so your hips jerk as you turn to liquid for me."

It takes all my control to keep from arching and thrusting my hips. Though there's nothing I can do about the hot wetness aggressively gathering between my thighs.

"Then I'll nibble and tease those perfect cupid bow lips of yours." His sigh comes out as a shudder. He closes his eyes and drops his head back as if he is entering the imaginary heaven he's painting with his words. "I want to lick at the top one before nibbling that full bottom petal until you gasp and pant."

I'm panting now. The air is too thick and weighty, making it difficult to breathe. My body is approaching molten temperatures, and a moan threatens to escape my throat despite the fact not a hand has been laid on me.

The hand on his thigh slowly inches toward the bulge now pressing against his loose slacks. Even from here I can make out the thick ridged length. More than that, something circular is pressing under the fabric along his sizable mushroom head.

I'd bet donuts to dollars it's a reverse Prince Albert.

I can't tell which I'm more desperate to know. What words are going to fall off his hypnotic tongue next, or what's under those slacks.

"And then once I finished torturing and abusing your perfect fucking mouth," the last part comes out a growl, "I replace my fingers with the tip of my tongue and taste your pert little buds—"

"No." The word shotguns out of my mouth as a near-panicked bark.

He freezes.

"I don't want your mouth on my skin." I don't want his teeth near my skin, on my body. Not anywhere but my mouth. The idea is an intrusion on the tension he's building.

Cocking his head to the side, Kaison studies me intently. For a moment, I think I've broken the game we were playing by editing his narrative.

"Then how about I just fuck you right up your tight little cunt with my big, thick cock?" He says it as casually as if he were suggesting we go to the movies.

My inner muscles clench down *hard*. Suddenly I'm aware of all my skin, how tendrils of my hair kiss the back of my neck. He's hypnotized everything in and around me until it's all liquid and pleasurable. Every word he speaks is a caress, igniting a fiery craving within me that wants more.

My fingers press into the sides of my legs so hard I wonder if they'll leave bruises later. I do my best not to visibly react, but I also don't tell him to stop.

Then he rocks up to his feet, slinking across the room toward me. It takes all my effort not to focus on the intriguing anaconda pushing against his pants.

When he nears, Prince Charming dips his head until it's mere inches from mine. There is no heat, but his body crackles with an energy that invades my space and makes me feel light-headed. "What do you think of that, my goth goddess? Do you want me to spread your legs open and fuck you until your voice is hoarse from screaming and you've gone blind from coming too many times?"

All I can do is swallow down over the lump stuck in my throat. Flutters in my Iron Maiden hint that he might be capable of getting me off just like this, describing what he would do to me.

As he awaits my response, his eyes darken with anticipation. "Tell me what you want," he husks.

"I want. . ." I finally find my voice, but my words trail off, the intensity of the moment stealing away my ability to articulate just what I need.

There is a devilish glint in his eyes as they roam hungrily over my body. He openly strokes the hard length of his dick through his pants. His breath ghosts over my lips with delicious promise. "Tell me," he urges.

"To go to work."

Kaison's expression smooths with surprise, his hand dropping from his crotch.

"What?"

"I want to work my shift and get paid," I say slowly. "It's time I get on my way."

Breaking his spell, I step away from his gravitational pull. I try to flush out the hot tingles racing rampant through my body. I swallow a couple times.

But I need to pull it together.

I refuse to end up another plaything for the prince, and it's almost time for my shift. Charming may want to fuck around and have fun, but part of me can't stand the idea of indulging him, perpetuating the idea that he can just stick it in anywhere, any time he wants.

Oh, but you would let him. You'd probably even enjoy it.

I bat away the thought.

If he's let down by my resistance to fucking, he doesn't let it show.

Confusion wrinkles his face as he reaches out to me. "How do you think you'll manage to do that?"

I shoot a scathing look at his hand before it touches me, and it drops.

"The same way I got in," I inform him coolly.

"You can't leave." His face darkens, and he steps closer as if he means to physically stop me.

I roll my eyes, ignoring the way goosebumps rise along my arms and the back of my neck. "I'll be back. But I have to go home. I have work, rent, and—"

His eyes, the deep hue of polished mahogany, narrow. "You can't leave even if you want to. The guards are instructed to stop us by any means necessary." His jaw ticks with anger and his eyes light up with the same intensity before it's gone in an instant.

Something about that look jerks me back in time to his face as a boy when he told everyone I was too disgusting to drink from. A serious command that doesn't fit with the man before me.

It takes effort to suppress a smug smile. "That won't stop me."

His face relaxes as he shoves his hands in his pockets. That insouciant grin has returned, and the slut muffins says something that utterly horrifies me.

"Well, wherever you are going, I'm coming with you."

CHAPTER 13

WHY DID I JUST GET HARD

CHARMING

"I'm not putting on the shoe. I'm going to break it and it will slice my foot off," I insist.

Cinder's bow lips tilt up before she looks away, hiding her smirk.

She's wearing the other shoe on her foot and trying to convince me to wear the matching piece. In one arm, she holds the dress she wore last night.

This feels like some kind of prank.

"It won't break, and if you insist on being with me, you'll have to come to the Common World, and this is how I do it. Though I'm not sure I should be sharing this with you," she mutters the last bit more to herself.

"Don't be like that, my little black cloud of cuddles. We are betrothed. We must share all our secrets."

I earn a glare for the newest nickname. My pulse quickens every time she scowls at me.

Maybe I'm too used to the 'yes sir' treatment of servants and those who adore me. Maybe I'm discovering I'm a masochist. I mean there was that time I let that dominatrix pour hot wax on my balls.

Painful yet so pleasurable.

Just like the blue balls she's given me.

Just like Cinder.

Though I doubt she'll appreciate the comparison.

"Stop being a little bitch and put the shoe on or stay here," she snaps at me.

Why did I just get hard?

Doing as I'm told, I wriggle some toes in the glass high heel. The fit pinches my foot with a strangling tightness, but I've got it mostly balanced in the shoe.

"Now what?" I huff, feeling blood flush my face from enduring the pain. This better be a quick trip or I'll end up having to amputate half my foot.

Per her instructions, I'm holding a pair of my boots in the other. She even gave me ten minutes to go and drink some blood. The evidence of my father's anger has already faded from my face.

I'm half surprised she didn't bolt while I was gone, but I threw every argument I had at her. I need to stick with her to protect her. There are plenty of people or agents who will be unhappy with our union and may even try to stop it. If I don't get out of this castle, I'll go crazy. I could really go for a cocktail, and I wouldn't be any trouble at all. She wouldn't even notice I was there.

In the end, she may have agreed simply to shut me up. Or dare I hope, she enjoys my company? More likely, she wants to see me put on a terrifyingly small glass shoe because she's a sadist.

She frowns, a little line forming between her brows. "I'm not sure exactly how to do this together, so uh hold my hand."

"Can we lace fingers?" I ask hopeful, taking her pale, elegant hand in my larger one.

"Only if you want me to cut them off," she says dryly. "Now shut up and let me focus on where we are going." Her lids drop shut as she concentrates.

We stand there holding hands, her wearing one glass slipper while I puff air out of my cheeks to keep myself from yanking my foot out of the tiny matching shoe.

I wait for someone to pop out with the flash of a camera yelling, "Gotcha, idiots!"

Not that it would be the first time I've been photographed doing something strange, but could we at least be naked?

The world tilts and colors swim before my eyes.

Oh fuck.

"Step forward," Cinder instructs. Despite being completely off-kilter, I follow her command.

The world solidifies under the step and suddenly I'm standing in a small apartment living room. It smells like mold and cinnamon baked goods.

When my vision focuses, I find the source of the delicious scent. A candle on the coffee table where a white-haired girl has her foot currently propped, nail polish posed over a big toe. It's the same girl from the Poison Apple, Snow.

"Hey," Cinder says casually in greeting, her face flat and expressionless.

Snow's brows raise in surprise. "Uh hey." Her ice-blue eyes bounce between the two of us, observing our joined hands, matching footwear, and state of dress. The question on her face is loud and impossible to ignore.

Cinder jerks her head toward me. "This is my fiancé."

Snow looks as though someone slapped her with a wet

fish. Though to her credit, all that comes out of her mouth is, "Cool."

~

APPARENTLY, Cinder hadn't told anyone where she'd been going. Or she had but hadn't explained herself fully. When she got to the Poison Apple with yours truly in tow, the questions came like a flood. Not from Snow, who seems content to watch us with the morbid fascination of someone observing bugs and trying to understand their mating patterns—but the blonde one sure as hell had a barrage of questions.

"I can't believe you got engaged before me," Goldie says, throwing her hands in the air.

The Poison Apple isn't as crowded as it was when I came last time, but then again, it's a much earlier hour. I take up a post at a nearby booth where I can kick back (in my own boots now) and keep an eye on the bartenders—bartendresses?—in between deliveries of dirty gin martinis to my table.

"I didn't plan it," Cinder says with a shrug.

"You know that makes it weirder, right?" Snow chimes in.

Goldie adjusts her pink pleather dress with a sniff. "Ted and I have been living together for over a year, and every time I bring up marriage, he changes the subject."

Cinder sets her hand on Goldie's shoulder. "Ted adores you. Don't worry about it. And besides, my engagement isn't even real. To Prince-follows-his-dick this is a publicity stunt, and to me, it's about getting the truth."

Goldie bites her lip and touches Cinder's shoulder. "I'm

so sorry to hear about your dad. I bet you guys will unearth something together."

"We aren't exactly working together, just using each other," she clarifies.

Ain't that the truth. If I had my way, I'd be using her for a lot more.

She can use me for anything she wants.

After the way Cinder responded to my words only a mere couple of hours ago, I've filed away that her attraction far outweighs her disgust for me.

The way her nipples stabbed at the silk robe, they were begging me to pinch, lick, and tease them. The scent of her blood and arousal filled the room, until I was near ready to blow in my pants from the promise of her alone.

The outline of her lace underwear also had me in a chokehold. I wanted her to slip that piece of fabric down before shoving it into my mouth like a gag so I could suck on her desire soaked panties.

Judging by her aversion to having my fangs near her skin, I imagine that might make her more comfortable too.

The fact Cinder wasn't averse to me kissing her mouth, but vehemently against me putting my lips anywhere else also hadn't escaped my notice.

Was she really so worried I'd just bite a chunk out of her arm like some animal?

I pretend not to notice the sweep of Snow's eyes as she assesses me. "Yeah, but maybe you should go through this engagement for real. Because that prince is a hot piece of ass I'd chain down any day."

I bite the insides of my cheeks to keep from grinning.

"He'd probably be into the chains," Cinder says quietly, maybe to herself.

I suck on an olive, careful to keep my gaze averted so I don't get caught eavesdropping.

She has *no* idea.

As the night continues, people ready to unwind from their daily responsibilities stream in until the bar is packed. Cinder commands the space behind the bar like a dark empress, all sharp edges and fuck-off attitude.

I'd waited in the living room of her tiny apartment until she came out dressed for work, and my cock instantly got hard again. My poor prick hasn't fully relaxed since.

In the layered dresses she wears in the Midnight realm, she is a haunting gothic phantom of beauty. But in fishnets, leather, and clothes with cutouts in all the strangest places, her hip bones bared but her legs covered, she is a forbidding dominatrix.

I would drop to my knees and lick her boots if she asked. Instead, she sweeps past me without a word, counting on me to follow her around.

Cinder is a slip of a thing, skinny as a wraith, but there's no denying the raw power she wields. It's there in the jut of her chin, the line of her brow as she stares down anyone foolish enough to test her.

And oh, how they try. I watch from my perch as a string of cocky bastards belly up to the bar, thinking they have a shot. Cinder shuts them down with a withering glance, those violet eyes flashing like shards of amethyst.

It only makes them hungrier for her.

I know the feeling.

It's a thing of beauty, the way she moves. Each pour, each shake of a cocktail is a dance, her lithe body swaying to the music pumping through the joint.

I lean back, savoring the burn of my second martini as I drink my goth princess in. She's a monochromatic dream, all black hair, black lips, and black lace barely covering her moon-pale skin. The only pops of color are the vivid tattoos winding up her arms, a serpentine tease disappearing beneath her sleeve.

Fuck, I want to follow those lines with my tongue, map every inch of her until I know her body better than my own.

I shift in my seat, trying to ease the tightness in my jeans. I'm here to watch over her, to make sure she's safe, to make sure she comes back with me, but damn if she doesn't make it a sweet kind of torture.

My attention snags on a rowdy group of finance bros shouldering their way to the bar. They're already shit-faced, with ties askew and eyes glassy as they place their orders. The ringleader, a hulking meathead with a thou-sand-dollar haircut and a spray tan, leers at Cinder like he's ready to eat her alive.

"Hey, hot stuff," he slurs. "How about you be a doll and get me a whiskey sour, extra sour?"

She gives a clipped nod.

One of his buddies with a bold-patterned tie nudges Hair Cut in the ribs, egging him on.

Hair Cut waves him off before saying, "Is it true what they say about goth girls?"

Cinder doesn't pause as she pulls out glasses and liquor bottles.

"I hear they are always into the kinky fucked-up shit. Is that what you are into?"

I want to laugh. Does he really think that will work? What an absolute fuck-nugget.

She doesn't respond, simply continuing to pull glasses and mix drinks for the group.

A thick tongue slides over his lips in what I'm sure he imagines to be a seductive move. "Why don't you come sit on daddy's lap, and you show me what's under all that fishnet?"

Again, his lewd comments are met with stony silence.

"I've always wanted to bang an emo chick. I hear they're crazy good at sucking dick. Care to prove me right?" he presses.

Cinder continues to ignore him, though I'm starting to have a hard time doing so. My hand grips my knee with an increasingly bruising force.

Hair Cut lowers his voice, and I strain forward to hear. "I heard a rumor that you pierced your pussy. Is that right?"

And there it is. The final straw. Snapped in two.

CHAPTER 14

CROSSING THE WRONG CHARMING

CHARMING

Half my body rises, urging me to do something, but Cinder can handle herself. I won't make the same mistake as this idiot and underestimate her.

Cinder slams a bottle on the counter, the sound like the bang of a gavel. Her expression could freeze hell itself. She regards him coolly, one pierced brow arched. "We're fresh out of sour. How about a nice tall glass of fuck off instead?"

"Oooooh," the crew taunts Hair Cut, in case he didn't realize he's getting his ass handed to him. His buddy pushes up his glasses and laughs nervously, watching Cinder with interest.

She slides the drinks across the bar to Hair Cut's friends, her expression stony. "Here you go, boys. Enjoy your night."

Aka, fuck off. Now.

As Cinder turns to walk away, Hair Cut's hand darts out

quick as a snake to snag her wrist. Cinder yelps in surprise when he yanks her forward, his other arm sweeping across the bar to send glasses and bottles crashing to the floor.

In a heartbeat, he has her bent backward over the bar, his massive body pinning her in place. One meaty hand finds her throat, squeezing just hard enough to make her gasp for air.

Even his buddies take a step back in shocked disbelief. The one in glasses nearly trips over a bar stool.

"I bet a little slut like you loves being dominated," Hair Cut growls, his face inches from hers.

Cinder scrabbles at his wrist, her nails leaving bloody furrows in his skin. But Hair Cut just laughs, his fingers pinching her cheeks, forcing her lips to pucker, preparing her for his disgusting mouth.

A visceral, white-hot rage explodes inside me at the sight of his hands on her. I'm across the room in a flash, my fingers clamped around his wrist in a vise grip. He yelps as I wrench his arm behind his back, bending him over the bar until his cheek smacks the sticky surface.

"I believe my fiancée said fuck off," I say, smiling through my fangs. "Or did you get a bit of your brains trimmed out with your last overpriced haircut?"

Murmurs ripple around me.

"Holy shit, it's the Prince of Midnight."

"I knew it was him!"

"Fuck, dude. He's gonna rip Alan's throat out."

Hair Cut whimpers, trying to wriggle out of my hold. Glasses Guy's fingers twitch nervously. His cronies look on in slack-jawed terror, knowing full well who—and what—I am.

It's not surprising people recognize me. Not only am I a royal, but I was required to spend two years of university in the Common World—a diplomatic exchange student system to keep good relations between the lands. Oxford is where I started developing the reputation of a careless party boy who was always down to bang the gong.

But my devil-may-care persona has all but evaporated, as cold fury pulsates in me with barely restrained violence.

"S-sorry, man," Hair Cut stutters. "I didn't know she was your girl."

Goldie is now poised next to Cinder, holding the soda tap like a gun, pointing it at Hair Cut despite the fact I've subdued him. Snow is on the other side of Cinder, icy eyes shooting hate and promising violence as she grips a full bottle of vodka by the neck.

I lean in close, my voice a dangerous purr. "Let me make something clear, *friend*. It's never okay to treat any person like an object for your impulsive tiny-balled pleasure, whether they're someone's girl or not. Do we understand each other?"

Hair Cut blanches, his throat bobbing as he nods frantically while he absorbs the blunter points of consent.

Cinder scoffs, crossing her arms. "I'm not anyone's girl, asshole." Despite the venom in her tone, I can't help the thrill that zips through me at the thought.

My girl. If only.

"You owe her an apology," I add.

I release the meathead with a shove, sending him sprawling into his bros. They catch him as they stumble back, nearly tripping over each other in their haste to put distance between us.

"Apologize." My voice is deadly calm. "Now."

Hair Cut swallows hard, his eyes flicking to Cinder. "S-sorry. Won't happen again."

Cinder gives him the look I have dubbed *the purple death*. "Whatever. Just get the fuck out of my bar."

They don't need to be told twice. The group practically falls over themselves in their scramble to vacate, leaving a wake of nervous titters behind them.

"Excuse me a moment, ladies, I think I'll see them out. Make sure they don't get lost." I say smoothly to Cinder and her friends who have now crowded behind her.

The room is a blur as I leave so fast the bouncer doesn't even see me pass by. I speed up until I'm behind the slow, bumbling group of men.

Hands in my pockets, I stalk them as they turn down a quiet street.

"Dude, we can't take you anywhere. Why you always gotta start shit?" one of the men asks Hair Cut.

Before he can answer, I do it for him. "Must be compulsive."

They all freeze and turn to meet my gaze.

"Hello again, gents. If I may have a word with that one." I point to Cinder's offender.

Hair Cut's face fills with blood, fueled by embarrassment and rage. The scent of it washes over me. While part of me wants to sink my fangs into his veiny, pulsating neck because I'm always thirsty, I wouldn't lower myself to drink from such a disgusting source. I have taste.

"Fuck off, man—" he starts, but I stop him. My pupils open up, and I reach out with my power. I grip him in it and he freezes.

In seconds, Hair Cut is a drooling mess, completely at my whim.

"Now, it may seem like I'm here for you, Alan," I say, rubbing my chin. "But I'm really here for him." I point to Hair Cut's clumsy friend with the glasses.

The three other men turn toward my true target while Alan remains slack-jawed and frozen.

"See, you made a mistake. There's no way this group of bros would let you in their group, wearing that *gouzasui*." I point at the mid-range time piece wrapped around his wrist.

Glasses Guy narrows his eyes at me, his loose, slouchy posture suddenly straightening.

"Tell me Alan, how much did he pay you to fuck with the bartender?" I ask without taking my eyes off the real threat.

"Fifty bucks," Alan says in an almost robotic voice.

My disgust forces me to double-take at the haircut. "You probably don't get up in the morning for less than. . ." I roll my fingers expectantly.

"A two-million-dollar deal," he finishes my prompt.

My lip curls up in a sneer. "So you did it for the sport of it, did you?" I'll deal with this son of a bitch, but not yet.

I turn my attention back to Glasses Guy, who's now watching me with a wary, calculating gaze. "So, who sent you? My father? Or maybe some other disgruntled court member who doesn't want a beater for their princess?"

A flicker of surprise crosses his face before he schools his features into a mask of indifference. "I don't know what you're talking about."

I chuckle darkly. "Don't play dumb. It doesn't suit you. I saw the way you were watching her, the way your hand kept twitching towards your jacket. You're here to kill her, aren't you?" I swipe my thumb across my lower lip. "What was the plan? A little reconnaissance? Wait until after she got off her shift at the bar then strike? Or was big meaty and clumsy over here a distraction so you could slip poison in her water glass behind the bar?"

His jaw clenches, and I know I've hit the mark.

"Ah, but you didn't count on me being there, did you?"

In a blur of motion, he lunges at me, fangs bared. He's fast, skilled, a trained assassin. But I'm faster.

I hear gasps of fear as the rest of the men scram, leaving Alan behind.

We clash in a flurry of blows, his strength nearly matching mine. But he doesn't know pain like I do. I took that pain and turned it into discipline, into muscle—into hours, days, months, years of sweat and movement.

Glasses throws a precise punch, but I easily duck and grab his arm. With a quick twist, I pin him against the wall, my hand around his throat. "You picked the wrong girl to mess with," I growl. "And the wrong Charming to cross."

None of this was necessary—like toying with a plaything before crushing it under my boot. But it was my way. I wanted him to know I could best him on my own.

But I had to finish this like a Charming.

I unleash my power, flooding his mind with a command. "You will drink your own blood until there is nothing left."

The assassin's eyes widen in horror as he raises his hand to his mouth, fangs sinking deep into his wrist. A muffled scream rips from his throat as he begins to drink.

It's the worst agony a vampire can endure.

I would know.

And I've doomed him to suffer that torment until he meets his end.

I leave him to his fate, turning back to Hair Cut.

"It's time to confess your sins. Alan, was it? Have you assaulted others before? Ladies or otherwise?"

With a dumb nod of his head, he confirms what I guessed.

"Despite our chat, I don't feel you've learned your lesson."

I sink my power in deeper.

The King is known to wield the power of thrall. The only vampire able to control the will of others.

What the world doesn't know is it's a family trait. And I absolutely fucking hate it. But right now, the ability is to my benefit.

Images flash in my mind, broadcast from his tiny pea brain. Women crying, struggling, or simply unconscious under his slobbering, meaty body.

Anger slices through me like a razor blade, sharpening me into a tool that can correct his supremely shitty behavior.

Cinder's face, that split second of fear that breaks her mask causes a storm to explode, detonating a bomb I didn't know was inside me.

I was going to thrall him into marching to the nearest police station, confess his every sin, and make him wildly proclaim to other inmates he truly enjoys being bottom bitch, but now...

Now I know too much. I know the girls' faces. I feel their pain. The need to protect Cinder from this monster overwhelms me. I catch the strands of thought floating around. He planned to return. He planned to catch her unawares in the back alleyway where she works and finish what he started.

That won't be happening.

Not ever.

I release him enough from the thrall that he is more present in his mind, but unable to move.

I bare my fangs, letting him know what's about to come.

I RETURN TO CINDER, concern tightening my face as I take in the angry red marks on her throat. "Are you alright?" My knuckle brushes the still wet smudge of blood on my jacket. Not that anyone would spot it against my black ensemble.

Cinder waves me off, but I catch the slight tremble in her fingers. "I'm fine. I had it handled."

I nod, knowing better than to push.

Unlike me, Cinder possesses pride.

"I know you did. But I couldn't just sit by and watch that asshole put his hands on you."

Something flickers in those violet depths, gone too quickly for me to decipher. Gratitude?

Nah, couldn't be.

And I very much doubt she'd feel gratitude if she found out the state I left those two guys in. Though no one will find them after what I did.

Loose cannon.

Irresponsible.

I've been called all of these, but the public at large is ignorant of the deep river of violence that flows deep inside me. The one that doesn't abide predators preying on the weak, whether they be fuck boys in bars or my father with his people.

Unfortunately, I also realize it may be the very trait that makes me most like my father.

Maybe the Mice are right to fear me. If they knew I had the power of thrall, they'd cut all contact immediately.

Cinder busies herself wiping down the bar. The angry slash of her mouth softens just a touch.

"You're impossible," she mutters, but there's no real heat behind it. As she turns away to tend to another customer, I swear I catch the barest hint of a smile playing at the corner of her lips. It's gone in a flash, replaced by her usual scowl, but it's enough to send a rush of heat straight to my chest.

One day, I'll coax a real smile out of her. For now, I'm content to sit back and watch my dark empress rule her domain.

Though for the first time, the idea of dissolving our little arrangement sends shoots of pain and anxiety through me. She's perfect because of what she is, but now I'm starting to believe she's perfect because of *who* she is.

She's a luxury I can't afford, a dream I have to let die before it even has a chance to take root.

If she learns who I truly am, she'll realize I'm just a shadow of the man I pretend to be. The confidence, the charm, the devil-may-care attitude—it's all a carefully crafted illusion, designed to hide the scars, the violence, the ugliness that's at my core.

Scars inflicted by a father who saw me as nothing more than an unsatisfactory heir, riddled with weakness. And no matter how much I want to believe in the possibility of us, a part of me knows that in the end, I'll only drag her down. It's all I know how to do.

No matter what I do, I will always carry a piece of my father inside me. A dark, twisted part that threatens to taint everything I touch. The darkness of my father's legacy seeps into every fiber of my being, staining me with the same cruelty and violence that runs in his blood.

I have no intention of subjecting Cinder to that.

When the time comes, I'll let her go. I'll watch her walk away and tell myself it's for the best.

So why do my chest tighten and my hands clench every time I think of letting her go?

CHAPTER 15

WAITING FOR THE SHOE TO DROP

CINDER

The last couple of days have been too intense. I've returned to my childhood home, laid eyes on my abusive stepfamily, got trapped in a castle, assaulted at work, and oh yeah, engaged to the Prince of fucking Midnight.

After that guy grabbed me, Snow ran over to see if I was okay. She'd been on her way to deliver an ass whooping, but Kaison beat her to it. I tried to play it off, but she told Goldie.

"You should have seen him, Goldie," Snow gushes. "He was a flash of danger. All he needed was some shining armor."

Goldie throws her arms around Kaison, squeezing him in a near back-breaking hug.

Then Rap finds out. She just about blows a gasket. My boss's face turns this mottled red color as she barks at the security guards to get the bastard's picture off the camera and make sure to call the cops if he ever comes back.

She tries to send me home. Usually what she says goes, but I tell her I want to finish out the night. It will make me feel normal. Otherwise, I'll stew over what happened. We compromise. I sit across from her and drink a cup of tea while she works on her computer. Then I get thirty minutes with some paper and the charcoals I have in my locker.

When I return to the bar, the crowd has died down and I find Snow and Goldie have created a fan club for Prince Charming in my absence.

The three of them fall into an enthusiastic discussion about Goldie's love life and the best brand of gin. I busy myself with cleaning glasses, trying to ignore the strange lurch in my gut as I watch them get along like a house on fire.

"So you keep thinking your beau is going to propose to you, but then he doesn't," Kai asks Goldie as he sips on another martini.

"I mean, I thought so." Goldie groans before dropping her head into her hands. "He set up this perfect picnic, and it was super romantic. He even made a pink heart cake, or tried to anyway, like I made him when we first met. But then the sky opened up and a torrential rain came down on our heads. The cake melted, and he practically scooped it into the picnic basket before we ran to the truck to keep from drowning."

I listen halfheartedly as Kai lets out a low, throaty chuckle. "The ring was in the cake."

"Shut up," Snow says, even as her face registers shock. "You can't know that."

"Oh yes, I can," Kai says with a knowing smirk. "You have to ask yourself, why would a man scoop up wet cake and put it back into a picnic basket?"

I roll my eyes at their antics, focusing on wiping down

the counter. But I can't help the twinge of envy that creeps up my spine. They are so at ease with each other, laughing and joking like old friends. And here I am, the outsider, the dark stone blocking the path of their effortless flow.

As their laughter rings out over some ridiculous joke, I feel myself retreating further into my shell, hardening against the warmth of their camaraderie.

Later, Kaison walks in silence next to me on the way to my apartment, his hands shoved in his pockets. I inhale deeply, trying to let the crisp chill of the Boston air calm me.

All I want is to put on my sweats, wrap myself up in a cozy blanket, and drink, eat, or smell something pumpkin spice. Or better yet, get my hands on some paints or charcoals again and lose myself in creating something outside of myself.

By myself.

I want to be alone.

"We need to get to Midnight," Kaison says once we are a block from my place.

"I know," I snap. "But I need to make another stop." I can't keep the irritation out of my voice. He doesn't say anything else or ask questions, just lets me lead.

I don't want to think about what's got me in such a shitty mood. While I can pin it on that asshole putting hands on me at work, it's more likely I'm pissed about how much Kaison gets along with my friends. Or maybe it's that he made this big public display of saving the day. That he defended *his girl*.

But I'm not his girl. And I told him that.

So why do I feel so fucking twisted up inside?

Because I wish I was?

We head up to my place so I can grab the ballgown

before immediately heading back out. It's only a fifteen-minute walk to a building where big neon signs glow above the door—the Pumpkin Coach Club. Kaison's face lights up, but I walk by the front door, opting for the alley.

"Wait, but aren't we going to—" he points at the front door.

I shake my head. "We are here for business, not to drink daiquiris and egg on the performers."

The prince juts his lower lip out in a pout and shuffles after me.

For fae fuck's sake, he's actually cute. I'm sure with that look he's gotten away with every little thing in his life.

My craptastic mood dissolves by half.

The Pumpkin Coach Club's back entrance is decidedly less glamorous than its glittering façade. I lead Kaison through the dimly lit alley, ignoring his continued pout at being denied the full club experience.

We find the Fairy Godmother in her dressing room. The muscular, Black drag queen sits as if she is on a throne, surrounded by a whirlwind of sequins, feathers, and wigs. She looks up from her vanity, her expression morphing from surprise to delight as she takes in my unlikely companion.

"Well, well, if it isn't the elusive Cinder," she trills in a honeyed voice, rising to her full, imposing height that easily towers over six feet, even without the stiletto heels propping her up. "And who is this delicious morsel you've brought to my doorstep?"

Kaison flashes his most charismatic grin, bowing with a flourish. "Prince Kaison Charming, at your service, milady. It's an honor to meet the legendary Fairy Godmother." Then he takes her hand and kisses the back of it.

I suppress an eye roll as Kiki practically swoons, batting

her impossibly thick false eyelashes. "Oh, my my my. The pleasure is all mine."

Clearing my throat I step forward, drawing her attention back to the matter at hand. "We need to talk. There's been a. . . development."

Her gaze darts between us, a knowing gleam in her eye. "Do tell, darling. I'm all ears."

"Prince Charming and I are engaged," I say the words quickly and efficiently. Like ripping off a Band-Aid.

The godmother's perfectly painted mouth forms a perfect "O" of shock before stretching into a knowing smile. "Engaged? Well, I did hear that you move fast, your majesty." She winks at Kaison, who grins right back.

Cheeky bastard.

There wasn't an ounce of genuine surprise in her reaction. She already knew. Though I'm not sure whether it's because she has an ability to divine the future, like she does in the crowd work portion of her act, or something else.

"It's not a real engagement," I quickly clarify. "It's a long story, but we need your help. I'll be spending more time in Midnight, so is there any other way to travel between realms besides the glass slippers? Sharing them is complicated." I side-eye Kaison. He blinks rapidly like the picture of innocence, acting like he didn't insist he stay glued to my side at all times.

Gratitude and resentment have been a strange mix inside me all night.

Dame Kiki taps a long, glittery acrylic nail against her chin, considering. "I'm afraid those slippers are one of a kind, my dear. Acquiring another pair would be tricky and will take time." A sly smile plays at the corners of her mouth. "But perhaps this shared mode of transport is a blessing in disguise, hm? A chance for you two lovebirds to get better acquainted."

Kaison grins wolfishly while my face heats.

"We're not—it's not like that. I told you it's temporary."

The Fairy Godmother simply laughs, a booming sound that fills the small space. "Of course, darling. Whatever you say." She winks again. Then her humor fades as she focuses on me. "Did you get what you went for?"

My spine stiffens, though I don't mean for it to. I'm careful not to look at Kaison to see if he's watching my reaction.

"Not yet," I say in a low voice. "But I also wanted to return this." I hand over the second ballgown I've borrowed. "Thank you for dressing me."

She waves a hand that could palm a basketball. "It was my pleasure. I'd offer to keep you in the bougie threads, but I'm sure his people will want to take over."

"I imagine so," Kaison says dryly, setting his hip against the vanity countertop. "The grooming of my future princess shall be top priority in the palace."

A warning of what's to come.

"Oh goodie," I say.

He gives me a wry, lopsided smile. A real one, just for me. My belly flips, then flops.

"Afterall, appearances are everything." Kai turns to look at the makeup lining the counter.

"Yes, but it's important not to focus on that so much you forget who you are and what you are about," Dame Kiki says, giving him a weighted gaze.

Kaison's shoulders stiffen almost imperceptibly as he blinks.

There is something serious and loaded with implications in her words, but I don't understand.

The smile he gave me remains but disappears from his eyes. "I never do."

I am definitely missing something.

I open my mouth to ask, but Dame Kiki turns to me. "And you, have recent events made you feel any more *powerful?*" She arches that drawn on eyebrow, loading the word 'powerful' up like a gun.

Almost two years ago, Goldie, me, and our friend Red ate cookies created by a powerful mage—Red's grandmother. Both Red and Goldie had developed level five mage powers, which is as rare as finding an ogre shopping for china at a mall.

Since the cookies, there has been this shoe hanging over me, and I keep waiting for it to drop.

While I'm happy to watch reality mage shows where level three magic-wielders who care too much about social status scrape, connive, and sleep their way to better alliances, I don't want to join in.

"Can't say that they have," I say flatly. The pressure of Kaison's gaze pushes against the side of my face and I know he's trying to figure out what we are talking about. My skin prickles under his scrutiny and I'm ready to get out of here.

I readjust my grip on the glass slippers. "I guess we'll make do with these, thanks Kiki."

She waves a dismissive hand, already turning back to her mirror. "Anytime. And do keep me updated on this delicious little development. I do so love a good royal romance."

Royal romance, my ass.

CHAPTER 16
PUSSIES LOVE A PRINCE

CINDER

The door creaks loudly when I open it to my apartment. It's time to jam our feet into those glass shoes and get back to Midnight. *After* I grab a few things to take with me.

My heart skips a beat with excited anticipation. That surprises me.

There is certainly dread coursing through me. There is danger and past pain, but a bigger part of me truly missed the Midnight realm. The kingdom has been irrevocably woven into the fabric of my being. Even those traumatic years after my father died couldn't change that.

But I also love the Common World.

I'm tired as all fae fucks from straddling two worlds, two time zones, and two lives. But it also feels so right, as if two halves of myself are coming together.

This time I'll be packing even more iron supplements and snacks to offset my anemia which is acting up like a bitch. The constant stress of swirling ballrooms, the shocking bombshells about my father's supposed murder, and enduring an unexpected public proposal have nearly put me on my ass multiple times now. It's no wonder my anemia has decided to rear its ugly head. The sheer exhaustion and emotional rollercoaster have drained me to the point where my hands tremble and my vision blurs at the worst possible moments. I hate the reminder I've had so much strength sucked out of me. Literally.

A clatter from our tiny kitchenette explodes in the apartment. It only takes a half step around the corner to see what's going on. Snow is in sweatpants and a tank top with her hair in a messy bun, making her behavior look all the more wild. She wields the bristle side of a broom at the hissing fluffy cat inside our cabinet. Lucifer pushes a glass off the shelf. It shatters on the floor next to even more shards of glass.

"Damn you, demon kitty from hell," Snow cries out.

"What are you doing?"

The question comes from behind me, where Kaison's chest brushes my shoulder blades, sending a shiver through my body.

Snow's head whips around. "This cat is out for blood. He won't be satisfied until he's burned this apartment to the ground after pissing in all our shoes."

As if to confirm, Lucifer hisses and swipes a clawed paw at Snow from his perch. My roommate shakes the broom back at the feline with menace.

Strong hands move me aside as Kaison walks into our kitchenette/living room, observing the scene closer.

Then without a care in the world, he gets between the two battling enemies, reaches into the cabinet, and gingerly pulls out the demon cat from our cupboard.

Snow's mouth drops open with the disbelief I feel.

In seconds, the fucking Satan cat is purring in Kaison's arms.

"What in the fae fucks is happening right now?" Snow asks in equal parts awe and disgust.

Kaison rubs the cat's ears and the purr double times. "What can I say? Pussies love me." Then he throws us that cheeky grin of his.

The broom hits the ground with a clatter as Snow stomps out of the kitchen. "That's it, I'm out." The door to her room slams shut behind her.

I grab the dustpan, pick up the broom, and start to clean up the broken glass. "Stupid ass cat."

Kaison puts the cat down in the living room and crosses over to crouch beside me as if to help.

I reach out and grab a large chunk of glass, but Kaison's proximity throws me, and my thumb slides across the sharp end, splitting the skin there.

I curse and suck the split digit into my mouth.

Kaison stiffens next to me. My heart thumps erratically, fearfully.

I'm bleeding.

In front of a vampire.

Slowly, I raise my gaze to meet his.

His pupils have swallowed his irises, and he stares at me with blatant hunger. Kaison's Adam's apple bobs in a slow, forced movement.

Fear skitters down my spine like a rodent on the run.

I bite on my thumb with my blunt teeth, as if to force the pain to drown out the sudden terror that grips me.

"Cinder," he says slowly, as if afraid of spooking me.

It's already too late.

Adrenaline pumps through me. Any second he's going to lunge at me. Tackle me to the ground and sink his teeth into me. He won't stop even when I'm screaming in agony, begging him for mercy.

"Cinder," he repeats, voice thick with emotion.

Faintness threatens to pull me under, fighting with the adrenaline.

"I'm not going to bite you."

It takes my rioting senses a minute to register what he says.

"I'm not going to bite you, Cinder," he repeats.

Even as he says it, he inches closer to me slowly, painstakingly. One hand pulls my wrist, removing my thumb from my mouth. But he doesn't go for my broken flesh. His dark eyes remain fixed on mine, trapping me in this moment.

I should whack him with the dustpan. I should scream. I should run like hell.

Instead, I remain perfectly still as his lips brush against mine.

My thumb disappears into my fist where I squeeze it tight to staunch the bleeding.

I'm not sure who releases the shuddering breath, him or me, but it mingles between us. Another light pass of pressure and my fear recedes as something else rises up inside me. Raw, powerful desire.

Neither of us close our eyes, the visual contact somehow important, vital to not ruining this.

Kaison doesn't lean in again but licks his lips. He's waiting for me to make the next move. Despite the fact I see the bloodlust clearly stamped on his face, he is in complete control, proving it to me.

His expression repeats his words, *I won't bite you.*

There is something under that message, something I'm missing, but I can't pull it out because there is too much swirling inside my body, my head, whispering across my lips.

With a hard swallow, I cross the distance this time, pressing my lips against his in a real kiss.

His mouth yields to me, letting me take control. Kaison's lips are firm and soft in all the right places. His hands frame my face gently, still letting me direct this. Something hot and burning passes between us that is almost painful.

I test the texture, the drugging delicious taste of him until my mouth opens, letting his tongue slide in. A low groan rips out of his throat and my body responds with swirling hot liquid in my lower belly.

There it is again. The fear. The arousal.

Fearousal.

Fingers slide into my hair, gripping tightly as he licks at my tongue. He must be tasting the blood there. He samples then devours my mouth with sensual expertise until I'm gasping, panting, and needy.

The burning intensifies. I must have got his lips with my teeth because I taste the metallic slickness of blood and it's not mine.

Kaison's eyes flutter closed as he kisses me more insistently, plundering my mouth. The piercing on his tongue swipes in passing mine. I test pressure on the hoop on his lower lip until we are more certain of each other. The kiss becomes more intense, confident, and intoxicating.

Though any traces of my blood must be gone by now, Kaison still ravages my mouth as if it's the most addicting thing he's known.

He breaks with another needy moan. "You taste like if heaven and hell combined for a smoke-infused ambrosia."

His words come out thready, needy, and though he's the

one with the fangs, able to rip out my jugular, for the moment it feels like he's at my mercy. Like I own him utterly and completely.

Then I see the blood on his lip. My silver tongue ring. That's what the burning is. Where the fresh blood is coming from. The silvers seared his flesh, yet he kept kissing me. *He* bled for *me*.

Something shifts inside me. As if an old, stagnant part of myself is dislodging and reorganizing. The block of intense emotions—terror, anger, fear, pain—that once anchored me begins to shift. Suddenly, there are two punctures in this block, allowing light to filter through the darkness.

My hands find his shoulders, using them to steady myself, hold on, or test the muscle underneath. Or really, all three.

"Fae lords, what you do to me," he says like a prayer. Kaison dips his head toward my throat.

His lips barely brush my jugular before I slam him back. He hits his ass and I'm across the room, panting, fear back at the forefront again and exploding like fireworks in my head.

"Sorry, sorry," he rushes to say, lifting his hands. "I forgot. No fangs near your body. I know."

My black lipstick is smudged over his mouth, adding a new layer of confusion and fear. Fear of how much I like my mark on him.

I fight for breath as if I've been running for miles. The erratic beat of my heart begins to drain my energy and I press to the wall, using it to keep me upright. Fae fucking anemia.

Twice in one night. This is some bullshit.

What he tried was bullshit.

That's what I try to tell myself, but the look of anguish and apology contorting his handsome features is difficult to ignore. The way he burned himself, bled for me just so he could kiss me.

You can't trust him. He's a vampire. He's one of them.

Pushing himself to stand, he grabs the broom and dustpan, gaze averted from mine. "You should go bandage that up. I'll clean this up."

My mouth opens but nothing comes out.

Too much, too much, too much.

Overwhelmed, my heart beats too fast in fluttery panic.

So I turn and leave, closing the door to my bedroom behind me. Putting a physical barrier between us instantly makes me feel more secure. My forehead rests against the mottled wood, hand still on the knob. A wave of exhaustion sweeps over me.

Words filter through the door as I catch Kaison presumably speaking to the cat. "I know, I know. I fucked up. Don't look at me like that. I know. I want to do it again, but I can't."

A sigh escapes me.

I know the feeling.

CHAPTER 17

CLIMBING THE LADDER

CINDER

Prince Charming is naked. Tied to my bed.

Have I entered some alternate—alternate universe?

After a day of being forced to learn Midnight's history until my eyes bled from boredom, I was grateful for a night off. But no, I've come back to my room to a very nude Charming, rubbing his ass on my fluffy duvet.

It's been weeks since our kiss in my apartment. Since I backed off hard and fast, unable to shake the heebie jeebies at having his fangs near my flesh. In that time, my faux fiancé has been the picture of respectful gentlemanly distance.

Until now.

"Hi there." Kaison's words are strangely muffled, something white and fluffy pushing under his lips.

"Are those. . . marshmallows on your canines?" Disbelief colors my voice.

"I've been thinking," he says around the sugary lumps,

"you don't do fangs. So I figured these little buffers might make you more comfortable."

Comfortable. The word hangs in the air, heavy with unspoken promise.

Despite my knee-jerk reaction to recoil, I take in the nude prince. I follow the lines of his tattoos, terminating at his groin. Of course, he doesn't have any pubic hair. Everything is exposed, fully on display.

Kaison is half-erect, giving me a glimpse of the horizontal barbells climbing up his shaft. A Jacob's ladder. And crowning the top is a reverse Prince Albert, a ring piercing that curves over the head.

The very idea of what that hardware could do makes me dizzy.

My skin flushes hot, my pulse quickening. My clothes are suddenly too tight, my palms tingle with the desire to touch his skin.

Moonlight plays over his sculpted body, making it glisten like silver. Each ridge of his abs is on display, the ink complementing his musculature. Even his thighs show striations that beg to be traced with fingers or tongue.

Even strapped down, he manages a shrug. "You can do whatever you want." His eyes darken, cock jumping as if he already has ideas in mind.

The truth is, having Prince Charming tied up and naked with his little fang bumpers is so indescribably perfect, any resistance inside me dissolves.

I cross over to him. "How did you manage to tie yourself up like this?" My voice is thick.

"A semi-willing servant helped out. Didn't seem very interested in knowing why."

I walk around him, fingers grazing his shoulders, dragging along inked skin and rough rope.

"So Cinder," Charming says, "What would you like to do while I'm in my current condition? Shall we talk about the weather? Discuss politics?"

He's giving me an out. Taking the pressure off while literally offering himself on a silver platter.

We sure as fae fucks won't be discussing the weather.

I take note of his tattoos. Where they begin, where they end, which are instantly my favorite. The one that strikes me most is front and center on his pelvic bone—the silver and jeweled crown of Midnight. It must have hurt like a bitch to get.

Whoever did the work is a pro, and I have high standards for ink.

I don't say a word, simply drink him in.

Kaison shifts in discomfort under my open assessment.

There are so many things I want to touch, maybe even taste. I give in to tracing my thumb over his bottom lip, sliding over the piercing. His brows scrunch, thrown by my choice.

I don't change course. I revel in memorizing the textures of his lip and the cold slide of metal.

His Adam's apple bobs as he stares at me in awe. A strange sight with marshmallows on his fangs.

I brush my lips over his cheekbones, trail them down his neck. Hot tingles race through me as I explore.

I've never felt this free. Never this. . . safe. It brings out a dark sensuality I've been suppressing for years.

"Wh-what are you doing?" I've stripped him of his mask, his certainty.

"Whatever I want." My fingers skim his chest, tracing cold contours.

Under my hands, Kaison shivers, cock stiffening despite the reservation in his expression. I go lower until he gasps.

I lean in, drinking in his scent. The heat of my lips bounces off his cold ones.

Then I kiss him.

The pressure starts light, experimental. He lets me set the pace, and opens his mouth when my tongue asks for entry. I gingerly sweep against his, keeping the marshmallows in place.

The kiss deepens, grows urgent. I tangle my tongue with his, the sweet bite of the marshmallows mixing with his intoxicating taste.

Cold meets hot, hard meets soft, and I'm drowning in the intensity of it.

I reach between us, wrapping my fingers around his thick length. He bucks into my hand, a strangled curse falling from his lips. The metal of his piercings is a delicious shock to my palm. He rocks as much as he can as we both build a rhythm for me to jack him off.

He's panting and straining. His tip weeps with precum, so I know he's close. I release him.

A frustrated groan escapes him.

"Whatever I want," I remind him.

He nods, expression drawn. The Prince of Midnight is putting himself in discomfort to let me decide how to proceed. It's a hard scenario to swallow.

"But if you're feeling kind, I'm dying to see your perfect breasts," he begs, words distorted.

"How do you know they're perfect if you haven't seen them?"

"Let's just say I'm a connoisseur." His lids lower. "I recognize the signs."

"Not a great time to bring up what a whore you are." Venom sneaks into my voice. I don't want to think of him with anyone else.

Why? This is a fake relationship.

Still, it lands heavy and ugly in my stomach. Maybe that Lord Vamp Douchebury who accused humans of jealousy was onto something.

Kaison rears back. "I believe my whoring lends itself to this moment. If I've seen so many and yours surpass them all, isn't that more validating?"

He's got me there.

The corset is too difficult to untie, so I push it down, drawing out my breasts until pierced nipples hold the neckline. I reach under my skirts, pull my panties off, and throw them across the room.

I straddle him. In this position, he's eye-level with the cobweb tattoo encircling my nipple, webbing outward to engulf my right breast.

"Fucking fae lords, I was wrong."

I'm about to move away when he cuts off the motion.

"I've never seen a pair even close to this perfection."

"Boobs aren't that great," I weakly protest. "More than half the population has them."

His eyes meet mine. "That's like saying a piece of art isn't great because there are a million other works."

Well, fuck me. That hits.

A fissure forms in the armor around my heart.

"Please let me taste you." A husky plea.

One I should deny. Fangs. A flash of him biting into me sends a quiver of fear through me.

Still, I nod. Kaison drops his head and flicks my nipple with his tongue.

The shock is immediate, electric. He didn't avoid my hardware. It must hurt.

"You'll burn yourself," I point out.

"I don't give a fuck." He says it with such intensity, I

believe him. Then he takes as much of my breast into his mouth as he can, sucking and moaning.

My head falls back as he lavishes attention on one bud, then the other. Desire gathers between my thighs in thick, swirling heat. If he's in pain, he doesn't show it.

He groans and suckles, feasting on my breasts while I work through the nervous knots in my stomach.

This is a test. His lips on my skin.

If I push too fast, I might freak out like last time.

That's why he did this. He tied himself up, put himself at my mercy. It's all me now. My pace, my control.

This is just about getting comfortable with sex with my fake fiancé who is incredibly bangable. Nothing lasting or permanent.

Something in my gut twists painfully, but I ignore it.

I brush my pussy lips over the cold metal of his ring and slightly warmer head.

Oh. *Oh.*

I slide over his length. Each press of his piercings is an electric kiss against my sensitive nerve endings. His dick slips between my lips as I fuck along his shaft. Heat sweeps through me until I'm an inferno.

The cool temperature of his body makes it all the more shocking and stimulating.

Kaison shuts his eyes. "Oh, sweet witchtits." Muffled between marshmallows and my tit.

I grind at a frenzied rhythm. My brain blanks, replaced by delicious fuzziness. Still, everything in me pulses, demanding more.

The friction of frigid balls has me riding harder, faster, dragging my clit over the bumpy terrain. I claw at his chest, trembling with want.

The scent of sex fills the air, mixed with a metallic tang and the musk of our mingling arousal.

"Oh fuck, are you going to come just from rubbing those pretty pussy lips over my cock?" Kaison sounds pained. As if the truth might kill him.

It might kill me.

My mouth waters, orgasm approaching.

"Fuck yeah, Cinder. Ride it, baby girl. I'm so hard for you." He licks his lips, one of the only movements he can make while restrained.

Then sharp pebbles of pleasure crash across every nerve ending. I scream and break on him.

Reality eventually cuts through the warm haze soaking my brain. "Have you had the birth control shot?"

"Naturally," he says, strained.

Thankfully, venereal diseases aren't a thing vampires contract or give. Another way they're superior to beaters. Not that I'd say that out loud.

Well, that's enough foreplay.

I'm so slick, his tip slides in easier and faster than expected.

We both curse, my nails digging into his shoulders. My thighs quiver. Perspiration breaks out over my skin. There's a rushing in my ears, drowning out most sounds as my senses focus on that spot between us.

"Holy fae fucks," Charming says. "You—you feel—"

He's at a loss for words.

Oh gods, this is unlike anything I've known.

It's incredible, foreign, cold, and impossible to ignore. I slide down further, inch by inch, allowing each piercing to rasp along my sensitive inner muscles.

Strange, animalistic sounds escape me.

The guys I fuck aren't usually pierced, certainly not like

this. The sensation of that ring is out of this world as I slowly envelop his head.

The guys I fuck also don't look at me like he does. Like I'm a goddess. Like he'd happily let me save or slay him.

My feelings of fullness, want, and need are compounded by emotion. Sex has never felt like this. Is this how it's supposed to feel? It's almost too much.

I avoid his intensity, staring over his shoulder.

"Just like that," he urges breathlessly. When I settle at the hilt, my clit piercing is trapped against his pelvic bone, sending spikes of sensation into clenching inner muscles.

"Fuck," he hisses. I jerk back.

"Oh shit, sorry." I remember too late that my silver likely burned him.

"No. Give it to me. Grind on me exactly how you need." Despite not needing to breathe, he sounds breathless. "I can take it. Please."

Unsure, I slide down, rocking back and forth, letting him stretch me, light up my every pleasure center.

"Oh, Cinder," he moans. My name becomes a prayer.

Liquid slides between us. I want to look, see if it's my desire or if I'm making him bleed.

"Don't you dare fucking stop," he warns.

That intensity again. Unexpected, bone-rattling.

I've brought a prince of bloodsucking fairies to the brink. It almost makes me believe I might matter. That I'm special. That this connection could be real, lasting.

Come on, Cinder. This is just another Tuesday for him. Take it for what it is.

Gripping his torso, I ride away the intrusive thoughts. Pleasure riots through me, assaulting my senses until I'm gasping, clawing, rocking myself on his massive cock, testing all the sensations.

Then I come.

I come so hard, head dropping, baring my neck. Eyes shut tight.

Later, I might realize I only feel safe enough to do this because of the marshmallows.

Who does that, by the way?

He's made himself completely vulnerable, put himself at my mercy with no real expectation. I know what he wants, but somehow, I know if I decided to leave, he wouldn't stop me. If I wanted to stop, he wouldn't force me to continue.

Not that I can think of stopping. Not when I'm connecting to things inside myself I've never had the luxury to explore before. I ride my way from orgasm to overly sensitized fullness, rolling right into building tension again.

Each drag of his piercings against my sensitive flesh is exquisite torment, pushing me higher, harder. The physical ache expands beyond the space between my legs, permeating my entire being. My hips slam down, wet sounds echoing.

I can't get him deep enough, close enough. It's both utter satisfaction and unchained desire for all of Kaison—his blood, his bones, his soul.

I want to paint it. Sketch his eyes, replicate that intensity when his mask falls away and the real him shines through. So I can look anytime, shiver under his scrutiny.

"So hot," Kaison grits out, "like fire around my ice."

His hips surge up to meet mine, his control slipping with every thrust.

"Let go," I whisper, "give it to me."

A snarl rips from his throat and he slams up into me, the force of it stealing my breath. His release is a cool flood in my womb, and I nearly lose my mind.

Pleasure spirals tighter, sharper, until I'm balanced on a knife's edge, ready to shatter.

"Come for me," he demands, his gaze searing into mine.

I come apart with a scream, my nails raking down his chest as I shake and shudder around him. He follows me over, my name a broken prayer on his lips.

In the aftermath, I collapse, my heart racing, running so hot I fear I might combust. His cool body calms me, though. He drops a kiss on the top of my head before he relaxes under me.

I should say something lighthearted.

This was fun.

It was an interesting experience.

Thanks for the safety bang.

But something has shifted, some fundamental piece of me slotting into place. I can't let any of those insipid nothings escape my mouth. So after a time, I get up, untie him, and then disappear into the attached bathroom, locking the door behind me.

There may not be electricity but thankfully there's running water. I turn on the bathtub.

Even as I pretend not to hear Kaison moving around before a door closes, I reassure myself.

Thank the fae lords I'm immune to his charms. Otherwise, I might be in some serious trouble.

CHAPTER 18
THE GREAT PANTY SMUGGLER

CINDER

Kaison looks like he's having a stroke. Or maybe an aneurism?

When he stepped into my bedchamber in the castle he started to say something, but the words died on his lips once he saw me.

His eyes widen, a flicker of surprise and something deeper, more primal, dancing in their depths. I watch as his gaze travels the length of my body, from the delicate pearls at my throat to the sinful sweep of my skirt. His Adam's apple bobs as he swallows hard, and I can't help the thrill of satisfaction that shoots through me at his reaction.

The royal stylists did in fact take over for Dame Kiki and even I have to admit they did me up right.

Before, I'd been dressed to be innocuous, to fit in. Now I'm dressed to stand out, a true royal.

I'm adorned in a cascade of rich plum that darkens to black as it tumbles to the floor. The bodice fits tightly to my chest, making it difficult to breathe.

The off-the-shoulder cut leaves my collarbones bare and exposed, feeling oddly vulnerable and yet defiant. Each billowing sleeve starts as a circle around my bicep, cinching at my wrists.

The skirt is a masterpiece. With each movement I make it flares and flows, layers of shadow and sin, echoing the whisper of leaves against ancient tombstones. It's drama and elegance. Beautiful, yes, but with an edge that says *approach with caution.*

The finishing touch is a choker of pearls at my throat, a stark contrast to the dark dress. It looks almost like a string of tiny moons captured and strung just for me. But I know it's a collar—a sign of bondage reminding me that tonight I am bound to a role I must play.

My mood turned absolutely brittle when they insisted on covering up my tattoos with makeup. Everyone knows who I am and what I am now. I tried to argue I shouldn't have to blot out my ink, but the bloodsuckers insisted I needed to look like a princess befitting Midnight.

I enjoyed the way the stylists backed away as I plucked out my bits of silver, as if concerned I'd chuck the harmful jewelry at their heads. I always get a little irritable when I have to take out all my visible piercings. Though to be fair, Kaison has to do the same.

I still need to ask him how he got them. Midnight isn't big on tattoos or piercings but he seems to easily straddle both realms. Maybe he got them in the Common World?

It's all worth it when for once, the silver-tongued prince seems at a loss for words.

He takes a step toward me, drawn by an invisible force. His hand rises, fingers twitching as if he wants to reach out and touch the exposed skin of my shoulder, but he lets it drop back to his side.

"Cinder, you look. . ." He trails off, shaking his head clear.

"Like a princess?" I offer.

"Like the most powerful, dangerously seductive creature I've ever beheld."

Heat creeps up my neck at the raw honesty in his voice and the way he says my name—so intimate. It's not the practiced flattery of a playboy prince but something more genuine, more vulnerable. For a moment I see past the mask he wears, catching a glimpse of the man beneath.

But as quickly as it appears the moment is gone. Kaison blinks, a slow, wicked smile spreading across his face. "You clean up nicely, for a goth girl."

I scoff, the spell broken. "And you're still an ass for a prince."

Though he also fits his station in matching burgundy and black colors, the leather gloves back on his hands and his collar pulled up to obscure his beautiful tattoos.

He clutches his chest in mock offense. "You wound me, my lady."

Despite myself a smile tugs at the corners of my mouth. This is the dance we do, the push and pull of our strange, unlikely partnership. But beneath the barbs and banter I can still feel the heat of his gaze, the weight of the moment we share.

It's a dangerous thing, this attraction simmering between us. I know I can't afford to let it distract me, to let him get too close.

As Kaison offers me his arm, his eyes glinting with a promise of mischief and mayhem, I can't help but wonder if it's already too late.

"You seem to be feeling better." Kaison smirks, propping his hip against a chest of drawers in the sitting room.

I want to tell him he's wrong, but I can't deny that my mood has improved. After another night at work, I forced him to stop at an all-night cafe so I could get a massive pumpkin spice latte and a slice of pumpkin spice sweet bread while we took the long way to my apartment through the graveyard.

Autumn is the best freakin' time of year and I come alive in these conditions, whether in Midnight or Boston.

Then I filled a backpack with my favorite pumpkin spice candles, my cozy fall sweaters, and some art supplies.

If I have to live in Midnight, I might as well make myself comfortable. And I feel infinitely better with my plushy of the Grim Reaper. You can turn it inside out and it turns into Anubis, the God of the Dead. I change my little Grim back and forth based on my mood.

We got to the castle with no one the wiser. We stayed up all night only to return to a flurry of activity as the day in Midnight began.

I was swept away to the dress designers where I had to stand for hours on end while they took measurements and tested different fabrics.

Then I was forced to sit through an interminable history lesson, followed by some boring meetings about philanthropic event planning, while being told approximately one million times my job was to serve Midnight as its future Queen.

Though every fairy who tried to get those words out choked on them a little.

Now we're dressed and prepped to attend a banquet in our honor.

Tonight is going to be a bitch. But to be fair, so am I.

"I would have never guessed you to go for such a cliche." Kaison crosses his arms over his chest.

I give him my best death glare. "Don't be a counter-culture snob. You only hate pumpkin spice because it's popular."

He shrugs. "It just seems like people make a lot of fuss in the Common World over the fall season and certain flavors."

His backpedaling is not going to get him out of this. "First off," I hold up a finger. "I know you mean *women* make a lot of fuss. Second," I raise another finger, "The world, no matter what realm you are in, can be a truly shitty place. Don't shame me for finding enjoyment in my hyperfixation. And the fact that it's popular? Well, how dare you enjoy blood, because, like, *everybody* in Midnight is into that. It's *so* overdone that you come off as a thoughtless sheep."

Eyes sparkling, his lips twitch as he tries and fails to suppress a smile. He raises his hands. "I surrender. Forgive me for besmirching the joy that is spiced anything, and may you flog me should I do it again."

I lift my chin in what I hope comes off as haughty indignation. "Don't tempt me."

"Oh, I think I might," he says in a low husk.

There is something impossibly. . . impossible about Prince Charming.

There is an ebb and flow to our banter that I can't but help get a spark of enjoyment from. And then there were those words he said, and the way his hard body submitted under mine allowing me to achieve pleasure in a way I'd never known possible.

A lusty fog rolls through my mind before drifting south. I sharply inhale through my nose, trying to mitigate the effect he has on me.

"I do have to warn you, my dark princess, this dinner is

going to be unbearably boring," he says dryly. "In fact, it promises to be so stifling and pretentious that we very well may die."

"Fantastic," I say in a flat voice. "Can't wait."

"Which is why," he draws out the last word like an excited kid, "I thought we could have a little fun." From his pocket, he pulls out a pair of dark purple panties that are strappy, lacy, and have something heavier set against the crotch.

"What are those?"

The question is out before I can stop myself.

Kaison looks back and forth between me and the scrap of fabric.

"Why, my darling bride, these are the answer to surviving a night of dull nonsense and barely restrained dismay."

"You want me," I point at myself, before pointing at the underwear, "to wear those?"

One dark brow dips as he regards them again. "Well, I suppose I could shimmy them on, but I do maintain they will be a far better time for you."

A far better time.

Oh sweet fae lords, the piece on the crotch is a vibrator. They are massaging panties, and he is suggesting I put them on. For dinner.

"How—how can those even work? There are no electronics in Midnight."

There's a devilish gleam in his eye. "I smuggled in *batteries.*" The last word comes out as a low hiss of conspiracy.

I shake my head despite the heat swirling and coiling around my lower belly at the thought.

"Oh, come on, Cinder," he says, his voice dropping to a

low timbre that has my nipples wrenching into tight, sensitive buds. I'm starting to doubt the decision to pierce my nipples, as it makes my reactions to Charming all the more intense.

"After all, my little black rose," he drawls, setting a hand on either arm of the chair I'm in, caging me in, "the panties don't have fangs."

His words are equal parts seduction and challenge.

With an unladylike snort, I snatch the underwear from his hands. His eyes widen as he stands back, giving me room. It's almost as if he didn't believe I'd actually do it.

It's not a good habit to fall into, intentionally trying to shock him, because he might think I want more of his attention than I do.

But I can't help but delight in the way he pales when I bend over, pulling them right over my feet to draw them up my legs.

Take that prince slut muffin. I can play too.

"Don't you need to take off—" He swallows hard while pulling at his collar.

"I'm not wearing any," I cut him off.

I want to laugh. Kaison, the fairy prince who has slept with likely hundreds, if not thousands of willing partners, is acting like a wolfish cartoon character whose tongue has rolled out of his head while his eyes turn into little fires.

His reaction is so satisfying I almost believe I'm not an idiot for putting these panties on.

CHAPTER 19
WOOF WOOF, MOTHERFUCKERS

CINDER

I'm an idiot.

An idiot who handed over control of my body to a prince who wants to play with it.

Seated at the banquet table in a grand stone hall, I can't even see the end of the attendees on either end; it spans so far and wide.

Dinner in the Midnight realm is about as fun as a bag full of nearly dead, gasping tuna fish. A blood liqueur mix is poured into goblets while I am offered a glass of expensive champagne.

I almost think to ask for a glass of whiskey, but I have already done enough to rock the boat. They'd likely look at me as though I've defecated in the middle of the floor. The fact I have to perform *that* particular function is just more evidence I'm a lowly animal compared to them.

Good thing I snatched that pumpkin bread and scarfed it down when I could because as predicted, there is no food being served here. Not human food in any case. Most vampires think it's disgusting when humans eat. Something about the way we chew offends them.

I know there are vast reserves in the kitchens for the familiars, but that stuff tends to be canned and past its expiration date. It's why I made sure to stop for that latte and cake. I won't be eating anything decent as long as I'm here.

Sitting at the center of the table with my prince doesn't stop the icy chill of everyone's disdainful gaze dripping down my skin. I'm sandwiched between Kaison and the Queen.

The Queen's smile is an absent mask of polite indifference, while the King's grin is a sharp-edged warning from her other side, daring anyone to question his joy over our impending marriage.

My stomach churns, a toxic mix of suspicion and anger swirling within me. If King Charming is responsible for my father's death, his brazen display of my father's work is a twisted mockery. Maybe it's like a serial killer showcasing the trophies of his conquests? Instead of nailing my father's body to the wall, the King uses his artwork to make the point.

Kaison dips over to me. "Whatever you are thinking, it is giving your already low-key expression a murderous edge." I'm sure he is making the whisper look romantic, like a stolen moment between us.

"So help me, fae lords, if you tell me to smile, I will remove your testicles with a blunt, rusty spoon," I whisper.

A beat.

"Fair enough," he says, leaning back and looking as unperturbed as before.

"Forming a union with a...human. How very forward-thinking, my King," one of the fanged dukes says from across the table. He's sucking up to King Charming so hard I want to hand him a straw.

"Per our agreement," the King answers, "my son picked his own match. Since the royal blood thrums through his veins, I cannot deny that his choice must be inspiration."

Despite defending his son and me to this duke, the King looks rather inspired to rip my head right off my body and use it as a volleyball he can spike across the room.

Eyes turn toward Kaison.

"Ah yes," the prince confesses, finishing up a sip of champagne, having sent his cup of blood away as soon as it was brought out to him. Did he do it for my comfort? I can't imagine why.

"I was inspired by Cinder's beauty and couldn't help but recall our times together as young children, bonded by our fathers' friendship."

I see my opening and dive in.

"Speaking of my father," I say, "I wish he were here to witness this union."

I try to match their elevated way of speaking, though I still get some looks as though the vampires can't believe there is a talking dog at the table.

Woof woof motherfuckers.

The expression of sorrow that crosses the King's face appears genuine as I scan it for any signs of feigned performance. "I do miss your father. We had such a. . . unique understanding."

An *understanding.*

Not a friendship. Not really.

My father was a lowly familiar and understood his place and provided a unique service of bringing willing human cattle into Midnight.

Resentment snakes through me before wrapping around my heart and squeezing with vicious intensity.

The urge to stand and punch this prick in the face is overwhelming. My hands clench into fists on my thighs.

A hand covers mine under the table. Kaison. With long, deft fingers, he unravels my seized-up digits before bringing our entwined hands up above. Resting his elbow on the table, he continues to play with my fingers in a lazy, affectionate manner.

I try to ignore the steady *boom boom boom* of my heart that seems too focused on his attention.

But I'm not the only one. Several eyes fasten to where our fingers are laced. A quiet, muffled indignation ripples out like a stone was dropped in a pond.

Kaison relaxes in his chair, a smile playing on his lips. "Yes, your father's death was rather sudden, wasn't it, my punishing petal?"

I'm tempted to kick his shins again at the nickname, but then I realize what he's doing. He's riling up and distracting everyone in the vicinity with our blatant PDA so the fangers drop their guard.

"We tend to forget humans lead such fragile lives by comparison," King Charming says, raising his brows in pity.

I don't miss the way his eyes narrow at our joined hands.

"Not as fragile as you think." Judging by the sharp look King Valdor gives me, I haven't hidden the venom in my words well enough. *In for a penny.* "In fact, my father was supremely healthy. His death was such a shock, I almost wonder. . ."

I stall out. I hadn't figured out how to phrase this. It wouldn't help to outright accuse the King of murder in the middle of an important banquet.

As the King's gaze intensifies, scrutinizing me, warning prickles wash over my skin.

The awareness that I'm utterly vulnerable here has never left me, but I'm not used to operating like this. It's been a long time since I worked so hard to blend in amongst the fairies and it takes a great amount of control and perceptiveness on my part.

"Wonder what?" The King's voice reminds me of the rattling of a snake about to attack.

"My dear, I think you need a top off," the Queen mutters next to me before waving over a servant to refill my glass.

The King and I don't break eye contact even as the thralled familiar leans over between us to pour more sparkling bubbles into my glass. My blood runs hot despite the chill of the hall.

Their eyes are so dead, so empty. I wonder if they can even take a shit without Valdor's say so.

"Wonder if perhaps there was foul play involved in your father's demise?" The King finishes for me.

The table quiets.

My lips flatten, suddenly glued together as my heart-beat moves to my throat.

The only thing keeping me from fighting or fleeing is Kaison's distracting play with my hand.

The tension presses in around me like a thick fog, making it difficult to breathe.

"I have sometimes wondered that myself," the King muses idly, taking a sip of blood, breaking the tension. "But then no one would dare hurt such a favored familiar of the King's," he says a little louder.

No one except you.

The Queen recoils between us ever so slightly at his

announcement. As if she knows the full weight of his power.

"Do you smell something burning?" the duke asks the prince.

Kaison shrugs, looking around briefly as if looking for the source of the smoky scent.

It is true. To attack any of the castle's familiars would be a treasonous offense, to which King Charming brings a swift punishing hand—fang?—down upon them.

I want to ask about what Kaison told me. About my father's final days sequestered. About what he and the King fought about. About why the King uses my father's art as the background for the social season.

Kaison's hand squeezes mine, hard. A silent signal.

Don't do it. You've already pushed the envelope enough tonight.

The message is received but not exactly welcome. Ever since Kaison shared that my father was likely murdered, it has been eating into the side of my brain like a hoard of flesh-hungry fire ants.

The King and Queen turn their attention away from me to converse with the guests on the other side of them. Kaison drops my hand and the scathing glances move on.

The stiff propriety of secrets, lies, and stuffy ass decorum in this place makes me want to jump and scream, shatter glasses, shake people by the lapels, and do something truly crazy to break the suffocating pattern that has existed for hundreds of years.

Just as I'm about to break and do something crazy, a buzz activates between my legs.

CHAPTER 20

THE PANTIES DON'T HAVE FANGS

CINDER

I can't bite back the moan before it escapes me.

The duke across from me shoots me a disapproving look as if the zoo animal is not behaving herself.

"Everything alright, my love?" Kaison asks airily as if he hasn't just remotely turned on the pair of vibrating panties between my legs.

That sonofabitch. That fae fucking evil—

Ohhhh dear god.

I swallow my groan as the vibrations against my vulnerable parts scatter my thoughts.

"Yes." My words come out shaky and on a half cough. Snatching up my champagne, I hastily sip my drink.

The duke turns away with a sneer.

The second I swallow, the vibration notches up to another level. My core turns to molten hot liquid. I instantly end up in a coughing fit, the sting of bubbles assaulting my nose from the inside.

More disgusted looks are cast my way until I get my coughing under control.

The panties don't have fangs.

And yet I am completely under attack.

Only by taking shallow breaths and squeezing my thighs together do I manage to keep still.

Fire licks up the base of my spine, as my clit undergoes an onslaught from the evil underwear.

As I turn pliant against the tiny motor, I feel Kaison's attention focus on me. With a quick look at him, I catch a positively devilish smug grin. Instantly I tear my eyes away from him and focus on the far wall. Even making eye contact with his sultry, knowing face heated my body several degrees.

With a deep breath, I will myself to suppress the overwhelming sensations. But oh god, I want to buck and moan and writhe like the animal everyone here thinks I am.

The fuck was I thinking, giving Prince Slut Bag this much power over me?

And when have I experienced this much pleasure? It's almost like since I met him my body woke up from a long sleep. Now it's party o'clock, and it is throwing out heat, shivers, desire, and anticipation in a big rave complete with music and laser lights.

This is a super inappropriate time for party o'clock.

And yet. . .

I summon every ounce of willpower to maintain a façade of composure. My hands grip the edge of the table with white-knuckled determination, anchoring myself in the storm of sensation threatening to consume me.

Kaison leans in close, his voice a feather-light whisper against my ear. "Having fun, my love?" he teases, his warm breath sending shivers down my spine. I bite my lip to stifle a gasp as the vibrations intensify yet again.

Holy fuck, did someone ask me a question?

I must make some sound resembling confusion.

Kaison lifts his champagne lazily. "Our guests are speculating on if you will insist on a white virginal dress the humans favor for our nuptials, or if you will take on our traditional colors for matrimony?"

He's completely unaffected, putting me on the spot on purpose. I want to smack him. I want to fuck him. I want—I want—

"I don't look good in white." My words come out so tight, they almost unravel into a lewd moan of pleasure.

"Au contraire my bride, I believe it could be quite a sweet look for you," Kaison coos.

I'm not sure if it's our sickening affection or my current state of approaching a bone-shattering orgasm, but I sense the discomfort at the table.

Also—*sweet?* I'll show him sweet. I'll beat him to death with my six-inch platform boots with the spikes on them until he's a bloody pulp—

The buzzing switches from an insistent thrum to a syncopated pattern. I bite my tongue even as I shiver.

"Oh my. Are you cold, my dearest?" Kaison dotes with false concern.

Forget beating him to death. I'm going to strap him to a bed and ride his face until he's tongue fucked me into next year. And long after his jaw is sore and popping from the effort, I'll make him do it again until I've come ten more times.

I'd have to pull his fangs first, but it'd be worth it.

Interest in us ebbs and people go back to their side conversations, allowing me the privacy to close my eyes and pant a little. I grip the side of my chair and Kai's hand with the other.

The decadent scent of Kaison's cologne swirls around me, filling my senses making me want to give in even more. Somehow, his scent of leather and icy pines evokes a sense of safety in me that encourages me to let go.

No, that can't be right. We have an alliance, but he isn't safe. No matter that he stood up for me at the bar and is working to entrap his father to avenge mine. We are still at the core, enemies—

Holy fuck bunnies on a pogo stick, I am going to come.

My teeth grit as my vision blackens, though my eyes are open.

Kaison's gaze burns into me like a brand, daring me to react, to succumb to the escalating chaos he has orchestrated.

Desperation claws at me as I struggle to maintain a façade of composure, to keep from giving in to the maddening pleasure that threatens to consume me. As conversations carry on around me, I remain ensnared in a secret battle.

My inner muscles clench and flutter, pushing me closer. . . higher. . .

Kaison's gaze pierces through me, his grin growing wider with each passing second. The sensation between my legs intensifies, pushing me to unravel right there at the banquet table. I shoot him a warning glare, silently begging for him to help me escape this humiliating predicament.

"I think I need to excuse myself," I say weakly, quietly.

"Are you sure you can walk?" Kaison asks with false concern. Underneath, he is brimming with mirth.

"Of course," I growl. I begin to stand and the panties

move to hit me directly on my swollen, sensitive clit and a rush of liquid escapes me along with a strangled moan.

"Oh dear, you better sit," Kaison says, tugging me down. I'm unable to resist, now that I know there is zero chance I will make it to the ladies' lounge to finish this out in peace.

Thankfully, no one is paying attention to us.

When I hit the seat again, the vibrating part of the panties push into my most intimate needy bits and now it's stuck there. I'm desperate for a finger, a dick to fill me up. Hell, I'd take the eraser side of a pencil as long as it penetrates me where I need it.

Oh fae lords, I'm going to come right here, right now, at the table of fairies.

A napkin dabs at my brow. "You're wet," Kaison whispers, his breath caressing the sensitive skin of my neck.

My body listens to him, another rush of desire coating the panties and slicking my thighs.

Kaison's other gloved hand falls to my leg, pulling it aside, forcing my legs open. They obey him as if he is master of my senses. The vibration presses tight directly on my clit piercing. The intensity jacks up so high and so fast, I become light-headed.

Oh fuck, fuck, fuck, fuck.

The pressure of the panties on my clit is almost unbearable, the sensation sharp and unrelenting.

Kaison seems to be enjoying my discomfort, leaning in until his scent surrounds me in a drugging cloud. "That's it," he murmurs against my ear. "Let me see you come in front of all these people, my gothic goddess."

He breaks me.

My vision fogs as I come, internally shuddering, splintering, coming apart.

Breath hitching, the temptation to arch my back and scream out in pleasure is nearly unbearable. My eyes flutter as the pulsating vibrations from the panties continue to overwhelm me, dragging out my orgasm and pushing it to last longer than it rightfully should.

Kaison's hand flexes on my thigh, agitation radiating through his fingers though the rest of him remains unchanged.

The vibrating panties slow their pace, releasing me from their grip as my body comes down from the edge.

Drawing in deep, ragged breaths, I manage to get some control over my body again. But fuck if my thighs and dress aren't soaked now.

It's time I make my excuses and get the hell out of here. Just as I'm about to rise, the panties start up with another whirr of power, causing my entire body to shudder as I grip the table for stability.

Casting a look at Kaison whose eyes are two hungry dark pools of obsidian, I realize that while *I* may be done, *he*'s not.

CHAPTER 21

THE PRINCE DESERVES A MEDAL

CHARMING

Cinder wheels around to face me in the hall outside our rooms, her cheeks flushed and her eyes bright with a mix of anger and lingering arousal. "Five times? At the table? Are you insane?" she hisses, her eyes narrowing to violet slits. Her chest heaves with each breath, straining against the confines of her gown in a way that makes my fingers itch to touch.

To say she walked funny out of dinner is an understatement.

When my mother commented on her strange gait, Cinder simply grumbled, "Back problems."

"Hmm." I'm somewhat disappointed by her number. "And here I thought I got you to come six times. Maybe I mistook one of those for aftershocks."

"You sadistic asshole," she hisses with narrowed eyes.

"Oh, baby, say it slow, and maybe step on my balls while you do."

The thing is, I mean it.

She wasn't the only one walking funny out of that dinner. Playing with her had been the most fun I'd had in I don't know how long. And there was that time with four of us in a kiddy pool of Jell-O.

Sure, the gelatinous orgy had been fun, but compared to this, it was a surface-level kind of fun that depended on the novelty of the situation rather than the actual sexual play.

But when Cinder put on the vibrating panties, fearless and defiant in the face of my challenge, something pinched in my chest. It was like a wild animal allowed me to put reins over its head, though we both knew she was the one who was truly in control. She could have stopped it at any time.

As much as she wanted to blame me for turning her inside out again and again, I knew she enjoyed it. The thrill of being caught, the way she masterfully controlled her expressions and reactions so those around us wouldn't suspect a thing. . . it washed over me in thrilling tingles again and again.

While everyone else had been oblivious, I was so horribly, completely in tune with each twitch, tiny gasp, and eyelid flutter. It was like sitting next to a bomb I was desperate to make go off.

I thought I was the reckless type before.

Now I know my previous antics were born of boredom and a hollowness I'd been trying to fill.

This is different. Interacting with my human bride sparks something inside of me, something truly alive. Cinder makes me want to raze everything to the ground just to break her eternally placid expression for a blink, a tiny curve of her perfect lips, or to earn a sharp inhale.

Cinder, usually so unflappable and in control, slowly coming undone by the buttons in my hand. The way she gripped the edge of the table, her knuckles white with strain. . . the barely stifled gasps and shivers that rippled through her body. . . the accusatory glares she shot me, tinged with equal parts frustration and desire. . .

Even before our tryst at the table, I suspected Cinder of being a master of concealment. The way her face gives nothing away, constantly exuding an almost bored disinterest. I wanted to see if it was a natural expression or something she'd schooled in herself.

Now I know the truth. It's a mask she wears, just like I have mine.

I got a glimpse beneath that tough exterior and caught the flicker of vulnerability, a hint of the passion she keeps so carefully guarded. Each time I increased the intensity of the vibrations I watched her fight to maintain composure, her breath hitching and her eyes fluttering closed as she battled the rising tide of sensation.

The true Cinder threatened to break out and she was so much more powerful, so much more. . . everything.

I didn't realize how handy those panties would be until she got so wound up, I feared she might do something rash and explosive in trying to find out what happened to her father. There is a difference between needling and pushing for information and trying to get it out with ham-fisted brute power.

But getting her to back off had been easy when I had access to her most intimate parts. Fuck, the self-control it took not to slither to my knees under the table and lick and play with the panties torturing her sex.

I deserve a medal of some kind.

But no, all I got is this massive hard on stealing all the blood from my head and making me dizzy.

As if reading my mind, Cinder's eyes widen, pupils

dilating with a fresh wave of desire. I'm not alone in this strange, exhilarating dance of wills and wants.

Taking advantage of her shift in mood, I lean against the doorframe to her bedroom, forcing her to look up at me. Cinder's arousal and blood sing to me in delicious notes, and my fangs lengthen a little. Her mouth is perfectly poised for me to dip down and plunder.

"So are you going to let me in?" I ask in a low voice.

Her breathing turns shallow as her gaze slowly drops to my lips.

Oh yes, my little tattooed treat. Let me in and I'll show you all I want to do to you with my tongue.

"Unless you get fang extraction, that would be a no."

Her bedroom door slams in my face. My hips jerk back only in time to not get slammed in my vulnerable protruding state.

Witchtits.

"Can I at least get those panties back?" I call through the door with a hopeful lilt. "No need to wash them, I'll take them as is."

A whistle catches my attention. Down the hall, I'm heralded by a vampire who, by all rights, should not be here.

I stalk toward the skinny vamp in a red shirt and green cap. "What the fuck are you doing here, Jack?" I glance wildly about to see if anyone else is around. "I should have never shown you the secret passage in and out of here," I grouse.

Jack's serious face is rough with stubble and his hair is limp and dirty. The scent of sweat mixed with dirt clings to Jack's body, as if he hasn't had a chance to properly clean himself in days. He's as out of place in this grand hallway as a child's fingerpainting over a masterpiece.

Not that I care about his fashion sense. Grabbing his arm, I haul him into my bedroom and shut the door behind us.

"If you get caught—"

"I won't," he grits through his teeth. "I made sure."

Walking to the window, I lift the edge of the curtain to see if the guards are scrambling on the grounds to catch an intruder. It all seems calm, but I've lost my cool.

"What are you doing here?" I ask again. "I sent a note."

Jack shakes his head. "I had to come see you. There's a lot of talk."

I'll bet there is.

"That's what I was hoping for," I say dryly. "Do they believe me now?"

Jack holds his hat in his hand and shifts his weight from one leg to the other.

"Oh for fuck's sake," I say, scrubbing a hand through my hair. Realizing I still have the damn gloves on to cover up my tattoos, I peel them off with an almost violent fervor. "What do I have to do to prove to the Mice that I am serious? That I want the King off the throne as much as them?"

Jack scowls. "It's not that simple."

Of course it's not. The rebellion has been running so far underground, they are known as Mice. No matter how many times my father or the kingdom has tried to exterminate their presence there is always another creeping out from a crack in the wall.

Despite my ire, I know the only reason their network has stayed active is because they have been so careful about who they trust. The son of the fairy King they hate the most is definitely not at the top of that list.

Taking a deep breath to calm myself, I relax into the mode that can handle bone-crushing pressure. "I took a human for my bride. Doesn't that count for something?" Despite my attempt to be at ease, I can hear the ice in my own words.

Jack's brows drop over his eyes. "There are still questions."

"Questions?" I draw out.

"She is the daughter of the King's favorite familiar."

"For cripes sake." I throw my head back in frustration. "That's the only way I could get away with such a move. Had I tried to propose to a human servant under thrall, do you think I could have gotten away with it? No. She's the only human that could get in under the line and even just barely at that."

Then I straighten and address the unasked question in Jack's eye. "Do the Mice think I'm feeding on her?"

Jack averts his gaze.

The Mice aren't just a rebellion network of vampires who demand the monarchy be dismantled. It's not just that they resent being kept in the literal dark ages when the Common World is granted access to electricity and freedoms that we aren't allowed on this side of the border. They are human sympathizers. They believe in the ethical treatment of humans, and they believe the King's thrall over humans denies them their free will to donate their blood to vampire kind. That mortals need to be allowed to choose each time, not just the first before they sink into unknowing servitude.

And though it hasn't been confirmed, I suspect a fair number of the Mice may even be humans themselves. I've heard of vampire/human relationships existing on the outskirts of society, but until my proposal it had been rare to happen amongst the fairy court. The last time was

Cinder's father who married a wealthy Midnight fairy who was seeking entrance to the court.

"I'm not feeding from her." My tone is a dark warning. "I would never. She is not a blood bag."

Jack winces at the reference before his upper lip curls in distaste.

It's not my term. It's a disgusting reference, and I keep a far distance from the fairies who use it.

"Listen, if the Mice want my father off the throne, I am their best bet."

Jack's eyes almost sink further into his skull as he warily regards me. "There is chatter that you want the throne for yourself."

My laugh comes out as a dry bark. "Me? Rule the kingdom? They must all be high. Everyone knows I'm not suitable to run anything, much less Midnight. I'm just the pretty boy who can get in places no one should be able to."

The only reason I'd take the throne is to give it away.

I'm no ruler.

The people don't need a fuck up for their leader. No, it's better I pass the ball to someone better. Really, *anyone* else is better.

I've been feeding the Mice information about my father and the castle for months, hoping to rally them into action. But they are hesitant to make such a strong move, especially behind someone they think may be leading them into a trap.

"So you are telling me, my publicity stunt did nothing?" I ask Jack, running a frustrated hand through my hair.

Okay, not nothing. I had that goth goddess shaking and coming in a room full of fairies, becoming the most enrapturing thing I've ever seen.

"The Mice are still listening," Jack says, yanking me

from my seductive thoughts. "And I do think Byung-He's daughter may be key. Keep showing up with your bride in tow, and I'll work on them."

"Cinder. Her name is Cinder." The violent edge in my voice surprises even me. I can't deny that I'm instantly irritated at hearing her reduced to the sum of her relations. She is her own person. Hell, she's a force of nature.

Jack's eyes widen in surprise before he nods. Something flashes over his face, like understanding.

He's about to leave when I stop him. "I'll put on a good show, but I need you to do something for me in the meantime."

After I give him his assignment he sneaks out of my room, going back the secret way he came.

Just because I can't leave the castle, doesn't mean I can't push my influence past it.

The idea of the Mice worrying I want to use them to take over my father's rule is laughable. I'm not cut out to lead anyone. Pick up any tabloid and they can see how ruefully ridiculous I am when it comes to acting responsibly. My entire history revolves around avoiding it.

I wonder when I changed enough to seek out the Mice.

It was somewhere between one of the ruthless beatings my father gave me and having to stare at the empty-eyed servants, pretending they weren't prisoners in their own bodies.

Even before I spent time in the Common World, I'd come to respect humans. Courtesy of my mother's guidance to treat everyone equally and the presence of a certain violet-eyed little girl who was always on the fringe of my awareness.

The girl who ran around with smears of paint on her face and hands. Who spent so much time with a father who loved and cherished her. At times I wanted to despise her for having something I couldn't, but in truth, I merely envied her.

Despite being cast out and separated, she seemed to form her own little world to live in between art and the dark countryside. I remember after a particularly brutal beating from my father for some weakness or another, I ran out to the cliffside and found Cinder. Her little legs dangled over the edge as she sat fearlessly, careless of the violent crashing waves below, absently humming to herself and alternating her attention between the stars and the ocean.

An invisible hand gripped the organ in my chest. I wanted to see the world through her eyes. To be so independent that I wouldn't have to answer to anyone.

Instead of approaching her, I found my peace in watching hers.

But the idea of Cinder ever becoming thralled or fed upon like a piece of meat makes my stomach curl and wither with disgust.

I would never in a million years do that to her.

To the basest root of my being, I've always known it's wrong to do that to humans.

Three years ago, it finally became too much. Maybe it was one too many beatings from my father, one too many familiars staring at me through sightless eyes, one too many days being crushed by cold, merciless oppression.

I decided I would be the one to help pave the way to a new monarchy. One without my father.

Where that left me in the end didn't matter. Though I'm starting to fear where that will leave Cinder.

CHAPTER 22
RAP WILL CUT YOU

CHARMING

If Cinder insists on going back to work her shift at the Poison Apple, I still insist on going with her. It's non-negotiable, especially after what happened last time.

Though I'm not sure why she feels so inclined to gripe about it. She's not the one who has to shove her foot in a tiny glass torture shoe that doesn't fit.

Despite the pain, nausea, and dizziness that comes with the teleporting shoes—or whatever magic they are harnessing to transport us—I'm damned happy to be in the Common World. If only to defy my father's orders to stay in the castle.

Fuck him.

Seriously, right off the throne and into a pit of crocodiles.

Thoughts of rallying a rebellion and playing the engaged prince to my people all fade away in the hustle and bustle of the Poison Apple.

Instead of hunkering down at the booth, I end up at the bar next to the bespectacled bookstore owner again.

"Prosecco and espresso?" I ask, raising an eyebrow at the two dainty drinks in front of her.

Belle's pink lips curve up even as she keeps her eyes on her open book. "It's the combo for champions."

She's been engrossed between the pages of a book with a cover of a man chest, called Chase Me—a Dragon's Love Curves novel by someone called Aidy Award.

"I'll have to try it sometime," I say, tipping my dirty martini to her.

"So, you must not care that much about Cinder," she says loftily, while turning a page.

My spine stiffens at her comment. "What makes you say that?"

Not that Belle knows our engagement is a ruse to help me incite a rebellion while Cinder investigates her father's murder. But I'm instantly irked by her comment.

"She's not wearing a ring," Belle points out.

My eyes track across the room to fall on Cinder's naked ring finger.

Shit. She's right. I did miss an element to this engagement, not only in this world. It's also a significant gesture in my own world. For a moment, I wonder why no one has brought this to my attention in Midnight.

Oh right, everything thinks she's human scum and doesn't want her as their princess. Not even my own father.

"It's on my list of things to do," I say airily before sipping my drink again.

"Mmm, hmm," Belle hums as if unconvinced or unimpressed. "You better if you want an HEA."

"A what now?"

She swivels to meet my eye. "An HEA. It stands for Happily Ever After."

I can't help but smile. "You really are a romance book lover, aren't you?"

A pretty blush springs to her cheeks. "Yeah well, I think the HEA is a goal for most love stories, fictional or nonfictional."

"You are very right about that," I add, tilting my head in deference so she knows I'm not teasing.

An unsettling pressure pushes at my chest. Not just because I missed a detail that helps the plan, but because now Cinder's naked finger legitimately bothers me. The need to circle that digit in some kind of binding metal to show that she is taken swells in me.

For the plan, I try to remind myself.

Not because I want to broadcast that she is off limits.

The memory of her normally placid face fighting off any indicator she was coming at the table next to me heats me from the inside out. A considerable feat since I'm always room temperature.

But fae fucks that was hot.

Normally after something salacious like that I'd happily wave goodbye to my partner and head off in pursuit of more depraved activities with others, but I'm hungry. Hungry to get her alone, to explore all her piercings and tattoos. I want to make her scowl, make her smile—like really smile. And I want to annoy the ever-loving shit out of her with the million more nicknames I cook up.

Hell, I could have grabbed any number of willing partners to take to my room and have them suck me off seven ways from Sunday. Instead, I jerked off in the shower, not once but twice, thinking only of those cupid-bows lips, violet eyes, and the smell of vanilla and charred cedar.

Even now, I can barely take my eyes off her perfect pout and flat gaze as she takes drink orders and effortlessly moves back and forth without even the hint of a smile.

Where I must constantly perform, pasting on a smile, schmoozing the masses of Midnight and the Common World, she doesn't perform for anyone.

Cinder doesn't do shit she doesn't want to and that hits me like a hammer to the chest. Is it envy, admiration, respect, or something else?

"You," a voice calls, "Come with me."

I turn to find the mohawked owner of Poison Apple crooking a finger at me with sharp, narrowed eyes.

Speaking of people not giving a fuck of what others think. . .

I follow the original badass of the bar to her office where she barks to shut the door behind me. Despite the rich, magical opulence of the bar, her office is minimalist and clean. A sleek laptop sits on the desk and a file cabinet is tucked into a corner. The only signs of personality come from the kitten calendar on the wall. The kitty hanging onto a ledge encourages me to *hang in there.*

Taking one of the seats across from the desk, I consider the possibility that Rap may literally hang me, judging by the dark thundercloud over her head. She's human, but I can't rule out the possibility she'd strike me with lightning from sheer force of will.

And I can't help but feel like she might be more than human, though I can't put my finger on why or what.

"Does she know about your connection to the Mice? What you are trying to pull? How you are using her?" Questions shoot out of Rap's mouth like speeding bullets.

Ping ping ping. Each question hits me dead center in my forehead.

"Uhh…"

Rap stands, slamming her hands on the desk with a loud thwang. "Don't fuck with me, Charming. You may be a pretty playboy prince, but no one messes with my girls. I'll cut off your little prick before you hurt Cinder."

I recoil into the tiny office chair as much as I can, even lifting a leg and crossing it over my precious bits protectively as I hold up my hands. "Whoa, whoa, I'm not trying to hurt her."

She snorts. Unlike Cinder's little huffs, this is that of a pissed off bull.

"We have a mutually beneficial arrangement here." Even as I explain, my brain is racing trying to figure out how this human bar owner knows about Mice, much less my involvement. "When we've reached our respective goals, the engagement will be dissolved."

Still bearing over the desk and me, Rap bares her teeth. "I asked if she knows."

Dropping my arm and legs slightly, I drop all measures of my likeable façade. "No, but I decided she didn't need to know."

Rap sucks in a breath as if ready to blowtorch me with the fire in her body, but I cut her off.

"She doesn't need to know because the less she knows the better." My voice has turned low and gruff.

"Why is that?" Rap challenges.

Taking a moment to calm myself, I lick my lips and articulate, "If she let it out, if my father ever questioned her, she'd be liable for my actions."

"And you intend to get your father off the throne," she says, still giving me the stink eye as she sinks back into her seat.

"That's the plan." I nod. "But the plan also involves

implicating him in the murder of Cinder's father. I'm not positive he did it, but I'm pretty fae fucking sure he had something to do with it."

Rap sighs and rubs her forehead as if I've gifted her an elephantine headache. "From what I understand of your father, even if Cinder doesn't know what you plan, if he even gets a whiff of this, he'll make her pay."

Acid coats my tongue and an invisible vise squeezes my spine. "I won't *let* him." It comes out a near snarl. The thought of him hurting her raises a beast in my chest I've only recently met. The same monster arose when that guy assaulted Cinder.

It's a feral protective animal who would chew off its own arm if it meant protecting her.

The reaction continues to surprise and throw me off balance.

The bar owner studies me. Her sharp green eyes seem to search my entire inner being like some kind of scanner. "You should tell her."

For a heart stopping second, I don't know what she means. Or rather, I fear what she means.

Tell her how you feel.

But then my senses return as I come back to our conversation. Rap means I should tell Cinder about the part she is playing.

Cinder is still under the assumption I'm rebelling against my role and trying to stick it to my dad.

Having her believe I'm the thoughtless, petty, unconcerned prince everyone thinks I am is better.

Better for her or for you? A voice in my head asks.

Better because if she thinks there is more to me, it might make things more serious. Even more serious than a coup and a murder investigation. Fae lords forbid anyone think I'm serious and capable.

Though that's exactly what I'm trying to convince the Mice of.

A commotion outside has Rap up and across the room, swinging the door open.

One of the security guards walks past her toward the locker room. Cinder clutches his arm as he escorts her there. Her face is drawn, a sickly shade, as she stumbles. The security guard steadies her, making sure she doesn't fall over.

I shoot out of my chair and am behind Rap in less than a second. She won't move out of my way, her body and arms blocking my exit.

"What's wrong?" I demand.

Rap's head tilts toward me. "She'll be fine. She just needs a minute."

"What's wrong," I growl out at her.

Rap stares at me with merciless passivity. Her gaze openly communicates that she doesn't owe me shit and she doesn't intend to tell me. "Guess you don't know everything either."

CHAPTER 23

A ROMANTIC STROLL IN A GRAVEYARD

CHARMING

CHARMING

"Why are my friends so obsessed with you?" Cinder asks with that searing judgment in her eyes.

After her shift, we stopped by her favorite all-night cafe again so she could get yet another pumpkin spice latte and sweet cake.

We stroll through an old cemetery as the crisp night air nips at us. I've learned this is my goth girl's happy place. One she reluctantly shares with me.

True to Rap's word, Cinder returned to work after twenty minutes of being in the locker room.

Though despite my asking everyone what happened, no one would answer me. Cinder rolled her eyes and told me to mind my own fucking business. The only one I could squeeze anything out of was the bookstore owner, who told me as much as she knew.

Cinder occasionally gets dizzy, disappears for about a half hour then returns no worse for wear.

The memory of her stumbling during our first dance flashes in my mind, and then there's when I had to hurry her out of the ballroom after our engagement was announced.

She seemed off-balance, weak. But she recovered soon enough. Still, I couldn't help but feel the prickles of annoyance at not being told what was wrong.

Not that I fix things or make them better, but. . . something in me wants to try. For once.

As I gabbed with her friends, Cinder almost deliberately seemed to stick to the outskirts. She listened, and only occasionally chimed in.

It seems as though another one of Ted's attempts to propose may have been thwarted. He cooked a romantic dinner at home complete with candlelight and a tie. He'd been telling Goldie how much she means to him when one of his brothers stumbled in with a girl on his arm, bringing the party back to Ted and Goldie's place. Things went downhill after that.

I've a mind to step in and help Goldie's lumberjack-esque bear shifter beau. But from the few times I've encountered him at the Poison Apple, I don't get the vibe that intrusion would be appreciated.

When I asked Goldie if Cinder would quit working to hang out, she responded that Cinder didn't always feel comfortable in group settings. That she equally loved and struggled with girl time.

Goldie didn't tell me the information with any judgment, only love and acceptance.

Snow nodded her head. "Yeah, she just needs space."

I wondered if Cinder knew how great her friends were, but I suspected she knew.

I kick a rock off a grave and respond to Cinder's question. "Your friends are catching me up on the shitty mage reality shows I used to watch when I was in university in the Common World. I haven't kept up in years. Not to mention I give great man advice."

"That's surprising considering you're only half a man," she shoots back before sipping on her impossibly large drink. Whiffs of cinnamon and cardamom invade my senses.

"Want me to pull my pants down and prove my manliness to you?" I ask with my best playboy smile.

Those violet eyes flash as she scowls. "Don't do that."

"Flash you my gigantic manly dick hose?"

She shoots me the purple death. "Use that bullshit fake publicity smile with me."

My heart clenches inexplicably. "I—"

"And don't tell me you don't know what I mean. I've seen enough to know when it's real and when it's not."

Well shit. Now a flutter has kicked up in my chest.

"Sorry." My apology comes out a little hoarse.

No one's ever called me on it before. Though I do possess an almost painful awareness of when I'm turning the lightbulb on and off for the Prince Charming show.

There's a pause that is weighted by her calling me out, so I shoot my shot again.

"What happened at the bar tonight? You got dizzy. It also happened in the ballroom after we got engaged," I point out.

Cinder shoves the last half of her spiced bread into her mouth until it's near bursting with the cake. Then she points to her mouth, indicating she can't talk.

"Jokes on you," I slip my hands in my pocket. "You just fucked up the chance to enjoy that for longer, and I got *all* the time in the world to wait you out. Unlike you, I'll live to be like five hundred years old. Maybe a thousand."

Cinder glares, awkwardly chewing over the mouth load. The purple death is much less intimidating when cake is involved. I cover up my smirk when I see her expression fall a little as if she's realized I'm right. I remain silent, walking by her side as she roughly swallows down the last big piece.

The silence is heavy between us, and I let it stretch between us. I pretend it doesn't make me uncomfortable, that it doesn't make me want to fill it with teasing or nonsense to yank her chain.

"I have anemia," she finally answers.

"Anemia," I shake my head. It sounds familiar, but I don't know what that is.

"I don't have enough healthy red blood cells, so sometimes I get dizzy or my heartbeat turns irregular. My feet and hands used to get cold all the time but that hasn't happened in a while. In fact, I'm usually running hot these days," she mutters more to herself.

Her blood smells plenty healthy to me, though I do my best to ignore that particular tantalizing scent.

It's not easy.

When her scent hits me, it's spiced cinnamon, cloves, and a hint of vanilla—warm and comforting. It's like a siren's call to me, a reminder of what I crave.

As Cinder talks about her condition, my mind drifts to the dangers that lurk within me, hidden beneath the surface of my calm demeanor. Most of the time I can ignore the fact she is a beater, but right now her heartbeat becomes my own, echoing in my ears.

I nod slowly, trying to focus on her words rather than the primal urge that whispers in the depths of my being.

The way her blood sings to me has my insides in knots. I clench my fists, willing myself to stay in control, to resist the temptation that dances before me in her every heartbeat.

The words hang heavy between us as we continue our nighttime stroll through the cemetery. My gaze is inexorably drawn to the gentle rise and fall of her chest with each breath, keenly aware of the rhythmic thrum of her pulse.

Heat rushes through my veins, an ancient hunger awakening from its slumber. I can almost taste the rich, coppery essence that flows beneath her skin—warm, intoxicating, utterly intoxicating. Desire coils low in my belly as vivid fantasies play out in my mind's eye, each more salacious than the last.

Forcing myself to meet her inquisitive stare, I'm transfixed by the molten depths of her violet eyes. They shine like precious gemstones, luring me into their fathomless depths until I'm utterly lost, consumed by want.

Without conscious thought I step forward, closing the gap between us until there's barely a breath separating our bodies. Cinder's back meets the solid rock of a weathered headstone as I cage her in with my arms, my fingers splayed against the cool granite on either side of her head.

Cinder looks up at me, concern etched on her face. She lets out a soft gasp, her pupils blown wide as her gaze flickers from my eyes to my lips and back again. I can hear the frantic cadence of her heart, sense the rush of blood heating her skin from within. The delicate flutter of her pulse at the base of her throat is a mesmerizing siren song that has my mouth watering in anticipation.

"Are you okay?" she asks, giving me a chance to stop. But I'm not sure I can. I'm obsessed, drawn in. Is this what it's like to be thralled? If so, it's not so bad.

Cinder goes stock still under me.

For a split second, I swear I see a flicker of orange flame dancing in the depths of her violet eyes. A trick of the light? Or something more?

She blinks and it's gone, but the air around us is charged, heavy with the scent of burning leaves—crisp, autumnal, a whisper of the season's change. It's entirely out of place and yet, inexplicably tied to her somehow.

Slowly, painfully slowly, I lean in until our lips are a hairsbreadth apart, our heated breaths mingling in the scant space between us. My eyes flutter shut as I savor the moment, every nerve ending in my body thrumming with unbridled need.

Just as I'm about to close that final inch, I stop.

Her blood rushes in my ears and heat emanates from her in intense waves, warming me to the center of my cold bones.

The beat of her heart.

It drums out at me.

An enticing message to every fiber of my being.

Fuck, I want to feed. I want to sink my fangs in her. I want to spear up into her tight little body with my dick and enter her every possible way while her liquid life flows down my throat.

I need to regain control. If I don't, I'm going to do something I regret. So I reach out and grab for a question to distract.

"How does one get anemia?"

CHAPTER 24
PULLING THE PLUG

CINDER

eat engulfs me, and I begin to tremble.

A feeling I can't name spirals up from the dark depths of me and whatever emotion it is, it is strong.

It's too strong.

It's too much.

No, no, no.

I don't want to be in my body, but Kai has pulled me back into it.

He kisses me like I'm the most precious, sensual gift to this world and I find myself fully inside my body, feeling every small movement, from the texture of his perfectly skilled lips to the way my stomach flips and flops in response. I'm not outside my body, not thinking of something I'll be painting later or how to exact proper vengeance on a stray cat. I'm *with* him. Fully and completely.

So when Kai interrupts the moment to bring up the

cause of my anemia, something else is immediately stoked inside me. Struggling to breathe evenly, the heat ebbs a bit even as my nostrils flare. I have to get away from this. Whatever this feeling is.

"Why didn't you let me question your father further last night?" I challenge Kai instead.

I'm hot all over and he's backed away as if he could feel the flames of fear and anger inside me.

I realize that's part of the terrifying concoction brewing inside me. Fear and anger at how close I let Kai get to me, in more ways than one.

There's absolutely no fae fucking way I'm telling him how I got anemia. I shouldn't have even confessed my condition to him in the first place.

Why the fuck does this ridiculous fairy prince have such an effect on me, pulling things out of me whether they are orgasms or secrets?

I should probably kill him. Just for safety's sake.

"You promised you'd help me find my dad's killer and the first chance I have to put Valdor on the spot, you force me to back off." I continue to lash out at him, desperate to get away from what's brewing inside. I even use the King's first name, trying to rip down his status as a barrier.

Kaison frowns. "You were pushing too hard. My father is dangerous, even more than you think. You need to tread carefully."

On top of being stonewalled, yet another day has passed without finding the Ember of Midnight. I have access to the castle, but I haven't had the time to search. My irritation has me at the snapping point.

"I'm sick of treading carefully," I snarl.

Suddenly I'm backed up against a headstone.

Charming bears down on me with a seriousness I've not seen before.

"Don't." He's so wound up he almost can't get the words out. The heavy metal rings shift as his knuckles flex in agitation. "Don't push him. There are things he can do to you. Things you can't imagine. Any rumors you've heard about him ruling with an iron fist, utilizing cruelty are all true and they only scratch the surface."

My surprise at his new side almost negates the twinge of fear at being cornered by a vampire. . . almost.

My skin prickles and shrinks away from him. All the fight drains from me.

Kaison blinks then backs away. "Sorry," he mumbles.

We walk the rest of the way to my apartment in loaded silence, though what it's loaded with is unclear. His sudden bout of seriousness throws me. Again, I get the sense I got a glimpse past the many masks he wears to something he shares with no one.

After a while, Charming breaks the silence. "We will get the information you need. We will find out what happens, but we have to work on playing the doting bride and groom. Thankfully our taboo coupling will keep people off their game. But my father is different. I want you to be. . ." He seems to struggle to find the word. ". . . safe."

I almost choke out a laugh.

Safe.

In Midnight.

I'm in constant danger of being thralled, assassinated, or drained because I'm human, upsetting the monarchy, and generally disgusting to vampires.

Instead of adding on, I glance at Kaison who seems lost in serious thought.

I do believe him. . . kind of.

Which scares me and makes me want to push him out of my inner sphere even harder. So I disconnect. Like pulling a plug, I let go of all emotions, feeling myself empty out.

I feel nothing.

Not for him.

Not even for myself.

This is the way things should be. I need to keep it this way. We can play but it's nothing more than that. We aren't friends. We are temporary allies, using our sexual chemistry to pass the time. Because that's all it is. Chemistry.

And I can walk away from chemistry at any time.

CHAPTER 25

A WEAK BAG OF BONES

CHARMING

"Hit the door with your face." My father's voice is cold and merciless as he commands it.

The insidious grip of his thrall takes hold, my body no longer my own. With rising horror, I watch helplessly as my face slams into the unyielding wood, pain exploding through my skull.

"Stop that," he barks, and my body jerks to a halt. Part of me still always hopes it will be over quickly, but he's far from done showing me his displeasure.

Not that I wasn't expecting this. This is a monthly, sometimes weekly known tactic of correction he's used on me since I was a boy. He's punished me for far less, and publicly shackling myself to a human bride is by far one of my worst trespasses.

"Punch the wall."

I grit my teeth, straining against the invisible bonds of

my father's will. But it's useless. I'm a prisoner in my own flesh, a marionette dancing to his twisted tune. The helplessness is almost worse than the pain, a sickening reminder of how utterly powerless I am. Unable to stop it, my knuckles crack into stone. Bones break, sending screaming pain through my body and brain. Blood covers my knuckles and drips onto the ground, and the swelling in my face is starting to make it difficult to see.

"You are worthless," he hisses. "You are weak."

Rage and humiliation war inside me, a toxic cocktail that burns like acid in my veins. I want to scream, to lash out, to make him feel even a fraction of the agony he's inflicting on me. But I can't. I can only endure, my hatred festering in my hidden depths.

By the time he's done, I can barely see out of one eye and my hands are as useful as two bags filled with broken shards of bone.

He pulls out a blue handkerchief from a pocket and dabs the droplets of my blood that landed on his hand. "You had *one* job. Marry. Strengthen our rule. Instead, you chose a lowly human to drag our name through the mud. You careless, insipid boy. You think of no one but yourself and play your stupid games. The next time you feel compelled to chase novelty, I want you to remember this. How when you follow your whims, you only hurt yourself."

Then he drops the handkerchief to the ground and leaves me there shaking with pain, rage, and the regret I didn't kill him.

The only thing that kept me from lunging at him with murderous intent—other than the fact I'm so beaten I've the strength of a kitten and he'd thrall me again almost instantly—is that I managed to make him believe I'm incompetent.

Soon, he will find out how very *very* wrong he is.

I begin the long journey to get blood, staggering like a drunk man.

Resentment simmers until it heats into anger.

Anger festers until it becomes rage.

And I know that's exactly what pulsates under my skin as I catch my blurry reflection in the mirror, taking stock of the damage in the castle corridor.

Rage.

Vivid mottled bruises swell across half my face. My knuckles are split and swollen, dripping blood along the floor.

Does the rage spring from a young boy who still wants his father's love, or if not that, his approval?

No. It's born from the fact my father does not even bother to lift a finger to inflict pain.

"Holy fae fucking hell."

The world around me is mostly dark, so I turn to see Cinder from the narrow slit of my good eye. She stands there, a gothic vision of royal enchantment and zero fucks. The only shift in her normally expressionless face is the downward tilt of perfect lips and a slight furrow in her brow.

Okay there may be one fuck lurking in her somewhere.

The court has been keeping us both ridiculously busy with tedious meetings and fittings, so I'm surprised to run into her alone. Two women emerge from the room where she was.

Ah there it is. The entourage attempting to shape up her etiquette for polite society and dance lessons. Interest and curiosity spark in their eyes. I need to get out of here, fast.

I try to smile. My lips instantly crack, filling my mouth with my blood. It tastes rancid.

"Really got to be careful not to sleep with married women," I say, playing off the wounds again.

Another couple of people emerge from the room. Ambassadors from the Common World. A half-elf and a human who both openly gape with shock.

"I mean it was a while ago. Of course I am only ever faithful to my bride," I rush to say. "Unfortunately, there is no statute of limitations on punishment for sleeping with another's partner." I do my best to throw a cheeky smile their way to put them at ease, but blood rushes faster into my mouth as my lip cracks open further.

Something crosses Cinder's features, but I'm not sure what. Disgust? Disbelief? Suspicion? No matter what it is, my battered brain won't be able to discern anything until I heal.

"See you tonight," I force out the words from the less bleeding half of my mouth with a curt bow before beating a hasty retreat.

Only when I've turned a corner do I resume my slower, limping gait until I reach my destination.

ONE SIDE of the castle's kitchens is lined with cold boxes that store blood while the far side has several wood stoves for heating it. It's still early when I enter the massive stone room. Later, familiars will be pouring and preparing a mass amount of blood and champagne to serve at yet another engagement ball.

It takes a painfully long amount of time to pour myself a chalice of blood and set it on the massive granite island that could easily fit forty people at its edge. A ridiculous design choice seeing how little preparation is needed for our food. The emptiness of the unnecessarily large kitchen echoes inside me. It's reassuring I can find places where no one will watch me, and I can just be.

My palms press against the edge of the countertop, causing my already injured hands to explode in a white-hot burst of pain. I grit my teeth and stare down at the chalice, forcing myself to feel the full extent of the agony tearing through my body and soul. Every nerve is on fire, sending bolts of electricity into my brain, screaming at me to release the pressure. But I can't. Not yet.

Focusing on the pain helps me compartmentalize what I'm about to drink.

I hate it.

I hate erasing all the marks he leaves. I hate the fact I need the blood to recover. Even the thought of the thick, viscous liquid makes me queasy.

To others, feeding is a pleasure.

To me, it is medicine for the afflictions I'm forced to act out on myself.

Worse yet, I hate knowing that this is how my people reduce the value of humans. To many, Cinder is just a blood bag. Just a chalice filled with something delicious but easily discarded after use. I don't know whose blood this is. If they gave it willingly. What their name is. This lack of detail always makes me uneasy.

The tendons in my forearms flex as I gird myself. Then I clumsily attempt to wrap my broken digits around the cup. When I find I can't successfully do so without sloshing most of the blood out, I'm forced to bend my knees and stoop to drink from the side as I tip it gingerly into my mouth.

Fuck. Ow. Shit.

Unsuccessful again, I set the cup back down.

I really need to start smuggling in big cups with straws from the Common World. A straw would be fae fucking life-changing right now.

A pair of thin, pale hands picks up the cup and I recoil on instinct.

My surprise turns into shock when I realize it's Cinder, who has somehow managed to follow me undetected.

I shouldn't be surprised. Hell, she may have used her glass slippers to transport here. Little minx.

Cinder offers the blood up to me. The coppery scent fills my nostrils, mixing with her unique scent.

I purse my lips, not about to let her feed me.

"I can do it myself," I grumble, trying to take the chalice from her, but my fingers are too broken, too weak to grasp it properly.

Cinder narrows her eyes, pulling it away from my mangled digits. "Stop being a stubborn ass and let me help you. "

Her words are harsh, but her touch is gentle as she brings the cup to my mouth.

I'm given a heavy dose of the purple death until I part my lips. Cinder tips the chalice ever so slightly so I can drink. Even in small sips, the blood slides down my throat, thick and heavy, coating my tongue with its metallic taste.

I hate it, hate the way it rushes to my core and spreads out, stitching my broken body together every time.

My senses sharpen until they are filled with Cinder. The heat of her body so close to mine, the sound of her heart-beat drumming in my ears, the sight of her slender fingers wrapped around the chalice.

The aroma of her blood grows stronger, a tempting blend of metallic and sweet. Its rhythmic beat whispers to me from just below the surface of her alabaster skin. My fangs ache with desire as I fight to control my thirst.

I try to step away, but she thrusts the chalice towards me again. The blood in the cup has cooled, the scent weakening, making her scent of charred vanilla and skin all the more prominent.

I allow her to push the cup to my lips again. At that moment, I am consumed by a wild and desperate craving, my body betraying me as I imagine sinking my teeth into her wrist, her pulse fluttering beneath my tongue as I greedily drink.

The self-loathing burns deep within me. I am no different from the rest of my kind, no matter how much I pretend otherwise.

Blood dribbles from my mouth and the edge of the cup. Wet droplets hit my shirt and the countertop in bright crimson drips.

I know, with a bone-deep certainty, that Cinder's blood would be the most delicious thing I've ever tasted. That if I were to sink my fangs into the delicate curve of her neck I would be lost forever, drowning in the essence of her.

The thought makes my body react with a fierce, primal hunger. Fangs elongate in my mouth and the room comes into sharp focus as my pupils expand with insatiable need. The blood from the chalice is like burnt plastic on my tongue compared to what I know would be the honeyed sweetness that flows just beneath her skin. And it's mere inches from me.

My cock thickens in my slacks as the ache builds in my fangs and my balls. An amazing feat considering the healing has barely begun in my body.

Cinder. I just want all of Cinder.

I need her.

In a flash, I have her pressed against the countertop. The chalice clatters to the floor, forgotten. My lips hover a hairsbreadth from her throat, her quickening heartbeat calling to me. A low, guttural growl escapes me as I inhale her scent, my fingers digging into her hips with bruising force.

I'm losing myself in her, drowning in the overwhelming need to consume her utterly. I am more monster than man, a slave to my darkest desires.

Cinder's breath hitches, her pulse racing beneath my fingertips. I revel in the heat of her skin, the way her body trembles. It's intoxicating, the power I have over her in this moment.

I lean in closer, my lips brushing her throat. She shivers, a soft gasp escaping her.

"Don't," she whispers, her voice a breathless plea.

Something from deep inside me has been unleashed and it will not be satisfied until it has tasted her essence.

"I can make it good for you," I rush to say. And I could. I know she's afraid, but if I'm pumping deep inside her hot little cunt while I sink my teeth into her skin, I know I can make her come so hard she'll see stars. "It'll be good. It'll be good for both of us." My voice is raspy to my ears. I'm giving her the promises of an inexperienced boy who is so desperate, he's on the verge of blowing his load.

My fangs graze her skin, a promise of the pleasure to come.

Cinder stiffens, her fingers digging into my shoulders.

"Please, Kai," she breathes. She's shaking under me. Violently.

My bride is begging me not to do the thing I promised not to do, the thing she's afraid of most.

I want her with a desperation that borders on madness.

But beneath the desire, there's a flicker of fear, a terrifying awareness of how close I am to losing myself completely.

I'm teetering on the edge of a razor, balanced between desire and destruction. One wrong move, and I'll slice us both to ribbons.

But oh, what a sweet fucking fall it would be.

CHAPTER 26

IT'S LIKE TEN THOUSAND CINDERS, WHEN ALL YOU NEED IS A STRAW

CHARMING

My muscles tremble with the effort of restraining myself, my jaw clenched so tightly I can feel my teeth grinding. Sweat beads on my forehead, my breath coming in ragged gasps as I fight the urge to sink my fangs into Cinder's soft, inviting flesh.

It would be so easy to give in, to let the monster inside me take control. But I can't. I won't. Even as my body screams for release, I cling to the last shreds of my humanity, desperate to prove that I'm more than just a slave to my thirst.

I jolt back to reality. I untangle my fingers from Cinder's hair and wrench myself away from her.

Even as the hunger howls its protest, I know I've made the right choice. I am more than my thirst, more than the sum of my darkest desires. And I will not let them define me, no matter how loudly they roar.

What the hell was I thinking? Not once but twice of late, I almost gave into my thirst for my human bride. I'm losing my fucking mind.

Cinder stares at me, her eyes wide with a mix of pure terror and something else, something darker. Her hand flies to her throat, fingers trembling as they trace the spot where my fangs nearly pierced her skin.

"I'm sorry," I mutter, running a hand through my hair. "I don't know what came over me. I wouldn't bite you without your consent." I give her a hard, searching look. My voice is hoarse with self-disgust. "I would never. . ."

Cinder narrows her eyes, her lips pressing into a thin line. "Really? Because it sure as hell seemed like you were about to."

I flinch at the accusation in her tone. She's right. I was seconds away from sinking my teeth into her, from taking what I so desperately craved.

Shame washes over me, hot and sticky.

"I thought I was. . ." she starts with uncertainty.

"What?" I ask, urging her to go on. Remorse and shame are drowning me. I'm desperate to know what she's thinking. I prefer she gives me the brunt of her judgment just so I can see what goes on behind those inscrutable violet eyes.

"I thought I was disgusting to you. What you said to the other boys that day." Then she shakes her head before looking away. Arms crossing over her body, she shrinks in on herself until she becomes even smaller. "Never mind, you probably don't remember."

"I remember." I'm deathly sober now, my body healing enough that my hands don't scream in agony, and I can see out of my left eye again. The muddled bloodlust has abated and I'm thinking clearly. And I know exactly what she's talking about. "Those boys were going to. . ." I didn't want to finish the sentence. It's what I almost did just now. Take. Bite. Claim. "...play with you," I finish grimly.

She swallows hard and nods. "Why would you want to bite me? You acted like—you said I was disgusting." Cinder pauses. "I spent most of my life thinking you despised me."

I take a step back, needing to distance myself from her words. It takes a moment to pull myself together. "No. No, Cinder. I don't think you're disgusting. I've never hated you. I've—I was trying to protect you."

Cinder sways a little on her feet before reaching out to grasp the counter edge. As if she's been so rocked, she can barely stand.

"I always thought we were kind of the same, you and I," I explain. "Children of the important figures of Midnight, separate from the rest. Now that I say it out loud, I realize how ridiculous that sounds."

She shakes her head slightly and I'm not sure if it's because she's assuring me I'm not ridiculous, or because she rejects the idea of what I'm saying.

Nausea burns through me.

"But even though I don't find you disgusting," even saying it is strange and so counter to the truth, it pains me, "I would never bite you without consent. And if those kids had tried anything with you, I would have ripped their heads clean off." The rage still pulsates under my skin, now transferred from the past.

It's transferred to the idea of anyone hurting the woman in front of me.

"I don't want you to protect me." She takes a step forward, her gaze flicking to the blood staining my shirt. "What I want is the truth. What really happened to you?"

My shoulders tense for a fraction of a second before I

fall back into the persona of Prince Charming. "It's like I told you. Jealous lovers from the past."

The truth burns on the tip of my tongue, but I swallow it back. I've learned the hard way that revealing my father's abuse only leads to more pain. Not just for me, but for anyone who tries to intervene.

But it's more than that. I don't want her to see me as a victim, to look at me with pity, or worse, to see me as weak. The role of the carefree, self-indulgent prince is a mask I've worn for so long it's become a part of me. It's my armor, protecting me from making reckless decisions driven by my pain. If I let that mask slip, even for a moment, I might give the old man a true reason to kill me.

Confident my face is healed enough, I cast a sardonic smile at her. "And shouldn't you be learning the latest dances right about now? There are only two hundred and twenty of them to memorize to be proficient at any Midnight ball."

She doesn't soften, only studies me with a serious, unrelenting gaze.

Under Cinder's scrutiny, my skin warms several degrees.

That must be the blood I just consumed.

"I told you," I exclaim with an exaggerated sigh. "We aren't even really together and now you are going to make a fuss about my past trysts? That will make the next couple of months quite difficult," I say airily.

I want Cinder to call me Prince Slut Muffin and think of me like everyone else does. A self-indulgent troublemaker who doesn't carry his pain like a brand. Better she think me a promiscuous ass than learn the truth. I'm a promiscuous ass who takes regular beatings from his father.

The lie goes down easier than the truth and my throat is raw.

Cinder's eyes flash with annoyance. "Bullshit. You expect me to believe some jealous husband did this to you?"

She gestures to my face, only moments ago covered in bruises and cuts. "I'm not an idiot, Charming. Someone beat the living hell out of you, and I want to know who."

Her gaze drops to where bright red spots mar my white shirt. I reflexively grip the crude color in a fist, covering it from her gaze before I know what I've done.

Cinder's violet eyes swing back up to meet mine. Something crackles in them. I expect it to be anger and disgust at drinking blood.

She pierces into me with invisible needles, searching for the truth. For a moment I almost wonder if she has the power of thrall herself.

You want to know what happened? I was punished because of you, my gorgeous demoness.

I can't ignore the anger still running rampant through me. It takes all my power to push my smile up into my eyes, and the effort leaves me exhausted.

I swallow hard and break eye contact with her to look down at the hand that still grips the spot that's likely already stained my shirt.

I need to distract her before she forces me to spill everything in a landslide of tar and sludge.

There are two main tactics of diversion I often resort to. One is lighthearted joking. Since that hasn't worked, I move on to number two. Sex appeal.

I yank the shirt off over my head. My muscles flex in a way that I know draws the eye.

Exposing flesh usually distracts, and even Cinder can't help but take a quick tour of my exposed body.

Wait. She isn't ogling.

Her eyes roam my body like she's checking for more injuries.

The idea she cares sends a powerful emotion swirling underneath my rage. It feels like a small seed being watered after years of drought.

No one knows who I am outside the persona. No one truly cares what I am when I'm not giving them pleasure or amusement. I'm not a person. I'm a thing. A performance to be enjoyed.

But that's not how Cinder looks at me. That's never how she's looked at me.

Even through the lace obscuring her eyes that first night I pulled her to the dance floor, I found myself entranced by her serious, probing gaze.

Suddenly I'm as vulnerable and wanting as a teenage boy again, watching the little human girl enjoying her own little world. The old pangs of longing to touch her solitude and peace shoot through me.

Good fucking witchtits. I've got to get out of here, I have to regain my equilibrium so I can be the Prince Charming that everyone knows and loves at tonight's engagement ball.

"Time for laundry," I say with a cheeky grin as I sweep past her, though I simply plan to throw the shirt out and have never done a bit of laundry in my entire life.

Instead, I stride out to the courtyard and begin a familiar sequence of martial arts moves.

Each strike is filled with pent-up anger and determination. As I twist and kick, I can feel the darkness pulsing through my body, but instead of succumbing to it, I use it as fuel to drive me forward.

With each move, I take control of the pain that doesn't

heal with blood, and I make it my own. My focus sharpens on what must be done. On why I've coerced Cinder into this engagement.

If only the Mice would come through and see this is the perfect time to put an end to an old fairy's tyranny. Because if they don't agree to help, I'm not sure what I'll do.

And that thought scares me, not because I'm afraid of what must be done. But because if I have to bring King Valdor Charming down myself, it may be the very act that transforms me into him.

CHAPTER 27
BURYING THE BRIDE
BEFORE THE WEDDING

CINDER

The smile plastered on Charming's face is so forced that I'm surprised it hasn't cracked under the strain. Despite his amazing ability to hide it, I can see the anger simmering just beneath the surface.

It's been there since I saw him bruised and battered, barely able to feed himself.

I play with the new engagement ring, an oversized planet made of opalescent diamonds, flanked by sapphires. Spinning it on my finger, I can't help but think it suits me.

But the way Kai casually passed it to me to wear before this event made my stomach twist in uneasiness. As if it were an afterthought—as if I were some kind of obligation he was fulfilling.

The dark energy is a living demon shadowing him, haunting and digging at him. I see it because it hovers next to my demons—who hung out with me so long I decided to friend them. The skulls inked on my arms are some of my very best friends.

Doesn't make it healthy, but I feel it makes the most of that darkness.

No one else notices, though. A few weeks ago, I might not have recognized it either. But I do now. I can't miss it. It's in his eyes, his posture, his very essence.

The pain and resentment within him are palpable.

Feelings I understand all too well. But I know how to shove those deep down into a lockbox before putting that in a different box and locking that one until I'm barely aware of what's at the center of my nesting containers of feelings.

I don't know what happened to him earlier, but the bruises and cuts that marred his face spoke volumes. And his hands. Sweet witchtits, they were beyond mangled.

My heart broke at the sight of them.

Or was it the way he tried to put on that Charming persona and brush it off?

He can't get anything past me. Not even that cock-and-bull story about a jealous boyfriend or husband kicking his ass.

Not that I doubt he's pissed some people off in the past, but that isn't the cause for that barely restrained violence I sense vibrating in him.

But now as we sweep through the ballroom arm in arm, he's the picture of a confident, proud prince showing off his bride-to-be. If only they knew the truth behind our little arrangement.

Though so far, I've gotten nowhere on my side of the bargain. I only grow more suspicious of the fairy court, of Kai's father, of the darkness I know is swirling underneath this glittering façade of Midnight.

Everywhere I look, the richness of the Midnight Kingdom is on full display, from the intricate ice sculptures to the dark, opulent tapestries with depictions of King Charming leading the realm into independence. The grand ballroom, bathed in cool, ethereal light, glows with hues of deep blues, velvety blacks, and rich purples.

Crystal chandeliers hang from the high, vaulted ceilings, casting a shimmering kaleidoscope of light across the polished marble floors. The air is cool, almost chilling, and carries the faint scent of night-blooming jasmine and ancient, cold stone.

The fairy court is in rare form tonight, their ignorance and disdain for humans on full display. I catch snippets of their inane questions, each one more ridiculous than the last.

While I tune it all out, Kaison is forced to answer for both of us.

"No, I'm not sure what you mean by the human musk being a potential issue," he says in an airy voice. "I find my bride's natural scent utterly intoxicating."

"I can't say I've given much thought to making burial arrangements for her just yet. My bride and I plan to have many joyous years ahead of us."

"Watching her eat doesn't make me gag. Yes, I've seen her do it many times and have coped just fine."

If this is what the court believes passes for polite conversation, I can't imagine what they must say behind closed doors.

With each question, I push away further and further from where I am. My eyes find solace in the massive paintings my father created, in the archways that frame the exit to the carpet of lush green grass under a sparkling sky.

I want to be there now.

A wave of lightheadedness washes over me and I blink rapidly, trying to clear the spots from my vision. Between the stress of the ball, the lack of substantial food, and my ever-present anemia, my body is starting to rebel. I down iron pills dutifully, but it's not enough.

Fuck, I hate this weakness. I'm determined not to let anyone notice I'm close to swaying on my feet.

Charming's hand flexes at his side, and I can tell he's struggling to maintain his composure. If I'm barely tolerating this, I can only imagine how he must feel, having to play nice with these priggish assholes.

There's been a distance between us since I helped feed him.

No, earlier than that.

Since he kissed me in the cemetery.

The memory of his lips on mine, the taste of his tongue, the way his body pressed against me—it's all seared into my brain, impossible to forget.

Prince Kaison Charming has bled for me. Has burned himself on my tongue piercing, and still kept in control to keep kissing me.

While I was scared shitless when he pinned me to the counter, a large part of me believed he wouldn't do it. He wouldn't bite me.

He controlled himself when I cut myself. He protected me from that guy who assaulted me at the bar. And apparently, he'd been trying to protect me from those boys.

That realization caused a pinch in my heart that has yet to release.

I thought I was branded by his scathing look, marked by his hate and disgust, but I couldn't have been more wrong.

Had the young, serious-face prince been trying to communicate a moment of solidarity?

Whoa, Nelly. I'm spiraling over here.

I can't let myself get carried away. This thing between us, whatever it is, can't be real. I'm just a means to an end for him, a way to piss off his father and thumb his nose at Midnight society.

Since the incident with the blood he's not come close to touching me again, giving me all the space I've said I need. Not even now. His hands are folded behind him in a royal posture. But a traitorous part of me wishes he would put his hand on my back or set my fingers at the crook of his arm. Anything to make me feel like I'm not just a pretty accessory.

What are you even saying, Cinder? You don't want him to touch you. Especially not after he almost lost control.

"Won't she get dreadfully jealous of all your other. . .dalliances? Humans are so emotional about such things, or so I'm told."

The question snaps me out of my thoughts, and I glance up to see Charming clear his throat. Several pairs of eyes bounce between us, searching for some kind of reaction. Some weak point they can needle into and then later wag their tongues.

Another rush of dizziness sways me slightly to the left. My gaze latches on the moving lips of the jerk speaking, but my vision swirls. Cotton might as well be stuffed in my head and ears, making it impossible to focus. Heaviness weighs my limbs down, but I stand my ground, refusing to fall.

"Now that I am an engaged prince, Cinder will not need to worry about me straying," he says, his hand finally coming to rest on the small of my back.

I stiffen at the contact. Not because I dislike it, but because I hadn't been prepared for it. As quickly as it's there, his touch is gone, leaving me strangely bereft.

The couple in front of us shares a knowing look, doubt and amusement plain on their faces.

"Come now, Your Highness. We all know your reputation. The playboy prince, always chasing the next thrill. This little experiment with a human bride is amusing, but let's not pretend it's anything more than another passing fancy, hm? You couldn't commit to a woman any more than you could to anything else."

I bristle at their words, the dismissive way they talk about me like I'm not even here. But before I can open my mouth to tell them exactly where they can shove their opinions, Lady Newcomb chimes in, her laughter grating on my last nerve.

"Indeed. A leopard can't change his spots, after all. It's only a matter of time before you tire of this novelty and return to your... usual pursuits."

Her husband nods in agreement. "As fun of a circus show this marriage is, do not fear, we all know how it will end. Managing a kingdom requires more than charm and good looks. It requires a steadfastness that, frankly, your history does not demonstrate. You clearly lack any aptitude to handle the throne and deal with the complicated decisions that affect all of us so."

I key into Kai enough to see the flinch. It's barely perceptible, but the blow this Baron Von Douchebag threw hit its mark.

It's one thing for them to think I'm unworthy scum, I'm used to it. But I'll be damned if I let these pompous windbags get away with talking to him like that.

"Oh, spare us your shitty, short-sided judgments," I drawl, my voice dripping with disdain. "You think you've got His Highness all figured out? Please. He's not some two-dimensional caricature you can dismiss with a wave of your bejeweled hand. There's more to him than meets the eye, but I wouldn't expect you to understand that, considering how far your heads are shoved up your own asses."

The group gapes at me, their shock and outrage almost comical. But I'm not done yet. The exertion of speaking up, coupled with my already weakened state, makes me sway dangerously. I grasp onto Kai's arm for support, trying to play it off as a casual gesture. Tremors vibrate through my hands, the telltale signs that my body is about to give out on me.

"Come on, darling," I say, rolling the pet name on my tongue. "Let's find more champagne and drink away the pain of such tedious company." I practically drag him away from the sputtering nobles.

Kai turns to me when we're finally out of earshot, his eyes searching mine with an intensity that steals my breath. Which is not good considering I need all the oxygen I can get right now.

"You stood up for me," he murmurs, his voice rough with an emotion I can't quite name.

I shrug, trying to play it off as no big deal. "Don't read too much into it. I just can't stand pompous windbags who think they know everything. It's not like I actually give a damn about you or your reputation."

But even as the words leave my lips, I know they're a lie. Because despite everything, despite the fact this is all just a charade, I do care. More than I should. More than I'm willing to admit, even to myself.

The lopsided curve of his lips says he knows I'm lying too.

Kai's gaze lingers on mine, and for a moment, I swear I see a flicker of something real, something raw and honest and vulnerable. But then it's gone, replaced by that familiar mask of charm and bravado.

And I'm left wondering if I'll ever truly know the man beneath the crown or if he'll always be just out of reach, a beautiful illusion that's never quite within my grasp.

"So I'm guessing you've forgiven me then?" he asks.

"Forgiven you?" I repeat, bringing a fresh glass of champagne to my lips while sneaking a longing glance toward the outside terrace.

My grip on his arm tightens as another wave of dizziness hits me. I blink hard, trying to will away the black spots dancing in my vision. Not now, I plead silently. Just let me hold it together a little longer.

Catching where my attention is fixed, Kai takes my arm and leads me in the direction I desire. As soon as we are outside, I suck in what feels like my first real breath all night.

"For losing control," he clarifies in a low, rough voice.

I lean heavily against the balcony railing, grateful for the support. My legs are jelly, my heart racing in my chest. I curse my stupid, traitorous body for failing me now when I need to keep my shit together.

"I—" Do I forgive him? Did I really think he would lose control? Everything he's done of late has been to protect me. Something I'm wholly unused to.

Kai's cool hand brushes my cheek, his brow furrowing with concern. "You're paler than usual. Did you take your iron supplements today?"

I nod wearily. Something warm curls in my stomach at his concern. "'Yeah, but some days they barely take the edge off."

"Psst," a voice from off in the bushes calls.

We both snap to attention and turn to the sound. I

catch sight of a lanky man emerging from the brush. He wears a loose beanie cap on his head, and loose clothes over his stick figure. The fangs give him away as a Midnight fairy.

Kai immediately tenses, checking the area to see if anyone notices the newcomer. "Jack, what are you doing here?"

The lanky vampire doesn't even flinch at the hissed question. "I got the info you wanted."

With that, Kai grabs me by the arm and leads me out of sight from the ballroom until we are in the shadows with this Jack guy.

"Tell me," Kai orders, his grip tight on my arm, but I don't tell him to let go. I'm barely hanging on now, the world tilting dangerously around me. I cling to Kai, my fingers digging into his jacket, as I try to focus on Jack's words.

Jack side-eyes me with hesitance but speaks. "You were right, Charming."

"What are you talking about?" I ask, a zip of heat goes through my blood as my attention sharpens.

Kaison nods to me. "Tell her."

Jack hesitates but turns to face me. "Prince Kaison sent me on a mission to unearth proof if your father had been murdered. We found original notes from the medical examiner, and he covered up Byung-He's true cause of death."

My breath freezes in my chest. "What was it?"

Jack winces as he tells me. "Exsanguination."

The shock and horror wash over me in waves, threatening to drown me in a sea of grief and anger. A part of me wants to deny it, but the unbearable truth settles in my chest like a lead weight. My heart pounds like a war drum.

My father was drained of his blood. Someone fed on him and killed him.

"Cinder? Breathe."

I vaguely hear Kai's plea, but it's muffled by the roar in my mind.

Part of me didn't believe it. Didn't believe Kai's claim. But now I have to accept the terrible fact that when I thought things were bad, they could still get worse.

My heart feels like a battlefield, torn between denial and acceptance. Part of me wants to believe it's all a twisted lie, but the other part knows that the truth is laid before me.

As the weight of realization crushes down on me, my world goes dark.

CHAPTER 28

A SPOONFUL OF SUGAR HELPS THE MURDER GO DOWN

CINDER

I'm being carried in two strong arms.

"Move."

Kai's voice. He sounds tense.

I try to open my eyes, but my eyelids feel impossibly heavy. I'm vaguely aware of voices around us, whispers and murmurs that I can't quite make out.

"Your Highness, is everything alright with your bride?" someone asks, their voice laced with false concern.

"She's fine," Kai says, his tone as nonchalant as it is dismissive. "Just a little too much champagne, I'm afraid. You know how humans are."

"Perhaps you shouldn't feed on her so intensely," another voice suggests, a hint of malice in their tone. "Humans are such fragile creatures, after all."

Kai's stiffens around me, and though his voice remains casual, I sense the anger simmering beneath the surface. "I appreciate your concern, but I assure you, she's my fiancé, not a blood bag."

There's a beat of silence, and then the sound of retreating footsteps. Kai continues walking, his strides long and purposeful. I drift in and out of consciousness, catching snatches of conversation as he carries me through the castle.

Finally, I feel him gently lower me onto a soft surface. A bed, I realize, as I sink into the plush mattress. I force my eyes open, blinking against the dim light of my bedroom.

Kai hovers over me, concern pinching at the corners of his eyes. "Well, well, my sleeping beauty awakens." He tries to tease, but his usual smirk is absent.

I scowl at him, trying to sit up. "I'm fine," I insist, even as a wave of dizziness forces me back down. "I don't need your help. You can get out."

Kai arches an eyebrow. "Is that so? Because from where I'm standing, it looks like you're about to pass out again." He leans closer, his voice dropping to a low purr. "If you don't let me help you, I might have to take drastic measures. Like cuddling you and calling you pet names until you give in."

I glare at him, but I can feel my resolve wavering. "You wouldn't dare."

"Try me, my black souled diamond. My ghostly damsel of distress."

There's that cocky smile.

I groan, realizing he's not going to let this go. "Fine. My iron pills are in that upper drawer. I need to take them for my anemia. And grab the box of Magic Morsels too. A snack can only help."

Kai nods, his playful demeanor fading into something more serious. He retrieves the pills and a glass of water, watching as I swallow them down.

"So," I say, breaking the silence. "You were right about my father. He was murdered."

Kai sighs heavily, sinking to sit on the bed beside me, handing me the box of snack cakes I smuggled in from the Common World. "I hoped I was wrong," he admits. "I didn't want to be right, not about this."

"Are we sure?" I have to ask. My brain is swimming in too much syrup to think it through myself.

I struggle to open the individually packaged Spice Spell Rolls. The rolled sponge cakes with pumpkin spice filling and a drizzle of white chocolate glaze are only available during the fall. Though I bet if I talked to Red, she could convince her grandma, the producer of Magic Morsels and owner and frontwoman of Grandma's House, to get me boxes off season it'd be possible. Even Martha Stewart would give her left arm and best rose bushes to run a home goods and food company like Red's Gigi.

He takes the rolls from me and rips the package open before handing it back. "You really should be eating spinach or red meat for your anemia. This is only going to make you feel worse."

I blink. "Did you research my condition?"

Pushing a spice roll into my mouth, I try to embrace the comfort that is anything pumpkin. Thankfully, when the servants light the candles, they light my personal ones as well so the autumnal scents swirl around us like a hug I desperately need.

"Maybe," he shrugs in an unexpected moment of modesty.

"Yeah, but this is for my feels," I say waving the second cake in the package. "Also I can do this now." I blink hard and a slight green film covers my vision, and I know my eyes are now green.

He frowns.

I do it again and my view changes to a sepia hue. I'm a brown-eyed girl now. Magic Morsels all have small, little magics you acquire for a short while when you eat them.

"Stop that," he says. "I like your eyes the way they are. And the cover up was sloppy. Likely no one believed anyone would bother to investigate the death of a human in Midnight, even if it was the most prolific one. Jack showed me the notes."

I nod, swallowing the lump in my throat. "Someone in Midnight drank all of his blood. And they managed to cover it up. It has to be someone powerful, someone with influence."

"My father." His jaw flexes visibly as darkness passes over his face. Again, I'm getting a glimpse of the side he doesn't let the world see. "It has to be him."

I close my eyes, the weight of this revelation settling over me. When I open them, the world is blue.

"But you aren't alone, Cinder," he says. "I'll help you find out what happened. You can trust me."

"Trust." The wry laugh sucks the energy from me again and I sink further back into the bed. "You know trust is earned right? And I don't think there is enough time in this lifetime for that to build between us." The exhaustion and weakness make my tongue loose.

"We can make a good team," he insists. Kai takes my hand, his thumb brushing over my knuckles.

I meet his gaze. For a moment, I almost believe him. I almost let myself hope that he means it.

But then I snort, pulling my hand away. "I doubt it," I say, my voice hard. "You're the playboy prince, remember? You don't do commitment or trust." I bite into the second spice roll though the sugar is making my teeth tingle.

Kai's jaw tightens, but he doesn't argue. He stands up, running a hand through his hair. "Get some rest," he says, his voice clipped. "We'll talk more tomorrow."

He turns to go, but pauses at the door and looks at me over his shoulder. "You're wrong about me, Cinder," he says softly. "I'm not who you think I am."

Something about the way he says it makes me think he doesn't even know if that's a good thing or a bad thing.

And with that he's gone, leaving me alone with my thoughts, a red hue, and the growing realization that when it comes to Prince Kaison Charming, I might not know anything at all.

THE NEXT NIGHT, I return from my vamp in training classes to Kaison trussed up like a naked sex slave on my bed again.

There is a strange, out of focus look in his eyes. Maybe he's had a shitty day?

Mine was certainly no picnic.

One more subtle warning that if I ever do anything so human as to burp or sneeze at the royal banquet table, I'll be excommunicated. It makes me want to show those presumptuous vampy fucks how crude I can be.

Unlike last time, I don't take my time. I rip off my panties and sit on Kaison's lap. Grinding on his hard cock, we both moan.

My body is ready for him, craving his touch like a drug. It's never been like this before. I try to chalk it up to the fact we have good sexual chemistry. *Atomically* good. Intrusive thoughts suggest it's more than that.

With an almost frantic fury, I position him at my entrance and then slam down on his cock.

His size and pierced texture blows my brains out of the top of my head. I cry out the same time a curse explodes from him. I don't check the ceiling to see if my gray matter is up there. Instead I lift and slam back down with all my power.

I want to fuck. Fuck until I can't think. Can't feel anything else.

All thoughts and worries disappear as I focus solely on the man beneath me, giving into the primal need to be connected to him. Kai's gaze remains fixed on mine, the intensity in his eyes stealing my breath. It's as if he can see straight into my soul, uncovering all my hidden desires. He seems to know what they are before I do. I didn't even know I had them until he swaggered up to me with his dark eyes and boyish charm.

It's more than that though. There's more to him than I thought, than everyone thinks. There's a depth to him, and I'm falling into it.

As I ride Kai in a punishing rhythm, I'm with him. There is a connection to the man under me, who keeps subjecting himself wholly to my power. He may be restrained but I'm starting to feel like he has tied me to him.

"You like that dick?" he asks.

I stop and open my eyes.

There is a look of knowing in Kaison's eyes. Not smugness, it's as if he has disconnected from his own body to make sure I'm having a good time.

The rising, all-encompassing euphoria rioting through me suddenly falls flat on a cold floor.

We aren't having sex *together*.

Charming is just playing the part of the party host, trying to ensure that I'm enjoying myself so he can pat himself on the back later and brag about it to anyone who will listen.

My lips pull into a frown. As much as I want to chase the feelings on his dick, I rise and step back. It almost hurts to let him from my body

The prince sputters. "Wait, what? Where are you going?"

I cross my arms under my bare breasts and raise an eyebrow. "*Whatever* I want, remember?" I repeat the earlier agreement.

"Didn't you like it? Don't you want more?" Confusion mars his face.

My body screams to get back on, to complete what I was chasing, but I tell it to shut the fuck up for a second. Somehow, I just knew he turned into someone he'd been with everyone else.

"Don't do that."

"Do what?"

"Do that thing where you put on a show. Yes, you have an impressive cock with a lot of piercings—" that feels fucking unbelievable and might ruin my velvet dungeon for all time. "—but don't think that makes you special."

His eyebrows raise.

The second he did that. . . looked for his A+ report card, he left me alone. Kaison wasn't there anymore. It was Prince Charming on his shit again, and I didn't like it.

Not that I hadn't fucked people with a fair amount of emotional distance, but it felt wrong. Not with the marshmallows, and the vulnerability pulsating just under my skin.

I don't want to be alone. I don't want to be some girl he impresses with his massive, pierced shlong. . . though I am impressed and thoroughly interested in riding that sucker like my life depends on it.

"If you pull that shit on me, I will leave you here," I announce. "Tied up."

"What can I do?" His voice is rough, and I can't read if it's from his arousal, shame, or frustration. I kind of hope it's all three.

What can he do?

If we are going to go through with this, I want Kaison here. Not Prince Charming.

"Ask me *nicely* to sit on your cock again." I drop my crossed arms and reach up to play with my nipple, heating my skin with the motion.

His eyes latch onto the movement.

"Please sit on my cock again."

"Mistress," I add with a sharpness that tells him who's in charge.

"Please," his voice is even more hoarse now. "Sit on my cock again, mistress."

CHAPTER 29
MY SAFE WORD IS PUMPKIN SPICE

CHARMING

*P*lease *sit on my cock again, mistress.*

How does she fucking do that? How does she know what persona I'm slipping in and out of at any time? She catches it before I even do.

And for a moment there, it was the Prince Charming show. The one I put on to entertain others. It gives me emotional distance so I can focus on the novelty or depravity of what I'm doing. It's about fun, breaking the bonds of my position, my title, my life.

This is different. If only because Cinder demands it.

Maybe I didn't realize what I was getting into when I decided to get tied up and put myself at her mercy. Something deep, dark, and lonely yawns open deep at my core, and suddenly I feel like I'm that boy again, wanting too much, too hard.

Shit, we should make a safe word.

Pineapples?

Pumpkin spice?

Stop touching me in my sensitive feely place?

Satisfied with my compliance, Cinder approaches again. While her perfect petite pierced breasts—the triple Ps I decide to call them—push her dress down in a lewd, sexual manner that makes me dizzy with horniness, I'm desperate to see her naked.

"Take the dress off," I rasp.

She pauses. Violet eyes narrow with merciless cruelty.

Then she turns on her heel and leaves the room, disappearing into mine.

What? Where did she go? Is she leaving me here?

The sound of drawers opening and shuffling filters in from my room.

"Looking for something?" I call out.

It's not long before she returns and there is a familiar implement in her hand. My cock swells with arousal while my balls shrink in fear. The slap of the riding crop hitting her palm resounds in the room. A positively wicked and triumphant smile curves her lips.

Uh oh.

Pumpkin spice! Pumpkin spice!

"You want me to take this dress off? Ask properly."

I swallow hard. "*Please* take your dress off, mistress."

Cinder nears me and puts the crop between my erect cock and stomach like it's some kind of shelf. She only briefly eyes the angry mark where her silver piercing burned into me.

I want to assure her again, but then she starts pulling at her dress, all the little fastenings until it loosens. Then in one fell swoop, it collapses to the ground, leaving her completely naked and me completely choked by awe.

Oh fuck, her tattoos curl down over her ribcage and under her breasts. One hip is engulfed by a massive phoenix and flies in majestic bright orange, yellows, and reds. I want to drag my tongue along it. In addition, to the skulls and flowers, I catch sight of little pumpkins and a cute pink cupcake with a little black dog peeking out from behind it.

And holy witchtits, I get my first full devastating view of her body. Precum leaks from the tip of my dick.

Despite the burn of silver, I'm so desperate to play with her cute little clit piercing, my fingers itch.

But then my attention catches on something else.

"What—what are those?" The question comes out in a harsh whisper as I take in the scars along her stomach, and full exposed arms. Now that I see the more prominent ones on her side, on her thighs, I see the ghost of those scars almost everywhere on her.

Worst yet, many had already been visible to me and I simply hadn't noticed. The tattoos, the jewelry, the fish-nets, and the long gloves covered them from view. She was bare of makeup to cover up the angry red bite marks that covered her.

Ignoring my question, she plucks the crop from where my dick was holding it. She snaps it on her hand. "Don't talk unless I tell you to."

My arousal is quickly siphoning off into fiery anger.

Someone has fed on her.

A lot.

All over.

"Who fucking did this, Cinder?"

I'm not joking anymore.

I've never been this serious in all my life.

Is this what happened at the border with those rogue Midnight fairies when she was younger?

I'll find them. I'll thrall them. I'll make them suffer beyond their imagin—

A sting explodes on my upper thigh, too close to the family jewels.

"Hey," she snaps, purple eyes burning. "Do not talk unless I allow you to."

Then before I can disobey again, Cinder drops to her knees before me and drags that sinful tongue from base to tip of my dick.

My murderous need to hunt down whoever did this to her fights with what she's doing to me, but Cinder is thorough in how she licks me back into full mast. She toys and plays with the ring at the top until I'm leaking precum, my head is fuzzy, and my balls draw up into my body.

I still have to know. Who did this to her?

Is this related to her supposed encounter with rogue vampires at the border? Was there some truth to the gossip? Did she nearly die?

One thing is for certain. This is the reason why she can't stand my fangs being near her body.

This is why when I tried to kiss her neck, she—ahhh fuck she's taken me completely in her mouth.

Cinder must have some unnatural power to open her throat because a shocking amount of me disappears. The scalding pressure of her sucking me off has me so close to popping, it's all I can do to thrust and groan and think of anything to keep from losing control right there.

Before I register the cold air on my cock, Cinder returns to her previous spot to begin the painstaking journey of taking me into her tight little body again.

"Oh fuck, oh fuck, oh fucking witchtitties on a toothpick," I curse, eyes clenched shut as I fight against the rope binding me. Again, the heat exchange between our bodies is so disparate, she is a hot, divine inferno of pressure, choke holding my dick.

Another stinging snap against my thigh has me jolting.

I'm not sure if I love or hate Cinder getting her hands on my crop.

"Open your eyes," she commands, though she can't keep the thickness out of her voice. She's also affected.

I do so but thrust into her with as much motion as I can.

She gasps and her head drops back.

There are only little grinding motions she makes on top of me and again I feel the pressure of her clit piercing.

It burns. It burns so fucking good. It pushes my orgasm closer to the edge while strangling it in place with biting pain.

I'm not sure if she's using the silver piece intentionally against me, or if she's fully forgotten as she takes her pleasure on my hard dick.

Her movements are so minuscule, she might as well not be moving.

I want to scream, beg, shout at her to move. To fuck me. To ride me like an animal she wants to break.

"Please, please, mistress," I beg. One of the marshmallows drops out of my mouth, but she catches it between us.

Cinder turns the dented mini sugar pillow over between her fingers then grabs my hair with her other hand, jerking my head back.

"Open," she commands. I do so and she pushes it onto my tooth again.

Despite her harsh act, the soft scrape of her nails along my scalp sends warm pleasure tingles throughout my body.

Her mouth crashes into mine with a fervor I'm not expecting. The kiss is hungry, desperate. She needs to escape whatever is inside her.

As our lips meet, a searing pain shoots through me, emanating from where her silver tongue ring presses to mine. It's a white-hot agony, the metal scorching my sensitive tastebuds. But I don't pull away. Instead, I lean into the kiss, savoring the burn as a tangible imprint of her touch.

The pain grounds me, anchors me to this moment. It's a different kind of pain from what my father inflicts—this is a pain I choose, a pain that connects me to her. So I deepen the kiss, ignoring the blistering sensation, pouring all my unspoken emotions into the slide of our lips.

She raises her hips and slams them back down. I grunt into her mouth, feeling the impact hit the middle of my bones. She does it again. And again.

Each time, her hips increase in speed, driving me into a frenzy. My entire body shakes with lust. Her impossibly tight, pulsing walls surround me, overwhelming me with pleasure. Her breasts, still bare and perfect, transfer their weight and heat to my body with each thrust like an electric current.

She moans into my mouth, the sound low and guttural. My animalistic noises echo hers, lost in the haze of our coupling. As I feel myself reaching the edge, I grunt and thrust upward as much as I'm able to with that half-inch of movement.

Her clit piercing scrapes against me, but her pace is so volatile, the bright sting of pain comes and goes.

Cinder's hips rock faster, harder, each thrust sending shockwaves of pleasure through me. I arch my back, trying to get deeper inside her, but she's in control now. Her nails dig into my sides, leaving little half-moons of pain that meld with the pleasure.

"I'm gonna—" my words are muffled by her lips.

"No." Her command is a sharp crack. "You will not come until I tell you." Even as she says the last words, she shudders.

"Cinder," I whisper. "Come. Come on me, I want to feel you."

Those violet eyes sweep down to me in surprise.

I'm not playing our game right now. I need to say her name, to feel her break apart around me. I can hold off like she said, but I want—no, I *need* to feel her come.

To drive my point home, I buck up into her again with that scant half-inch of hip room I have to work with. But I fill her up so much, it still rocks her back with a squeak of surprise.

With that, her thighs shake like earthquakes, and the most glorious, sex-sodden wail escapes her throat. Cinder's hips rub and buck desperately, while her inner muscles strangle me in alternating waves.

I war between shutting my eyes to keep hold of the fast-unraveling threads of control and forcing them open to watch my writhing tattooed fake fiancé take my throbbing erection deep inside her orgasm-shattered core.

Sweat and exertion have destroyed her normally perfect line of bangs. She's flushed, messy, and so very fucking hot. Hotter than anything I've felt or known.

By some fucking miracle, I hold back as she fucks out two more orgasms on my dick before she says the magic word with a kiss at the corner of my (still full) mouth.

"Come for me, Kai."

My name on her lips has me exploding like a party popper. My body strains against the rope as a tortured half-groan, half-cry escapes me. The blood disappears from my head and gravity doesn't exist. Nothing exists except the fingers stroking my chest and the lips softly laying trails of kisses down my throat.

I thought I came in here to have fun. To scratch an itch around this need I have for Cinder. But even as I'm still inside her, I realize that whatever this is. . . it isn't that.

It's not just fun.

She isn't a novel amusement ride to try out before moving on.

I already know I'll be playing this memory out over and over in my head. I'll be counting minutes, seconds to when I can touch her again, see her face vulnerable, open, and breaking from pleasure, from when I can hear my name pass on her lips.

Despite being part of the royal family, I realize with a solid block of ice dropping in my stomach, she's charmed *me*.

For a moment, I think she's right there with me. Falling. Feeling. Succumbing to this thing between us.

Then something shutters down in her gaze, and I'm locked out. Her walls are up, the doors are sealed, and as she lifts off my body to stand, I know she's retreated to the internal fortress she's built.

While I sit out here, with a softening dick and a different kind of need inked all over me in plain sight.

A need for Cinder.

CHAPTER 30
INKED BY TINK

The fluorescent lights of the tattoo parlor, Inked by Tink, are a stark contrast to the warm seductive lights of the Poison Apple where the girls just finished their shift.

Cinder moves with purpose, her combat boots thudding against the linoleum as she strides up to the counter. Each time they connect to the ground, I get a little harder. She's back in fishnet, adorned in her many piercings, and dark makeup. And I'm obsessed.

Goldie and Snow flank her with their ripples of laughter, their camaraderie a living thing in the cramped, ink-scented space.

"We need a tattoo," Cinder announces to the artist.

My bride downs the last of her massive pumpkin spice latte and chucks it into a trash bin a couple feet away like she's done the exact same movement here at least fifty times.

Behind the counter stands a figure almost too vibrant to

belong to the dreary surroundings—a pixie-like woman whose punk-rock presence is topped with a wild mane of spun gold. Her bangs are curled perfectly, and a kerchief that screams 1940s glam falls back to her high, full ponytail. Her tattoo-laden skin is a vibrant tapestry telling tales of deep magic and wild forests.

The delicate features of the tattoo artist's face are enhanced by bold makeup and piercings that glint under the fluorescent lights. Her skin, a golden tan like sun-kissed sand, seems to radiate with its own inner glow.

More than that, two iridescent wings tinged with pale green and purple extend out behind with ethereal elegance. Tink doesn't hide the fact she is pure fairy, though she operates on the edge of the densely human population of Boston.

Tinkerbelle, the tattoo artist whose name is whispered in both reverence and awe across the Common World, smiles at Cinder. The artist's needles weave not just ink but with a touch of fairy magic, capturing the essence of one's spirit in her art.

Tink arches a pierced eyebrow, her gaze sweeping over us like a beacon through her heavy-framed green glasses. "Looks like we've got a party. Who's first?" Her eyes blink in recognition when she catches sight of me. "Long time no see, Kai."

"Tink," I say with a quick salute.

The girls turn to stare at me with surprised expressions.

"You've been to Inked by Tink before?" Goldie puts a voice to the shocked look on Cinder's face. Which is really only a slight widening of the eyes, but for her, the reaction is as earth shattering as I've seen.

"Not exactly," I say, slipping my hands into my pockets.

"Princey-Poo gets whatever he wants, so years back he

flew me out to Europe to tattoo him," Tink explains with a smug little smile.

I shrug. "It was during the two years I spent at Oxford in the Common World."

"The ink did look familiar," Cinder says almost to herself as her eyes drop down to my exposed chest. Hot prickles race along my skin under her probing gaze.

"Didn't have time to jump across the pond," I explain, clearing my throat, "so I had her come to me."

"And I did, in fact, come," Tinkerbelle says slyly.

The slow sweep of her lashes reminds me of the mini party we had after she finished my tattoos over the course of three days. We'd soaked ourselves in gin and sex for a job well done. We parted as friends.

Cinder stiffens. It's almost imperceptible, but it happens in her shoulders and face.

My stomach inexplicably drops at her change in demeanor. Is she . . . no.

Wait, is she jealous?

Snow steps forward, a mischievous glint in her eye. "Okay, enough ogling princey-poo." Snow addresses Tink. "I've heard about how awesome you are, and I want to be tatted. I want something fierce, like me."

Tink's grin broadens as her wings flutter, "Well come on back my dear and I will divine your design."

Snow follows dutifully. "I want something that pops. Can we do that? I know my skin is really dark."

The artist lets out a tinkling laugh as she leads Snow behind a curtain. "Oh don't you worry, it's gonna be pure magic."

Goldie follows Tink and Snow.

Before Cinder can do the same, I grab her arm and spin her around. "It was a long time ago." I rush to explain.

"Sure," Cinder says. There's that distant, untouchable expression on her face again. As if she couldn't give a single solitary fuck about me. But I'm learning to see through her mask. And I know she's bothered.

Pulling her to a different curtained area where Tink administers piercings, I press my lips to hers the moment we are alone.

For a little human with anemia, she's surprisingly strong as she pushes me back. I obey, letting her.

"I don't care," she says with vehemence, as if I'm annoying her with my attentions.

Hell no, you can't run away in your little glass slippers from this, my dark-wing darling.

"*I do.*" I envision pressing the words into her skin until she believes me.

For a minute, I'm sure she's going to sweep out of here to join her friends.

She yanks me down so our lips collide in a hungry kiss.

"I don't care," she reiterates, albeit breathlessly as she claws me, devouring me with the same fervor that I'm giving.

Liar.

Instead I say, "I know."

Cinder climbs me like a tree until her legs wrap around my hips. My hands easily scoop her tiny, perfect little rear as we continue to kiss like the world is ending.

Though she tries to keep me from pressing my tongue into her mouth at first, I persist until she gives me access. I don't care that her piercing burns my tongue. I tangle mine with hers, tasting her dark sweetness.

Soon the coppery taste of my blood mingles between our mouths. She tries to pull away, but I grip her by the throat. My fingers weave in between the spikes on her collar. Unlike her piercings, the jewelry and adornments on her clothes aren't true silver, so I can touch all I want without consequence.

For a moment, I think she'll freak out. She likes to be in charge. I'm breaking the rules.

An erotic half groan, half mewl escapes her.

Oh. *Oh.*

So it really is just the fangs that freak my little spicy Queen.

Or maybe she is learning to trust me?

Something inside me laughs at that. *You aren't worthy of her trust, she knows that. No one would trust you with a plant even if you were born in a greenhouse.*

Cinder's hips buck against the crotch of my black jeans forcing a friction that makes my aching dick throb.

Oh fae fucks I'm so hard, I could drill into a wall. Instead, I set her on the edge of a counter and reach under her skirt. My other hand is still wrapped around her throat.

"Do you know what these fishnets and these little skirts do to me?" I rasp.

She shakes her head, purple eyes glazed and unfocused. Every part of her communicates what she wants—*more.*

"You make me rock hard. It's almost impossible to keep from unzipping my pants and fisting my dick whenever I set eyes on this little getup. I wouldn't even care if anyone saw me jerking off to the punk princess of two realms."

The fishnets are thigh high, held up by garters.

Fuckity, fuck godsdamn.

Don't blow your load, Charming.

Putting my raging arousal aside, I run my index finger up along the pleather underwear that keeps probing eyes from seeing too much when she's dancing up on the bar.

They are too strong a fabric for me to easily rip or even

pull aside. Her hips buck harder as I rub the underwear against her most wanting part.

Catching sight of the reclining chair for Tink's customers, I get an idea. I effortlessly pick her up—gods, she's so small I need to make sure she's better fed in Midnight—and swing her around, depositing her on the chair. I drag her underwear down her legs before spreading them. I lift her skirt, putting that pussy on perfect display. It's so wet and ready I just know my fingers or prick would slip right in so effortlessly before she strangles the cum right out of me.

When I step away, she growls.

Literally growls.

Fae lords, she's incredible.

"Now, now," I say as I snap a pair of surgical gloves on. "Don't be like that. daddy's gonna take care of you."

"Daddy?" she says flatly, raising an eyebrow. Despite her unimpressed expression, her fingers turn bloodless where they clutch the arms of the chair and her thighs glisten with her desire.

"Shh," I hush her. "Or you won't get dessert."

With that, I swipe a gloved fingertip up her slit. Her body jerks as if hit by a live wire.

"Fuck." She bites her lower lip as if it's too much. "It's never felt like—"

She cuts herself off.

"Oh no. That's not going to fly," I say. "You are going to finish that statement."

I sweep the digit up and down her glistening seam, occasionally dipping in ever so slightly.

Those pale cheeks flush as she shuts her eyes against either my demand or the sensation. My other hand wraps around her throat again. It forces her eyes open. They are even more dazed and glazed than before.

"It's never felt like what?" I ask.

I roll my gloved thumb over her clit. Protected by the latex, I don't have to worry about the silver burn.

Cinder is moaning and thrusting her hips, still holding onto the chair arms for dear life.

"Tell me like a good girl, and I'll give you what you want." My voice is rough with need.

Her eyes meet mine with a fiery purple defiance. "It's never felt this good. Like I want more. Like it's not a chore. Like I don't want it to end." The words come out like an accusation like she's angry. She resents the confession being forced from her. But I'll make it worth her while.

My chest swells to nearly the breaking point even as I plunge two digits into her sweet cunny. She chokes on her gasp of surprise.

"Good girl," I coo as I pump my fingers into her.

Her moans of pleasure get louder as I finger fuck her. "Whoa there, baby. You're getting a bit loud and while I love it, I don't want anyone to come interrupt us." With that, I move my hand from her throat until I'm pushing my fingers into her mouth. She gladly takes them in, her tongue undulating against them, sucking them as if they were a dick.

I keep talking to distract myself from the almost uncontrollable urge to unzip my pants and shove my cock down her slutty little throat. "Not that I'd stop. All your friends could come in along with Tink and I'd still pump this lil' snatch until you're frothing and coming your brains out."

Cinder's hips buck and she moans and sucks at my hand harder. My thumb rolls over that piercing. It's a game to keep generating this little sound she makes at the back of her throat and the flutter of her eyes. Every time I hit it, I gain five points. Like a video game.

"Because you're my bride. And even if this engagement is fake, I'm yours for the duration and you're mine." Five more points to me. "I don't want anyone else. In fact, there is no one else now that there is you and this perfect little cunt." I remove my fingers from her mouth to push her top up. She's not wearing a bra and those little piercings glint devilishly at me from her erect nipples. I tweak and squeeze them until she's left gasping.

Her legs begin to close so I extract my hand. A needy sound of protest escapes her. I land a sound slap on her pussy and she jerks. "Be a good girl and keep those legs open for daddy."

"Please," she begs. Another five points. I'm up to thirty-five total.

"You want to come for daddy?" I taunt, giving the other nipple an extra squeeze.

"Please, Kai."

Kaboom.

Her use of my name breaks my every wall, like a bull-dozer exploding through cement bricks.

It's then I go to work. My fingers piston into her, curling up to hit that spot I know makes her lose her mind. Even when my wrist starts to ache, I don't slow down. I'm a prince on a mission.

Her hips lift and raise back almost as if it's too much for her, but I know I'm pushing her higher and higher until—

The cry of sexual pleasure that escapes from her mouth is coupled with her body shuddering and bending. I don't stop pounding into her, chasing her orgasm, elongating it.

"That's it, let them hear you. Let Tink hear how I plea-sure you. You may not care, but I sure as fuck do. I need you to know I only want to do this for you, *to you.* Because you come more beautifully than anyone I've known."

I can tell from the way her eyes flutter and how her cries choke off that she is trying to suppress it now, so no one does hear, but it's too late. Cinder can't suppress what's been set into motion. She can only come on my hand as I grip her by the throat and force her to finish.

"And if you let me," I choke out. "I'd feast between your legs. I'd lick up your desire like a starving man. Like it was my last meal and you're the only thing that can sustain me."

My mouth turns dry as I think of tasting her pussy. And I cannot deny her blood sings to me as much as her body does. The lust is folding me over and over until I'm a tense knot of want. I want to sink into her, I want to take from her. I want her blood sliding down my throat. I want to penetrate her with my dick and fangs. I want to claim her, mark her, so everyone knows she's mine, and I'm hers.

Swallowing hard, I close my eyes, pushing the need back. I won't do that to her.

Lost in my thoughts, I don't consciously notice how we've both slowed down until she pushes my hand from between her legs. A reedy little moan escapes her even as she does it. The flush of her blood pressing against her pale cheeks, throat, and bare breasts only causes my bloodlust to surge.

I have to stay in control. Even though she's left a little sexy mess on the chair. *Oh fuck me...*

"Kai," she says, pulling my attention back. She pushes off the chair and on wobbly legs walks to the counter, sits on it and spreads her legs, putting her at the perfect height. "Fuck me, daddy."

My hand flies to the bulge of my pants as I squeeze myself to keep from popping off right then.

But I don't need to be told twice. I unzip and thrust into her, making sure to keep my lips on hers.

I can't control myself. My hips rampage into her impossibly tight, hot wetness. She strangles my cock, dragging extra friction of force across my piercings only heightening my need to come. My balls are so tight and ready to shoot off.

In mere moments, I'm spurting my release into Cinder, gasping and moaning, completely at her mercy. Cinder's grip firmly tugs at my hair, grounding me as I lose all reason and sense. There is only my dark princess.

"I'm yours, only yours, my gothic goddess," I punctuate with a kiss.

One half of her lips quirk up in a smile that doesn't reach her eyes. "For now," she confirms.

Maybe it's because I exerted the fuck out of myself just now, but I suspect it's what she just said that has my heart sinking, spiraling down into my stomach cavity.

For now.

The tinkle of the front doorbell signals new arrivals to the parlor.

"Hey, if you guys are done fucking in there, make sure to clean up before you come out," Tink yells.

Cinder buries her head in my chest as I suppress a chuckle.

"Got it, boss," I yell back before we go about righting ourselves. I pocket the gloves, knowing one day they may be all I have left of Cinder.

It'll be for the best. She deserves better. But I can pretend I deserve her. For a little while.

When we step out of the curtains, I'm surprised to find

a very tall silver-haired man with a scar running down his face standing next to a striking redhead. They both are damp from the rain coming down outside now, dripping a little puddle onto the tile floor.

"Uh hey," the redhead greets Cinder, her surprised expression slowly morphing to a smug knowing grin.

They know each other.

"Hey Red," Cinder says, her mask of indifference back on despite her messy bangs and the smell of sex permeating the air.

Ah yes, Red. The other friend who got engaged before Goldie. The blonde bombshell told me all about it.

The silver-haired man is staring me down like he is trying to put spikes through my head.

"Prince Kaison Charming, a pleasure to meet you," I say, sticking my hand out to the alpha male.

He simply stares at it before his lip curls with a slight sneer.

"We're here to support Snow in getting her first tattoo," Red explains, her green gaze bouncing back and forth between us.

"Cool," is all Cinder says.

My nose wrinkles. "Does it smell like wet dog in here to you?"

CHAPTER 31
SPEWING THE WOLF

CINDER

In record time, Prince Charming scores an invite to Red's wedding, despite insulting her werewolf betrothed.

Brexley was only slightly less thrilled than me, and I was shocked to find it was because Brexley is protective of me. I saw him act like this when Goldie first started seeing Ted, and we were on the same side of that protectiveness. But now to be the object of it?

Super weird.

Once Tink finishes Snow's tattoo, we all decide we aren't done with the evening. Boston is pretty much closed down at four A.M., so we went to the best place we knew to hang out.

The Poison Apple.

"I have to confess it's kind of weird you guys still want to hang out here after you spent all night working," Kai says, leaning against the bar. "And won't your boss be pissed?"

"Rap loves us. She doesn't mind if we hang out as long as we clean up after ourselves and don't take advantage of her too horribly." Goldie waves a dismissive hand before putting it back around Ted's neck, who is sitting on a bar stool with his girlfriend draped all over him.

Unlike us, the big lumberjack-looking bear shifter is a morning person, but he doesn't like Goldie being out late without him and is often coaxed out well past his bedtime to hang with us.

I am more than a night owl. I come to life. I live for the darkness to fall. It's one of the reasons my heart sings whenever I step into Midnight. I'm covered, shrouded, and held in perpetual night.

Thankfully, Ted owns his own business and finds ways to manage the opposing schedule. For being a big serious, grumpy looking guy, he's an absolute slave to the pink and leather bombshell that is my best friend.

I wonder if he really is trying to propose to her, and if he'll catch a break. She deserves all the happiness in the world. Though I can't help but notice how his hand keeps returning to a certain suspicious boxy outline in his pocket.

"Have we ever crossed the line of taking advantage of Rap too much?" Red asks, rounding the bar to pour herself a glass of red wine and a whiskey for Brex that she then slides over to him. She has a real, adult job as an accountant now, but once a lost girl, always a lost girl. She has the Poison Apple tat on her left arm to prove it. We all get it eventually.

"Maybe we aren't trying hard enough," I say, cracking my fingers in preparation. "Pumpkin spice martini, anyone?"

"I'll try one," Snow volunteers, though her gaze is still fastened to the new tattoo that spans the length of her inner forearm—a hand mirror. The ink practically springs off her smooth skin in glowing silver lines. The mirror is beautiful, broken, and hazardous all at once. When Snow asked Tink what it meant, Tink shrugged and said the magic is in the ink and it does the speaking for itself.

Snow needed some ink for herself, but I intend to push the Lost Girls' branding on our next visit. The Poison Apple logo with the words 'pick your poison' underneath it.

"That sounds dangerous," Kai says, referring to my drink.

"I thought you were brave," I shoot back as I pull out the RumChata, vanilla vodka, and Irish cream.

Snow, Red, and Goldie break out in a chorus of 'oooo's, letting him know I've definitely thrown the gauntlet down.

"In that case," Kai says. "I'll take two."

I roll my eyes, but I can't stop the smile spreading across my face.

"Holy fae fucks," Kai says under his breath, even as the others continue to discuss Snow's new ink.

"What?" I ask, even as I measure out a bit of syrup over the pumpkin puree.

"I just—I've never seen you smile." Kai's tone is full of shock and awe.

My brows pinch, but he's right, I can't keep my mouth from its upward curl.

"I smile," I protest in defense.

"Small ones. Crumbs barely big enough for birds to eat, but this, this on your face is a real smile. I can see your teeth and everything."

"Shut up," I laugh.

"Forget the martini. I'd like to order a hundred more of these."

"Smiles? You are the cheesiest, most ridiculous person I have ever met. And don't you think the pumpkin spice might be the reason I'm smiling?"

"You want me to believe pumpkin spice has this much power over you?" Kai leans in until his delicious male scent wraps around me.

"Maybe it's because I get to make my favorite martini, or maybe it's having my friends gathered in one of my favorite places in the middle of the night." He's right. I am in a particularly good mood.

Kaison tilts his head, probing me with a private, sultry gaze. "Nothing to do with the multiple orgasms and fantastic fucking?"

I shrug one shoulder and work to suppress the smile that threatens to validate everything he's saying. The pressures of finding the Ember of Midnight and uncovering the truth about my father seem so far away right now.

"Pumpkin spice is the way to a girl's heart, but it's possible the second best way is, in fact, via some fantastic fucking. I think I read that in a book once."

Kai looks hungry, and not for food. Heat sweeps through my body. Only the barest hint of fear zips through me at the idea he might be thirsting for my blood. The way I've started to trust him so fast it's scary.

I push the martini over to him, hoping it will keep his thirst at bay.

"Do vampires live forever?" Snow asks, breaking our private moment as she reaches for the third martini. "Like are you actually in your twenties, or do you just look that age while you are hundreds of years old?

I bring my martini to my lips and sip on the perfect cozy cold concoction that heats my belly immediately with pumpkin, cinnamon, and nutmeg. If only Midnight had more pumpkin spice and less a-hole bloodsuckers, it might be my perfect haven.

Kai laughs, looking down at the creamy, light orange liquid that I sprinkled cinnamon on top of. "Midnight fairies age at a normal rate until we hit our mid-twenties or early thirties and then it slows down from there. So, I will likely live hundreds of years if I keep in good health and don't get murdered." With that, he cheers Snow and then sips the liquid.

A spew erupts from Kai's mouth. He turns his head away from Snow just in time so as not to plaster her with his mouthful. "Gah, that is disgusting." He smacks his lips and pushes his tongue out as if he can rid himself of the taste.

Unfortunately, while Kai avoided hitting Snow, he sprayed Berkeley fully across the face. The room collectively sucks in its breath. Even I wait to see if Brex will massacre Kai on the spot.

"Oh, sorry, man. I didn't mean to get you like that." Kai grabs a napkin to dab his own dripping chest.

The tall wolf shifter stands, the stool scraping loudly across the floor.

"That's it," he growls. "You're uninvited to the wedding."

"No, you're not," Red assures Kai, without missing a beat. She hands a clean bar towel over to Brexley who is too busy glaring at Kai to clean himself.

"Even if you were uninvited, you'd obviously just come as Cinder's date," Snow pipes up.

"Oh my god." The distressed voice distracts me before I can respond.

"Goldie?" I prompt when I see her eyes glued to her phone, brows furrowed with concern. She's even extracted herself from Ted as she takes in whatever she is reading.

"That guy, remember the one who fucking assaulted you?" Goldie's nostrils flare with anger at the memory.

My stomach sours a little. "Yeah."

Her big brown eyes turn up to meet mine. "They found him dead."

CHAPTER 32
WELCOME TO MY DARK SIDE

CINDER

The news hits me like a sucker punch to the gut. It wasn't just my attacker, there was another man too.

Snow rushes over to look at Goldie's phone, but I remain rooted to the spot. I feel Kaison's gaze on me, heavy and searching.

Their corpses were entwined in a jumble of limbs. There's no mention of the cause of death.

I know. I know it was Kaison.

A part of me is relieved, grateful even. That monster can't hurt anyone else now. But another part, the part that clings desperately to the tattered remnants of my morality, knows that murder is wrong. No matter how justified.

"How was he killed?" I ask, my voice sounding distant to my own ears. Suddenly, I'm staring down at an empty martini glass. When did I down the whole thing?

"They don't know yet." Goldie shakes her head,

scrolling for more information. "He was totally mangled and left in a dumpster."

I meet Kaison's gaze, steeling myself for what I might find there. Remorse? Regret?

But his eyes are unreadable, a carefully constructed mask that I'm all too familiar with. It's the same one I wear every day, the one that hides the broken, jagged pieces of my soul. But what is he hiding?

No one comments on how quiet I am over the next hour, and we don't speak of it again.

Not even as Kai, Snow, and I make our way back to my dingy apartment. Not as I start packing my suitcase for our return to Midnight. But the weight of the unspoken hangs heavy between Kai and me, a palpable presence that threatens to suffocate.

It's not until we're alone in my bedroom, surrounded by the chaotic jumble of my paintings and art supplies, that the dam finally breaks.

"You killed him," I say matter of fact, the words tasting like ash on my tongue. "That man from the bar. You killed him for me."

Kaison swallows hard, his Adam's apple bobbing. "Cinder, I—"

"Why?" I demand.

He rakes a hand through his hair, a gesture of frustration, of helplessness. "I couldn't let him hurt you again. I couldn't—"

"So you decided murder was the answer?" I cut him off, my tone sharp as a blade.

"Cinder, please." His voice is deeper, darker. The side of him he hides is coming out and I wonder if it's the real him. "You have to understand. He didn't understand the word no. A man like that can't just be allowed to walk around doing whatever he wants."

"Funny," I say coldly, "Hearing that from a Charming."

I regret the words as soon as they leave my lips. I see the way they slice into him, the flash of hurt that he can't quite hide.

Because the truth is, Kaison is nothing like his father. He's not the ruthless, power-hungry tyrant ruling Midnight with an iron fist. But in this moment, with the blood of my assailant on his hands, it's hard to separate the two.

Kai bears down on me, backing me up to my bed. He's so fast, I barely have a chance to skip backward before I'm trapped.

"Don't say that," he snarls. "I'm not my father. Do you know why? I don't view you as property. I don't view you as less than me, but we are engaged. It may be a fake one, but it makes you mine for now, and I refuse to let anything happen to you. You want me to be sorry? I can't be. Not when I know what that bastard has done," he points out the window, "what he would have done to you. And I'd kill him a hundred times over if I could for even thinking he could take you by force."

"Kai," my voice shakes. My entire body trembles. I need my iron pills. A shot of whiskey. Anything to fortify me against his storm.

Realization enters his expression. Kaison turns and stalks away, putting his back to me.

The silence pulsates between us.

"The other man," Kai says in a low voice. "He was there to kill you that night. The meathead who put his hands on you was a paid-off distraction. If I hadn't been there, the assassin from Midnight would have taken you out."

I drop to sit on my little, unmade bed. "What?"

He turns so I only see half his face. "The assassin was likely sent by someone on the Midnight court, or maybe even my father. Though I imagine if the King knew we were traveling back and forth between Midnight and Common, I imagine he would put a stop to it."

I open my mouth then shut it.

"If you want me to be sorry, I'm afraid I have to disappoint you." He brings up his knuckles, looking at the heavy rings adorning them.

There it is. The part he hides.

A cold, powerful killer. A shrewd one at that.

Now that it comes into focus, I wonder why I didn't figure it out sooner. So many signs, so many signals that he's not what everyone says.

It's as if I've seen the dark side of him no one else is supposed to. The parts he works so hard to keep hidden. I should be shaking with fucking unbridled fear, but I'm not.

But it is a lot to take in. He's killed someone, for me. To protect me, and he's saying he would do it again. It causes something to open up inside of me. Something I'm not sure I want opened.

I stand up again and take a step towards him.

Lucifer streaks past, a blur of black fur and bad attitude. He swipes at my ankles, leaving angry red welts in his wake. I trip over the demon cat, about to plummet.

Witchtits!

My arm smacks into the covered painting in the room, but I don't hit the ground. Kai is there, holding me up, drugging me with his intoxicating scent and the intensity of his fury.

"Damn cat," I breathe.

I hate that I want to kiss him. That I want to lose myself

in Kai, right here, right after he confessed to killing someone.

Kaison's gaze falls to a spot over my shoulder. It's landed on my painting, the twisted, tortured expressions of my innermost demons. The mostly done painting of a girl's face, eyes closed as thorny vines surround her, dig into her flesh until red drips from everywhere they bite into her.

"It's supposed to be you?" he asks in a low voice.

I don't respond, because he already knows. I didn't mean for him to see it.

I move to block it from view, a reflexive action born of years of hiding, of burying my pain deep where no one can see.

As Kaison steps forward to intervene, Lucifer winds around his legs, purring like a damned engine.

The insult isn't lost on me—the way my demon cat accepts the fairy prince without question, after attacking me for no good reason.

I can feel myself slipping away, retreating into that empty, numb space where nothing can hurt me. It's a defense mechanism, a survival tactic that's kept me sane all these years.

"I've never seen your paintings before," he says in a voice that seems far away.

Unable to stop him from looking, I make my way to my dresser and pull out my pills. I dry swallow two of them, leaning heavily against the mottled wood. "Can we go now?" I ask.

"Yes, of course," he says, his edginess all drained away.

As I slip on my glass slipper, ready to return to the poisoned paradise of Midnight, I can't shake the feeling we both gave up an important hidden part of ourselves.

Things that should drive the other way.

But it only makes me want him more.

CHAPTER 33
MOON RIVER IN MIDNIGHT

CINDER

Roaming the halls of a castle for vampire fairies alone with all this delicious blood pumping through my veins probably puts me in the dumb category. The same category as a girl who suspects there's a slasher murderer in her house before she loudly announces she is going to take off her clothes and hop in the shower.

I still haven't found the Ember of Midnight and my heart aches with every pounding beat, stretching out toward wherever it is. It must be in the castle.

Though it is always Midnight in the realm, there are the same eight hours of rest afforded that there is to the Common World. It's just offset which makes for a perfect complement of straddling worlds. Though it doesn't mean I get much sleep after stepping back into Midnight from the Poison Apple shift only to have to get ready and put on a show for the fairies.

Not to mention the intermittent fuck sessions with Prince Charming.

But right now, it's my time and I'm going to take it.

The halls are forbidding. The flickering candlelight casts eerie shadows on the ancient stone walls, making the portraits of long-dead fairies seem to watch me with cold, judgmental eyes. My footsteps echo in the silence, each too loud in this labyrinthine castle.

I pause before a particularly ominous painting, the subject's eyes seeming to follow me. A shudder runs down my spine, and I hurry the hell up to get away—the urge to find the Ember growing stronger.

As I turn a corner, a draft of cold air brushes against my skin, raising goosebumps in its wake. I frown, glancing around for the source. My gaze lands on a small, nondescript door, half-hidden, half-open in the shadows.

A fresh breeze sweeps through it, carrying the scent of fresh grass and roses, and spreading a chill along my skin.

Curiosity piqued; I approach cautiously. The door creaks open at my touch to reveal a narrow, winding staircase. My heart leaps into my throat. Could this be it? Could the Ember be hidden away in some secret hideaway with the rest of my father's art?

Excitement wars with trepidation as I climb, the stairs steep and uneven beneath my feet.

Finally, I emerge onto a small balcony, the night sky stretching out above me in an endless expanse of stars. The moon hangs low and full, casting a silvery glow over the scene.

And there, leaning against the railing with a lit cigarette dangling from his lips is Prince Charming himself. The neon green earbuds he wears are a striking contrast to everything else in this place.

He turns at my approach, eyes widening in surprise. The shadows cast dark swaths over parts of his face, concealing half of his expression. His white shirt is unbuttoned, exposing ink and muscle. The sleeves are rolled up, revealing the strong tendons of his forearms.

Pulling out an earbud, he says. "Well, well. Fancy meeting you here, my dark princess." Despite his teasing words, he doesn't smile.

I freeze, my mind racing.

But as he takes a drag of his cigarette, the tip flaring orange in the darkness, I realize that he seems just as taken aback by my presence as I am by his.

"I couldn't sleep," I say by way of explanation, moving to join him at the railing. The cool night air is a balm against my flushed skin, helping to clear my head as I scan the landscape. The dark crashing waves violently hit the cliffs and somewhere inside me.

Charming nods, blowing out a stream of smoke. "I know the feeling. These walls can be suffocating at times."

There's a weariness in his voice that catches me off guard, a hint of the man beneath the perpetual smirk and bravado. In that moment, he seems almost. . . human. Relatable, even.

"Why do I get the sense that there's more to your restlessness than just wedding jitters?" His gaze pierces as it meets mine.

I look away, my fingers gripping the railing. Can I trust him with the truth? Can I afford not to, if I want to find the Ember?

"You're not supposed to have that here," I gesture to his earbuds, pointing out the obvious.

Kai pulls a small brick from his pocket, it fits in the palm of his hand. An mp3 player.

"Don't tell anyone, but I've "become quite the smuggler over the years."

"Oh," I breathe.

Kai's face is shades of black and blue, his lip is split again, and the left cheek is swollen.

Tilting his head down to look at the player in his palm, he says, "Thought I'd come drown out all my angst in some music for a while. You've somehow found my secret hideout spot, though I shouldn't be surprised. You manage to get into all types of places I've never imagined." The last sentence is a low, thoughtful murmur and I wonder if he means into the fairy balls or something else.

"Your father?" I guess.

Fingers curl around the small music player. I watch his Adam's apple do that slow long bob down then up again, whenever he seems to be holding onto a particularly intense emotion.

"He didn't care for my *attitude* today." He flicks the ash off his cigarette, enunciating his words more sharply than usual. "I still haven't learned how to act like a Charming. Though it seems you would think otherwise."

Regret and dread roils through me like a chainsaw.

"It's what happened the night we went to the Poison Apple too, isn't it?" I point out, already knowing the answer but needing him to say it.

Kaison only gives me a short nod.

"Why are you up here? Why don't you go have some. . . blood and heal what he's done to you."

The moonlight casts a slice of light across Kaison's eyes, and they are suddenly alight with rage. "I don't want to forget just yet. And I don't particularly care for blood."

"Excuse me?" I must have misheard.

He manages to cast a wry, pained smirk at me. "Don't get me wrong, blood is literally life, and sometimes. . . it can smell so sweet, so enticing." His gaze drops to my throat, and the skin under his scrutiny prickles with fear and anticipation. Kaison shuts his eyes and turns away. "But I don't enjoy the dependence. I don't really want to need it."

"I don't understand."

I really didn't. I needed food, but I also wanted it.

"I don't ever want to forget where it comes from. I don't want to take that shit for granted." His hands curl around the stone edge, the bones turning taut from tension. "My father views blood as power, and he abuses power. I don't want to be like him."

"So what?" I let out a little laugh of disbelief. "You intentionally starve yourself to keep from being like your dad."

His jaw flexes.

Oh. Oh my fae lords.

"You realize that's insane right? You need to eat. I need to eat. We all need to eat."

His head leans forward, that unruly bit of hair hanging in his eyes doing that trick where he goes from handsome to devastating. Still, he doesn't answer.

Coward I am, I change the subject, "What are you listening to?"

Kaison holds out an earbud. I pop it in, bringing our faces closer together so it can reach.

Whatever I was expecting it wasn't this.

Sure, some club music, or maybe some pop hit sung by a hot chick, but no.

It's a cover of the song *Moon River*. Peeking at the screen, I see in tiny digital words, Frank Ocean. The song is layered, complex, beautiful and. . . sad.

There's a wistfulness in it that wraps around my heart and doesn't let go. My gaze lifts and I meet his. That same wistfulness, an intense hope shines from his eyes. His poor bruised eyes. He's holding back drinking blood, forcing himself to feel the pain.

Whatever Prince Charming the world thinks it knows, they are all wrong. I was wrong too. He's not a killer. He's a protector. Protecting others because no one can protect him. Because he knows what pain and suffering is.

I know the same truth, but instead of protecting others, I withdraw into myself. Disconnect from the world to keep from feeling any further.

I'm seeing the real Kaison right now. I recognize the same look he gave me when we were young. It holds such intensity, such undirected need as if he is desperate for a freedom he can't even fathom.

As the song begins to fade out, I ask, "Play it again?" It's a whisper. I'm desperate to keep this moment from ending.

He wordlessly hits the button to start it over again. My heart flutters, unsure of how to beat as Kaison stares at me with unrestrained, open longing. Not for my body, not for my blood, but for *me*.

Our faces move in as one until our lips connect. We've kissed before, but there is a new weight to the pressure as our lips find one another's. It's like meeting a new person, and the effect of the kiss makes my heart thump so hard my chest rattles. My skin turns into one giant hungry organ, desperate to have him everywhere.

His hands find my hips before sliding up to my rib cage, pulling me closer to him until our chests are pressed together.

My lashes flutter enough for me to see Kaison's face is contorted as if in pain as he meets my mouth with passionate intent.

Kai pulls back suddenly, looking at me with surprise. "Your tongue ring. It doesn't burn," he says in amazement.

I lick my lips. "When we were at Inked by Tink, I had her take me to the back room and we swapped out all my silver for something a little more. . . fiancé friendly."

My pride pinches a little at the confession. The silver always gave me a sense of comfort, a layer of protection. But I traded it in for the vampire in front of me.

Next thing I know, I'm lifted onto the edge of the castle wall and he's attacking my mouth with a fervor and husky *thank yous*. I pull up my skirts, his hardness meeting my hot, needy center.

We gasp against each other's mouths as our sensitive straining parts meet.

"Cinder," he rasps against my mouth. Then he reaches into his pocket and pulls out a handful of marshmallows. He pushes a couple on his sharp canines.

Like a man walking around with condoms should the occasion arise, Prince Charming is packing sugary fang bumpers. . . for me.

I could laugh. He presses his hips against mine, a primal and possessive move. I instinctively grab onto the hair at the back of his skull, tugging harshly as our bodies collide with an electrifying force.

The song rolls out and restarts again. He must have hit repeat.

We struggle with our clothes briefly until I feel the cool and even colder contact of his cock and piercing respectively. I let out a whimper, needing more, needing so much more, maybe even all of him.

When he pushes in, we both gasp and moan, taking in the overload of sensations.

CHAPTER 34

'I SMELL SEX & BLOOD

CHARMING

Her lips part in a breathless gasp as I rock my hips forward, sheathing myself fully inside her scorching heat. "I'm sorry, I can't wait."

Cinder would have responded, but I've robbed her of speech, sealing my mouth over hers in a searing kiss. I drink in her little whimpers and moans as I move with increasing fervor.

Her fingers tangle in my hair, grasping almost painfully while I anchor her hip with one hand. The other cups her jaw, holding her for my devouring kisses as I plunge into her welcoming depths over and over.

"You're so hot, almost scalding," I murmur. "I want to burn to ash in you."

Cinder's inner walls flutter and clench around me in addictive waves. The molten grip sends licks of fire dancing along my cold, perpetually chilled flesh. I'm drowning in the searing sensations overwhelming my system.

I'm careful to keep my mouth on hers, though I'm desperate to lick, kiss and suck up her neck. To tongue the perk little peaks of her nipples to see if I can get her to squeal and writhe.

It's getting harder to resist her. It's getting harder to pretend the scent of her blood doesn't grip me by the throat and squeeze with insistence.

I want to drink from her so badly, my balls tingle painfully.

More than that, I want to bash down her emotional walls. My cock drives into her with punishing thrusts as if I could batter them down. I want to pierce her throat with my fangs, dissolve her barriers, and drink all she has to give until I'm as full of her as she is of me.

Desperate for more of her branding heat, I slip my hand beneath the hem of her dress. I clutch and knead the juncture of her hip and thigh, using my thumb to rasp over the sensitive flesh.

Cinder's back arches violently as a broken cry escapes her. Her release detonates around me in rippling contractions that constrict with unrelenting pressure. Part of me wants to let go and join her in that shattering rapture.

"Oh fuck, I can't hold on if you keep tightening around me like that," I grit out, fighting the crushing urge to lose myself utterly.

Her inner muscles seem to grasp me even tighter in response to my strained words. I grit my teeth and squeeze my eyes shut, forcing my hips to slow to an aching grind as she rides out her climax.

When Cinder's shudders begin to subside, I gradually increase my pace once more. I chase that blazing peak relentlessly, driving her higher and higher until she shatters apart a second time.

This time, when Cinder's release slams into her, she throws her head back in complete surrender. The sinewy column of her pale throat is bared in a display of trust and vulnerability.

I can't tear my gaze from the throbbing pulse at her delicate neck.

For a suspended moment, the primal need to mark her, to seal that tempting flesh between my lips and taste her very soul wars against the fragile bonds of control I desperately cling to. Resisting the impulse becomes more impossible with each gasping breath and arch of her lithe body.

It's madness to keep starving myself while she's around. Drinking blood around her feels so wrong, but now I realize how much danger I've put Cinder in, how much I've weakened myself.

Because all I smell is sex and blood, and it's driving me crazy. I latch onto her lips, anchoring myself there, plunging my tongue into her sweet mouth to keep from doing anything that could destroy either of us as she comes around me with such trust.

"Cinder, oh fae lords," I choke out in a ragged rasp, her name tinged with equal parts rapture and anguish. My hips jerk erratically as I shoot everything I have inside her.

Cinder's warmth seeps into my cold flesh, chasing away the chill that has settled in my bones.

For a moment, I allow myself to imagine a future where we're not bound by the constraints of our worlds.

Where I'm not a vampire prince and she's not a human caught in the crosshairs of a looming rebellion.

Reality comes crashing back all too soon. This thing between us isn't real. It's a temporary respite from what I must do. Yet, I find myself clinging to it, to her, like a drowning man to a life raft.

But I won't let her drown with me. I'll let her go. Though every day the thought gets harder and harder than the day before.

CHAPTER 35

RETURN OF THE STEPS

CINDER

The Midnight garden party is in full grotesque swing by the time the King sweeps onto the grounds. I've spent the last hour fielding more thinly veiled insults and disdainful sneers, each vampire guest eyeing me like a toxic stain they wish would vanish.

Of course, they do their best to tamp it down in front of the ambassadors from the Common World. The humans and fae from the Common World are a constant background presence, always watching.

I get the sense they are waiting to find something amiss. Anything to justify taking a political move against King Charming. While I might be compelled to throw the King under the bus with them on sheer principle, I have my own agenda to see to.

I still have this burning need to find out if he killed my father. My frustration only grows as Kai keeps telling me to be patient and we'll find a way to get information soon.

Thank the fae lords for the overflowing champagne

fountain—at least nobody bats an eyelash when I gulp it down like a camel in the desert. The bubbles help dull the sting of their muttered barbs about my "unsuitability" to become a princess.

Pfft. As if I actually want the fucking job.

Though I have to confess I'll miss this place when I'm gone. It's not like I'll be allowed to waltz back into Midnight after Kai and I call things off.

"You've sat on the cliff's edge?" the vampire with an Indian accent and curious brown eyes asks. "For fun?"

I've shockingly found some of the court members aren't as heinous as the rest. The fangers are still ignorant in many ways about how humans operate, but I've been asked some questions out of genuine interest. Questions about my father's life and art, or how I maintain such pristine skin as a human, or which part of Midnight is my favorite.

The cliffs.

Still, I can't keep my eyes from finding Kai across the lawns like he's a magnet.

Even dressed to the nines for this stuffed shirt soiree, the Charming prince radiates an easy sensuality that has more than a few noblewomen—and noblemen—fawning over him.

Kai serves all of them the same publicity smile that I know to be part of his act. A strange buzz generates in my belly when I realize I may be the only one here who knows him beyond the mask he presents.

The predatory glint in his eyes every time they flick my way promises all sorts of deliciously filthy things if we can ditch this freak parade early. I squirm a little at the thought, downing another glass until the bubbles fizz low in my belly.

Maybe I shouldn't read too much into that hungry look —physical desire is fleeting at best.

But I agreed to my part of this arrangement and that means keeping the wolves at bay.

"Would you excuse me?" I ask the two fangers I've been talking to.

As I make my way across the grounds, I pretend not to hear the hushed whispers.

"Do you believe this farce?"

"She clearly has no interest in our prince."

"Do you think she's been thralled for this PR stunt to please the ambassadors?"

"I wouldn't be surprised. Her demeanor is downright robotic."

Heat pulses in me. They think I'm thralled. Really?

I glide in between the women and select men who are cooing over Kai.

A beautiful Black beauty stands before him, flashing her teeth and fluttering her lashes. "Your Highness, why don't you let me rub your neck. I'm sure there are many knots from all the stress you've been going through lately."

I catch the woman's hand as it snakes up to my fiancé's shoulder. "That won't be necessary. My prince prefers his knots be untied in private."

Before Kai's surprise begins to register, I cup the back of his neck and kiss him. I press against his strong lips until they yield, just long enough to put heat and a bit of tongue into our exchange, but not so long that it would be considered obscene. Then I back away, pretending to give an embarrassed blush. "Oh so sorry, I forget myself when you are near, sl—sweet muffin." Even I hear how ridiculous the endearment sounds in my deadpan voice. At least I caught myself before I called him a slut.

"Not at all, my punk rock princess." Kai sounds a little out of breath and looks a little too pleased.

The disappointment of the crowd around me ripples palpably. My appearance is oddly inspiring them all to disappear one by one.

The Midnight fairy who'd been attempting to feel up my man barely restrains a hiss in my direction before she wanders off. I briefly think of trying to set her up with a certain demonic cat as they both have the same behavioral traits.

It's not long before we are alone. Kai's cold mass fills the space next to me, giving me the strangest sense of comfort and protection.

"Enjoying yourself, my raging beauty?"

There are few times he's not glued to my side, and I have to admit his presence affects me in a way I've never known. In the way only a massive pumpkin spice latte can usually achieve.

An alarm goes off in the back of my head.

Don't get used to this.

"I love the gardens," I admit.

My heart expands in Midnight in a way I'd almost forgotten. The silver rays of the moon stretch so bright over the lush green lands and the brine of the ocean from the cliff sides mingle with the fragrant flowers that grow here.

"It makes me want to paint," I breathe the words even as my hands itch to wrap around a paintbrush.

"You should," he says, a sudden intensity focused on me. Yet again he holds a glass of champagne instead of blood. It's not even tinged with pink to indicate drops of blood present.

The vampire who hates drinking blood.

He's insane.

"Maybe later I'll sneak away to see if there are any supplies left in my father's studio. If it's even still there, that is."

l also need to spend more time searching for the Ember of Midnight.

"You seem tired," he says, softly.

Guess my concealer isn't cutting it when it comes to hiding the little baggies dragging down my eyes.

"Yeah well, between shifts at the Poison Apple and then coming back to a full social schedule at Midnight there hasn't been much time for sleep. This place *does not* have enough pumpkin spice lattes for me to keep up. Not to mention, when I'm here I have to subsist on old packets of ramen and stale bread and cheeses."

My eyes catch on the human servants milling about. Are they trapped inside their minds? Are they blissfully unaware of what they are doing?

Kaison frowns and I think he's about to say something when he's interrupted.

"Lords and ladies," the King's reverberating voice cuts through the tittering crowd. "I'd like to take a moment to address the future of our families."

"What is he talking about?" I mutter to Charming as my fingers flex around my empty glass.

"I have no idea," Kaison says darkly.

Apparently, he doesn't think Daddy Dearest has good intentions either.

"Our two families were once entwined and after Byung-He's death, I fear to say we fell out of touch," The King's voice drips with regret, but his eyes sparkle with undisguised triumph as they find me in the crowd.

The horror of what he's talking about slowly dawns on me.

"Ladies and gentlemen, permit me to rectify this. I am so very grateful to find our families have the very best reason to strengthen our bonds."

"Oh, oh fae lords no," I whisper even as my throat feels an invisible leather strap start to pull.

I scan the grounds.

As if summoned by dark magic, the three figures I'd tried so hard to erase from my memory materialize alongside the King, resplendent in glittering jewel tones that would make a debutante weep.

Marisela glides across the marbled pathway followed by her vicious daughters. Anastasia and Drusilla flank my stepmother like sleek, malevolent jackals, their movements practiced and predatory.

Every muscle in my body goes rigid as stone as Marisela's chilling stare settles on me. Her perfectly glossed lips curl in a poisonous facsimile of a smile.

"Cinder?" Kai asks next to me in a low voice.

I can't blink. I can't breathe. I can't move.

Suddenly, I'm twelve years old again. My father is dead and I discover the true meaning of family.

Rejection.

Punishment.

Pain.

"Cinder, you're shaking," Kai whispers, panic lacing his voice.

He's right. I have to stop. I have to pull the plug on my own thoughts, disconnect from what's happening before it destroys me.

Though staring into the eyes of the vampires who tore into me with their sharp fangs over and over whenever they felt like it makes it difficult. My throat is suddenly hoarse as

I remember begging them to stop, pleading because the pain was too much.

Around me, the party's atmosphere chills to a sub-zero degree. Dozens of eyes bore into me, sharp and judgmental as their whispers reach a fever pitch. I can practically taste the scandal and intrigue like fine port on their tongues.

Only the ambassadors from the Common World seem to genuinely clap with enthusiasm as my stepfamily makes their way toward me, escorted by the King.

His face is twisted into a cruel, triumphant smile. His eyes gleam with smug satisfaction, revealing the true depths of his intentions.

He knows.

He knows I fear my family.

This is a trap. A manipulation orchestrated by the King to strip away my composure. He wants me to lose it, to rail, to fight, to accuse my stepfamily of all they've done. Or maybe just reject them. Because that's all I want to do. Turn on my heel and run. Find a dark corner and shut down every one of my wild emotions.

It would damage the relations between the Common World and Midnight to reject the family that allegedly raised me. The King is appearing to be gracious and accepting of our mixed families, so I would look like the asshole here.

It would give a perfect excuse to dissolve the engagement so Kai will have to marry a fairy.

"Cinder," Kai hisses this time. Fingers slip into mine, but I jerk away, rejecting his touch.

I don't realize I've done it until it's too late.

There is an almost imperceptible gasp. Everyone is watching.

I don't want to be touched. Not now. Not while my skin crawls as if turned into a giant mass of wriggling maggots.

But I can't explain that.

The perfectly timed misstep on my part will give them all the excuse they need. And even though I can't choke my way past my visceral reactions, I become even more certain that the King had something to do with my father's death.

"Right," Kai says with resolved acceptance.

The icy tendrils of panic wrap around my throat as I meet my stepfamily's gaze. I force my lips into that simpering smile I've seen every other noblewoman wear. It's all I can muster.

"What a joy it is for us to all be joined together," Kaison says, breaking the tension, opening his arms, and stepping forward to greet my stepfamily.

Suddenly it's the Prince Charming show, and I've been demoted to cast extra.

Kaison kisses my stepmother, Marisela on either cheek, taking her hand. Then he moves and repeats the gesture to greet Anastasia who tilts her head, almost in offering to him. Her colorless eyes blatantly promise him dark, dirty trysts. Her platinum updo is a complicated set of braids that mimic a crown. A placeholder until she can get her clawed fingers on the real thing.

Meanwhile, Drusilla's hungry gaze remains fastened to me. It burrows under my skin, and oily nausea sloshes up my throat. The glossy chestnut hair tumbles over either shoulder and I'm still amazed at how much she looks like a child.

...from a horror movie.

With a theatric sweep around, Kaison rushes to embrace me. "Is this not fortuitous, my beautiful bride?

Your family is here." I'm too frozen to keep him from pulling me close. His mouth falls even with my ear.

"Don't let them smell your fear. They want you to break. I will get us out of this."

I swallow hard as his words penetrate. He's right.

I can't give them the satisfaction. No matter how many bloody memories flash behind my eyes, no matter how hard my heart hammers, I am Princess Cinder Charming for tonight.

And a Charming always gets the last laugh.

The King isn't laughing now though. His eyes narrow at his son who is effectively diffusing the bomb he set to go off.

Marisella, Anastasia, and Drusilla drop into shallow curtsies before me, and I can't make my knees work to mirror the gesture back.

That, or every fiber in my body fights the thought of bowing before them.

Never again.

"We are so happy to celebrate the union of our families," my stepmother says in that voice that reminds me of dark red wine.

Marisela doesn't want to give it away that she had no idea I was in Midnight, much less about to get engaged to the prince.

I'm sickened by the realization that she still always knows the right thing to say. The thing people around her want to hear.

You are my daughter, just as much as them.

We're family now, Cinder.

Even if they are blatant lies.

Anastasia's eyes are fastened hungrily to Charming as if willing him to engage in a randy bout of eye fucking. He artfully dodges her intense stare, as he smiles at subjects in the garden.

"Well, my dear," the King says smoothly to me. "Aren't you pleased to include your family in the celebrations? I've made sure they shall be at *all* of our soirees and events, fastened to your side in support."

A roaring kicks up in my ears.

They'll be at every event? At my side?

For the foreseeable future?

My heart thumps sluggishly, battering at my ribs with all they can muster.

I'm going to pass out.

Or scream.

Either way, it's not going to end well.

CHAPTER 36

BREAKING BY THE GARDINIUMS

CHARMING

A crash explodes off to the side, a hail of shattering glass.

A heavyset Caucasian man is now surrounded by a scattering of broken glasses from the tray he dropped. The hulking familiar is almost round as he is tall with dark hair and a generous beard. He stares at the mess by his feet as if trying to discern what has happened but is too thralled to truly comprehend.

Something about him brushes against my brain with familiarity, but I don't have time to dig into my memories. I'm going to take advantage of the distraction.

A second ago, everyone's attention was fastened on us, but the crash has broken the tension and they've all gone back to their own conversations. Cinder is barely keeping her shit together while her stepfamily looks on the mess in shock and annoyance.

My father frowns, realizing he's lost the spotlight to the shit show he was trying to choreograph.

"Oh, that's a shame," I say lazily. "What a waste of good champagne and blood." I grin too wide at Cinder's stepfamily.

Anastasia's body sways toward mine by inches and I can tell she can barely hold herself back. To say she's thrown herself at me in the past is quite literal. The number of times she's dropped a handkerchief for me to pick up, or swooned in faints I've needed to save her from is a number so tedious I haven't bothered to keep count.

"If you'll excuse us, I think I'd like to show my bride the gardinium flowers of the hedge maze until this mess is cleaned up." I sniff in distaste, then lead Cinder by the arm toward the opening of the maze.

When we are far enough away, I turn her around to face me. Cinder's already pale skin is now white as a sheet. Her eyes are sunken black pools of dilated pupils, and she's trembling.

"What's wrong? Tell me," I urge, not keeping the panic from cutting through my voice.

She shakes her head.

Okay, so she can't tell me why they rattle her so much. I have my suspicions, but my wild imagination conjures up too much to be trusted.

The scars flash in my mind's eye.

A murderous flame flares inside me.

Calm down. You don't know anything. Don't assume anything.

"What do you need?" I ask, sliding a hand up her cheek, running my thumb across her jawline, keeping her eyes on me. I can find out the facts later, but Cinder needs me right this second.

What *does* she need?

Water? Her iron supplements? I have some in my pocket along with a snack bar. Does she need to sit down? If only I could get her a pumpkin spice latte—

Her mouth collides with mine with a fervor I'm not expecting. The kiss is hungry, desperate. She needs to escape whatever is inside her.

"Are you sure?" I break long enough to ask.

"I need it, now," she practically growls.

This I can do. It's what I'm good at.

Stepping fully into her space until I'm looking straight down at her, I cup her face with both hands as I push my tongue past her teeth to sweep inside her mouth. I taste and tease her until she sags against me, still trembling but less violently.

Black polish nails scratch at the nape of my neck sending goosebumps careening along a path over my chest and arms to where I'm already stiffening.

"More," she rasps.

Her hand sweeps over my hardening length and I groan into her mouth. Now she's not the only one who's desperate.

Oh fuck, I want to drop to my knees and tongue at her cute little clit piercing—before sliding my fingers up into her, exploring her depth and heat.

So I do. Dropping to the ground, not caring about the dirt, I push her skirts up.

Cinder's grip on the back of my neck tightens painfully.

When I tilt my head up, I'm met with that same wild fear I saw in her eyes as her family approached.

"Not that," she confesses breathily.

For a moment, my lust fogged mind doesn't understand. Then I do.

My fangs.

A desperate twitch clenches in my cock as I realize I won't be tasting her.

But it's not about what I want.

Cinder needs control. Safety.

And sex. My dark goddess absolutely needs sex. A bone-shaking orgasm that will sweep everything else away, and I want to give it to her so badly the muscles in my body hurt from the tension of holding back.

"Right," I say, hoarsely.

Standing, I grab her hand and practically fly further into the maze, dragging Cinder behind me. Eventually, I find what I'm looking for. A wrought iron bench.

Technically this gives credence to my story. The white gardiniums curls and curve around the hedges here, filling the air with their potent floral scent. Similar to gardenias of the Common World, these flowers only bloom in Midnight. And when they do, they open with little soft sighs.

I turn around and fall to my knees again and reach under her skirts. Instead of pushing them up this time, I find one of the layers of fabric to her dress and rip.

Cinder jolts at the sound of tearing cloth coupled with my violent motion of separating it from her.

I pull out a long piece of her dress.

"It's not marshmallows," I confess, "But hopefully, it's enough."

Understanding dawns in her violet eyes. "Tear me another," she demands.

I don't question her, I just obey.

"Turn around," she orders.

My brow dips in confusion, but I do as I'm told. She pulls my arms back and uses one of the strips of fabric to tie my wrists together.

Oh fucking witchtits, I just got harder.

Then the other cloth goes over my head and into my mouth as she ties it around the back of my head.

Looks like my idea doesn't suck after all.

As I congratulate myself on the spark of genius, I realize I should have unbuttoned my slacks. But then Cinder is there, fingers deftly releasing me from my confines. Faster than I anticipate, her small hand sweeps up and down my fast-hardening shaft.

My groan is muffled into the cloth, as my vision blurs from the intensity of sensation she inspires.

"Sit on the bench," she orders.

I do as she says. At first it's tricky, but I manage to position my arms through a gap in the bench so I'm not in danger of squishing or ripping my limbs off.

Cinder approaches as soon as I'm settled, a wild gleam in her eye. In no time, her hot heat sinks down on my cold, hard shaft. So shocked by the blazing heat of her, I nearly suck the gag down my own throat.

Oh fuck me sideways on a stake.

She's so tight.

Scorching hot.

And if I don't focus on something else, I'm going to shoot off like a prepubescent teen.

My eyes roll up to the heavens as I work on counting stars.

My wrists are bound with a strip of fabric, the rough and tight texture digging into my skin. Cinder's body is hot against mine, her silky skin igniting a fire within me.

She rides me hard and fast as little sounds of pleasure escape her throat.

The controlled, placid Cinder is gone, replaced by something fiery, unquenchable and addictive.

Right now, I'm not the prince of Midnight, I'm not even a playboy down for an inventive roll in the hay. I am here solely for her release. I'm hers to use, to abuse, desperate to give her whatever she wants however she wants it.

I have a fleeting thought that I'm in real danger of letting her cover me in honey and spanking me with a tennis racket while a women's knitting club watches us fuck isn't out of bounds.

Not that I would say no to it. Sounds like an amazing story to recount at parties.

But it wouldn't be for the novelty of it. It would be because *she* simply wanted it.

Hell, she wouldn't even have to ask. She'd only need to lift that one dark brow a mere fraction to indicate it's what she'd want, and I'd hand her the tennis racket myself with an "if it pleases you, mistress."

Just when I think it can't get any more intense, Cinder shifts her body, her slick heat tightening around me, and I'm forced back into the moment where I'm painfully aware of every sensation.

Fucking fae lords, I need to focus, or I'm going to explode in less than a minute. I try to block out the intensity of the moment, but Cinder's body is like a living, breathing inferno, consuming every inch of me.

As I struggle to keep myself in check, she picks up her pace, riding me harder and harder with each passing second. My hands clench the fabric, the makeshift ropes tightening as I grip them with all my strength, trying to keep some semblance of control. The world outside of this little corner of the gardens fades away, leaving only Cinder and me, lost in the primal dance of her taking what she needs from me.

I want to taste her, and knowing she won't let my fangs near her pretty pussy infuses with me a desperate edge of frustration I've never known before.

It's so easy to get what I want, but not with Cinder. Nothing is just given, and I can't take it.

It has to be her decision.

My hips thrust up into her as best they can as I try to give her all I can.

Then she's shuddering, clawing, and moaning as she comes on top of me.

My eyes roll into the back of my head as she milks me, beckoning me to go over the edge with her. But I refuse. I can't just yet.

Cold air replaces her tight heat and a pathetic whimper slips out of me.

Real dignified, Charming.

"I need more," she rasps. Cinder pulls me to my feet, and I almost fall over in a dizzy spell. My focus snaps to attention when Cinder bends over the edge of the bench. She lifts her dress, and I can see her perfect lower lips glistening with desire. Her legs spread a little more, allowing me a view that might kill me.

Prince Charming.

Came into this world a regal heir.

Taken out of this world by a human girl's derriere.

RIP me.

My arms are still tied and I'm gagged, but I understand the assignment.

Stepping up behind her legs, I direct my cock back into her perfect channel. She's even tighter in this position, but I can go deeper. Taking my chance, I slam into her with all the power I possess.

The sound that comes out of her throat is animalistic, at once conveying I've hit the spot and also please, fuck, hit it approximately one million more times.

She keens and moans as I piston my hips into my princess, my mistress.

"Oh fuck, yes, just like that. And don't you dare fucking come. Do you understand?" she hisses.

My balls draw up into my body with unexpected vigor. I already know that when she finally lets me come it's going to be harder than I've ever come before.

I fuck us both into oblivion as Cinder becomes the center of my universe.

"Oh fuck," she grits out as her fingernails scrape for purchase on the bench. She shakes and breaks apart around me and I don't stop. I continue to pound into her. The need to conquer her consumes me, pushing me closer and closer to that razor's edge of control.

"Don't stop," she begs, and I don't. I draw out her orgasm as her back arches. What I would give to reach a hand into her silky black hair right now.

Tossing me a dark look over her shoulder, Cinder's eyes shoot straight through me like a sharpened sword.

"Come for me, Kai."

I'm not sure if it's the commanding way she delivers the order, or if it's my name falling off her lips, but my body obeys before my mind can catch up. Stars sting and sparkle behind my eyes as my muffled moans reach my ears, as I pour into her. No, I *explode* into her. Even as I release, her inner muscles tighten and clench around me until she's pulled every last drop from me.

Before I know it, we're both sagged on the bench, panting and sweating. My wrists are free.

Cinder visibly shivers.

With numb hands, I remove the makeshift gag.

"Fuck me sideways," I breathe.

"I think that's what you just did to me," she points out between pants.

I tilt my head. "Touche." Then sense filters into my brain. The way she reacted to her stepfamily was not normal. "What did they do?"

She stiffens, then as if she is unable to hold any tension in her body after what we just did, she melts into the seat again. "I don't know if I can do this."

Panic zips up me with a sharp sting.

I need her. I need her to play bride. I need her to help me convince the Mice to overthrow my father. Without her, none of this works.

Though something deeper inside me rips at hearing her say *she can't do this.*

Is it my pride? No, something else. Something that bleeds.

I shove it aside.

"Cinder, I need you."

She shakes her head. "I can't. I shouldn't have come. I'm going home."

Even when she's breaking, she's remarkably poised. She's back to her usual mask of indifference. Her face flatlines. Brooks no arguments.

But by the gods, I'm going to argue.

Her only tell is her weak, shaky voice, and that rip inside me gushes more blood.

"Wait, just wait until tomorrow," I beg. "I have something to show you. It's the thing you most want."

By the spark in Cinder's eye, I know I have her intrigued, curious.

Which means I better find out what happened to her

father.

No. That's too complicated a task to resolve in such a short amount of time.

But if I get this Ember of Midnight I know she still roams the halls for. . . I'll secure her again.

Now, I just need to figure out what the hell it is.

CHAPTER 37
PUSSY DOESN'T LIKE YOU

CINDER

Charming asked me to give him until tomorrow, but I'm not sure I can.

After the garden party, I practically fled to the Common World. Grateful for my shift at Poison Apple, I ground myself in the motions of serving drinks, remembering who the fuck I am.

Even with Kai sitting mere feet away, watching me, it's easy to remember who I am when I'm surrounded by other badass females. Snow flashes me a quick gleaming smile just before she hauls six shot glasses up onto the bar in one motion.

Goldie's ass shakes as she takes a quick break to groove with one of the bar patrons who dances with her from the other side. Both of them sing loudly along to the popular tune. The lights turn pink, bathing Goldie in her signature color. Ted sits at the bar, his eyes locked on her as if she is the only thing in the universe.

"Hey, you good?" a voice interrupts. Rap is behind me, taking some numbers for stock orders.

"Yeah, yes," I say, going to fill a pitcher of beer. My boss's sharp eyes never miss anything. She doesn't ask for more of an explanation, but she continues to work.

I will be good. Once I break things off with Kai and return to my normal life.

After my shift, Kai insists on dragging me to some mystery location. I'm exhausted and my nerves are still raw from the confrontation with my stepfamily, but he's relentless.

"Where are we going?" I demand, struggling to keep pace with his long strides.

"You'll see," is all he says, that infuriating smirk playing at his lips.

We stop in front of a nondescript building. Kai ushers me inside, ignoring my protests. But the moment I cross the threshold, the words die on my tongue.

It's a studio. A real, honest-to-gods art studio. The space is open and stacked with art supplies. The faint scent of paint and creation lingers in the air, beckoning me.

"What is this?" I round on Kai, my voice sharp.

He shrugs, hands in his pockets. "It's yours. For as long as you want it."

Kai's words hit me like a punch to the gut. A studio? For me?

My heart clenches painfully in my chest. The offer is tempting, dangerously so. The studio feels like a trap, a shiny lure designed to lower my defenses.

I scoff, crossing my arms. "I don't need your handouts. I'm not some charity case for you to fix with your endless riches."

Something flickers in his eyes, but he keeps his tone

light. "It's not a handout, Cinder. It's an investment. In you, in your talent."

"You don't know anything about my talent."

"Don't I?" He steps closer, his gaze intense. "I've seen your paintings. The ones you hide away, the ones that come from your soul. They're incredible, Cinder. The world deserves to see them."

My heart stutters. He's seen my art. The pieces I've never shown anyone, the ones that are too raw, too real.

Part of me wants to melt at his thoughtfulness, but another part still bristles. I don't need him to swoop in and save me. I've survived on my own for years.

Even as I think it, a small voice whispers: *Maybe it's not charity. Maybe he really believes in you.*

"That's also why I got you a show," he goes on. "At a gallery downtown. Whenever you're ready."

Anger surges through me, hot and bright. How dare he presume to know what's best for me, to make decisions about my life and my art. It's just like Marisela all over again, pretending to care while secretly plotting to control me. The sour taste of bile rises in my throat at the thought. No, I won't let myself be fooled again. Trusting others only leads to pain. "I don't want your pity showcase, Kai. I'm not some pet project for you to parade around."

He's trying to trap me. Bribe me into staying. But I won't be forced to spend time with my steps.

Though fuck him for pulling out all the stops on what I want. He knows me too well and it borders on scary.

"It's not pity," he says, his voice low and fierce. "It's belief. In you, in what you can do." He takes my hand, his touch searing. "You have a gift, Cinder. Don't let your pride stop you from sharing it."

I yank my hand away, my skin burning. "My pride is all

I have. It's what's kept me alive, kept me fighting. I won't let you take that from me."

Kai's eyes soften. "I'm not trying to take anything from you. I'm trying to give you a chance. To show the world who you are, what you're capable of."

I turn away, my throat tight. The temptation is so strong. To take what he's offering, to let myself believe that I could be more than a servant, more than a survivor.

But it feels too easy. Too good to be true.

"I won't interfere," Kai says quietly. "The studio, the show. . . they're yours. What you do with them is up to you."

I don't respond. I can't. If I open my mouth, I'm afraid all my secrets will come spilling out.

It's everything I've ever wanted - someone who believes in me, who supports my dreams without trying to control me.

The bitter voice in the back of my mind won't be silenced. It whispers insidiously, reminding me of all the times I had dared to hope.

"If you are trying to convince me to stay in Midnight, you are fucking up real bad." I run my hand over the smooth wood of the easel. "Because all I want to do is hide in here."

"This isn't the thing I wanted to show you," he says, slipping his hands in his pockets. "This is just a necessity. Because of your talent, the refuge and convenient hiding place is just a byproduct." Kaison gives me a lopsided smile.

I can't return it. Something is clawing under my skin and burrowing its way into vital organs. Gratitude? Attachment? No matter what it is, I can't trust it.

Kai sighs. "We should get to Midnight. Before we're missed."

Numbly, I follow him out of the studio and to my apartment trying not to love every single fucking thing he's just given me.

Trying not to love *him*.

It's just another reason to leave the whole situation. We were never going to end up together. The agreement is going to come to an end whether it's now or later.

The only reason I agree to return is because I need to get my stuff. I'm not leaving my grim reaper doll for anyone, and iron supplements are expensive as shit. I'll go, get my stuff, and let him make his final plea before I peace out to the Common World, never to look back again.

As we slip on the glass slippers, preparing to return to Midnight, a black streak comes hurtling out of nowhere.

Lucifer attacks with a vengeance, yowling and clawing. I cry out, trying to fend him off, but it's too late. The world tilts, reality bending around us.

We land in a heap on the cold stone floor of the castle. Lucifer hisses once more before darting off into the shadowy corridors.

I lay there, my heart racing.

"You okay?" Kaison asks.

"Yep," I say popping my 'P,' not bothering to hide my irritation.

"The cat kind of sucks," he confesses with a grumble.

"Guess pussy doesn't love you as much as you thought it did."

CHAPTER 38

THE EMBER OF MIDNIGHT

CHARMING

I lead Cinder into a storage room. The smell of must and acrylic paint thickens the air until my eyes water.

The dark is oppressive, even for me, and I can see in the dark. It takes a couple of moments to light the candles. I've already located the item and hung it on a wall, on display for Cinder.

Once the room is illuminated, Cinder's eyes turn round and glassy. "The Ember of Midnight."

I found it.

I fucking found it.

I deserve a medal. Or at least my own detective series complete with a roguish cap and pipe as I solve even more mysteries.

The painting is a beautiful skyline of the Midnight cliffs. Byung-He has perfectly captured the crashing waves below. The starlight seems to stretch out to me with a hundred magical winks that make it feel like a benevolent divine being is giving me a cheeky nod of knowing. I see you. All is well.

Fucker always had a talent for art.

But the best work he ever did is standing next to me, clutching her heart as if it might pop out of her breastbone.

"Took a bit of doing to find it," I say, forgoing modesty to let her know I hunted like a dog to figure out what she was looking for. "Would have helped if you told me it was a painting from the get go." I scratch the back of my head, not about to admit I had to pull on Jack's strings for information.

Cinder spares me the briefest glance before she's glued again to the painting. "It's bigger than I remember," she breathes.

"Yeah. If your plan had been to swipe it and return home, I'm not sure how you'd get those slim little arms around it to make off with it."

"I would have managed." She says it with all the piss and vinegar in the world. Which tells me she also has no idea how she would have got it back to the Common World.

Then Cinder lowers to the ground, crossing her legs, settling in. I drop down next to her and sit in silence.

In the foreground is a woman with jet-black hair that gleams beautifully against the deep blue and indigo hues of the night sky. Her pale skin glows like moonlight, and only half of her face is visible as she stares out at the ocean with loving awe.

I don't consider myself particularly sentimental, but even I have never been able to deny that Byung-He's work moves me. Perhaps this one more than any other.

To my knowledge, he never painted people or portraits. The woman's dark eyes are filled with so much love I can almost feel it swelling inside me like a second heart growing in my chest, crowding out my non-beating organ.

While it's kind of creepy feeling, it also creates a sensation of fullness and companionship. Like I'm suddenly not alone.

A silence falls over us, and the moment feels sacred.

This is important. This matters, and I won't ruin the moment. Cinder risked coming back to Midnight, risked facing an ugly past just for this and I've been desperate to find out why. I do my best not to stare at Cinder as she drinks in the painting with a blatant thirst.

Though her eyes remain glassy, tears never fall.

The question of why burns my throat. It presses on me with increasing pressure, but I fight it with everything I have. Cinder needs this moment more than I need my question answered.

"Ask it," she finally says, her voice a little ragged.

"What is so special about this painting?" It comes out in a whisper.

Her shoulders hitch and I can't tell if it's a hiccup or a swallowed sob.

"It's my mother."

I suspected. Knowing gives me a strange sense of relief that I'd guessed correctly. The eyes, the hair, they are Cinder's.

"She died in childbirth. It's the only picture I've ever seen of her." Cinder's voice is thick with emotion. "And it's painted by my father's hand. When I'm with this painting it's my family, all of us together."

"You look like her," I point out, nudging her with my shoulder.

A lop-sided smile springs to her lips.

I swear my heart almost beats.

I'm ready to let the silence fall around us again, but she goes on.

"When I sit in front of this painting, it's like I'm with them. I can feel my mother's love. My father used to tell me how excited she was for me to come into this world. That she wanted a girl more than anything, and she would be so proud of me. When I look at this painting, I'm part of a family unit and I'm not alone anymore. I actually. . . belong."

"You belong with your friends," I point out, trying to ignore the almost painful squeeze in my chest.

You belong with me.

"Yeah."

"Wow," a laugh burst out of me. "That was completely unbelievable. Do you really not think you belong with them? Goldie, Snow, Rap, all of your friends at the Poison Apple adore you."

Cinder shrugs, avoiding my gaze. "It's very nice," she says again in a completely unconvincing tone.

I study her for a moment, realization dawning. "But you don't fully let them in, do you? You keep a part of yourself locked away, even from the people who love you most."

Her eyes snap to mine, a flicker of defensiveness in their violet depths. "That's not true. I'm close with my friends."

"Are you?" I press gently. "Because I've seen the way you are with them. You laugh and joke, but there's always a distance, a wall you keep up. It's like you're afraid to let them see the real you."

Cinder opens her mouth as if to argue, then closes it again. Her shoulders slump almost imperceptibly.

"And it's not just them," I continue softly. "You do the same thing with me. We've been through a lot of the same things, but I still feel like I only know a fraction of who you are. You're always holding back, keeping me at arm's length."

She stays silent, but I can see the truth of my words hitting home in the way she worries her lower lip between her teeth, the way her gaze darts away from mine.

"I think I understand why," I murmur, turning to look at the painting once more. "After what happened when you were young, after your father died. . ."

Cinder inhales sharply beside me, and I know I've struck a nerve.

If I could find those fucking monsters who attacked Cinder as a child. . . Perhaps when I'm not on Castle-arrest anymore, I'll go hunting for some rogue vampires. Make them pay for what they did to her. For the scars they left behind.

We sit quiet for a moment, the only sound the distant ticking of a clock echoing through the empty halls.

"But this painting," I say at last, "it's different, isn't it? With your family, captured like this. . .it's safe to feel that connection, that love. They can't hurt you here. Can't let you down."

Slowly, Cinder nods. "When I look at this, I'm part of a family again. I'm not alone anymore. I belong." Her voice cracks on the last word, and she clears her throat. "But out in the world. . .it's not so simple."

"No," I agree quietly, "it's not."

She doesn't respond, just continues to stare resolutely at the painting. As if she has refuge as long as she has her eyes on it.

I know, deep in my bones, that I want to be one of the people she lets in. One of the ones she trusts with her whole, unguarded heart.

No matter what it takes

I don't deserve her, but fucking hell I want her more than I want anything else.

"It's not safe." It's barely a whisper from her perfect purple-painted lips.

"What do you mean?" I ask, instead of giving into the almost overpowering desire to kiss her.

"You can never know who to trust. Not really. I know my stepfamily was never the most affectionate or loving, but I figured we were still family. I was very wrong." Her voice drops to a low, dark pitch. "The moment my dad died, they turned on me. They hated me and I had no idea. So not only was I devastated over my father's passing, but I found my family wasn't really my family at all. Suddenly I wasn't allowed out of the house. They locked me and forced me to clean like a servant. It was like that for four years until I couldn't take it anymore and left when I was sixteen."

"Sixteen," I echo, stunned. I often wondered what happened to the human girl after her father died, and now I know. "How did you get past the border?"

Without my necklace or Cinder's shoes, there are portal points between the realms—gates guarded on both sides. My father is strict on border patrol.

She shook her head. "Dumb luck. I was so small, I was able to sneak by. But the constant blood loss took its toll. By the time I escaped, I was severely anemic. The iron supplements help, but it's a constant battle to keep my levels up."

And it doesn't help she's been living two lives, her head spinning from one emotional shock after the next.

"I lived on the streets of Boston for a while until I found jobs here and there. Then I met Goldie. She introduced me to Rap and the Poison Apple. I got some actual money and put myself through college for art. But this. . ." She sighs at the stretch of canvas. "I'll never be this good."

"You should stop comparing yourself. Your father was talented, but so are you. In a completely different way that's unique to you." Then I lean back, observing the painting closer. "Did your parents love each other?"

She nods. "My father adored my mother. But I bet if they lived long enough, they would have been disappointed in each other, or maybe even in me. But here in this painting, there is so much love. It can't be taken away. It can't turn into bitterness, resentment, disappointment."

With that, Cinder pushes up to a standing position, dusting her hands off. I'm on my feet in a second.

Something in me says she's been too vulnerable for too long and she's trying to shut it down. But I won't have it. I got past her defenses for just a little while and I'm fucking addicted to it. I could live off her hardness, any scraps she'd throw my way. But now that I've brushed against her naked underbelly, I can't stop until I'm nestled in there, a permanent fixture in her softness.

"Your parents would never be disappointed in you. If they were here, you would have been safe and loved." The word comes out almost ferociously.

Cinder shakes her head. "I used to fantasize about that, but the more I know the world, the more I realize people live too long. Not just fairies. Live long enough and I think we'll find everyone ends up hating one another or at best, drifting apart. At least you and I have a straightforward agreement."

I swallow over a lump in my throat. I want to tell her she's wrong. I've seen the way she completes the Poison Apple, the way her friends look at her with such love and acceptance. Even her boss would protect her from the likes of me. I want to show her that's not how relationships work, but truthfully, I wouldn't know.

I turn and run my hand along a crate of paintings, almost wishing for the stab of splinters.

"I've never had that acceptance you spoke of. My father only views me as an heir to his throne, a pawn of power. I still remember the day I found that out. I began training at twelve in martial arts, and when I won my first tournament, I went to my father after to share the pride I felt. I worked my ass off."

I remember stepping into the training arena, my heart pounding with a mixture of anticipation and nerves. "At twelve years old, it was my first real martial arts tournament against other young nobles learning the warrior disciplines."

All eyes turned toward me as I made my way to the center mat. The King's icy gaze bored into me from his ceremonial throne. I could feel the weight of his expectations like a lead vest strapped to my chest.

"The referee called the first match, and I faced off with a wiry boy a couple years my senior. We exchanged the traditional formalities and then the bout began."

Months of rigorous training took over as we traded blows and grappled. I had been drilled mercilessly on form, tactics, and sheer ferocity. Mentors beat those lessons into me until they were deeply ingrained instinct.

"Eventually I landed a decisive strike, sending my opponent sprawling. The referee's hand shot up, declaring me the victor. A primal sense of accomplishment surged through me. I had proven myself, overpowered my adversary through sheer skill and fortitude.

"As I turned with a flushed smile toward my father, desperate for his approval, his expression remained chillingly impassive."

As I tell Cinder the story, a painful coldness extends out from my center.

The King's voice had cut through the arena like a blade. "Continue."

I didn't understand. The other kid was on the ground, dazed. I'd won.

My father's eyes narrowed to slits. My chest deflated as surely as if he'd struck me. Before I could respond, he continued in a booming proclamation. "Continue."

Realization dawned. The word hung in the air like a sword suspended above the captive onlookers.

I stared at my downed opponent, already battered and beaten. A sudden pit opened in my gut as I realized my father demanded I continue wailing on him well past any honor or decency. Simply for the sake of dominance.

"And no one on the court would stop either him or me. I was to make an example of our power, our ruthlessness. I was meant to inspire fear and let everyone know the Charming throne ruled all."

When I opened my mouth to protest, my father's granite expression turned any objection to ash on my tongue. The truth was laid bare—the approval I so desperately craved would not come through upholding virtues like honor or mercy.

"At that moment, I understood my father did not view me as his son, only as an instrument to wield and shape into the most ruthless extension of his will. And if I failed to become that heartless embodiment of his power. . . then I was nothing at all to him." The wood of the crate cracks under my hand. I didn't realize I'd been holding it so hard. I step back and wipe my hand down my pants.

"Did you do it?" Cinder breathed after I told her what happened. "Did you keep beating the other kid?"

I shook my head. "I wouldn't do it." I paid for that.

It was the first day I learned what true pain was, but it wouldn't be the last.

"Since then, I've almost made it my mission to disappoint Daddy Dearest." The partying antics, the sleeping around, they were partly proving that I was exactly what he said I was—useless, irresponsible, and no real royal. The rest was because I was trying to fill that hole inside me where I imagine parental love should be.

"But your mother loves you," Cinder points out even as she crosses her arms over her chest. "At least you have her, still."

I nod and grip the back of my neck. "My mother does love me, as much as she can, but she doesn't have much to give. I don't know when it happened. I was too young to realize it for a while, but something in her is broken. I've no doubt my father is responsible," I finish darkly.

Yet another reason on top of the pile of cruel sins he's committed that he needs to pay for. If only I could get the Mice to help me with making him pay for them.

"Cinder," I start again, dropping my arm. "About the scars."

A pair of perfect lips press against mine, and my question scatters.

CHAPTER 39
EATEN BY A VAMPIRE

CINDER

Our hands explore and pull at clothing until we are naked and exposed under the dim candlelit storeroom.

"We don't have protection," I say, suddenly.

"Hold that thought," Kaison says, pushing up to stand then he disappears behind some stacked crates.

He comes back with a couple packing peanuts in his hands. After some finagling, he thrusts them up into his mouth, covering his fangs.

My heart squeezes so tight, I fear it might explode.

The proud grin he gives me is goofy, and I hate how my heart beats faster and feels lighter.

"What does my mistress want?" He waggles his eyebrows, but then his face darkens.

How does he do that? He skates almost effortlessly between light and dark. As if he could laugh and kill in the same breath.

His complexity has my throat thick with want and my heart pounding with need.

"Kneel," I command.

We aren't in a position for me to pillage the depths of his sex closet for dominatrix tools, but I intend to continue the dynamic we started.

As he does so, I grab a small rickety stool from a corner of the room and bring it over, setting it in front of his naked body.

"Put your arms behind your back and keep them there."

He does as I say, crossing his wrists over each other as if invisibly tied. Kai's eyes drink me in hungrily as I sit on the stool before him, but I see the question lurking there with displeasure.

Where are the scars from?

Who did it?

But I don't want to talk about that. I don't want to go back there.

I won't.

So I spread my legs and lay a hand on his head so it's even with my sex.

Kai's brow smooths and he suddenly turns serious.

"You'll let me?" he rasps in disbelief, already anticipating what I'm about to order.

Fear pulsates just under the surface, making my heartbeat erratic. It's risky, but when I'm with him I want to push the envelope. I want to face my most intense fears, or at least some of them.

Am I trying to prove that he can be trusted, or is some part of me setting him up to fail?

Do I expect him to fail my tests and disappoint me?

The second would almost be easier to take in some ways. He's confusing me with the way he is always there with a joke, defending me, or shielding me in any given situation. It makes me want things.

Things I can't have.

Things that don't exist.

Like lasting trust and love.

"Lick me," I order. My order comes out a little hoarse to my own ears.

"Yes mistress," he says in a thick voice that makes me think he might already be on the verge of coming. His dick is hard and erect, little metal balls winking at me with cheeky promise.

Leaning forward with painstaking slowness, he runs his tongue from the bottom of my slit to the top.

In one swipe, all the air squeezes from my lungs and my organs refuse to fill again.

Kai closes his eyes and moans as if he's tasted heaven.

Okay, he can't be that excited about—oh fuck me his tongue is so long.

Again, he swipes up my part and I grip his hair tighter.

"Do you like that, Kai?" I almost use a pet name on him, but I realized long ago he has plenty of those. No one uses his real name.

No one except me.

Proving my point, he shudders. "Fuck yes, mistress."

Kaison continues his long swipes, before switching to quicker shorter ones. Then the tip of his tongue burrows until it taps my clit. The pressure pushes in my own piercing and my head snaps back as hot, liquid tingles fuzz my brain like a broken television.

A gurgling sound escapes my throat.

"Mmm," he hums in pleasure, repeating the motion. Kaison probes and pushes and tongues my clit, as if it's some kind of video game controller he's manipulating.

Even I can't deny he's fucking winning.

"You taste like spice," he groans.

"And everything nice?" I finish for him.

Impossibly dark eyes turn up to meet mine. "No. Like you're my forever vice."

Before I can remark on his cheesy rhyme, he pushes his tongue past my lower lips as far as he can. I'm uncertain which is more erotic, the way he penetrates me or how he looks at me as he does it.

Like he owns me, even from on his knees, hands poised behind his back.

The packing peanuts are acting as bumpers and part of me wants to take them off. I want him closer. Closer than I've ever wanted anyone before.

Then he presses his mouth against me and licks and sucks with new fervor. My feet lift until my toes curl around the rungs of the unsteady stool.

Kai keeps his wrists crossed and his hips gently pump as if fucking the air, thinking about me.

"Fuck Cinder, you are so hot. So delicious. I'll do anything you want," he says with his mouth still full of fang bumpers and my cunt.

"Take off the packing peanuts." It comes out a whisper and even I wouldn't be sure I've said it, except that Kai goes deathly still. He looks up at me again.

"Are you sure?"

No.

Yes.

I'm not sure

I swallow over the planet-sized lump that's suddenly sprouted in my throat.

Keeping his lips glued to mine is an easier way to feel

safe, but down there with my femoral artery pumping so close to his face. . .

He could kill me in seconds. The pain he could cause if he lost control. . .

I know he wants my blood. He pretends to be in perfect control, but I recognize when bloodlust turns his pupils into massive pools of ink and has his nostrils flaring.

Charming wants me. He wants me in every physical manner. He wants to eat me.

And fae lords help me, part of me wants to let him.

Unable to find my voice, I can only nod.

I've learned his Adam's apple slides down then back up his throat only when he's under extra duress and I find it hypnotizing every single time.

"You have to say it," he says far too seriously.

I expect a pithy nickname. I'm almost angry he doesn't throw one out. He's not letting me out of the weight of this moment where he gets my consent.

It's a big deal. We both know it, but I want him to joke and pretend it's not.

"Yes."

It costs me to say it out loud.

Or maybe the price will be collected later.

Keeping his hands behind his back, Kai doesn't break eye contact. He tongues the puffy peanuts off his fangs and spits one after the other onto the ground.

Those pupils grow even larger, so there's only the thinnest band of maple brown framing them.

Unencumbered, he presses his mouth against me again and there are more points of contact. I'm engulfed with even more fervor and hunger than before. He moans and licks and sucks until lava-infused spirals curl through my belly and I can't catch my breath.

He eats me out like a starving vampire. Like he'll die if he stops. Like he's unable to stop.

The stool creaks under me as my hips rock underneath his mouth. The tension coils and stretches, reaching up, up and up until I'm begging.

"*Please*. Please, please, please Kai." The words tumble over each other in an incoherent mess. "I have to come."

He throws my legs over his shoulders, and I have to cling to the back edge of the stool to keep upright. He latches onto my clit, while a finger slides into me. I cry out.

It's so godsdamn satisfying yet not nearly fae fucking enough.

"Ah," I gasp, my hips rocking even faster chasing the sensation. I'm there, teetering on the edge. If I lose the thread to the orgasm, I might rip the hair off his handsome head.

A loud creak followed by several cracks is my only warning the stool is breaking under me. My bare ass meets thin air, but Kai picks me up. My legs are still balanced over his shoulders. Hands pressed to my spine, he balances me against his still licking and suckling mouth.

The violence of the shift is too much for me and I break. My fingers fly to dig into his hair, holding on as I cry out for dear life as my body riots and shudders, clenching around nothing, missing his finger penetrating me, and needing more.

My back meets the cold stone floor as he never breaks his pace between my legs. "Kai," I gasp. "Fuck me."

CHAPTER 40
THIRSTING FOR CINDER

CHARMING

"Yes mistress," the words drip from my lips, still glistening with the essence of her desire. My dick twitches every time she says my name.

She owns my name. She owns my everything whether she knows it or not.

So easily, I could crumple in the palm of her hand like a piece of paper.

Then I'm there, pushing forward, sheathing myself in her scorching heat with all my flesh and hardware. Her greedy body pulls me deeper as her fingers flex against my shoulders.

"Oh fuck," I can't help but groan at the exquisite sensation.

My head dips, ready to trail open-mouthed kisses along the tempting column of her throat.

At the last second, I jerk back, denying myself. My teeth cannot go near that delicate skin. Not her limbs either.

Only two places are safe harbors—her luscious mouth

and now, her perfect pussy. As long as I stay there, burying myself in one slick heaven or the other, she'll be safe.

Well, not exactly safe. Not with the way her internal muscles are already fluttering and clenching around me like a velvet fist. Not when her breathy whimpers undo me completely, making my fangs ache to pierce her flesh and drink down her cries.

Gritting my teeth, I fight the primal urges rising up.

I have to stay in control, for her sake. I'll ravish her body with everything but my bite, ensuring only euphoric cries spill from that perfect mouth.

Yes, for now, her mouth is where I'll stake my claim, swallowing each of her delirious moans. Drinking her in utterly, yet denying my scorching thirst the ambrosia pulsing through her veins.

I sink into her molten velvet depths and nearly lose my fae fucking mind.

A broken sound escapes my lips.

Don't lose control. You're a grown damn man.

Again, I'm gripped with the need to pierce her, to spill that vibrant essence and drink from her neck. To mark her as mine, so everyone knows who she belongs to.

I want it so bad, my fangs ache.

But I can't. I won't.

Cinder is giving me her trust and I refuse to fuck this up.

She lets me do this even knowing the darkness in me. The violence, the thirst, the parts that take men apart for grabbing her by the neck.

Why is this so hard?

I've never had this intense of a reaction. This intense desire to feed from a human.

Cinder's bucking hips erase the thought as she comes

underneath me, muttering the word please on repeat like a prayer.

She milks me so intensely, I know I'm finished.

Doing my best to keep the pace going, I pound into her, drawing out her orgasm even as I'm gripped by mine.

A strangled cry escapes me as I explode, shooting my cold desire into her.

I can't help but imagine her skin under my fangs, her blood rushing over my tongue. It must taste as smoky and sweet as she does. My hunger rages like a firestorm, threatening to consume me whole.

Cinder's eyes flutter open, still dizzy with the aftermath of our encounter. Her expression is soft and trusting. I don't know which is more responsible for it, finding the Ember of Midnight for her, or the sex.

I'm hit in the chest with a sledgehammer of unworthiness.

I'm scum.

I'm worthless.

I am not suited for responsibility or anything of importance.

And the only girl who can see through all my masks is looking at me like I matter.

CHAPTER 41

THE STARLIGHT TEA

CINDER

So I'm not bailing, like I planned. Somewhere between the studio, the Ember of Midnight, and coming on Prince Charming's way too talented mouth, I caved.

And now I sit stiffly beside Kai, at the Starlight Tea, my untouched teacup in front of me. And to make matters worse, my stepfamily holds court directly across from us.

At least the setting is picturesque, with the gardens surrounding us and exotic flora indigenous only to Midnight. But even in this beautiful vista, I can't relax.

Candelabras are lit all around, their flickering light caught by the diaphanous white curtains that serve as a partition. The chairs are plush and luxurious, but the seating arrangement is a cage.

If it were my friends gathered around the long tables instead of these fanged haters and my evil stepfamily, I could see this being a magical time. What girl doesn't enjoy a tea party?

I can't bring myself to stomach even a sip of what's in my china cup. I already know it will taste like bitter resentment and forced interactions.

The only reason I can handle being here now is Kai. He came over to my room in the middle of everyone dressing me beforehand, caught one look at my face, and ordered them all out.

Then he spent twenty minutes fucking the absolute sense out of me until I couldn't worry about what was to come.

How the fuck did he know I was knotted in so much anxiety it was making me sick?

Kaison took the edge off for me, but the longer I sit here, the higher my nerves begin to climb again.

Marisela is entrenched in conversation with the King, her purple-painted lips curving in a calculated smile. Anastasia keeps throwing Kai sultry looks from beneath lowered lashes, while Drusilla's unnerving stare darts between us, lingering on me just a bit too long each time.

I grip the table edge until my knuckles turn white, fighting the urge to bolt. Kai must sense my unease, because he reaches over and takes my hand in his, lacing our fingers together in a pointed display of unity.

It does little to deter his admirers. If anything, their giggling intensifies, their eyes sharpening with predatory interest. Apparently, being engaged to a human only makes the prince more desirable.

I'm just about to excuse myself, propriety be damned when a familiar approaches our table. The scent of cinnamon wafts through the air as he sets a plate down in front of me.

"What is that?" Anastasia wrinkles her nose in disgust, eyeing the offering like it's roadkill.

Kai leans back, slinging a casual arm behind me. "Humans are accustomed to cake with their tea, and my bride deserves the very best treats."

I glance down at the plate, my heartbeat stuttering. There, in all its golden glory, sits a generous slice of pumpkin spice cake.

In Midnight.

Shock ripples through the table, the other ladies aghast at the audacity of serving human food at their precious tea party. Even the ambassadors are not served food in the Midnight realm.

I barely register their horror rippling around me. I'm too busy staring at Kai, a silent question in my eyes.

He raises a brow in return, a ghost of a smirk playing at his lips.

You did this for me?

Of course. Don't you want it?

I swallow hard, my chest suddenly tight. As I reach for the fork with trembling fingers, I can feel every eye on me, waiting for me to make a spectacle of myself.

My eyes flutter shut in pure bliss as I take that first bite. The rich spices dance on my tongue, the moist cake practically melting in my mouth. I can't contain the soft moan that escapes me, lost in a moment of unadulterated pleasure.

When I open my eyes again, Kai is watching me intently, his gaze molten. There's a heat there that has nothing to do with the tea and everything to do with the way I savored that sinful bite.

I'm suddenly hyperaware of his arm brushing mine, of the way his fingertips draw idle patterns on my shoulder. The air between us feels charged, electric with unspoken desire.

"I didn't know you were so flexible to get your foot *there*," Kai husks into my ear.

I'm still busy enjoying the cake, but I say around a happy mouthful, "Put my foot where?"

Kai jerks so hard the entire table clanks, the China shuttering in outrage. He draws the attention of almost everyone.

His forehead scrunches up as he stares at Anastasia with accusation. My stepsister flutters her lashes at him coquettishly.

Oh.

Not *my* foot.

"Are you alright, Your Highness?" she asks Kaison with feigned concern. "Sometimes the outdoors can be so. . .agitating, would you like me to escort you indoors?"

I nearly choke on my cake.

I don't remember my stepsister being so transparent. Or dumb.

"I'm fine, thank you," Kaison grits out, his jaw clenched.

That's when Marisela's voice raises as if wanting everyone to be part of the conversation she's having with the King. "Indeed, if our prince is to marry, it is only right that he show his commitment to our traditions." My stepmother's tone is saccharine. "What would show our people that this is a true union is if this young couple went through with the marking."

Ice slides down my spine. The marking?

That doesn't sound good.

The King chimes in, his eyes glinting with malice. "Yes, the marking would indeed uphold the values and commitment to tradition and the Midnight fairy ways."

I turn to Kai, a question in my furrowed brow. But

before I can voice it, he squeezes my hand in warning, his face carefully blank.

Stay quiet for now, we'll talk later.

Marisela smiles at me, a cruel twist of her lips. "Why, it's only the highest honor, my dear."

Kaison's grip tightens, grounding me even as I feel danger pulsating all around me. "Surely you see how inappropriate that would be," he says, his words clipped. "She cannot leave a mark on me. Perhaps when she has acclimated more—"

"Nonsense." The King cuts him off, his tone brooking no argument. "The consummation of your union must be sealed by the marking. Marisela is absolutely right. It's paramount to unite the bloodlines and prevent. . .friction within the monarchy."

Silence falls like a heavy hammer.

But as I meet Kaison's gaze, I know whatever we'd just been committed to is not good.

"Are you going to tell me what the fae fucks we just agreed to?" I ask as soon as Kaison and I are out of earshot of the others. "What is the marking?"

He pulled me away, telling the others he needed a moment alone to impress me with the swath of Midnight roses. I can't focus on the full blooms of blackish-blue petals all around us that smell like a floral licorice.

I understood Kai's signal and kept my mouth shut, but I knew from his reaction we have a problem. A big problem.

"They want me to bite you." Kaison doesn't mince words, he simply comes out with it.

The voice disappears from my throat in a puff of smoke as the air squeezes out of my lungs.

Kai watches me carefully, letting me react, letting me travel back to the conversation and put it in context of the 'mark her, or this marriage won't happen.'

I'm trembling now, my heart rabbiting against my ribs. The thought of Kai's fangs piercing my skin, of being bound to him like that. . .it's too much.

"I—I can't." I force the words out despite having no breath.

Kai's face is flat, expressionless, which scares me even further. "I know."

My chest tightens. The flowers swirl and blend in a dizzying array of color. I can't breathe.

"Why?"

He takes a few steps away from me, caressing the head of a rose as he explains. "Midnight fairies mark each other with their bite mark—it's called the Seal of Amaranthe. No matter how much blood a Midnight fairy drinks, that scar does not disappear. It's a true signal of dedication, loyalty. Your stepmother and my father are trying to call our bluff." His fingers close, crushing the flower head in his grasp.

"Is there some supernatural binding to the bite?" I ask.

This sounds like mating.

I already know full well that weres have mates and it affects them physically to the point where if they break ties, it can mean death. I'm not sure what scares me more. Trusting Kaison to bite me and drink from me, or being bound to him beyond our deal?

Kai licks his lips slowly. "Not exactly. It means that. . ."

I don't know why he is hedging now. "What? Spit it out."

"It means that your blood will have power over me for the rest of my life."

"Power over *you*?" I ask.

Kai rips the flower head off the stem and throws it into the brush. "No other blood will ever taste as sweet as yours. It's like an addiction I'll always crave. Sex and blood."

"And the same goes for me?" I guess dryly, even as panic crawls up my throat, threatening to choke me from the inside out.

"I don't know," he shakes his head, expression tortured. "I don't know of any human who has been marked or what the effects would be."

Great. Fae fucking fabulous.

"I—I'll be right back," I stutter, backing away.

"Cinder," he says, trying to stop me.

I need space. I need to breathe. This is all spiraling out of my control.

Was it ever in my control?

I'm gone before he can stop me. I race through the gardens, headed toward the only place I can breathe. My eyes sting and my chest seizes, and I'm unable to catch my breath.

I only stop when I'm at the cliffside. Gasping for air, I curl my arms around my middle as the world threatens to tilt.

"I can't believe you came back."

My spine stiffens at the words.

Slowly turning, I find myself staring down the devil herself. Marisela.

My stepmother walks next to me and looks out over the crashing waves.

"I'd hoped you'd died," she says airily.

"Ditto," I say darkly.

A flash of a smile appears on her face before disappearing. "Yes, how strange to have such similar hopes and now to be in a helpful position for each other."

"Helpful?"

My skin crawls. Goosebumps rising up.

Would she throw me over the edge onto the jagged, deadly rocks below? I wouldn't put it past her. Hell, I was thinking of doing it.

Could I be like Kaison? I knew what she was. I knew the evil inside her. It could be so simple—just throw her over the edge and be done with my demon.

"Yes," she goes on as if murdering each other isn't imminent. "We need back into the good graces of the Midnight court, and you need to make it to your wedding. I believe we can have a mutually beneficial understanding. One that will lead us all to resuming a life as one big happy family." The smile she gives me is one I've seen far too many times. She lied to me for years, but I spent nearly as many learning to see past them to the ugly truth inside her.

"You mean the life where you help the King edge me out so your dearest darling daughter can take my place?"

Marisela's face tightens.

That's right you ol' bitch, you can't get anything past me anymore. I know what you are.

"Well, I can't say I tried." She tuts insincerely. "But since you also can see where this is headed, don't you think it's best you just leave now?" The threat lingers just below the surface.

I want to scream, pull her hair, cut her up into tiny little ribbons the way she did to me for years.

I thought she loved me. The way she brushed my hair in front of my father. The way she pretended to be concerned about my fitting in with the other children. The way she told me I was just like my dad in a way that made me warm to my toes.

My father died and the rug was pulled out from under me, and I never stopped falling. Not for years. Not until Goldie, Rap, Red, and the Poison Apple.

"I'm not going anywhere. I'm here to get justice for my father, and I won't leave until I get it."

Her smile flickers as one eye twitches. "You think your father was some saint? You think he was a good man? I may have married him to get on the fairy court, but I'm not the monster. He was."

She can't be fucking serious.

"You're as deluded as you are greedy."

"You wouldn't know," she hisses, her mask of decorum dropping like an anvil. "Not his precious Cinder who he doted on. Not his darling daughter who was better than everyone else. No, he never laid a hand on you. He never left bruises on your precious skin. He never left you a bloody pulp. It wasn't even the adultery that bothered me, at least that way he was taking it out on some other whore rather than me."

"You're insane." Whatever happened to Marisela in my absence, it really turned her brains to scrambled eggs to come up with these ridiculous victim stories.

"Insane? No. You think I only married your father to get close to the court? I have no qualms admitting I sought prestige, but he had his own agenda. Your father wanted so desperately to be one of us. He didn't want to remain a familiar, he wanted the King to turn him into one of us, a Midnight fairy."

"That's impossible," I scoff. "No one is turned vampire. You have to be born that way."

She sniffs. "Maybe, maybe not."

Oh dear fae lords.

It is possible?

She gives everything away. Familiars worked to get close to the vampires, but none were under the delusion they could be changed. But Marisela dropped her façade and she can't hide the truth.

My father knew he could be changed into one of them.

Holy witchtits.

Knots tighten in my belly.

"But your father was too useful to the King to be turned," she goes on in a disgusted tone. "He was the bridge to the human world and brought more obedient, willing familiars, more fresh blood to our lands than had ever been accomplished before. It's what made him truly valuable." Her face darkens. "It's also what made your father so angry. He'd made himself indispensable in such a way he could never become one of us. And he took it out on *me*."

I scoff. "Even if what you are saying is true, the idea he could hurt you is laughable."

Marisela is a vampire. He was a human. The power dynamic she's describing doesn't make sense.

Her face turns to stone with a seriousness I've never seen her exhibit before. Something else flickers underneath it and I can't believe what I'm seeing.

Fear.

"You think the only way to hurt someone is by biting them? You think he was disarmed because he didn't possess fangs? You couldn't be more wrong. The man could charm a snake out of its skin one moment, but then he'd fly into such a rage the next. The countless times he'd grab the nearest heavy object and take his fury out on me. . ." she trails off, as if drawn back into some horrific memory.

"You're a vampire," I reiterate, unable to indulge in her bullshit for even a moment. If she is going to lie, it should at least be a good one. Knowing what a nefarious schemer she is, I at least expect better on this front.

Marisela doesn't speak for a moment. "I am. And even the vampires know better than to invoke the thrall of the King. You displease his favorite familiar and it brings the wrath of King Charming, himself. I may have been physically stronger than your father, but I'm no match for our King. So I showed my strength by dragging myself off the floor, riddled in burn marks from those nasty cigarillos, bloodied and broken from the lamp he shattered over my head, from the dresser he'd push onto my body, drink some blood, heal, and pretend it never happened."

My teeth clench, the skin on my jaw threatening to snap. This conniving bitch. How dare she spew such bullshit from her mouth when she is the real monster. This is... this is all ridiculous.

My father would never. He was good. Unlike her. She's fucking delusional.

Every working cell in my body freezes as realization slams into me.

"You killed him."

My stepmother licks one fang, not blinking. "Can't say I had that particular pleasure, though I did have my suspicions someone else might have put an end to his miserable existence. And to be frank, I'd gladly cheer to their chalice of blood if I knew whoever it was."

That's it. I'm going to show her the wrath of a human. The way she callously makes up these lies about my dad who did nothing but serve this kingdom and give her what she wants.

My blood boils at the audacity of her words. How dare she slander my father's name, the man who had given everything for this kingdom and for her?

Without thinking, I lunge at her with murderous rage.

A strong arm wraps around my waist and pulls me back.

Kaison. His dark eyes are filled with concern and confusion.

"Cinder, what is going on?" His deep voice reverberates around me, causing me to take a hesitant step back. He stares back at me with an expression of confusion and detachment as if I'm a stranger to him.

He doesn't know me.

Maybe I don't even know me.

I wrench my wrist from his and turn and run, run like my life depends on it.

Tears blur my vision as I run from something that's dug its way under my skin. Her lies are enough to drop a seed under my skin, and it sprouts tiny little leaves.

No. No, my father was my everything. He was a good man.

A memory ignites. He had grabbed paint buckets and flung them at the art I'd thought was so pretty. His curses would flow in violent streams of Korean as he lashed out at the source of his frustration.

He was envious of the vampires, he wanted to be one of them. He'd lash out in anger if a canvas wasn't speaking to him. But he was an impassioned artist. That was just his thing.

He never turned that energy on me. So he would never turn it on anyone else.

Another sprig sprouts on my seed of doubt. Acidic bile shoots up my throat until I fear I might throw up.

Part of me wants to jump in my glass slippers and disappear back into the Common World, leaving all this ugliness and confusion behind. But I know that's not an option anymore.

More than ever, I have to find out who killed my father and why.

CHAPTER 42
BITING BACK THE TRUTH

CHARMING

"What happened? You almost pushed your stepmother off that cliff." I don't wait to follow her into her chambers.

I threw open the door to find Cinder already half-undressed. I drink in her pale moon skin and those perfect nipples that taste as sweet as the rest of her. My body responds instantly with a primal need, throbbing with desire and desperate for her touch. But I push aside my physical cravings, knowing that there are more important matters at hand. "If you did that. . ." I couldn't finish the sentence. Humans didn't kill fairies in Midnight. If she had done it, it would mean certain death.

There wouldn't even be a trial. With my father looking for any opening to rip this engagement apart, he wouldn't even have paused before thralling Cinder and putting her to death in some creatively fucked up manner.

Fear has me amped up to the max. She doesn't know how close she came to fucking dying tonight.

Cinder shakes her head.

"Tell me," I urge. Power expands in me. My vision turns clear and precise.

Tell me, Cinder. All my thoughts pinpoint on her, willing her to bend to me.

I whirl away, shutting my eyes tight, realizing I almost thralled her to find out what was wrong.

Fuck, she's got me turned inside out. Killing humans, kneeling before her, trying on women's shoes. . .

"I need you to bite me."

Her calm statement has me turning around. Cinder stands there, piercings back in, sans makeup. Her glossy black hair is wind-blown from being outside and her violet eyes are so clear, it makes it all the easier to see the storm raging underneath.

"Cinder." My words come out strangled. "No."

"You have to," she says taking a couple of steps forward. "You heard them. If you don't mark me then this whole thing is over."

She draws near and I catch sight of a strange fury in her eyes, as if she's possessed.

"We don't have to do this, Cinder. We can call off the engagement." I scrub a hand over my face, trying to ignore the physical effect she's having on me. This has all gone too far. The way her stepfamily affects her. . . it's painful to watch. Which is nothing compared to how she must feel being in forced proximity to them. I can't imagine having to be forced to fraternize after they turned her into a slave in her own home.

"No." She shakes her head. "I *have* to be here. My father

was drained by a vampire. I have to find out who did it. If we break it off, I'll never find out."

Sidling up to me, she pushes the strap of her dressing gown over her shoulder before tilting her head to the side. The long sinew of her neck is perfectly offered up to me and my mouth turns to cotton. Something primal pulsates inside me.

Feed.

Bite.

Fuck.

Claim.

My hands squeeze her arms, and I have to keep from using bruising force. The pressure in my chest is building so quickly, I fear my ribs will blow open in a matter of minutes.

Oh fuck. She's giving herself to me. If I bite her, everyone will always know she's mine. My balls tighten at the thought of seeing my teeth imprinted into her flesh as I fuck her.

My nose slides over her collarbone as I take a shuddering breath I don't need.

She's right. We need to do this for our engagement. And then after I take the throne from my father, she would still be mine. I'd be hers.

She doesn't have to mark me the same way. I'm already fucking hers, body and soul.

"I know you want it," she whispers in a ragged voice.

What she says stops me cold.

Underneath her words, there is resentment, or maybe disgust. It turns my stomach.

I release her so fast, she stumbles.

"Wh-what are you doing?" Her eyes turn round as the 'O' of her lips. She's dazed from my about-face. The gown strap dips, revealing a pert, pierced nipple. I swallow hard, ignoring her state of undress and my raging needs.

"I'll tell you what I'm *not* doing," I say with a cold stiffness that sets up in the core of my being. "I'm not going to let you think you are just some blood bag to me."

Cinder's eyes narrow and I know before she even opens her mouth she's about to hit below the belt. "You're afraid of yourself. Your own power. So instead you throw away all your real power and pretend you are this shallow well. That you've never had a real thought and you are only good for a fuck and a good time. Prove me wrong. Show me you can do this."

I try to laugh it off, but my face is tight and a weight presses down on my chest.

"I'm afraid of myself? Well, you're afraid of *everyone else*. You don't even trust your close personal friends. I can see that, so I bet they can too. How can they miss that you always hold a part of yourself back? No matter how much you love them, you are always waiting, expecting them to turn on you. You're waiting for them to let you down, betray you, leave you."

"You don't know anything about me," she hisses.

"No? I know you suffered inhuman torment and pain at the hands of monsters after your father died. That even before that you were so lonely you feared you'd cave in on yourself from the hollowness that loneliness carved out of your soul."

Was I talking about her anymore? Yes and no.

"But then you got out, and instead of fully living you protect yourself from inside the safety of a fragile, hollow shell."

Accusation and hurt glint in her eyes. "I am not fragile, and I'm not hollow." Her words come out in a ragged rasp.

I've hit the mark and she hates me for it. I don't blame her.

"Yes, you are and it's fae fucking beautiful. You say *I* pretend nothing bothers me? Well, we have that in common, my little black parade. You pretend nothing can get to you. But we are both two live nerve endings, so sensitive the slightest real touch hurts us so deeply, so ferociously, that we think we might die."

My lips hover over hers now. Our breaths mingle, though I have no true need to pant like I do. But she makes me feel like my heart is beating, like my blood could boil.

I'm laying everything I feel at her feet, and it feels like dying. Like jumping over the Midnight Cliffs, plummeting toward the waves of ice water crashing over jagged rocks that will gore me in moments.

In my head, one thing repeats over and over as I glare down into her flaming violet eyes.

Let me love you. Let me love you. Please, fuck, let me love you, Cinder.

"I'll never break you. Not even when you beg me too."

Even as I say it, I question if it's a lie. Could someone like me promise anything like that?

Fear fills her eyes as they search mine.

I take a step back, too affected by our proximity. "This started out as a transactional agreement, but you didn't know what you were agreeing to," I say coolly.

"Yes, I do." She sighs with exasperation, shooting me the purple death.

It's time she knows the truth. As much as I want her, she shouldn't trust me. I've done nothing to reward her trust. Rap is right. She needs to know I've held back secrets, that I've used her.

Then she'll give up this insane idea to go through with the marking.

"No, you don't. I didn't ask you to be my bride because I needed help fending off the husband hunters. While it certainly hasn't fucking hurt to be known as yours to keep them all off my backs, the true reason is I am using you. Using you to inspire the rebels to go through with a coup against my father. I want the Mice to bring down the crown."

I don't know if I'm trying to be honest or hurt her. I only care that this rattles her enough to give up the idea I need to bite her. No matter how much the larger part of me wants that—to claim her, to devour her, to make her mine for all of time.

That gives her pause. "That's insane, Kai. You are part of the crown."

She adjusts the strap, covering up again, thank fucking witchtits.

"I know," I say through gritted teeth. "But it has to be done. And the only way is to get the Mice to trust me by using you as a symbol, as a sign that I am to be trusted."

The stunned silence reverberates around me.

"Jack," she says. "You've been trying to convince Jack to get the Mice on board. He's one of them."

I nod my head, feeling defeated. "Yes. They think I'm a trap set out by the King. But you have been helping convince them I'm not like my father."

There. I've given up my dirty secrets and now she can hate me. Maybe she'll cut off this engagement and go back to the Common World. I'll figure out some other way to deal with my despotic father. The thought of her leaving tears me apart but I refuse to be the one to make her confront her worst fears. I won't be the cause of her pain and suffering.

Cinder sucks in a sharp breath. "Then let's do it. Let's show them."

That throws me.

"What?" I expected anger, outrage, another knee to the nuts maybe, but I didn't expect acceptance. "Aren't you pissed I lied to you?"

She shrugs. "We were both using each other, that was always the deal. The specifics are less important. Seems more like your business than mine."

It's as if an entire castle's worth of stone walls come slamming down. This Cinder has no feeling, no connection because she is a brick wall. And I fucking hate it. Just when I think I'd been disassembling the fae fucking thing, it's back up in my face.

"And now that you've unburdened yourself of this secret. . ." Her lips thin with determination. "Kai, we have to go through with this. The engagement can't continue unless you mark me."

"I don't give a flying fuck monkey. I'm not going to hurt you."

Why doesn't she get it? Why is she pushing me away? This is about more now, and I can't hurt her. I refuse to.

"If you don't do this, I can't find out who killed my father." Her tone is even but her violet eyes flash with fear.

"Maybe it's better you don't know. The deeper you dive into this, the more it crushes you. You should go home, Cinder. Forget all this. Work at the Poison Apple with your friends and leave Midnight in your past."

Leave me in your past.

She shakes her head. "I can't do that anymore. I need to know what happened. Marisela told me. . ." She nearly pulls her hair out as she paces to the bed and back. "She said all this crazy shit about my father abusing her. That he was a monster. Which has to be bullshit, but some of the things she said. . . the cigarillos." Then as if cutting off her stream of thought, she stops and stares up at me. "I'm going to find out the truth about who he was and why he was killed."

"Why?" My arms fly out. "Your father doesn't define who you are. It shouldn't fucking matter what he did or didn't do. He's dead, and you're alive."

She closes the space between us until her devastating scent wraps around me like a warm blanket.

"Kai, I need you to bite me." Her voice drops to a low, commanding tone.

You'd never know right now that I'm the one with royal authority.

Slender fingers skate up the back of my neck before her short nails scrape lightly against my scalp, pulling me to the crook of her neck. I inhale her deeply, my nose brushing along the soft pale skin of her neck again.

Underneath me, she shudders.

Oh fuck. I want it so bad. To sink my fangs into her, to let the blood that calls to me slide down my throat. I want to leave marks so that everyone knows she's mine. Every time she looks at it or closes a dog collar over the raised scars my teeth left, she'd know I possess her body and soul.

My hands curl around her impossibly tiny waist. So small, so fragile. So broken. But shattered into a hundred even more beautiful pieces I'd gladly cut myself on if I could hold them in my hand.

I'm fully shaking now. The bloodlust, the need for her roars to the surface, demanding.

Pierce her.

Drink her.

Mark her.

Fuck her.

So I do what I must.

I drop the softest kiss where her neck meets her shoulder before I step away, forcing her to let me go.

"No."

When I pull back, I see an expression that far exceeds the purple death. If she could incinerate me with her outrage, she would. In fact, I swear I almost smell something burning.

"Why?" Her question is a blend of pure agony and hatred.

I have to scare her off this idea. Off this entire endeavor. It's getting too dangerous. It's going to hurt her no matter what, I see that now. So I'll do what I never thought I'd do.

Show her the real me.

"Because I love you."

I close the door between us, locking it for good measure. My chest is in danger of caving in on itself, and I press a hand to it to brace myself.

There's a crash and then something shatters against the adjoining door.

For the first time, I realize neither of us are going to come out of this unscathed. I'd been a fool to think that taking the crown wouldn't create a body count. I just didn't count on it being like this.

CHAPTER 43

CORNERED BY PIRANHAS

CINDER

Another fucking ball.

Another fucking bullshit evening, and I can't even pretend I don't want to set fire to this entire castle.

Worst yet. I'm here by myself.

I was told by one of my royal dressers that the prince would not be attending tonight. He's "not feeling well."

It was a message.

This is over. You can't do this without me.

Well, Prince Charming can go fuck himself off a cliff and right in his own butthole. Because I'm tired of holding back on everything.

He said he loves me. Loves me!

I only wish I'd had time to go home to tell Goldie, Red, and Snow about his dick move.

If he thinks he can manipulate me with his so-called charm and woo me into doing whatever he wants, he's got another thing coming.

Because that's what it is. *A manipulation.*

He doesn't love me.

He can't.

We had an agreement and sure, we may be fucking, and the chemistry is blow-the-roof-off hot, and he's worked his ass off to make me comfortable and trust him even though he possesses a set of fangs as lethal as his pierced dick.

And okay, so he's helped me find the Ember of Midnight and shared gory personal details I don't think he's shared with anyone else while allowing me to do the same. But it's all a play.

He said it himself. He's using me to overthrow his father. To inspire the Mice to creep into the castle and take over.

That's all I am.

It feels as if my heart is on fire and I'm struggling to tamp down my feelings of anger, outrage, and. . . and. . . something else.

Something I do not want to admit, or even fucking consider.

That he means it? Or that I feel it too?

No. I have to focus on why I came here. And then I can cut ties to Midnight and all of Charming's bullshit.

I'm still equally suspicious of the King and Marisela. Despite what she said about not having killed my father, I can't trust her. And I certainly can't trust what she said about my dad.

She is the abuser.

I hate the way my stomach roils whenever I think about what she said.

"All alone this evening?" Anastasia asks. Drusilla is behind her. A head shorter than her sister, her dark plaited back hair is a perfect contrast to her blue dress. She stares at me with those colorless snake eyes with a hunger that makes my skin itch and gives me a need to get as far away as possible.

"The prince isn't feeling well," I say for the twentieth time in half an hour.

"I think I have an idea of what's making him sick," Anastasia smirks knowingly.

"Yes, well he thought it'd be rude to tell you to lay off that skunky perfume, so he chose the classier route of staying safe behind closed doors from your stench and bad attitude." The words flow easily off my tongue as I search the room for the Queen.

Maybe she knows more about my father. She's a resource I haven't used before. And without Kai protecting her from every interaction threatening her little world, maybe I can get something out of her.

"You little bitch," Anastasia hisses.

Drusilla's eyes dart back and forth between us with an anticipatory grin on her face. As if she's excited by the prospect of blood being spilled in front of her.

"Now now, is that any way to talk to your future Queen?" I ask, turning to look my older stepsister in the eye.

Anastasia is moments away from lunging at me and either tearing out my hair or my throat. I almost want her to do it. Let everyone witness what an uncontrolled animal she is.

Just like vamps detest the sight of red, they can't stand uncouth displays that are considered uncivilized. My presence alone has nearly pushed them past their limits.

"Ah Cinder," the half-elf ambassador calls out, coming to my side. "I wanted to ask you about your wedding attire. I know there is much pressure for you to adorn the black dress of a Midnight fairy, but I believe a white gown heralds the Common World values and would help cement this blending of cultures."

I can never remember his name, but I always wonder if it's a coincidence he smells like plums when his skin is a light hue of lavender up to his pointed ears. Either way, I let him lead me off to talk about the vapid details that somehow further his political agenda of pulling power and influence in not one, but two realms.

An hour later and I have to admit that as tough as I thought these gigs were before, without Kaison it's fucking excruciating. He takes so much of the social pressure off me while making me feel like I'm not alone.

When I spot the Queen, I catch her slipping from the ballroom. It's not unusual. She doesn't seem to have the stamina for these things either and often retires before the evening concludes. I decide to follow her, leaving the murmurs and music of the ballroom behind to head down a corridor. I don't see her, but I head toward where I know her chambers are.

When I turn the corner, I come face to face with Drusilla. Despite being a half-head shorter than me, the grin on her face would make the devil pee himself.

"I've missed you, sissy," she purrs like the predator she is.

I start to back away, feeling I've made a massive mistake.

"That makes one of us," Anastasia says from behind me, arms crossed barring the way. I could chip a couple of ice cubes off her face if I needed a cold drink.

"Y- you can't touch me here. They'll know. I'm engaged

to the prince." My words seem infantile to my own ears. Suddenly I'm that twelve-year-old trying to convince two vampires that they are sisters, friends even.

They did an excellent job of clearing up that notion back then.

"Why do they think that?" Anastasia asks, cocking her head to the side. "Is it because you dress like one of us, pig?" With that, she grabs the necklace at my throat and yanks.

My hands fly to the jewels that choke me instead of breaking.

"These should be *my* jewels," Anastasia says through gritted teeth. "This should be *my* dress. And he should be *my* fiancé."

"They dressed up the piggie," Drusilla says with a gleeful little clap. She was always the truly sadistic one. "Like a yummy bloody present to open." She grabs my sleeve and rips it away. It flutters to the ground which seems to send Drusilla into a frenzy. She grabs the other sleeve and rips that off too.

I can't stop her because I'm too busy trying to keep Anastasia from choking me, even as black dots appear in my vision.

Nails scratch at me. Someone pulls at my hair.

"Stop," I gasp.

"Aww, little piggie wants us to stop, Dru," Anastasia mocks. She shakes the necklace like a collar, and it cuts my throat. Fear flares like a supernova as I feel my blood slide down my neck.

Dru gasps in delight. "Let me bite the piggie."

"Not yet—" Anastasia says, but she never held any real sway over her younger sister.

Drusilla jumps on me. The necklace breaks against my throat sending Anastasia stumbling backward.

I slam to the ground, the breath knocked out of me so hard I lose my bearing for several seconds. A cold, thick tongue swipes up my throat as greedy fingers grip my hair to keep me in place.

"I forgot how good you tasted, piggie," Drusilla pants in my face.

Fear turns me ice cold. I know what happens next.

I'm desperate to disconnect from my body, to be anywhere but here. Just like I used to, I want to send myself elsewhere to colors and shapes in my mind where it's safe, so I feel no pain. But I've spent so much time being inside my body, letting Kai into it. I'm too grounded to let go.

Oh fuck, oh fae lords, I'm going to have to feel it all. Be agonizingly present while she tears into me. Tears slide out of the corners of my eyes and trickle into my ears.

If I were going to manifest those powers latent in my body, now would be a great time. I could use a fireball, the power to fly away, anything to save me.

Reearrrr! A pissed off feline yowl fills the hallway.

"Gah, get it off!" Drusilla jerks away from me.

A darting figure of black fur clambers over her. I scramble back, not wasting any time.

"Ana, get this beast off me," Dru screams as her sister flails uselessly at the offending creature.

Lucifer. Lucifer is attacking my stepsisters.

Between them and the cat, I'd bet on devil kitty any day. So I turn and fucking run. I slip at first but regain my bearing, determined to get as far away as fucking possible.

I don't get far before I slam into something solid. Two hands grip my shoulders, holding me still despite my struggle.

"Cinder. Cinder, it's me."

I look up and find Kaison, fully dressed to the nines. I

sag in relief as he holds me up. Fuck, I hate how much I need his strength, but I'm seconds from bursting into some very messy tears.

"You weren't going to come down tonight," I say, the words not making sense to my own ears.

"I couldn't stay away," he says with a lopsided smile that vanishes as he takes me in. "What happened? Your dress is torn. You're bleeding." With each observation, his tone tightens as his nostrils flare and his pupils visibly expand. Whatever effect my blood is having on him is over-powered by his concern.

I throw a look over my shoulder, trying to see if they followed me.

"Cinder," Kai gently takes my chin and directs me to look at him. "What the fuck happened. Who did this to you?" Darkness enters his face.

I should be afraid. I should be afraid of him for so many fucking reasons. And definitely still pissed off at him. But one night without him and it was too fucking much.

"My sisters," I whisper. Then I do what I never thought I'd do. I tell him the whole story. Clenching my eyes shut, it all pours out of me. "After my father died, I was no longer a family member, I became a servant. I served them by cleaning house, by trying to cater to their every whim. I kept thinking if I did a good job for a while they would accept me as a family member, that they were hurting too at the loss of my father. But then they. . ." I couldn't say it. I could feel myself go flat as I moved outside my own body. As if it was too much to stay in this meat bag.

Oh great. *Now? Now* I can detach from my body?

Where was this ability five minutes ago?

"They fed on you." Kai finishes my sentence with a snarl so hateful and brimming with wrath, it suddenly snaps me to awareness. I take in the way his muscles bunch and coil, from his shoulders and pecs, to the way veins now throb at his neck.

"It was a long time ago," I say, trying to keep the events far in the past. But they are here, I am here, and it feels like only yesterday their fangs tore into my flesh as they sucked the lifeblood out of me with uncaring savagery.

And it almost happened again just now.

To this day I can't figure who was worse—Anastasia, with her blatant hunger for power—power over me, power she gained from me—or Drusilla. Being younger, her fangs ripped and shredded my skin with a lack of precision. Like a tiny piranha out of its mind with bloodlust.

"The scars on your body," Kai whispers, almost to himself. "It wasn't rogue vampires. It was your family."

Then that rage disappears and it's as if his emotions have flatlined, like mine do all the time.

"I'm going to kill them." He turns on his heel and I'm too late in realizing he's not reacting like me at all. He hasn't detached. He's simply made a decision and now he must execute.

"Kai, no," I run after him, clawing at his arms, trying to hold him back, but I can't.

The entry hall is empty except for my stepmother and sisters and two thralled familiars helping them into their coats. Ana and Dru sport numerous visible and deep scratch marks on their faces from a certain devil cat.

"You," Kai snarls. "You three aren't going anywhere."

CHAPTER 44

THE POWER OF CHARM

CHARMING

"Y**ou hurt her. You fed on her, you fucking monsters. She was just a child." My accusations erupt in a torrent of rage.

Marisela's face contorts into a mask of fear and panic, her features frozen like a helpless animal backed into a corner. Then slowly, her muscles relax and the tension shifts to her calm and composed demeanor.

"What happens in my household is my business, Your Majesty." She drops into a slight curtsy, her eyes darkening with an ill-concealed sense of superiority as she gazes up at me through her long lashes. She thinks she has me.

She doesn't even try to deny it.

"Now if you'll excuse me, I must take my daughters home. They have apparently been attacked by some beast let loose in the castle," she sniffs.

"It was massive. It has to be some kind of monster from the forest," Anastasia cries. Dru only scowls with what appears to be disappointment.

There are no explicit rules against feeding on humans. It's one of the main reasons I want to dethrone my monstrous father.

"You think you can treat her like a blood bag? Why don't you see how it feels?"

My eyes lock on the woman who caged and fed on an innocent child. A fiery red blurs my vision, and my pupils expand, swallowing the whites of my eyes.

I rope in the sisters—who are just as guilty—until I know I have all three of them under my power. Thrall lassos around them, and a deep satisfaction blooms inside me as I watch them become as helpless as Cinder was.

"Feed on yourself."

My words come out with a monstrous intonation.

All three women bite into their own wrists, red dripping from where their fangs penetrate. Whimpers of pain escape all of them. Drusilla lets out a muffled scream.

I know what they suffer all too well. It's the worst pain any vampire can endure, a kind of self-imposed canni-balism that twists the guts up before a stabbing sensation relentlessly drills into the entire body.

Our blood howls, a tortured symphony of agony that courses from our fangs to our toes. The brain cannot escape any of it, held captive by something so wrong that it's captured entirely by the horror of it.

"Enough." Someone else's words cut through my thrall, releasing the women.

They drop into sobbing heaps.

No! I'm not done with them. They aren't finished reaping the rewards of their sins.

I turn to find Cinder blinking at me with either surprise or horror, but behind her is the one who broke my thrall, the King. His brows are furrowed and there is a dangerous glint in his eyes. I can practically feel the anger radiating from him as he takes a step towards me

He can try. But not before I kill these monsters.

"You can thrall," Cinder murmurs.

Her words break through my fury. Making her family repent can wait. I need to get her to safety.

"It's okay now," I assure her, taking a step to hold her in my arms. Cinder recoils, stopping me in my tracks. My arms drop.

"What's going on here?" More voices add to the din as people file out of the ballroom, with the ambassadors at the forefront. I watch my father's demeanor shift like a snake's, to appear levelheaded and cool though I know he wishes to punish me violently and without remorse.

"They attacked my bride," I snarl. "And it isn't the first time. But I guarantee it will be the last."

My chest and shoulders heave from the intensity coursing through my body. The women cry piteously, but I have no sympathy for them.

More chatter kicks up, mainly discontent from the ambassadors. My father's eyes slide over to them, calculating, measuring.

"This is unacceptable," the King finally says in a loud tone that causes the hallway to quiet. "We cannot stand this threat to the crown, to the relationships we are trying to build."

I can't believe it. My fucker of a father is using this moment to pander to the ambassadors.

"You three are despicable. We do not treat our familiars or allies with such callous, abusive regard. For this, you three are all banished from this kingdom. Stripped of all title, rank, and wealth. You are to live with the rogues on the outskirts."

Marisela's eyes roll up with a wild look, the whites nearly consuming her irises. "No, you can't." Her protest comes out with a desperate shriek.

"I can and it is done." My father says, staring at her with disgust he doesn't have to fake.

The ambassadors hum in approval around him, and I realize I may have inadvertently given him more power than he had before.

And if there's one thing I know, it's that the more power King Charming has, the more he abuses it.

CHAPTER 45

THE SUN ALSO BLEEDS

CINDER

I want to go home.

I'm going back to the Common World, and I might not come back. But I haven't had a moment alone since my stepfamily got banished.

I can't say it wasn't satisfying. Watching everything my stepmother ever wanted get ripped from her greedy, power-hungry hands. But I've had enough of the ugly side of Midnight.

However, I find myself escorted to my chambers by Kaison and the King himself.

"I am so very sorry for your misfortune this evening, Cinder," the King says, though the wheels of his brain seem to be spinning too fast to be that sincere. "But I am now seeing the benefits of your presence. I believe the best course of action is to move up the date of the wedding."

"I—I don't think I can." I feel numb and cold all over.

Kai shoots me a strange look. Is it hurt?

I'm too in my own emotions to parse his out.

371

"Nonsense," the King says, walking to my closet. "You simply have cold feet, but I know what will help with that." He pulls out my glass slippers and I practically choke.

Kaison goes deadly still.

Before either of us can react, the King sets them on the ground and stomps down, smashing them to bits. They are nothing but powder by the time he is done with them.

Shock and panic war for dominance within me. I can't catch my breath. I have no way home. No escape. The guards aren't going to let me waltz out of here and cross the border. I am truly a prisoner of King Charming. A scream builds but gets trapped in my throat, rubbing it raw with unexpressed anguish.

I want to lash out, to claw at the King's smug face, but I can't move. I'm frozen, paralyzed by the enormity of what's just happened.

"Get out," Kai says in a low tone.

The King regards his son with new appreciation. "Perhaps you aren't the disappointment I always thought you to be."

"Get the fuck out," Kai repeats, his gloved hands clenched tight.

The King merely chuckles. "You can keep your pet after all, my boy. Turns out there are many doors she can open I hadn't considered." With that he sweeps by and out of the room, the door shutting behind him.

Kai and I meet eyes. The intensity in his gaze sends a shiver down my spine. There's anger there, yes, but also something else. Something that makes my breath catch in my throat.

He swallows hard. "Cinder, I—"

"You can thrall." I state it as a fact. A terrible truth. You'd think I'd get used to facing them by now, but it still turns my stomach and prickles like needles at the nape of my neck.

"Yes, I can, but I almost never use it. Cinder, you can trust me. I promise I would never do anything to hurt you." He rambles, his words tripping over each other to assure me.

"Kai, I know."

"You. . . what?"

"I know you won't hurt me." The words come out almost defeated. Because despite everything, despite all logic and self-preservation, I do know. I feel it in my bones.

"You know," he says slowly, disbelief coloring his tone.

He sounds like a parrot, and I'd normally rib him for it, but I'm not in the mood.

"I know you won't hurt me because you love me."

It hangs in the air between us, heavy with implication. I see pain flash across his face, quickly masked but unmistakable. My heart constricts, aching for him, for us, for this impossible situation we've found ourselves in.

"And Kai?"

"Yeah?"

"I love you too."

The vulnerability of the confession terrifies me. But I can't hold it back any longer. Not when everything else has been stripped away.

We stare at each other. A beat passes between us. And then we cross the distance to collide in the middle, a mix of mouths and limbs. His cold is calming, soothing, reassuring, and I want to surround myself in it.

I meant it about leaving Midnight, but I planned to take Kai with me. One night without him, and everything turned to shit. Not just because my step-monsters attacked me, but because I wanted him by my side. I want those stupid fucking nicknames he doles out. I want to make sure he doesn't feel alone in a crowded room.

This time there aren't any games. My dress was already practically pulled apart at the seams, and Kai dismantles the rest. He's perfectly dressed, but I waste no time pulling off his coat, ripping off his shirt, and dragging my tongue up his abs.

"Fuck, Cinder," he hisses.

I need him, I need him so bad, I'm fucking molten between my legs. Still, I pull down his pants so I can take him into my mouth. The feel of his velvet flesh and cold piercings raking against my tongue and the roof of my mouth only drive me wilder. When I gag a little on his reverse Prince Albert, he lets out a feral groan, hands tangled in my hair.

"Please baby, please. . . fuck. . . let me taste you," he begs. He tugs my hair, gently pulling me away from his cock. With a sweep of his arm, he clears the dresser of all my little spooky pumpkin spice tchotchkes.

"Hey," I protest.

"I'll buy you more," he reassures me before pushing my knees apart and dropping down. Sliding two fingers into me, he attacks my clit with his mouth. A gasp slips from my lips, and I grip the edge of the dresser, rocking into him.

"Say it again," he mumbles into me, a raw vulnerability in his tone.

"I love you."

"With my name, say it with my name." He's desperate, a cross between a feral beast who is claiming me and a lost little boy who needs me to give him something he's never had before. And I can't help but give it to him.

"I love you, Kai."

Whatever he does next can only be described as supernatural. The speed at which he licks, sucks, and thrusts into me has me coming in seconds. I scream even as my nails dig into the wood.

I barely blink before I find myself on the bed.

"Been hiding your vampire speed much?" I ask breathlessly.

"What can I say? I've wanted to take my time with you." He covers my body and engulfs one of my breasts in his hand, squeezing and pinching me into a higher fervor.

"Fuck me, Kai," I tell him, grasping his shoulders.

"Thought you'd never ask, my unholy hottie." He gives me a lopsided grin that makes my heart skip two beats then somersault.

He slides into me and for the umpteenth time I'm overwhelmed by his girth, and the piercings I am now climbing with my cunt, pulling him into me. My blunt nails bite into his shoulders, trying to gain purchase as Prince Kaison fucking Charming claims me from the inside. All my parts. All of my black shriveled soul. All of my broken pieces and my ugly past. He wants it all.

And I want all of him.

"Cinder." My name escapes him in a pained, pleading moan. "I've never wanted anything, anyone more than you. I've always wanted you."

A bubble swells in my chest, creating a confusingly full pressure against my ribcage. If it pops, I'll explode in a gory mess.

His words penetrate the haze. "What?"

"I used to follow you to the cliffs. I'd watch you paint for hours and I wished you knew me. I wished we could be friends because I was certain you were the only one who would truly understand me. I loved the way your eyes got serious whenever you were lost in drawing. I used to wish you'd draw me."

Each vulnerable confession is punctuated by a long drive in and out of me, making it hard to focus.

Is this for real? The bright heat inside me swirls and tightens, pushing me toward a feeling that could shatter me.

"I think I've always loved you," he says. Fingers tangle in my hair, angling me to look at him.

"Kai," I arch my back, thrusting up into him, needing more. He's so deep, he fills me so much but it's not enough. "Bite me."

He stills. I want to squirm and force him to move again, but I hold his gaze.

"You said it can be good for me. I want to feel it. I want to feel it with you."

"I—" he swallows hard. "I can't do it without marking you."

Kaison clenches his jaw, attempting to hold onto his composure.

"Hey," I yank his hair a little to get his attention. He blinks and refocuses. "You already have."

With a surge of dominance, I flip us over, straddling Kai's hips as I take control. His fingers dig possessively into the flesh of my waist as I rise up and then sink down onto his thick length. A filthy moan rips out of me—I can't help it. Being so full of him this way hits different.

I ride him hard, chasing that high I'm desperately craving. Kai stares up at me with hungry, glazed eyes. Then he surges, crushing our bodies together as he piston-fucks up into me. My head drops back on a garbled cry, his hand fisting in my hair to hold me in place.

I tense, readying for that familiar pain as his fangs

pierce my flesh. But it never comes. Instead, the glide of his teeth into my throat is the most incredible fullness—like his mouth was crafted to fit the sensitive curves there. It's as if his bite was designed specifically for me, his fangs settling into the sleek divots of my flesh with bone-deep precision. It's so perfect, so right, like the final piece slotting into place after being empty for far too long. With his cock buried to the hilt and his fangs in my neck, I've never felt more deliciously complete.

Then Kai sucks, and every nerve ending in my body ignites with ecstasy.

My stomach tightens and I almost come right then.

"Oh fuck," I pant, my walls fluttering around him. "Oh fuck, it feels so good."

Like he can read my need to be even more full somehow, Kai shoves three fingers into my mouth, stretching my lips but not far enough to gag. I swirl my tongue around the digits shamelessly, savoring the taste of him mixed with the tang of my own desire.

He doesn't let up, driving up into me with relentless thrusts that leave me breathless and scrambled. I'm overwhelmed in the best way, stuffed full of Kai on every level—his cock demolishing me from the inside, his fangs embedded in my throat, his fingers dominating my mouth. Yet I still crave more of him.

Power unfurls within me, a searing wave of heat that blossoms from my core and spreads outward in scorching trails along my veins. It's as if molten gold has replaced my blood, pulsing in time with my thundering heartbeat.

The fire spreads upwards in searing trails until it spills over into Kai's mouth with every pull of his lips against my neck.

He moans around the wound, the vibrations resonating

through me as he clutches me closer like I'm made of precious fucking stardust. When he finally wrenches away, he's trembling hard, staring at me with a mix of awe and primal hunger.

"Cinder," he rasps, voice tight with an emotion that borders on reverence. "Oh fae lords. . . you taste like. . . like the sun."

He latches onto my throat again and the heat entwines us, surrounds us in glowing heat. Every nerve is alight in a storm of blistering ecstasy. We're fucking and ascending and boiling and nothing can be this good.

I didn't think we could get any closer than fucking but Kai is in my blood, in my heart, in my soul, and I want him there forever.

An ancient power roars through my veins, that eldritch force that's been shackled until this moment of complete surrender to Kai. The realization is staggering—for too long, I was the victim, the prisoner, the gutted little human. But not anymore. With this vampire between my legs, owning every cell of me. . . I become Death, the motherfucking ruler of a crimson empire that burns hotter than a thousand suns.

The orgasm detonates—a scorching supernova that rips me apart atom by atom with blinding intensity. I throw my head back on a scream so guttural, so earth-shattering that I feel it reverberate in my fucking fillings. My body suspends as waves of rapture crash relentlessly through me.

Kai isn't far behind, my volcanic walls milking that icy release straight from his balls. He lets out a sound so visceral that it shudders straight into the base of my spine. The clash of those frigid jets colliding with the magma in my veins only amplifies the high, dragging out each shattering pulse of ecstasy until I'm sobbing through it.

I've no concept of how long we remain locked in that elevated state, our energies crashing together in a continuous cosmic tempest. Time is meaningless when we're bound in this single, transcendent moment of fucking rapture.

I'm not sure how long it goes on before I find myself wrapped in Kai's arms, his tongue worshipfully lapping at the shallow punctures in my throat. "My dark goddess. . . fuck, so sweet. . . spice and sunlight. . ."

"Probably because of all the pumpkin spice," I say, still feeling lightheaded.

"Then we better keep you flush in the stuff," he says seriously.

CHAPTER 46
THE DAMSEL'S GREAT ESCAPE

CINDER

We lay there for a long time before the pillow talk comes. I never thought I was a cuddler or one for pillow talk, but with Kaison it's different. It's everything.

"I thought it was rogue vampires." He brushes my hair back from my face, before slowly skimming his fingers down my neck, gently caressing the bite marks he left. Shivers of delight run up my spine. "I thought you were attacked, maybe even left for dead when you left Midnight the first time."

I shake my head. "There were no rogue vampires. There were. . . dissidents."

"The Mice," he says, with understanding.

Right. The name of the rebel faction against the Midnight monarchy, but they operate so quietly most people aren't even sure they really exist.

And Kai is using me to inspire them to overthrow the King.

I still haven't fully wrapped my head around that one.

"I'll never let your stepmother or stepsisters hurt you again." The words are strained as if he's desperate to convince me of this fact. "They'll never step foot back in this kingdom, I promise you."

The corner of my mouth twitches and something releases in my chest. I believe him. They'll likely find their way to another fairy realm and make a new life, but they'll never climb up the ranks to what they were.

Would I prefer them dead and gone? Maybe.

But I almost feel letting them live in exile is more of a punishment. They were hungrier for power and status than they ever were for blood, so I know they are living their literal nightmare.

I do know I'm fucking relieved they will never bother me again. I'll never have to fear running into them or be forced to be in their presence. This assurance they are far away and miserable triggers a healing in me that I didn't know I needed.

"What *did* happen when you escaped?" Kaison stares at me so intently, I can almost feel him burrowing under my skin, slipping into my veins, infusing with my soul.

I swallow hard and avert my gaze.

"After my father died, my stepfamily showed their true colors. They didn't think of me as family. I was barely tolerated. I found it out right after the grand funeral."

The day had already been exhausting, devastating me more than I thought possible. I could at times still pretend that my father was in his studio caught up in his next painting and I'd turn the corner and there'd he be. But the funeral brought it all crashing down around me. I had to face my grief head on, in front of everyone, and there was no hiding from the truth anymore.

My father was dead. Truly dead.

I wished I was more like the placid faced prince who stood next to his father, dressed in ornate funerary garb. His expression was perfect parts distressed and reposed, while snot dribbled out of my nose as I unsuccessfully tried to stop the sobs wracking my body.

Only once did our eyes meet and I saw a familiar strange expression cross over the prince's face. A glimmer in his dark eyes betrayed a hidden emotion, maybe a mix of sympathy and concern? But just as quickly, it vanished behind a curtain of stoicism.

I remembered the words that accompanied this very same look the last time after he discouraged those boys to keep them from sinking their fangs into me. I knew it was a look of disgust. I was disgusting to him and everyone else.

If I knew then what I know now. . .

"As soon as we got home, they moved me out of my bedroom and stuck me in the servants' quarters. My room was locked from the outside. I was demoted to staff and forced to clean up after them. Scrub floors, wash windows, clean the fireplaces. They barely fed me better than a dog. And then. . ." I work around the lump in my throat. It's time to get it out. It's not like he doesn't already know the gist.

I just haven't said it out loud before. Not once.

Not even to Goldie and Red.

"My stepmother brought my stepsisters into my room, and they all took turns biting and drinking from me."

"Fae lords of hell," Kai whispers in equal measures of disbelief and rage.

I shut my eyes, suddenly right back there watching myself. "The pain was agonizing. My blood turned to rivers of ice as I was pierced and drained over and over. I screamed. I screamed a lot. I begged them to stop. I begged them to tell me why until my voice was gone. Once, Marisela flew into a rage and told me she despised me, that she despised being married to a filthy human just to gain entry to the Midnight Fairy Court. How the King was not treating her with the respect and deference she deserved. So I would feel her pain. I would give her girls the strength they needed to rise in the realm. As the years went on, I continued to clean and serve and act as a human blood bag. Eventually I learned to disassociate from the pain."

My throat turns dry as year-old pumpkin bread.

A cracking noise draws my attention, pulling me out of my memory. It was Kai's fist, flexing and releasing in that way I knew meant he was barely holding onto his self-control.

"Then after four years, I got my chance to escape. One night, after they'd fed on me, they forgot to lock the door when they left." The effort it took to stagger to my feet was nearly impossible, but I hadn't heard the click. The little click that signaled I'd be locked in my dark room until they needed me next.

When the door handle gave way under my hand, I almost couldn't believe it. I'd learned not to hope for a long time, but it turned over and the way out was clear. So I ran."

Okay, I didn't run, I had to brace myself against the walls and propel myself off them to get out of the house, barely feeling the thick cushion of Midnight grass under my feet as I pressed forward. Even though I was out, I wasn't sure I'd make it. They drained me of blood so many times that I'd become prone to passing out regularly. Later, I got a prognosis of anemia and iron supplements to help.

"I headed straight for the portal to the Common World. I knew it was the only way I'd be safe from my stepfamily."

"Did you have a plan when you got to the border?" Kai's tone is soft with gravel underneath.

I lick my lips and give a wry laugh. "Of course not. But turns out, I didn't need one. When I got to the border, the guards were completely preoccupied. They were under attack. Vampires and humans were crossing the border, trying to get out to the Common World. Or maybe they were trying to get in? I was too dizzy to really understand as I hid behind a tree. I watched everyone fight, occasionally some of them disappearing through the portal or coming through. So I did my best to find a window, then snuck past everyone, straight through to the other side. Nobody even saw me." My voice sounds small to my own ears now, and I realize my body is closing in on itself. As if I could shut down the feelings, the memories, the past.

"Hey, you're safe now." He tilts my chin up. "And I swear we'll get you back to the Common World, to your friends, to the Poison Apple."

"I like it when you talk like that."

Half his mouth curves. "Like what."

"Not I'll get you back, but we'll get me back. Like we are a team and we do things together."

Kai's half smile spreads into a full-on grin. "I'm not an idiot. I know I don't stand a chance without you. Honestly, I need you to save me." He covers his heart. "I'm so very often a damsel in distress yet no one comes to my rescue."

I smack a pillow in his face.

How can things feel so light, so right, when I'm fucking trapped by an evil King in another realm?

Sounds like one of the books Belle sells at Chapter Three.

"That being said," he adds. "I think it's time we maybe extend beyond our little team and get some outside help."

CHAPTER 47

THE RED ROOM

CINDER

Apparently Jack knows the ins and outs of the castle. Kai left a note behind a loose stone in the court-yard and only a couple of hours later, we're meeting with the mouse at the storeroom where the Ember of Midnight hangs.

Looking at the painting now causes a strange topsy-turvy feeling inside of me, like I don't know what to trust.

Though why I should trust an evil bitch like my step-mother over my memories doesn't make any sense.

"Can you help get her back to the Common World?" Kai asks.

"*Us*. Can you help *us* get back?" I correct.

Jack gives us a look as if he sees more than he should. "That will be tricky. Border patrol has doubled since the wedding announcement. Congrats on the pending nuptials, by the way."

He seems skeptical, as if ready for one of us, really me, to protest the event.

"Yeah, I'd prefer if it weren't at the hand of an insane, power-hungry King," I say dryly. "I would have preferred Vegas."

"Ohh with an Elvis impersonator?" Kai chimes in hopefully.

"Sure," I shrug. "Whatever blows your tits off."

Kai grins at Jack. "She treats me so well."

"And who is this?" I ask, when Jack is joined by a much larger man. He's as tall as he is rotund with a close-shaved beard.

"The familiar who broke the glasses when you were confronted with your family," Kaison says, a sly smile tilting his lips. "I knew I recognized you. I've seen you with Jack before."

The hefty human blushes as he tugs the green shirt which doesn't quite cover his large stomach. "I thought you needed a distraction."

"I've told you before," Jack says impatiently to Kai, "the Mice have eyes everywhere. Gus has been posing as a thrall for a while now."

I frown, taking a few steps to confront the impossibly large man. "You thought right." I push up onto my toes and kiss his cheek in thanks. The pink tint of Gus's cheeks turns into a full-on tomato red.

"Hey now," Jack says, running his arm through Gus's with a possessive scowl. "Don't be trying to seduce my man."

Kai's brows shoot up in surprise. "Your man?"

"Didn't know you were such a homophobe," I say, addressing Kai's shocked reaction.

Kai sends a scathing glare my way. "I'm *surprised* because I didn't know there were more human/vampire pairings." Then in the most mature Kai fashion, he sticks his tongue out at me.

I'm tempted to snatch it and hold it.

"Wow," Jack says to Gus, "They aren't what you said they were. They are so much worse."

"Hey," both Kai and I say in protest at the same time.

"As fun as this is," impatience tinges Jack's voice, "we need to tell you what we found about that night. We know what they were arguing about."

"Something called the Red Room."

Kai stiffens, his back turning ramrod straight.

"What? What's the Red Room?" I ask him.

Jack and Gus wait for him to answer as well, but Kai turns to pace away from us before coming back. He runs an agitated hand through his hair.

"And why would there be a place called the Red Room when vampires consider red to be so vulgar?" I throw in for good measure.

"That's a PR statement," Jack answers this time. "We don't consider it vulgar, it's ah. . . how do I explain this." He pinches the bridge of his nose. "It's basically a massive aphrodisiac to us. We see red, we want blood. It makes us lose control."

"Kai, what is it?" I push again.

"It's. . . it's a place where vampires take familiars they want to play with," he says hesitantly.

"What?" I ask the question though I don't really want to hear more.

"It's a space reserved for the Midnight court to play and feed on beaters. The beaters don't usually walk back out."

My gorge rises. He's describing a torture and kill room.

"Repulsive," Jack says, spitting off to the side before his

voice raises in outrage. "Treating humans like they are cattle, playthings, like—"

Gus grabs his hand, silencing Jack.

"Do we know what was said?" Kai asks.

"Byung-He and the King were discussing the beaters for the Red Room. It was a disagreement about which ones would go in and which ones wouldn't."

"Who usually goes in?"

Kai clenches a fist. "Thralled familiars."

"And no one fucking knows about this?" Gus asks his pitch a little higher than before.

Kai shakes his head. "My father is careful. If he sent a familiar in there, he'd have to make sure they fit a certain profile. No family, no friends, no connections. If they disappeared, they couldn't be missed."

"You know this for sure," I ask, not liking the slithery, sliding feeling in my gut.

Kai shakes his head. "No, but it's my best guess."

"You think like him," I say, not liking it the moment it's out of my mouth.

His nose wrinkles with dark disgust. "My father sent me to the Red Room when I was fifteen. Telling me I wasn't a man until I knew how to feed and fuck."

Just when I think the King's cruelty and disregard for his son tops out, he outdoes himself again.

"I didn't do it," he says, looking at me in earnest. "I shut my eyes." The look he gives me is half pleading, half probing. As if he's desperate for me to believe him. Then a dry smirk lifts his lips. "I cemented his belief that day that I would always be a disappointment."

"I believe you," I say.

Kai lets out a breath. This time when he runs a hand through his hair, I spot a tremor. "It's still only one of the hundred reasons why we need to get him off the fucking throne."

"No shit," Jack says.

Kai perks up at that. "So you'll do it. The Mice will help?"

"Can you actually help?" I can't help but add.

Jack speaks in a low voice, "The Mice grow stronger each day. We recruit more members, gather weapons, and learn of the King's weaknesses. We are not just rebels, but an organized resistance."

Gus nods with pride, his eyes shining. "We have waited for the perfect moment to strike. Your engagement to Cinder truly has provided us with that opportunity. The people are ready for change, and with our numbers, we can finally overthrow King Valdor."

Jack gives Gus a meaningful look that makes my heart feel too big. "We're in."

"All of us," Gus adds as he entwines his fingers with Jack's.

The door cracks open and hot staticky panic explodes in my chest.

Someone is about to walk in on our secret meeting with members of the rebel faction.

We are royally fucked.

CHAPTER 48
THESE BOOTS ARE MADE FOR WALKING

CINDER

The door swings open and in sashays the Fairy Godmother herself, Dame Kiki Eleganza, resplendent in her signature powder blue and glitter. Her cream-colored wig is teased to new heights and her heels could beat up my combat boots in a fight.

"Well well, if it isn't the happily engaged couple," she drawls, one perfectly arched brow lifting in amusement.

"Not that I don't appreciate the surprise visit," I say, "but how the hell did you get in here? The King has this place locked down tighter than a hipster's skinny jeans."

Kiki waves a dismissive hand. "Please, child. I've been sneaking into castles since before you were a twinkle in your daddy's eye. Speaking of. . ." Her gaze turns shrewd. "I hear you've been cooking up quite the magical storm lately."

My brow furrows. "What are you talking about?"

"Oh don't play coy with me, Cinder. You think I can't sense when a fellow sister is coming into her power?" Kiki

393

stalks closer, her heels clicking ominously against the stone. "You've been tapping into something ancient, primal. Something in your. . ." she pauses for dramatic effect, "...blood."

I swallow hard, my mind racing. Is she talking about my strange reaction to Kai's bite? The searing heat that flooded my veins, the way it felt like being bathed in sunshine.

"I can only imagine it has to do with prince studly over here." She jerks her head toward Kai, who looks equally mystified.

"Me? What did I do?"

"Made her feel safe," Kiki says simply.

Her words are a gut punch.

The Fairy Godmother is right. With patience, a sense of humor, some ass kickings and a pocketful of marshmallows, I feel safer than I ever remember. I'm pretty sure the rope played a big part too. . .

But regardless, I've always been a little detached, a little floaty, keeping my distance from my friends, the world, hell, myself. Inch by inch, Kai reeled me into my own body giving me experiences it was worth being present for.

Maybe becoming grounded was the bridge to coming into power.

Not that I'm sure how to harness the power of blood that tastes like sunshine. . . Sounds a bit like a lame hand I've been dealt, but I've got more important things to worry about.

"So she's a witch?" Kai asks. "*Oof.*"

Kiki smacks him with a closed fan in the gut. "That's an outdated term, princey-pie. We call wielders of magic mages, and yes. I imagine Cinder is a mage at a level commensurate with that of her friends."

"You're here because I'm a super powerful mage?" I ask, feeling a bit of whiplash from the last twenty-four hours.

"No, honey," she draws out. "I'm here for your wedding. I got this, what would you call it, sixth sense you might need some friends now. And maybe a new pair of shoes." With a snap of her fingers, Dame Kiki summons a pair of boots from thin air.

They're glossy onyx black, studded with gleaming silver spikes and with platform heels that kill. Deadly and delicious.

My heart skips a beat.

"To replace those glass, shank traps I had you in," she says with a wink. "These beauties will let you come and go from this pretty palace as you please. Because if you are going to get married, you'll need to assemble your wedding party."

"My wedding party?"

"Your maidens, your posse, your squad. Every Queen needs her court. And honey, it's time to rally yours."

"It's going to be difficult for anyone to shove their foot into that tiny devil boot to transport," Kai points out.

The Fairy Godmother turns to him with a skeptical look. "What do you mean shove their foot in the shoes? Only Cinder needs to wear them. If she wants to bring a boo, they only need to hold hands with her and they'll travel with her just fine. Hell, she could make a daisy chain and they'd all make it with her." Her expression smooths with surprise as Kaison's face blanches. "Have you been sticking your big man foot in one of her shoes to travel back and forth? Sweet baby ogres, did you cut off your toes to get that honking thing in there?" She gestures to his feet.

Kaison mumbles something about nearly becoming an amputee and it would have been nice to know earlier.

"Yes well, stop that," Kiki barks before turning back to me. There's a glint in her eyes as Kiki presses the boots into my hands. "It's time to show Midnight what happens when you mess with the Lost Girls."

As I clutch the boots to my chest, I feel a new resolve taking root. Kiki is right. I'm done being a passive prisoner, a pawn in this twisted game.

I am Cinder Park. Goth Queen. Mistress of my own fate.

And I'm ready to raise some hell.

CHAPTER 49
MY RED WEDDING

CHARMING

The day of the wedding comes all too soon, and my bride-to-be has spent the entire day being prepared.

My father assures me that the Red Room has been readied for me. I'm a man today and I should feed and fuck before my wedding night. After all, we need Cinder alive now. She's great for public relations.

For now anyway.

Fucker.

The grand hall is resplendent, decked out in the royal indigos and silvers of the Midnight court, yet there is an undercurrent of unease rippling through the gathered crowd. Anticipation and disdain create a heady atmosphere, yet I'm oddly calm.

I stand tall at the altar, my posture impeccable, my expression carefully schooled. This is it. The moment that will make or break not just my future, but the future of the entire Midnight realm.

The doors swing open, and a collective gasp rises from the assembly.

It's not Cinder who walks down the aisle.

It's another human.

Goldie is a bombshell in a bubblegum-pink leather sheath, her blonde curls tamed into a messy updo. On her arm is her large, bearded beau who has somehow managed to cram his bulk in a suit.

Then comes Red, fierce in a corseted silver gown, her arm linked with her werewolf mate. In a suit, Brexley is a slick lethal force to contend with.

If I weren't so secure in my own masculine power, I might be threatened by the men in the bridal party, but I have way more appreciation for their Moxy to show up in style. I've always had an affinity for a well-dressed man.

Next comes Snow. She's an ice princess in frosted blue, her silver-white braids woven through with delicate chains. Rap is her escort, mohawk higher than ever, her heavy black eye shadow and scowl ever intact. I'm a little surprised to find the bar owner in soft pinks and purples.

All the women wear spiked dog collars and both Ted and Brexley sport smoky eyeliner and black painted nails.

The mutterings of the crowd grow with discontent. They came for a traditional royal Midnight wedding. Instead, humans and fae make their way down in nontraditional pops of color with goth accents.

"Is this your doing?" I hear from my side.

"Why yes, father. Cinder wanted to make this soiree her own and who am I to deny my bride her bridal party or the wedding of her dreams?"

The ambassadors seem to be the ones enjoying the spectacle, humming and nudging each other in the ribs as if they are witnessing celebrities come down the way.

Which means my father's hands are tied. The PR stunt is doing its job. And soon Midnight will be known as a beacon of power and strength because we have ties to the Common World.

I try to suppress my chuckle when I catch my mother touching her own neck almost wistfully as if she too wishes she'd been supplied a collar of her own.

I always knew she was a rebel.

Then the crowd hushes and the orchestra takes a back seat to the strings section as they perform "Paint it Black" by The Rolling Stones.

I crane my neck, eager for my first glimpse of my bride, and the breath leaves my lungs in a dizzying rush.

A spiked platform boot steps onto the cerulean carpet.

The gasps of shock and cries of outrage ripple through the room with a vengeance.

Cinder is a vision in red.

Her dress is a deep, blood-red masterpiece adorned with intricate black lace and beading that catches the light and shimmers with a dark allure. The strapless bodice, with its plunging neckline and detailed embroidery, highlights her slender frame and the soft curves of her shoulders, while the voluminous skirt cascades around her in a wave of luxurious fabric.

The gown is lifted at the front, so her footwear remains on display.

My bride's choice to wear red on the day of our wedding is nothing short of scandalous. The entire ensemble is a visual riot, a direct affront to the Midnight Kingdom's decorum. The deep crimson hues flicker and dance with each step she takes, causing whispers of outrage to ripple through the crowd.

Even her lips are a glossy cherry red. The choice is

nothing less than a disgrace, and I have never loved her more.

I take the time to shrug off my jacket before turning it inside out. I adjust the high collar, proud to now match her dress.

Though he says nothing, I sense my father's displeasure ratchet higher.

Cinder is led by the Fairy Godmother who sticks to light blues, her wig a towering confection of ocean-colored curls.

Cinder's bridal party assembles up front, the gentlemen taking their places in a line by me, including Rap. Cinder's Lost Girls, her chosen family.

They are a force to be reckoned with, these women. Powerful, passionate, loyal to the bone. And they are here for her. For us.

As Cinder glides down the aisle, the rubies at her throat catch the light, scattering sanguine flecks across her collarbones. She is a dark enchantress, and I am aroused in every possible way.

"At least you had the decency to mark her," my father hisses at me.

The necklace perfectly frames my bite marks which tells everyone here that this girl is mine.

I take her hand as she reaches me, marveling at the heat of her skin. She seems ready to catch fire. Despite her broadcasting that fantastic fuck you to everyone that I so love, I can tell her nerves are rattling underneath. I give her a squeeze to let her know I'm here.

The wedding begins with an officiant chosen by my father.

"In the eternal darkness of Midnight, we are gathered here today to witness the union of Cinder Soo-Yen Park and his highness, Prince Kaison Qing Constantine Minghao Wei Ambrose Jiayi Ignatius Charming.

Cinder mouths at me, *Ignatius? Really?*

I give her hand an extra squeeze and make a face at her.

"Prince Kaison, do you take Cinder to be your lawfully wedded wife, to have and to hold, to bite and to cherish, from this night forward, till death do you part?"

"I do," I reply. "But I also take an oath to lead Midnight into a new era of equality and justice."

"What are you doing?" my father demands in a low voice, rising from his throne behind the officiant.

If things hadn't been shaken up before, things are busting wide open now.

My gaze locks with my father's, unflinching, resolute. "The old ways must die," I continue. "The time for change is upon us."

I raise our joined hands, my voice ringing out through the cavernous hall. "Today marks a new chapter for Midnight," I declare, my tone sharp, commanding. "A new era of unity, of equality, of progress."

The King's face contorts with fury. "You disappointing little bastard," he roars, spittle flying from his thin lips. "You presume too much. I will never yield my crown to a mewling pup and his mortal whore."

Cinder's hand tightens in mine.

"You have no choice, father." My words are icy, laced with a calm certainty that belies the fear running rampant through me. "The people have spoken. Your reign of terror and oppression ends today."

The doors at the back of the hall fly open once more. Figures pour into the room, a tide of righteous fury clad in the patchwork motley of the rebel faction known as the Mice. They surge forward, eyes blazing, weapons glinting.

Screams erupt from the crowd as panic descends.

THEY DON'T CALL HIM CHARMING FOR NOTHING

CINDER

Kai jerks me out of the way, forcing me to flee. Not that I want to face down a very angry King Valdor Charming, but he's not the only one to worry about.

Half the court surges to fight off the Mice, a mix of humans and vampires, while another portion targets us.

Thankfully, we brought reinforcements.

Brexley easily breaks the faces of several fairies, putting them down, hard. Ted bowls through the ones standing in our way like a human wrecking ball. Not that my girls are any less active.

Red has picked up one of the guest chairs and wails on a guy. Snow miraculously procures several daggers that are all poised between each knuckle. Judging by the reaction of one of the recipients of her daggers, the way they scream and carry on, I easily guess they are made of silver.

There is a lot I still don't know about my roommate, I realize.

A woman screams as she flies by me. I turn to the right to find Rap dusting off her hands.

"Way to go, boss!" Goldie says with a fist pump. She's more a lover, not a fighter but refused to be left behind just because she's better at moral support.

The Fairy Godmother whips out a magic wand and starts turning vampires into toads. Each one leaps and croaks in a fearful frenzy as they shrink and turn green.

"Enough," a voice booms.

Something ripples over my skin, a power that triggers my basest sense of flight or fight. Mainly the flight. My bones would escape my skin if they could and run for the hills.

Things turn almost quiet. The Mice and vampires are still fighting down the way but all of my friends are frozen in place. I grab Kai's hand and pull, but he doesn't move.

I tug harder, but when I turn, I see Kai is under the same power as all the others.

Thrall.

King Valdor Charming takes the steps down the dais with a lazy pace, a sneer on his face. "Bite yourself."

I turn to see Kai's hand rise to his mouth, his movements rigid and mechanical. With a sharp flick of his wrist, his fangs slice through his own skin, spilling scarlet blood down his arm in winding streams. The crimson droplets splatter against the ground with a haunting rhythm.

Kai's muffled scream is that of an animal beyond reason or thought, only one enduring unrelenting torture. His face is twisted in agony, every muscle contorted in torment.

"Stop," I scream, even as I run to Kai and try to pull his arm away. I continue to scream and pull, but Kai is unmovable as he is forced to inflict agony on him.

"Enough," comes another command.

At last, Kai lets go with a ragged breath, but Kai doesn't move again. Wetness streams from the corners of his eyes. His eyes plead with me to run even though he's stuck where he stands.

"Interesting," the king muses, sight trained on me. "Seems you are resistant to my thrall, but no matter."

I turn to face the monster as anger and fear flicker inside me in long hot snapping whips.

I also don't know why he can't thrall me. Maybe my powers do have more punch than I gave them credit for. I step in front of Kai, protecting him with my body though I know there is little I can do. I'm desperate to get Kai to safety.

"You killed my father."

A scoff erupts from the merciless King. "Is that what all this is about?" Then he turns serious, his beady eyes glinting with malice. "I hate to disappoint you, but you have completely missed the mark. But I shouldn't expect anything less from a weak-minded, insipid human. No, Cinder. I did not kill your father, as I've said before."

"You fought the day he died. It was about the Red Room." Why won't he give up the truth? Why won't he confess? He seems to have no problem confessing to his other sins and cruelties.

Valdor's jaw clicks as he levels me with a cool look. The tension in the air is palpable, his gaze piercing and calculating as he sizes me up.

"*That* I can attest to. We did argue." He pauses as if debating whether he should continue, but then he seems to throw restraint to the wind. "When he was instructed to bring in. . . younger blood, your father balked." A sneer curls up his piteous mustache. "No children, he said. He'd no problem selling out any person from his homeland, but he dug his heels in at adhering to a certain age. But many of our court members had specific tastes that needed to be appeased. I tried to tell him, it may even be better for the young ones since they don't usually understand what's going on anyway."

Dear witchtitting fae lords.

The King wanted to slave out children and my father said no.

"I can only imagine his devotion to you had something to do with his sudden scruples." The King rubs his thumb along his fingers with evident distaste.

Nausea crawls up my throat even as he comes to stand in front of me. I reach back and hold onto Kai's frozen hand.

I won't let him hurt you again, I promise silently.

"Perhaps if he lived longer, it might even have resulted in a falling out in which case, yes it would have been necessary for me to dispose of him," the King mused as if he were debating what outfit he would pick out for a future event. "But your father was highly valuable in bringing an influx of familiars to our gates. And for a human, I can honestly say I considered him a friend." Affection crosses his eyes.

I'm starting to realize my father could only earn the esteem of such a monster for a reason. He had to be a bit of a monster himself.

"So no Cinder, I didn't kill your father. In fact, what little deference I've given you is only because of him. But you aren't a child anymore, and your father's graces have now expired." Those tufty brows draw down over his eyes. "I should have done this a long time ago."

Valdor grabs me with surprising strength and whips me around so I'm facing Kai. I struggle but it's no use. King Charming's fangs rip into my throat. White-hot pain explodes through me as my blood gushes into his eager mouth. I try to cry out, but only a choked gurgle escapes. My vision blurs, darkness creeping in at the edges. The King savagely drinks from me like an animal, ripping flesh, going deeper than is right. Blood pumps out of me, drenching my shoulder, splashing down my dress. The pain screams where I am unable to.

I try to fight back, but Valdor's hold is unbreakable. My body convulses with agony while Kai watches on, his eyes blazing with helpless rage and torment. His dark orbs are glassy, fingers twitching in their menacing poise to attack his own father to protect me.

I am trapped in this nightmare, unable to escape or defend myself. With each passing second, I feel my life force draining away, cooling on my skin and clothes.

The familiar instinct to separate myself from my body, the pain, the horrific reality knocks at my brain, insisting it's time. Time to detach from what's happening.

If I do it, I know it will be for the last time.

But I can't this time. Something is keeping me here, in my body, in the pain. Not something, *someone.*

Kai.

His face contorts with anguish, eyes wide and trembling. We are both held captive in the moment.

Pain is always something I've suffered alone, but not now. My pain is his and I can't leave him with my pain while I step out of my body and go somewhere else.

I don't want to leave him alone like that.

So I ground myself in my body, forcing myself to endure the pain and horror of my life pumping out of my throat just so I can look in Kai's eyes, and let him know I'm with him. I'll be with him until the last.

My body should be cooling, weakening.

Instead, an internal heat kicks up at my core like a

generator being turned on. It thrums and throbs through my veins even as I hemorrhage and I swear I can feel the path of my blood entering the King's mouth, swirling down his throat and hitting his stomach.

I'm dying. I know it. Fatigue and pain crash over me as if I've run a hundred miles, but that internal power flows through me even as my heart slows.

The King releases me and I drop to the floor like a sack of potatoes, my head spiking with pain and fuzziness. Kai's face turns blurry. I'm losing him. It's a knife through my heart. I don't want to leave him. I want to be with him.

I don't want to go like this.

I'm not ready.

King Charming gasps as he stumbles back a few steps, and I can vaguely make him out.

The magic cookie I ate, along with my righteous vengeance unleashes a cataclysmic force within me. The sheer magnitude of this power terrifies me, but I don't fight it.

The rage I've tamped down. The pain, the injustice. It flows through my blood, even the blood outside my body. It heats over my bare shoulders, collarbone, and dress. I can feel the King's blood boiling within him, connected to mine in an intense shared heat.

He spent his life controlling others, and I can't stand it. The bruises and breaks in Kai's body. Those familiars who survived his wrath and those who didn't.

"Wh-what?" The King sputters and looks at his own hands. They are covered in my blood and like that mess on his mouth, they are smoking with heat. Just like my blood is now doing in his body.

"No—" he chokes off.

I can end this. I have the power. My rage. Fueled by my

last bit of my life, I try to stare the King in the eyes though I can barely make him out.

His veins light up as if lava runs through them. He sizzles and screams as steam and sparks sizzle through and off his skin, floating into the air around him.

He doesn't stop screaming even as his hands blacken to ash, as his jaw disintegrates in a burning mass before falling off his face altogether. The fire blazes hotter as I burn him with my blood magic.

In the midst of the scorching chaos, I sense a thin silver tether connecting him to all of my friends. Tethers as delicate as fishing line yet strong as steel. With a slicing power of my own, I cut the connection he has to them.

The pain and agony are almost sweet as I exert my power over his body until he completely crumbles into a smoking pile of ash.

All my strength leaves me in one sharp exhale and I collapse, gasping for air that never seems to come.

I always feared I'd die at the fangs of a vampire. But now Kai and the others will be safe from King Charming's thrall.

CHAPTER 51

BITING EVER AFTER

CHARMING

Whatever nightmares my father has visited on me through my life, they all pale in comparison to watching him rip Cinder's throat out in front of me while I'm helpless, unable to do to a fae fucking thing about it. My mouth and voice are frozen in place, but inside I'm screaming as she bleeds. As he feeds.

Murderous rage pumps through me in a way I've never known before.

Agonizing pain and despair rip through me like a pack of howling wolves.

Not her. *Not her.*

I promised I'd keep her safe.

Fuck everyone else. I'd hand over every last human and fae to my father to save her.

My body strains uselessly against the thrall as her violet eyes lose focus and she drops to the ground.

No.

Fucking no.

I can't lose her.

I won't lose her.

Then my father begins to smoke and burn. Wonder pierces the rage and fear as I realize it's her blood.

While I felt the sun from the inside out, her heat is burning my father alive. And he won't survive.

The unquenchable hunger of a monster overtakes me as I revel in watching my father scream in agonizing pain until he is no more.

The second my father is dead, his thrall breaks and I'm instantly by Cinder's side, lifting her into my arms. "No, no, no, come on. Come on, stay with me." Tears clog my throat and fall onto her face which has gone ashen and gray.

"Oh fae lords, there's so much blood," a small voice says from behind me somewhere. Maybe Goldie.

"Can't you do something?" Brexley asks.

"I'm sorry honey," the Fairy Godmother replies. "This amount of healing is beyond me."

"Cinder, stay with me," I beg.

After some effort her violet eyes find mine. They are dazed, as if she's already lost touch with where she is, who I am. Who we are to each other. Her essence is already detaching from her body, preparing to leave for good.

"Please don't leave me," I beg. "I can't live without you."

But I will. I'll be here. For centuries. Without Cinder.

I can't fucking stand the thought.

I need her to speak. To say something cutting or snarky, but her throat is ravaged as are her vocal cords.

My body shudders with wracking sobs. Anger and fear crack my heart in my chest and I'm sure I'm about to die alongside her.

You are weak. Men don't cry. You are a disgrace.

The words of my father hammer into me, but they can't hurt me anymore. She's worth being weak for. She always was.

None of this was worth it.

"I shouldn't have involved you," I blubber. "I should have kept you in the Common World where it was safe. Forced you to stay there. Far away from Midnight."

I am what everyone says I am. Selfish. I should have let her go, but I wanted her with me. And now she's paying the price.

I'm paying too, punished for my greedy idiocy.

Cinder's eyelids flutter as her muscles relax. She has moments left.

A calm settles over me.

Things won't end like this.

She's my happily ever after.

I'll prove everyone right.

I am a selfish, impulsive son of a bitch, so it's time I act like it. Even if that means doing the forbidden.

I bite into my wrist and push it to her lips. "Drink."

She's too weak, she's fading.

In a last, desperate attempt, I gather every ounce of my power and focus it on Cinder. Pupils dilating, all the horrible details come into painfully clear focus.

My thrall, fueled by the depth of my love for her, surges forward, enveloping her. She resisted my father's ability, but I have something more powerful than he could ever understand. Her trust and consent.

That night I marked her, she let me in and I let her inside of me. I just pray to the fae lords it's not too late.

"Cinder, drink."

What little life is left in her responds and she attaches

her lips to my wrist. Her suction is weak, barely there, but she's drinking.

She can take my life. All of it. If she drinks me dry in exchange for five minutes more of life, I'd gladly give my future away for her.

Five minutes so she could drink one last pumpkin spice latte, hug her friends, so I could show her that I love her more than anything in this realm or the next. That I'm not scared to be who I am anymore. I'm not my father. Because I love. I love her more than myself. And that's something he could never understand.

My head turns light and dizzy as she drinks.

Her hands curl around my arm as she becomes stronger, taking me in faster, harder.

Ravaged skin knits together and I let out a thankful gasp.

"That's it my gothic goddess, take all of me." My voice is reedy to my own ears.

Cinder's head drops finally, her eyes shutting tight as if she's overwhelmed by some emotion. When they open again even the whites are completely swallowed in black.

"What did you do to her?"

The question comes from Snow who now stands next to me.

It takes a moment to get my throat to work.

"I made her like me." I use the word she'll understand. "A vampire."

Snow's hand squeezes my shoulder. I'm not sure if it's in solace or anger.

"She might not want this." Snow's words are barely audible.

I pick Cinder up in my arms and trudge along the

blood-drenched floor, stepping directly on my father's mottled remains.

"She can kick my ass when she wakes up."

CHAPTER 52
WAKING UP

CINDER

When I wake up there are two things I notice. One, I feel remarkably healthy for a dead girl. Second, I'm thirsty as hell.

"Thank fuck," Kaison says before crushing me to him.

My brain can't catch up to what's happening or where I am.

Strangely, my skin recognizes the air, and it's not Midnight. I'm on my own bed in my own apartment. It's daylight but my blinds and curtains are closed tight and only the slightest wisps of sunshine creep in from the windows' corners.

"I can't breathe." My muffled words go into his shoulder.

He doesn't pull away, continuing to crush me, when I realize something absolutely wild. I'm not breathing at all.

"Uh, Kai? I'm not breathing," I say when I pull back.

My prince's eyes are red-rimmed, and he looks like absolute shit. His hair is a tousled mess, and he's sporting some patchy dark stubble. I didn't even know he was capable of growing facial hair. All Kai has on is a wrinkled set of jeans and some chains around his neck.

There is a wariness to his expression as if he's expecting me to lose my shit. "I know," he says, then clears his throat before taking my hands. "You were dying." His voice cracks over the words. "I couldn't let him take you from me. I couldn't let you die so I. . . I. . ." Suddenly, the prince of Midnight is a lost little boy, scared of what he's trying to tell me or what my reaction will be.

"He turned you into one of us," another voice answers from the door.

I turn to find Kaison's mother, Queen Mei-Ling Charming, standing there in full Midnight regalia, her blue and black skirts filling the entryway to my tiny bedroom.

She looks so out of place, I almost think I'm hallucinating or dead after all.

"Oh," is all I can say.

I'm a vampire.

A Midnight fairy.

A bloodsucker.

"So, that's why I'm so thirsty," I say in a low voice over a dry throat.

Kai leans over and grabs a massive takeout cup covered with a lid. He hands it over. "Drink this, you'll feel better."

At least it has a lid so I don't have to face the bright red blood I'm about to consume. Sipping on the drink, my eyes widen. A mixed medley of pumpkin spice and something sweet and savory hits my gut in a satisfying ker-pow. "Well that's the best thing I've ever had in my mouth," I say taken aback after I've swallowed half of it in one go.

"Well, that's hurtful," Kaison says with a pout.

"Kaison," his mother snaps.

His shoulders hunch a little. "Sorry, Mom." Then to me he says, "It's half pumpkin spice latte, half Goldie, with extra cinnamon."

I stop drinking at that. "Did you say Goldie?"

"Yeah," he gives me a wry smile. "She and Red fought for a while about whose blood you would drink first but Goldie won that fight pretty quickly. All your friends donated blood because they wanted you to feel supported and loved through your transition to this new, erm, lifestyle."

I'm fully fucking floored. "Wow." I should be grossed out or weirded out but I'm just strangely touched.

"You have pretty awesome friends," he says, squeezing my thigh, his hair dipping into his smiling eyes.

"Pfft, I knew that," I wave off. Then my eyes move back to the Queen of Midnight so casually standing in my doorway. The usual disconnected glaze in her eyes is notably absent as she focuses in on me.

"I owe you an explanation," she says evenly.

"An explanation?" I ask.

Her lips tighten as if she's bracing herself against something unpleasant. "As to why I murdered your father."

CHAPTER 53
THE AFFAIRS OF AN ARTIST

CINDER

We move to the shabby couch and chairs in the living room. I find the space is significantly more cramped than before. The ornately framed Ember of Midnight barely fits against the far wall. My heart twists painfully. The painting that once made my family whole now feels tainted by my father's past and I don't know what to think of it.

Snow is out, but Kai texted everyone that I was awake and okay. The text thread exploded in so many excited happy crying gifs that both Kai and I had to turn our phones to silent to hear his mother out.

"Your father wooed me the way he did everyone else," Kai's mother begins. "He was brilliant, romantic, and saw the beauty in everything. Even a heartbroken, hollow Queen."

"Mother—" Kai starts but she silences him with a lifted hand.

"We fell in love. And it was a torrid, wonderful affair," she says wistfully.

I keep my expression neutral, though inside my mind is reeling with this new information about my father.

A sad smile tips up at the corner of the Queen's mouth. "Many months of sneaking around in Midnight began to bring me back to life. Your father was the embodiment of passion, and he lived it in his art and in his life."

Kai scrubs a hand down his face, and I can sense his discomfort.

"But with that passion came volatility," her voice darkens. "As time went on, he became more frustrated by my husband's unwillingness to turn him into one of us. He'd fly into fits of rage, screaming how it wasn't fair, how no one loves Midnight more than him. He'd fall into ramblings of how his dreams would never come true, and no wishing upon any Midnight star would get him what he wanted."

I stiffen at her words. "That was our thing. We'd wish upon stars. We'd wish for things like ice cream, or to paint the greatest piece of art in the history of all time." If there was any doubt as to her story about the affair, it dissolves with that detail.

The Queen nods as if finally understanding something about her past. "I see. Well, his devotion to me turned after a matter of months. I went from being the Queen of his heart to an adversary. He'd beat me."

"You're a vampire," I protest, my voice weak. It's the same defense I laid out to Marisela, but it sounds far less convincing to my ears this time.

The Queen's brows knit together. "Just because we are fairies, it does not mean we are immune to pain or power."

Kai stares at me, and I wonder if he's trying to convey

that despite our differences, we both hold power over each other.

"Why didn't you go to your husband?" I ask.

The Queen and Kai exchange a look, a shared understanding of deep pain. After all, they'd been in the trenches together all these years under Valdor's thumb.

"He did learn of the affair and he believed that I deserved every bit of pain. He did not care about me as a wife. We had not been intimate for decades. My husband made sure to tell me in explicit terms that he didn't care who was between my legs as long as I kept my affair under wraps because if the kingdom knew I was screwing a human, he would kill me." She sounded like she was paraphrasing.

"Then something began to deeply bother your father," the Queen continues. "I believe it was related to an argument with my husband, but he wouldn't tell me the details. I only knew that my husband offered him the thing he wanted most in exchange for a task."

Valdor would change my father into a vampire if he trafficked human children into Midnight. I rub my arms as a shiver rips through me, leaving a trail of goosebumps in its wake.

Mei-Ling shakes her head. "He only became more agitated, keeping to his studio, sequestering himself to his art. But one night, your father came to my chambers. Consumed by jealousy and resentment and a madness I've only seen the tip of before, he took a pair of pliers, and he removed my fangs." Her head is held high, but there's a tremor in her voice.

I shake my head and stand up, my hands rising to cover my ears. I pace, trying to absorb this new, horrifying information about my father.

I don't want to believe it. This is not the man I knew. He would never do something like this.

Marisela's words come back to haunt me. *You wouldn't know. Not his precious Cinder who he doted on. Not his darling daughter who was better than everyone else.*

When I've calmed my nerves enough, I sit back down.

"The worst part was," the Queen says softly, "I still loved him. I couldn't understand why he could despise me so, cause me so much pain when I was so devoted to him. But I learned to fear him more, and that act was the final thing that broke me." She folds her hands in her lap and looks down at them. "So after he left, I fed, and my fangs grew back, and then I decided what had to be done. I found him in his studio. He was distracted from a fight with my husband. I didn't waste any time. I told him I could give him what he wanted. I could change him. I lied. And then I drained him. It was easy to bribe the undertaker to make it look like a heart attack, and that was that."

A heavy silence falls over us, the weight of the past, the violence, and the regrets pressing down. If only I'd known what my father was. If only Kai knew what was happening to his mother. If only there'd been another way.

"I don't expect you to forgive me, but I seek your forgiveness regardless," the Queen says to me, her eyes glassy and full of remorse. "I robbed you of your father, and I now see I subjected you to a fate worse than what I endured. Had I the chance to do it again, I would have chosen a different course of action."

I stare at her, my mind working to process everything. Part of me wants to lash out, to make her feel the pain I've carried all these years. "You fucked up my childhood," I finally say, deciding to be direct.

"I did," the Queen admits softly, open remorse in her voice.

"I had no way out and no one to help," I continue, as she listens intently. "And that kind of sounds how it was for you, too."

I see a glimmer of hope in Kai's eyes.

I hesitate to forgive the Queen. Part of me wants to hold onto my anger. I paid a heavy price for her decision. But another part recognizes the trapped, desperate woman she'd been. Wasn't I fighting against that same kind of powerlessness?

"I'm not sure I forgive you," I say carefully. "But I understand why you did what you did. I understand the fear of someone else having that kind of power over you, even if it was my own father." I close my eyes and swallow hard, still struggling to reconcile these new facts about my father with the man I thought I knew.

AFTER THE QUEEN LEAVES, returning to Midnight via her charmed necklace of transport, Kai goes to the kitchen. The shiny new espresso machine and milk frother look so very out of place on the chipped laminate counters of the kitchen.

"You learned how to make lattes for me?" My heart squeezes to a near-painful point despite not pumping anymore.

He shrugs with a half-smile as he pours out the pumpkin spice syrup. "It's nothing."

It's definitely not nothing.

I sit at the counter watching him make my drink,

pulling a carafe of blood from the fridge labeled "Red," in my friend's handwriting.

Kaison passes the coffee cup to me and I stare into it for a while, my thoughts a tangled mess of confusion, hurt, and a tentative understanding.

"I don't know what to think of my father anymore. For so long, he was my everything. My hero. Nothing could knock him off the pedestal I put him on."

"And now?" he asks hesitantly.

I lick my lips slowly, feeling pain and confusion and a hurt I've never known before tumble around in my chest, making my temples throb. "Now, I see what he was, or at least more of him. He was greedy, abusive, and a temperamental manipulator whose behavior I chalked up to him being an artist. My father made beautiful art and committed horrible crimes against my kind and even yours. I can't say I blame your mother, which hurts even more." When my mouth goes completely dry, I pause to drink the deeply satisfying concoction Kai made for me. "Do I absolve him of any of his sins because he drew a line at children? Does he get any points for loving and protecting me? I don't know how to add up the score."

Kai rounds the counter, taking my hand to lead me back to the couch with my drink in hand. "You're trying to make it black and white, and I think it's because you might be trying to figure out if it's still okay to love him."

A bubble swells inside my chest and I feel the sob trapped there. Kai is right. How can I love someone so. . . so fucking awful? But how can I not love my father who was the shining star of my childhood?

I don't even know how he treated my mother. If he'd always been a bastard or if maybe my mother's death inspired a fall from grace? I'll probably never know.

"I won't lie to you," he says, "I struggle to relate. My father has never possessed redeeming qualities, but I still yearned for his approval. The closest I can come is that while I love and adore my mother, I don't think she did the right thing either. She shouldn't have entered into an affair with your father. She shouldn't have suffered in silence. She certainly shouldn't have murdered him."

"Shouldn't she have?" My vision blurs from the tears gathering, but I refuse to let them fall.

Kai goes silent. Maybe he's thinking of the man who assaulted me and how he killed him because it was better for everyone. How he has made similar choices and while it doesn't make him good, it doesn't make him wrong.

"There's two ways to this that I see. You land on a side of love or hate and let go of everything else to reinforce that decision to give yourself peace. Or two, you won't ever make sense of your feelings about him, and you have to live with the messiness, the jumble of confusion where your adoration for him and his despicable behavior will always be at odds inside of you."

Ugh. That sounds so hard, so awful and confusing.

"The second path is certainly much harder, and most people would choose number one. It's easier to narrow the scope and force everything else out to give yourself certainty and peace. But," he pauses, taking my hand into his. "I have a feeling you'll end up taking the second route. Because only the strongest people can hold things that are at odds inside themselves for the sake of truth rather than comfort."

A tear drips onto our entwined hands as I laugh a little. "I hate how well you know me."

"No, you don't." The words come out husky and serious.

"No, I don't," I repeat. Meeting Prince Kaison Charming's intense gaze, I let him in to see all of me. No matter how ugly or conflicted, or hurt or broken he teases out the beauty of it all. He empowers me in whatever way I need.

To the world, the Prince of Midnight is this two-dimensional caricature, but to me he is everything. Funny, serious, thoughtful, protective, intelligent, and of course, charming.

"So what now? Are you going to rule Midnight?" *Or run away from responsibility and your power?*

I know he can't hear my thoughts, but he shoots me a knowing look at what I've left unsaid. Kai sighs heavily.

"I never wanted to be King."

"True."

"And this realm would be better left in the hands of the Mice."

"Maybe."

"But they keep going on about how I show leadership qualities that can help us all transition to a new Midnight."

I flatten my lips to keep from putting in my two cents.

"They think instituting a parliament structure will help bring new balance. A house of Midnight fairies, a house for beaters, and the monarchy. Which means I would be taking a leadership role, but I would be sharing a great deal of the responsibility and decision-making with the other houses, so I could still live my life. To be honest, there's really only one real thing holding me back from committing to becoming King."

"What's that?"

"What my Queen thinks?"

A lightning bolt strikes through me at his words. *Queen.*

"We don't have to get married right away," he rushes to say. "I'd be happy courting you all over again, for real. But the important thing is that you're by my side. Sniping me down when I get too cocky or unfocused, and I'm not ashamed to say holding me up when my knees get wibbly wobbly under the pressure I'm not used to. But mainly, because if you don't want to build a life in Midnight, I'll give it all up in a second and move in with you and Snow in this shitty little apartment where I'll get a job flipping burgers and make it my goal to scour the city for pumpkin spiced anythings to lay before you."

I press my lips to his as my non-beating heart clenches tight again. I believe him. He really would leave it all behind to slum it with me.

"It depends," I say seriously, putting my mug down on the coffee table.

He perks up. "On what?"

"Would I be known as Queen Spooky Babe or Queen Goth Girl?"

When he goes for my throat, tackling me back on the couch, nipping and kissing, I can't help but laugh.

EPILOGUE

SIX MONTHS LATER

CINDER

Mmmpffmppsstrsmpf.

After pushing my sweaty bangs back, I lean forward to unclasp the ball gag, taking it from Kai's mouth.

"What did you say?" I ask even as I lift and fall over his cock. My stomach clenches tight and I'm close to coming all over the King of Midnight.

It's not necessary to tie up or gag my royal husband because of trust issues, but it sure as hell remains a hot as fuck thing to do.

"Mistress, please let me bite you," he rasps even as his head falls back, and he arches his hips with what little movement he has strapped to our massive bed of black satin sheets.

The crop lands a sharp strike over his pubic bone. He jerks then lets out a low, pleasure-filled moan.

"That's Queen Mistress to you," I correct.

"Queen Mistress," he repeats. His lids lower. "My night-shade nymph."

Another strike, and he hisses. I drop my head and sink my fangs into his chest, right over his heart, riding his dick hard and fast, chasing the mind-melting friction from his piercings that rake along the inside of me like he owns me.

He gasps and writhes as I drink his blood. I do it over the mark of Amaranthe I made on him.

Just as he said, after the marking Kai's blood is the most delicious, heady thing I've had enter my body. . .other than his cock of course. And yes, that even includes pumpkin spice lattes.

That piercing on the end of his mushroom tip slams into just the right spot in me that makes my thighs quake and sweat bead between my breasts.

I'm hurled over the edge of a bone-quaking orgasm, and I release his flesh to present my neck to my husband, my King, my forever slut muffin.

Kai bites me without hesitation and my orgasm doubles down with a vengeance even as Kai lets out a muffled cry, shooting his release up into me. The bed quakes under us, creaking from the strain of the fight Kai puts up.

Like the first time, warmth spreads out from my center and travels to Kai engulfing us both in a heat so intense it feels like being embraced by the sun. It's fucking beautiful and perfect. Tears prick the backs of my eyes and emotion swells in my chest so intensely I fear I'll burst.

Another shot of arousal spirals through me when I pull back to see a little of my bright red blood smeared on his lips.

It reminds me of our wedding night when I marked him. We eloped in Vegas after all and I got to wear the black purple and spiked goth gown of my dreams and Kai got his Elvis impersonator as an officiant.

All my friends were there, and we partied the entire

weekend in the hotel penthouse of the most luxurious hotel on the Strip that's modeled after a pyramid.

Even Rap let loose a little and got smashed on brown liquor and kept repeating that she was so proud of us. She's a savage winner at flip cup too it turns out.

Goldie was glowing, dancing with her hands in the air showing off her new pink diamond engagement ring even as she was wrapped around a stiffly swaying Ted.

He managed to finally land that perfect proposal but he had to call in back up. Aka Goldie's mother. They went to her family's home in the Midwest for a long weekend and he proposed to her over a family dinner. Goldie describes it as intimate, heartfelt, and absolutely perfect because it was him. He even invited his two bear shifter brothers who Mama Goldie kept in line so Ted could finally get on one knee.

Brexley turned out to be a surprisingly good dancer and stuck to Red like glue as she held a glass over her head—a virgin decaf mocha martini. The wedding plans have been postponed until she gives birth to the little pup growing inside her. If Brexley was insufferably overprotective before, now he's ten times worse.

When we got back home to Boston, I thought I could resume my split life in equal measure but that became quickly unsustainable.

Running Midnight with Kai is a lot more duty than I expected and also far more pleasurable than I could have guessed it would because it involves fairies, humans, fae, and even my friends. Midnight has become the place I always wanted it to be—magical, dark, and frankly, home.

Though I need long stretches of time to myself to paint, draw, and sculpt. The one gallery showing Kai got me launched me to a new level he swears he had no hand in tipping. I've got more showings coming, one that also co-features my favorite artist, Lala Drona. I almost died on the spot when I met her.

For Mei-Ling Charming's crime of murder against Byung-He, which she confessed to the new powers that be, it was decided she was to be banished from Midnight. Despite my attempts to step in to convince them of a less harsh punishment, my mother-in-law assured me it was for the best. She's already moved to a fairy-friendly retirement home in the Common World where she plays mahjong nightly with her new friends and is even dating a nice man down the hall, another Midnight Fairy who had been exiled from Midnight two hundred years before. Mei-Ling says a new life is a gift she doesn't deserve.

Word got back to us that my stepfamily led a miserable existence. They fled to the fairy Realm of Roses where they tried to ingratiate themselves with King Stefan. Anastasia tried to seduce the kingdom's princess to gain favor. She disappeared after that night.

Then a blackmail and murder scheme came to light, devised by my stepmother. It all came to a head when Drusilla attacked one of the court members, and then they lost theirs. Their heads that is. Now I really don't have to worry about the old fam knocking down our castle doors come Christmas time.

Underneath me, Kai grins like an idiot, knowing the gift I've given him. The one we share.

The ability to walk in sunlight.

I still prefer the darkness, but many days are now spent chasing my husband along beaches with tubs of sunscreen while he soaks in the sunshine without bursting into ash. He may be immortal, but I still worry about the number of bad sunburns he's been racking up.

My mage power is a reassurance to all of Midnight since I can't be thralled, and I can sense and break thralls on anyone else. The familiars have all been broken free of their bonds and now choose for themselves what they want to do. Some left, some stayed, and some beaters defected to Midnight specifically to be of service to Kai and me.

A knock at the door has me releasing Kai's straps as I wrap a robe around myself to answer.

I pass the easel with my latest creation. Sometimes I want the paintings to invade my dreams, so I move them to the bedroom. This one is a hauntingly beautiful portrait of Kai, his eyes filled with darkness and depth no one sees. I doubt I'll ever publicly show it. Kai doesn't need the world to know who he really is as long as I do. Not to mention, he may be far more than anyone gives him credit for, but he also enjoys being a celebrity ham.

The large human familiar, Gus, stands waiting when I open the door. His eyes drop to the spiked platform boots I'm still wearing. I'll have divots in my ass for a week from sitting back on them repeatedly as Kai and I fuck, but it only adds to the fun.

"What is it?" I ask, not mincing words though Gus knows I don't mean anything by it. I'm just direct.

"Your Majesty,"

"Gus," I warn.

"Cinder," he corrects. "It's the beast again."

I thought we may have reached a truce, but the devil cat apparently relishes his new role as causing chaos in the castle. No one can catch him, but every night I leave out a dish of tuna in thanks for saving me and attacking my step-sisters.

Kai steps up behind me, a comforting presence. "What'd Lucifer do this time?" he asks, slipping an arm around my waist. He hasn't even bothered to put on clothes, the immodest little freak. I feel his softening dick against my back.

"I'll tell you what he did," Jack answers, walking up the corridor in a storm cloud of pissed off.

Gus and Jack are probably Lucifer's biggest adversaries. He seems almost to delight in terrorizing the couple daily as they now live in the castle too.

"The little feline fucker scratched the shit out of your thrones. And that's not all," Jack rants.

"Let me guess?" I ask. "He pissed on them too."

At their nod, I realize that while almost everything in my life has changed, some things never will.

WANT TO MEET THE NEWEST LOST GIRL?

Head to www.hollyroberds.com and check out the bonuses to read!

BLACKMAILING BELLE

Preorder the next Lost Girls book now, and we'll meet back
at Belle's Bookshop in Spring of 2025.
Reserve Your Copy Now!

LOVE THIS BOOK?

ENJOY MORE BY THIS AUTHOR

Vivien woke up with no memories and a terrible thirst for blood.

The Grim Reaper must destroy all blood suckers.

The reaper dogs just want to get pets and loves in between fetching the souls for the Afterlife.

Read this COMPLETE trilogy and you'll laugh, you'll cry, you'll absolutely die.

Vegas Immortals: Death & the Last Vampire

*Available on Audio and Kindle Unlimited

WANT A FREE BOOK?

Join Holly's Newsletter Holly's Hot Spot at www. hollyroberds.com and get the Five Orders Prequel Novella, The Knight Watcher, for FREE!

Plus you'll get exclusive sneak peaks, giveaways, fun lil' nuggets, and notifications when new books come out. Woot!

Acknowledgments

A massive thank you to my assistants, Leah Crowell and Tara Volpenhein. I can't stress enough what a massive impact you two have made on my business, my time, my life, and honestly my satisfaction. I feel we are the three lost girls rocking our way through fantasy smut books and life. There are only more awesome things to come for us.

Thank you to *Calliope's Children*, my monthly plotting group. To Kim K., Kim M., Brooke you continue to help pour fire into my cup of inspiration on the regs. Thanks for plotting my books, k thanx bye! I'm wildly in love with all of you!

Thank you to my Tuesday writer friends – Aidy Award, M. Guida, Shannon McLaughlin, & Nikki Hall. The way our group supports and genuinely celebrates each other's success is so fucking wonderful and I'm so damn grateful. Thank you for supporting my journey and being genuinely happy for me.

Thank you to Sarah Urquhart! I love the writing vibes we've created and that we remember in between writing chapters to actually live life!

Thank you to my editors Theresa Paolo, Havoc Archives & Athena Franks, every time I send you my novel I'm like *pssshhh* this thing is damned near perfect and then I get all the red pen back and I'm like good Christ how did I miss all that?!?!? You take my book and make it shine in ways I'm absolutely not capable of doing on my own.

To my special reader fan group, *Holly's Hellions* – you are my heart and I love how we play in that group. I bring a lot of questions and problems to you and get immediate and unhinged responses. I fucking love it. Let's always Read Books and Raise Hell!

To my Patrons – YOU GUYS ARE SO FUCKING AWESOME! Thank you for giving me a place to throw all my messy drafts and playing with me. I didn't know how much I would love playing with you guys and it's only going to get better.

Thank you to l'husbun, Chris, my very own Prince Charming. The way you have believed in me and supported me is beyond magic. Also, I will never stop biting you for no reason. Jk the reason is you are hot and delicious. Om nom nom.

A LETTER FROM THE AUTHOR

A Letter from the Author

Dear Reader,

Thank you for reading!

The main reason I keep writing more Lost Girls books is because of you. I'm so grateful for the enthusiasm over this series that continues to blow me away every day.

Want to make sure you never miss a release or any bonus content I have coming down the pipeline? Make sure to join my Patreon: Holly Roberds Books

And definitely sign up for Holly's Hotspot, my newsletter, and I'll send you a FREE ebook right away!

You can also find me on my website www.hollyroberds.com and I hang out on social media.

Instagram: http://instagram.com/authorhollyroberds

Facebook: www.facebook.com/hollyroberdsauthorpage/

And closest to my black heart is my reader fan group, Holly's Hellions. Become a Hellion. Raise Hell. www.facebook.com/groups/hollyshellions/

Cheers!
Holly Roberds

ABOUT THE AUTHOR

Holly started out writing Buffy the Vampire Slayer and Terminator romantic fanfiction before spinning off into her own fantastic worlds with bitey MCs and heart wrenching climaxes as well as other errr climaxes...

Holly is a Colorado girl to her core but is only outdoorsy in that she likes drinking on patios in Denver.

She lives with her ever-supportive husband and surly house rabbits who supervise this writer, to make sure she doesn't spend all of her time watching Buffy reruns.

For more sample chapters, news, and more, visit www. hollyroberds.com

www.ingramcontent.com/pod-product-compliance
Lightning Source LLC
Chambersburg PA
CBHW070401310726
48977CB00003B/518